The
Cost
of Living

The
Cost
of Living

A NOVEL

Christopher
Zenowich

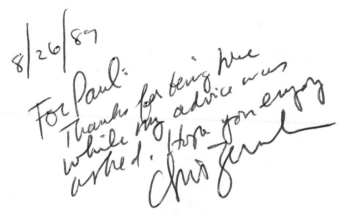

8/26/89
For Paul:
Thanks for being true
while my advice was
asked. Hope you enjoy
Chris

1817

HARPER & ROW, PUBLISHERS, New York
Grand Rapids, Philadelphia, St. Louis, San Francisco
London, Singapore, Sydney, Tokyo

FIRST EDITION

Designed by Nina D'Amario

Library of Congress Cataloging-in-Publication Data
Zenowich, Christopher.
   The cost of living: a novel/Christopher Zenowich.—1st ed.
      p.   cm.
   ISBN 0-06-016044-6
   I. Title.
PS3576.E537C6   1989
813'.54—dc19   88-45539

89 90 91 92 93 AT/HC 10 9 8 7 6 5 4 3 2 1

For my father and my mother

Toe to toe
Touch and go
Give a cheer
Get your souvenir

 —Mose Allison

The
Cost
of Living

CHAPTER

1

I think this is the town we've been looking for," Irene said. "That sign seals it."

Bob Bodewicz glanced at the sign, which read: Sterne, Home of Kwik Kake.

Irene pushed aside a strand of hair that had stuck to her forehead. "You know Kwik Kake, don't you?"

Bob shook his head and arched his back away from the seat to help dry out his shirt. It was late afternoon and hot even for August. They had been driving through towns since ten that morning, looking to rent an apartment in an old house. That was Irene's idea. Around noon, the air conditioner on Bob's company car, a white Caprice Classic, quit. Bob was ready to call off the hunt, but Irene insisted on continuing.

"Kwik Kakes," Irene said. "They come in those little blue boxes. Just add water and bake. We ate them all the time at boarding school. For the munchies."

"Let's take a break," Bob said.

"And scarf some Kwik Kakes, too?"

Greater Sterne had the look of a town that had passed its prime a half century before without realizing it. There were the visual signs of complacent decay—empty buildings, peeling paint, sagging porches—and an ambience of missed opportunities that appealed to Bob in a literary way. Still, he couldn't

see the point of living this far from Ann Arbor. But Irene felt
it was important, once she deferred her admission to the law
school for a year. She didn't want to be around a campus.
Fewer distractions, fewer parties, fewer people. "I need to dull
out for a year," she told Bob, who wanted to think of their first
few months together as a little better than "dulling out."

They stopped at the town's only traffic light, directly in
front of two railroad tracks. Everything in town seemed defined
by its perpendicular or parallel relation to the tracks. The Kwik
Kake plant straddled both sides of the tracks to the south, a sky
bridge connecting the buildings at the third floor. The plant was
made of the same red bricks as every other building on Perry
Road, the main street. Dusty metal silos rose from its roofs,
each with a metal chute running down to the tracks. When the
light changed, Bob drove over the tracks and into the parking
lot of a diner named Olive's.

The see-through yellow film shades on the diner windows
warped the reflection of Bob and Irene as they got out of the
car—"the pimpmobile," Irene called it. It couldn't have been
more out of place in Sterne, whose main street looked like a
used pickup truck dealership. The Impala had a gas-guzzling
six-cylinder engine and a powder-blue suede interior. It was
bigger than any car Bob's father had owned. Even Byron Cutter, his regional manager, thought it was odd that the company's lease arrangement, a lottery of availability, had coughed
up this vehicle. "Do yourself a favor," he told Bob. "Don't let
anyone else know you've got an Impala."

The tint of the windows cast their movements in a dis-
torted, sepia shade. Their dress appeared as out-of-place as the
car: Irene in sandals, white shorts, blue tank top, and dark
sunglasses; Bob in loafers, painter's pants, and a red and blue
striped Land's End shirt. They looked like two tourists from
California who'd made a bad choice of an exit off the thruway
in search of rest rooms.

The air conditioner above the diner's front door hummed
furiously, but inside it was no cooler. They sat at one of the
three booths and waited for the waitress to notice them. There
was no one else in the diner except for a man at the end of
the counter. He held a cup of coffee in one hand, a cigar in the
other. The waitress leaned, propped on her elbows across the

counter from him, listening. When he finished his story, she walked over to Bob and Irene, laughing softly.

"Those Kwik Kakes?" Bob asked, pointing to a case behind the counter.

"What else?" she said. Her blue uniform was clean, but stained with faint pink blotches.

Irene ordered two slices of vanilla Kwik Kake and a Coke; Bob a cup of coffee. The waitress set the slices in front of Bob, as if there were some sort of etiquette involved in dining on Kwik Kakes in Sterne. He slid a slice over to Irene.

"One bite and you'll be a convert," Irene said.

Bob put a large forkful into his mouth, and before swallowing, said, "If I go into catatonic sugar shock, the keys to the pimpmobile are in my pocket. She's yours."

"You love me that much?" Irene asked. She rolled her eyes, her lids dropping slowly. "My madeleines. One taste, and poof—I'm back to the spring term of my prep school senior year. We got stoned every afternoon and ate Kwik Kakes for the munchies."

"Yeah, but you can't move to a town like this just because of that." Bob sipped on his coffee and waited for her response.

"We can at least look."

"Somehow, Sterne doesn't seem quite like your kind of place," Bob said.

The waitress wiped the counter slowly, moving toward them. Her eyes had the craved look of a gossip who hadn't heard a good rumor in a week. Irene had lit a cigarette and now tapped the ash into the saucer of Bob's coffee cup. There was no ashtray at the booth. "What makes you so sure?" she asked.

Bob stared at the slurry of ashes and coffee at the bottom of his saucer. He and Irene had been together nine weeks. And every time he thought he had a fix on her, she would do something like knock her cigarette ashes in his saucer. It unsettled him. Not because he felt he needed to predict her every action. Only that he hadn't gauged the currents correctly. He had a knack for anticipating where people were headed after knowing them for a while. But with her, his instincts were off. It humbled him.

"Well?" Irene asked. "Are you just passing through, or looking for a place to stay?"

"Even a man like me needs a place to hang his briefcase once in a while. What do you have in mind?"

"More Kwik Kakes," she said and grinned.

"Not for me," Bob said. He pushed his empty cup and the saucer to the center of the table and took the check to the register. He asked the waitress if she knew of any apartments in Sterne.

"You want to live here?" she said.

"Why not?"

The waitress shrugged. "It's your life," she said, and gave them directions to a couple who had an apartment to rent.

They found the Gunderwalds without difficulty. It was the only brick house on a street that had several large houses on it. As he got out of the car, Bob noticed that beyond the houses cornfields lined both sides of the road. The town seemed to end abruptly.

An elderly man and woman sat in chairs on the front porch. Bob introduced himself and Irene, and asked if they were the ones with an apartment for rent.

They looked at each other, then at Bob and Irene. "It isn't the same anymore," the woman said. She stood up. She was stout, and wore jeans rolled at the cuffs.

The man was thin and balding, and he rose slowly, as if he was in pain. He held a Stroh's in one hand. "We split it in two."

"Is it free?" Irene asked.

"Why, of course not," the old man said. "We want a hundred and fifty dollars a month for it."

"She means vacant, Charlie," the woman said. She turned to Bob and Irene. "Ignore him."

"It's a hot one," Charlie said.

"You have a job?" the woman asked Bob. He nodded.

"And what will you do?" she asked Irene.

"I'll take some graduate courses in January, and start law school in a year."

"Oh, a lawyer. I've never met one before starting school. You seem nice enough."

"You don't get rotten until after," Irene said. "Lots of us are okay at the start."

The woman laughed and slapped Charlie on the back. "She's got me pegged."

"How about a beer?" Charlie said. "I'm getting one."

"Will you hold off for a minute," she said. "Let the last one pass through."

Irene tugged on Bob's shirt. "I like them," she whispered.

"Now I don't mean to pry," the woman continued, "but are you two married?"

Bob figured they would be asked this and he answered without hesitation. "Last week," he said. "In the Ann Arbor town hall." He waited for Irene to jab him in the ribs, but she pulled her role off perfectly, wrapping her hands around Bob's elbow and leaning against him.

"Aww," the woman said. "No family? If you move in, I'll bake you a cake for Labor Day." She opened the door. "Do you want to see it or not?"

Bob and Irene followed her inside. "My name's Rita," she said. "We don't rent to just anyone who shows up. But you two look all right. You've got to be fussy with a house like this."

Only then did Bob notice what she meant. All the trim and the stairway were made of oak, ornately carved and well cared for. There were two doors at the upstairs landing.

"The whole upstairs used to be the apartment," Rita said. "But we split it in two. We're keeping the smaller part open for company. The one through this door is yours if you want it." She opened the door to a small, furnished living room with a tiled fireplace. The oak mantle had a hunt scene carved in relief and swirling overlaid vines at either end.

Rita slid open a thick dividing door. On the other side was a bedroom furnished with an Art Deco bedroom set. "All the furniture in here used to be ours. This style doesn't go with the house, but there aren't many of them left." She looked at Irene and said, "I hope you don't mind."

"Not at all," Irene said. "It's beautiful."

"If you've bought your own stuff already, this isn't the place for you."

"No," Irene said. "We haven't bought anything yet."

Bob was walking around the bedroom. There was an oak

secretary built into the wall. The room was brilliant in the afternoon sun. "We'll take it," he said.

"Don't you want to see the kitchen?" Rita asked. "I wouldn't take an apartment without seeing the kitchen. It's got all our old appliances, but they're in good shape."

Bob and Irene obliged her by inspecting the kitchen.

"All we ask," Rita said at the end of the tour, "is that you keep the place clean and pay your rent on time. It's a good starter place, don't you think?"

Bob hadn't heard the expression before. But now that he thought about it, it did seem like a good starter place.

CHAPTER

2

B ob hadn't been friends with Irene in college. She was in a couple of his classes, but ran in a faster crowd. Her boyfriend, or at least the guy he saw her with most often, was president of the most elitist fraternity on campus—the only one that kept out nonmembers during house party weekends. Knowing this, Bob avoided her when he found out they were both renting rooms that summer in another fraternity.

But during the first week there, Lipton, the business manager of the house, told Bob that Irene had made Phi Beta Kappa and been admitted to every law school to which she applied, including Harvard, Michigan, and Stanford. The news made him curious. It was the first time he realized she was more than a high-class party animal. He tried to recall if she ever spoke up in the English classes they had taken together, but remembered nothing. He could see her, though. She was hard to miss. She was tall and thin and had the skin that swimmers always seem to have—smooth, well toned—although he had no idea if she was a swimmer. Her hair was blonde and sometimes seemed to have a red tint. She kept it short, just above her shoulders. She got to class late, usually just ahead of him. Once in a while she would smile at him and nod, as if they had something in common beyond their tardiness. But at the time, he couldn't imagine what that could be.

At the end of the second week at the house, Lipton organized a small party for everyone to meet one another. Bob
looked forward to meeting Irene, if only to find out whether
she was as smart as Lipton said. The heart of the party was on
the back porch of the fraternity, where the kegs were. He
caught sight of her there early in the evening, but after thread-
ing his way through the crowd could no longer find her. Instead he found himself boxed in among a set of foreign science
students who could not afford to return home for the summer.
They were in a festive mood, and although Bob had little to
contribute to their conversations of vector space and neutrinos,
he was close enough to the keg to listen and nod when asked
a direct question. He was ready to call it a night when he heard
Lipton's squeaky voice saying his name.

"Now Bob's a man of my own persuasion," Lipton was
saying, "opting for the world of commerce rather than law
school."

"I'm not sure I would link myself with any of your per-
suasions," Bob said, turning. Irene stood next to Lipton.

"What commerce is that?" she asked.

Bob couldn't tell if she was really interested. And he felt
a little embarrassed hearing Lipton describe him in those words.
"You know what a Saturday Night Special is, don't you?" he
said.

Irene nodded. Lipton appeared confused.

"Well, I've taken a job with a firearms company, one of
the larger manufacturers of the weapon. They've given me a
company car equipped with a police radio, an expense account,
and four boxes of Saturday Night Specials. I'm to drive around
various towns in the Midwest on Friday and Saturday nights,
trying to extend what is now primarily an urban market for
these weapons to smaller towns and cities."

Lipton laughed in a series of sharp intakes, like a dog with
hiccups. "Oh, God, that's dark. Really dark."

"Are you drunk?" Irene asked. "A lot of people wouldn't
find that too funny."

"Sure, the same people who get heated up about the issue
after some white wine. Can I get you some?"

Irene's expression softened, and she smiled. "If there is
any. And only if you tell me what you're really doing."

Bob was impressed. She had fielded his retort effortlessly. He considered that a sign of intelligence. Her composure made her even more attractive.

Bodewicz believed that only people with an effortless intelligence were worth knowing. He had come to this conclusion at the end of his junior year while breaking up with his girlfriend of three years. She was ploddingly smart, with the looks of an attractive nun. They had begun a series of skirmishes during the winter, after Bob had walked out of a final exam that he considered irrelevant to the class that had been taught. She thought he was immature. She brought it up repeatedly, and when he countered by saying he didn't care about flunking the exam, she would say "And what about your cume?" as if that were an irrefutable condemnation of his decision. It was during one of these skirmishes that he first noticed she kept the books in her room in alphabetical order. She had two small bookcases, one for British literature, the other for American. He couldn't believe he had never noticed it before. It bothered him. He kept his mouth shut about it until she finally tried to organize his books, which he kept loose in liquor cartons in his closet. Everything fell apart at once. He told her that her organization drove him nuts. The severing blow came when he brought up her habit of gasping *veni, veni, veni* when she came during sex.

"No white wine," Bob said when he returned. "Just beer."

"That's what I was drinking," Irene said. "Now what are your real plans?"

"I'm not too interested in talking about it," he said. "Really, I'd rather hear about you."

Irene shook her head. "You first."

Bob exhaled slowly. "Oh, God. You'll laugh."

"Only if you give me the cue."

Bob told her just what he had been told by the guy who hired him. He would be a district inventory coordinator for P&V drugstores. The chain was what the guy called a "new concept in retailing." They had the standard offering of toiletries and headache, cough, and nasal remedies, drugs and magazines. Then they also had "innovative" areas—hardwares, auto parts, electrical supplies, and foodstuffs—based on a calculus of good deals and local interests. Most of the hardware came from the Far East; the foodstuff from whatever distributors wanted to unload—potato sticks one week, chunky-style soups the next.

"I guess I'll be traveling from store to store," he concluded, "making sure everything is selling as it should and helping the managers fine-tune their inventory. At least that's what I'm told I'll learn at the training session."

"You have to be trained to do that?" she asked.

He nodded and took a seat on a porch chair. Irene leaned on the wall beside him.

"You don't seem very excited. Why did you take it?"

"It seemed like the thing to do. You know, pay back the loans. My folks are ecstatic for me."

Irene smiled. That was the first time Bob had noticed her smile. Each tooth was perfectly white and straight. He suspected a smile like that, genes aside, cost a lot of money.

"Actually law school is a family affair," she said, the tone of her voice shifting down a notch, as if the subject dictated it.

"Lipton said you got into Harvard and Stanford and a few others. Why did you apply if you were going to Michigan anyway?"

"To let Dad know that I could do well enough on my own, that's all. Family is a capital *F* word in my house."

"Sure—but who does that help?"

"It helps me," she said, lighting another cigarette. She took a long drag and looked at him, from top to bottom. "You surprise me."

"Do I?"

"Yeah," she said, shaping her lips in an O and blowing a smoke ring. "You were always bringing up the worker's point of view in class, with a touch of cynicism. Somehow I can't imagine you working for a drugstore chain."

"I'm a worker I guess," Bodewicz said. "Besides, it's a job." His voice sounded distant and foreign.

"Don't you have any other options?"

"None that would pay back the loans, other than postponing them in graduate school."

"How about some time off? A little travel. Goof off?"

"Goof off? If I could find someone to underwrite it. I'm not as lucky as you are."

"It's not luck. It's fate."

"When you don't have it, it feels like luck. Bad luck."

"The world never gave Jefferson his due, did it? All our natural aristocrats are measured by their money-making prowess."

"And luck has a lot to do with that."

"You must despise someone like me." Irene blew out smoke with a slightly exaggerated force, marking a boundary.

"Sure," he said. "I probably despise someone like you. Whether I despise you, I can't say. Not yet anyway."

"Take a guess then. What's the bottom line? Do you, or don't you?" She grinned.

Bob grinned back. He could play a game. "I don't guess if I can help it."

"Oh, come on. You have a few pertinent facts. I've told you enough."

"But you haven't shown me enough," he said, returning her top to bottom stare.

Irene stood up, snuffed out her cigarette, and saved the last lungful of smoke for his face. "Of course. Sex—the first battlefield of true class warfare." She looked at Bob as if she were just assigned a dull topic for a paper. "What do you see when you look at me? A hostile country? Something to be stormed and invaded?"

"I was hoping for a demilitarized zone."

Irene nodded. "Good. Maybe there is some capacity in you for compromise. I don't know if I want to be a demilitarized zone."

"What then?"

"I don't know yet. Maybe a DMZ isn't a bad place to start. But don't surrender your principles in the process. Who knows, you might be able to use them on the job."

"Yeah, right," Bob said.

Irene waved good night and left. Bob got another draft and took a seat away from the keg and the lights. As much as he wanted to find some reason, some safe reason to dismiss her as a frivolous rich girl, he couldn't. There was something else about her that got to him. He felt almost overpowered by her. Not by intellect alone, nor by her looks, but by her ability to shift, to move quickly. By her gamesmanship. He hadn't expected that. It made him feel for a brief moment that he had his own prejudices. His own perceptual constraints.

Bob didn't see Irene again until the following Tuesday. He was eating sardines out of a can in the kitchen when she walked in with a bag of groceries.

"Are you conducting some sort of research for the job, or simply eating?" she asked, tossing several vegetables into the sink.

"Simply eating," Bob said. "It's a shame I need a fork to get these out. It would be easier if I could plop the whole tin into my mouth at once."

"There's a thought," she said. "Perhaps pulverized sardines you squeeze from a toothpaste tube. Save on cleanups. Great for snacks. Decorate the tops of cakes. Kids, use it with your toothbrush to fool Mom. And Mom, don't forget to put an extra tube in your child's lunch box."

"Sounds like you've got something," he said.

"Oh, you had it. If you had seen yourself eating—wasn't that what you called it?—you would have thought of it too." She smiled at him and washed a head of lettuce in the sink. "Care to join me for a salad? I call it 'dinner.' "

"No thanks," he said. "I was planning to swallow a few spoonfuls of mayonnaise—kind of a tuna salad effect. But I'll skip it. My stomach needs a rest."

"Eat like that all the time and it's a wonder it doesn't need a transplant."

"Naw," Bob said. "A stomach's like a muscle. You've got to exercise it to keep it strong. Get into the habit of a regular dinner and it'll go soft in no time. The goat is my model."

"I usually think of goats as associated with other appetites."

Bob grinned. "But first and foremost for their ability to digest anything. They survive anywhere."

The door swung open and Lipton came in. "This kitchen is rank," he said, marching to the counter and lifting a dirty plate with his fingertips. He dangled it in front of himself as if it were a pair of soiled underwear. "God, look at this thing. There's something on it that's alive." He turned to Bob. "Is this your doing?"

"He doesn't use plates," Irene said. "I'll vouch for that."

Bob waved off Lipton and turned to leave. Irene ignored him, too. She shred the lettuce into a bowl.

"By the way," Lipton said. "I meant to ask you—where will you be stationed?"

"Stationed?" Bob didn't like the sound of the word.

"You know, where's your district?"

"They haven't decided yet. They might keep me in the office for a few months until they open stores in Chicago. Or they might send me to central Indiana or Michigan."

"Well, if you have any say in it, I'd tell them, 'Keep me in the office and I'll open Chicago.' That way, you give management a good look at you. That can help your career."

"Yeah, my career," Bob said. "Lipton, I don't have a career. And if what you say is true, I'll push for Indiana or Michigan."

"Where in Michigan?" Irene asked, suddenly drying her hands on a towel.

"Lansing or Ann Arbor."

"Ann Arbor would be more fun," she said. "Especially with me there." She raised her eyebrows and tilted her head to the side as if to say, isn't that obvious.

"Oh, what's this?" Lipton said, breaking into his hiccuping dog laugh.

"No one has fun in law school," Bob said, turning to leave once again.

"That's only because I've never gone," she said. "Care for some salad, Lipton?"

Wednesday night Bob returned to his room and found Irene writing a note for him on the pad attached to his door.

"Hi," she said without looking up. She signed it. "Here, have a read."

> Bob: Curious to know whether you can swallow your distaste
> for the good life long enough to join me in the Adirondacks
> this weekend. Let me know—I'm leaving noon tomorrow.
> Irene

"How am I swallowing any distaste for the good life by going on a camping trip?" Bob asked, still staring at the note to avoid her eyes. He was more than a little surprised.

"This isn't camping," Irene said. "My parents have a cottage on Upper Saranac Lake. No one is there now. We'd have it to ourselves."

"As in a date or something?"

"As in call it what you want." Irene gave her head a quick shake and exhaled slowly. "I took the first step. Are you going to take one?"

"One question . . ."

"Just one?"

"What became of that other guy?"

"Brent? He gave me the classic blow-off this past spring. Thought it was time we both saw some other people. Actually, he beat me to the punch by about a week. So, here I am. I'd like to see you."

"As a project?"

"Look—if you're going to ask questions like that, forget it. I don't need any projects right now."

"Bad joke," Bob said, holding his hand up to signal that he meant no offense. He could smack himself over how defensive he felt whenever luck seemed to go his way. "Let me try again. What do I need to bring?"

"That's more like it," Irene said, jabbing him gently in the chest.

Bob carried his brother, Carl's, letter with him for an hour or two before he opened it. He waited until there was no one around and took a seat on the porch out back, shutting the door behind him. He did not like to read letters from his brother in front of anyone else. Most of the time they were a lot of fun. But he had not heard from him since he wrote telling him about the job. That had been a month ago.

Carl came right to the point:

So you have a job, but I would never have expected it to be for a drugstore chain coordinating inventory. Is this the brother who sat there during spring break of his junior year trying to convince the old man that only art mattered, and that only the esthetic experience could create a capacity for moral behavior? I never did get your reasoning. In any case, I trust you have more up your sleeve than counting shampoo bottles.

Tell me what else is going on? How do you keep occupied during the days up there in the summer? Do you smoke a pipe and take long walks, or is that all behind you at this point?

For me, it's still a lot of fun. Like Bertrand Russell, I want to throw a tobacco pouch into the air in the excitement of a new insight. I hope I never do lose that. Of course, I'm still waiting for a big intellectual breakthrough. I've tried throwing the pouch, but it doesn't produce the insight.

Lately I've been translating Trakl and have applied for an extra semester over here to keep at it. Also: a paper on the relation between George Grosz in Germany and George Grosz in Hollywood.

Do you know that there is a show called the "Kick of the Week" here. It shows these phenomenal acrobatic kicks for goals by the best German strikers. Sort of like "This Week in Baseball." Sponsored by a beer company. I swear, over here, kids catch a Frisbee with their feet before they can with their hands. I have been running again, and now weigh, in spite of the heavy German beer, what I did in high school. I look forward to hearing from you, especially about the job. I'm very curious.

Bob put the letter back in its envelope and at first thought about throwing it away. He felt as if Carl were teasing him with things he might have done. But instead of tossing it he tucked the letter in an old notebook. He would keep it there—at least for a while.

CHAPTER

3

Rain fell all the way to the Adirondacks. Irene drove an old BMW that belonged to her parents. By the time they were near Blue Mountain Lake the clouds hung so low overhead that Bob couldn't see the mountains. Irene kept two hands on the wheel. She didn't say a word except to curse the streams of run-off that covered the road in spots.

Bob felt it was up to him to break the tension, to say something clever. But seated in a BMW in the midst of the Adirondacks—both firsts for him—he didn't feel resourceful. Instead he watched her as she drove. As she downshifted around a corner he could tell she was an excellent driver. When the rain fell blindingly hard, her shoulders tensed and curled toward the wheel. Bob would have pulled over and waited. But she wasn't like that. She kept on going.

"Is this typical rain up here?" Bob asked.

"Only when I want to come up."

"Why don't we pull over for a while and see if it lets up?" The windshield looked like someone had turned a fire hose on it.

"It would seem worse. Besides, we're almost there."

"How much farther?"

"Not that far. Maybe an hour or two in this weather."

"That long? You want me to drive for a while?"

Irene turned on the headlights and patted Bob on the knee. "It's not the right day to drive up here for the first time."

Bob settled back into his seat and felt that he had taken her mind off the storm for at least a second. He shut his eyes and listened to the assault of the rain. He remembered running with his brother once in a rain like this—only it had been a thunderstorm. They were alongside a reservoir, about a mile from the caretaker's house, where they could find shelter. Suddenly a tree exploded right next to them. He never saw the lightning. Chunks of the tree, ripped by the explosion, fell around them. Then the upper part of the tree began falling in pieces: limbs, leaves, whapping them from all sides. More lightning close by, another explosion. They kept running at the same pace, as if it would make no difference to speed up. By the time they got to the caretaker's, the heart of the storm had passed. "What were you thinking?" Carl asked. "I thought we were dead," Bob said. "But I didn't think there was a god-damn thing we could do about it." He kept his eyes closed as he remembered.

Just before they reached Upper Saranac Lake, Irene took a side road. A short cut, she said. The road wasn't much wider than the BMW, but there was no other traffic. After a few miles, she turned onto a dirt road. It was a mess. The rain had eroded the edges into gullies. Twice Bob got out to direct the car. Nothing on him was left dry. When they got to a one-lane wooden bridge, Irene stopped the car and got out. Bob followed. The rain had slackened off, but the mud-brown stream ripped down the hillside, only inches beneath the bridge's deck.

"Want to leave the car?" Bob asked. Irene said nothing. He realized she couldn't hear him. "The car," he shouted. She turned quickly. "Should we leave it?"

"Naw," Irene shouted back. "It's a mile yet."

"Could we get any wetter?"

"Probably," Irene said.

They got back into the car, its windows steaming up now. Irene spun in the mud and drove across the bridge quickly. The bridge vibrated as they crossed.

"It's been knocked out twice in storms like this," Irene said.

"Thanks for waiting to tell me," Bob said.

"You're welcome," she said. She grinned at him and wiped a strand of wet hair from her forehead. For the first time, she drove with one hand on the wheel, the other on the stick shift. The woods on either side were thinned with an eye to appearance. As they rounded a bend, Bob saw an immense roof over the rise straight ahead. One more bend, and the house beneath the roof came into view—all four stories of it. Bob assumed the lake was down the hillside, but he couldn't see it through the mist and rain.

"This is what you call a cottage?" Bob asked. He heard the gawky, gee-whiz tone in his voice. And he resented the way Irene had led him to believe they would be staying in a cottage rather than a summer mansion.

"Actually it's an old Queen Anne–style sanatorium. But everyone up here calls their house a cottage. That or a camp. My grandfather bought it in the thirties. It was owned by a doctor who was in competition with the Trudeau Sanatorium. He had about five wealthy TB patients a year. He'd bring them up for the summer."

The road dipped toward the front of the house and split into two branches. Irene took the one leading to a circular driveway. The grass island had a garden at its center. Irene stopped the car at the steps leading to the porch, which ran the length of the house.

Bob knew now he had made a mistake. There was no way he belonged in a place like this. But Irene was already running up the steps, waving for him to get going.

When Bob caught up with Irene at the front door, she was trying to work her key. "Damn," she said. "It looks like they've changed the locks. Nobody told me." She turned and slapped her hands against her thighs. "That's great. I suppose I could break in, but maybe we should try something else first. Come with me."

Irene stopped at the car and pulled two bags out of the backseat. Bob grabbed his. She led him quickly down a stone walk toward the water. As they passed beneath several large spruce a boulder and stone boathouse came into view. The boathouse was bigger than his parents' house.

"This should be open," Irene said. "At least we can get out of the rain until Mr. Himmel gets here."

"Who's he?"

"The caretaker. He lives in the village. He's been taking care of the place since before I was born."

The water slapped against the sides of the boathouse and the dock. Irene opened the front door and beckoned Bob in first. There was a large hall with tables and chairs stacked at one end, and a stone fireplace at the other.

"By the end of the summer, this is one big party room. There's a balcony over the water. You can dive right in, it's deep enough."

The water sounded as if it were directly beneath, ready to break through at any moment. Bob cracked the door to the balcony, but the wind and spray of rain forced him to push it shut. Irene was already stacking logs in the fireplace. Bob walked around, studying the photos framed and hanging on the wall. Most were of men holding drinks or beers or fish. But there were several of Irene, one of her as a girl jumping backward off the rail of the balcony. She wore a one-piece bathing suit, her hair cut short. Her face was freckled more than it was now. She had a hand raised that held her nose, the other hand was straight along her side. There was an expression of calm on her face, her eyes wide open and staring flirtatiously into the camera. She could have been falling into a bed or the arms of someone she loved rather than into a lake fifteen feet below.

"Skip the family history," Irene said. "You'll choke on the dust. Help me get this fire going."

Bob broke handfuls of thin branches for kindling and stuffed them beneath the log rack. Irene doused the logs with kerosene and lit the fire. The heat felt good. Irene fumbled through one of her bags and pulled out a small package wrapped in foil.

"Chicken salad sandwiches—for the trip up—but I forgot them in the rain. This weather makes me nervous."

"I gathered."

"Was it really obvious? I wasn't rude, was I?"

"Rude—oh, no, not rude." Bob rolled his eyes.

Irene tossed a sandwich like a Frisbee at his chest. "You know what I meant. Give me a break."

Bob leaned against the stone face of the fireplace. He watched Irene eat slowly. "I don't always know what you mean. For instance, what are you doing with me?"

Irene swallowed before answering. "Don't act like I kidnapped you."

Bob shook his head. He was glad she had invited him. "It just seems a little too good to be true. I barely know you."

"That's why I invited you. To get to know you better. Besides the weather, what's wrong so far?"

Bob waited for a large bite of chicken salad to squeeze down his throat. "Nothing. I feel out of place, I guess."

"Oh, come on," Irene said. She tossed a napkin into the fire.

Bob watched the napkin burn to ash. "Whatever you say."

"There you go again."

"Sorry," Bob said, although he knew he didn't sound it. That was the big difference between Irene and him. She could say sincere things without sounding inflated or sarcastic. When he tried to say sincere things, he sounded sarcastic. And most of the time, he was. But he was trying to change. Right now he was trying.

Irene stood and walked slowly in a circle in front of the fireplace. She pulled a cigarette from her bag and lit it. "I hadn't planned to make it an early night. But I'm really tired. I'm going downstairs to the storage room to see if I can find some sleeping bags. Would you throw a few more logs on the fire? The wood-box is over there."

Bob listened to Irene as she walked down a stairway out of sight. Then he pulled an armful of large split logs out of the wood-box and dropped them on the hearth. He put two on and left the others for later. He sat with his back to the fire and listened to the slap of the lake against the boathouse. He could smell the water now. It didn't have the salty pungency of the sea or the thick scent of decay like the stagnant lakes of Connecticut. This was a crisper smell, a combination of clean water and clean air. He shut his eyes and concentrated on breathing in rhythm with the waves. He wanted to relax. He didn't notice Irene until she spoke.

"No sleeping bags," she said. She held a stack of gray wool blankets in her arms. "These were all I could find." She put two next to the fire and spread the third out on the floor. "Once this stone gets warmed up, it'll keep the floor warm. When I was a kid, my parents came up here every September to see the leaves. I'd stay by the fire the whole time."

Bob took off his shoes and put his feet on the ledge. It was just warming. Irene turned the blankets to warm them all the way through. She took another pair of jeans from her bag and made a pillow out of them. Bob did the same with a sweater from his bag.

"Is there a bathroom?"

"Afraid not," Irene said. "Just the great outdoors. I ran out while I was looking for the blankets."

"I'll be right back," Bob said, putting his shoes back on. The rain was heavy again, the wind blowing it into his face. He felt like he was walking through a car wash. He chose a spot right outside the door. There'd be no evidence in a downpour like this. After he finished, he lingered, facing the wind, letting the rain soak him through again. The force of the rain took his mind off Irene for a moment. It felt good not to think, just to feel, to feel that something could sweep him away and obliterate him, for the rain was that hard. But it didn't carry him off. He gave up and headed inside.

"Stay out there any longer, and I would have called for a search party," Irene said. "Jesus, look at you."

"Toss me a blanket, will you?" he said, taking a seat by the fire. He took his clothes off there and draped the blanket around him. The wool was scratchy, but felt good.

Irene covered herself with a blanket and curled up on her side. Bob wasn't certain what the sleeping agenda was—whether he was expected to sleep beside her or pretend they were brother and sister. He first needed to get warmer, so he stayed by the fire, tossing two more logs on. After a few minutes, he slid across the floor and lay beside her, sealing the space between them with his blanket. "Is this okay?" he said. When she didn't respond, he rose up on his elbow and glanced at her face. She was asleep. "See you in the morning," he whispered.

The wind blew all night. Bob felt drafts of cold wet air passing his head. The water slapped and sloshed, one-two, one-two, one-two-three. Sometime during the night, Irene rose and put more logs on. Bob couldn't get into a deep sleep. He dozed, woke, and listened. If he concentrated, he could hear Irene's breathing, slow and soft, beneath the sounds of the water and wind. In the dimming glow of the fire, he thought he could see his breath. It was getting colder. Each time he woke, he found Irene closer to him, her breathing more noticeable. The last time, he closed his eyes and let her breathing lead him back into sleep.

When Bob woke next it was light. The rain pelted against the lakeside windows. His arm was draped over Irene, her hair close enough to his mouth to move when he breathed. Her sweater had pulled to one side during the night, exposing the top of her shoulder closest to him. He moistened his lips and kissed it softly. Nothing. He kissed again, this time running his lips up toward her neck. She sighed and rolled toward him, opening her eyes. She stared at him for a moment as if he were a stranger, then smiled.

"Are you taking advantage of a sleeping woman?" she whispered.

"I thought you might be cold now that the fire's out."

"Oh," she said, pulling him toward her.

Irene led him by the hand and ran to the side of the house. It seemed even larger, its edges sharper in the muted daylight of the storm. Bob had the feeling in sunlight it would appear immense. They were starving—and out of food.

"Well," Bob said, pausing by a cellar window.

"Go ahead," Irene said.

Bob pressed his foot to the window frame and pushed—it shifted but didn't open.

"Don't be hesitant—it's no big deal given the situation."

Bob gave the window a quick kick. The window popped inward, a pane falling to the floor below. Bob threw the bags inside and slid down through, mud covering his shirt. He dropped to the basement floor, which was farther down than he expected. He caught Irene as she slid down, equally muddy. They kissed, the glass shards crunching beneath their feet.

"Well," she said. "It seems you know how to get inside one of these houses after all."

"Other than by invitation, it's the only way," Bob said.

He turned around, his eyes adjusting to the dark. Irene led him through a maze of boxes stacked on skids to a horizontal freezer. In the freezer's light, Bob could see a moosehead on the floor to the side.

"Crap," Irene said. "There's almost nothing here except venison, frozen smelt, sausage, and peas. How's that sound?"

"Right now, anything sounds good."

Irene grabbed an armful of packages and shut the door, the absence of light temporarily blinding Bob. He followed her footsteps to the stairs and up.

The kitchen was large—stained pine cabinets up and down and windows overlooking the lake.

"I'll bread the smelt and fry them for lunch—they've got to thaw first. The venison will be for dinner. Why don't you get a shower while I cook the sausage and peas. Upstairs." She nodded toward a swinging door.

"You sure?"

"Sure. Go. Let me get on with this."

Bob pushed the door open and walked into a small pantry area, which led to a formal dining room. A long oak table with high-backed chairs dominated the room. He felt disoriented— he had no idea where the stairs in this house were. He continued through, into what he guessed was a parlor, furnished with stuffed Victorian chairs and Tiffany lamps, and through that room into a central hallway, dominated by an oak staircase leading upstairs. There were other rooms beyond—but Bob didn't feel like exploring. It was overwhelming, a house like this as a summer cottage. He had worked in houses as large— but never with freedom to roam. He almost expected someone to pop out from around a corner and demand to know what he was doing there. He paused on the landing to look out toward the lake. The rain still fell heavily, and he couldn't see much of it. There was a six-car garage he hadn't noticed the night before. Irene's car was parked down from that near the boathouse.

Bob froze when he heard the sound of a bathroom shower. His first thought was to call Irene—but then he saw her muddy shirt draped on the handle of a door halfway open.

"Irene?" he shouted above the sound of the shower.

Irene pulled the shower curtain to the side. His breath left him the way it felt when he missed the last step on a stairs. The lines of her body were smooth and continuous without being soft. In one quick motion—sliding the shower curtain open—he saw a grace and confidence that was at once foreign and everything he had ever sought. Looking at her, he felt a rush of excitement—not just sexual but heady, as if he had been summoned to the big leagues after years in the minors.

"What took you?" she said.

"How did you get here?" he asked, pulling his clothes off in a clumsy rush.

"The servants' stairs."

"I should have guessed. They had to be here somewhere."

"They make for a lot of shenanigans whenever the house is full," she said, pulling the curtain around behind Bob. He moved into her arms beneath the warm spray of the shower.

Later, Irene made breakfast. They ate, and Irene took him on a tour of the house. In the parlor, she took her shirt off and unbuckled Bob's pants.

"What is this," he said. "The Olympics?"

"A little contest," she said. "I want to see how many rooms we can do this in before it degenerates into a standard house tour." She pushed Bob back into an overstuffed couch and jumped on top of him, her breasts pressing against his face.

"First, I want to know," he said, pulling his pants down, "how many rooms are there in this house?"

"Enough."

"For what?"

"To know you've been on one heck of a tour." She pulled her pants down and straddled him. "Those screwed-up Victorians," she said. "They never knew what to do with this much stuffing in a chair."

From room to room they went—the parlor, the family room, two studies, and a downstairs guest bedroom. Hide and seek, rough play, affection, war. Bob lost all track of time, conscious only of one sensation after another. High ceilings, oak trim, wainscoting, oriental rugs that chafed and couches that squeaked and slid. Somewhere near the kitchen, in a small room Irene claimed was just for laundry, Bob begged for a re-prieve. "Sustenance," he cried, leaning against a stack of beach towels.

Bob woke to the smell of hot oil and a spattering sound coming from the kitchen. He had dozed—not for more than a few minutes. But his mind had regained its edge. He rose and retraced their path from room to room in search of his clothes. He wasn't sure if at first he had attempted to bring them along. The rooms were quiet—no loose boards. Their formality seemed odd in the midst of the woods. It took money to have leisure, leisure to get out of a backseat, to transcend the Friday night party, the drive-in, the game, to avoid the awkward fumbling of redressing at the sound of the parents' unexpected return. It took the space of leisure, and the leisure of space to imagine the limits of one's potential for pleasure. Irene knew this. It made Bob feel like a plaything for a rainy day.

In the white light of sunrise in a clear sky, Bob recounted the events of the previous day as if they could be stolen from his memory without warning. Irene slept, her face turned to-ward him. A digital clock on the bureau read 6:04. There was no sound of rain. He lifted the sheet from his body slowly—Irene rolled over—and crept out of bed carefully, using his hand to slow the rise of the mattress as he slid out.

Bob walked to the window and surveyed the grounds. The grass in front was a brilliant green—wet and glistening. A rust-ing white Ford pickup was parked in front of the garage. Bob walked to the door and opened it slowly, listening. There was no sound in the house. He closed it and walked quietly to the bed. He lifted the sheet without waking her and traced with his eyes the slope of her flesh down from her ribs to her waist and its gradual rise to her hips. Her rear was paler than the rest of her. A tuft of red-tinted hair showed through at the juncture of her hips. He slipped beside her without rocking the bed and reached for that hair, his fingers loose and exploring. Her legs lifted slightly, and he found her there, moistening without waking, and he closed his eyes, allowing his fingers to sense everything. She exhaled, and rolled to him.

Bob slept lightly. He heard Irene rise and dress. She left the room and returned, the smell of fresh coffee thick in the air. When he felt the mattress depress beside him, he opened his eyes. She had set a cup of coffee for him beside the bed. "Mr. Himmel's here," Irene said. "C'mon, I'll introduce you." The clock read 8:57.

A white-haired man in khakis and a navy blue sweater emerged from the garage with a chainsaw in hand. He set it in the bed of the pickup before noticing Irene.

"Hello, missy," he said. "Saw your car and figured you were about somewhere. You come up in this blow?"

"As always. It was pretty nasty."

"I'll say. Took down a big cedar on the road in. Must've been during the wind last night. Popped the chain cutting her up. Just enough out of the way to make it past. Who's this here with you?"

Irene introduced Bob. He shook Himmel's hand. There were age spots on the back of it, but his grip was firm and his palm callused.

"You better get yourself a big breakfast if you want to keep up with her," Himmel told him.

Bob grinned and nodded.

Bob found Himmel working on the cedar. He was still trimming the branches. The heavy work remained. "He looks like he could use a hand," Bob told Irene. "Do you mind?"

"If that's what you want to do, sure," she said. "He is used to it. But I'm sure he'd welcome the help. I'll head into town and get some groceries. I'd like to go sailing later, though, so don't wear yourself out."

"A little sawing is the least of my worries as far as that goes."

"And I thought you were a long-distance guy."

For lunch, Irene brought Bob and Himmel sandwiches. They used two logs as stools and ate without speaking. Irene had gone down to the boathouse. After he finished with his sandwich, Himmel cleared his throat. "Get on," he said. "I'll finish up here."

Bob caught up with Irene in the boathouse. She was about

to lower the sailboat from its hoist. "Before you get that down," he said, "I should tell you I've never been sailing. Don't know how."

"Oh," Irene said. "Why didn't you say so earlier. I wouldn't have pretended I knew how to work this damn hoist."

"I didn't wreck your afternoon, did I?"

"No, not at all. Let's just take a rowboat out, okay?"

"Sure," Bob said, relieved that there had been no expectations other than for the sailing itself.

"You've been rowing, haven't you?"

Bob paused to think for a second. "I guess I have. Once or twice, fishing."

"A canoe would be more fun. I guess we let someone borrow ours."

"The rowboat's fine," Bob said. "That way, I can act the part of the gallant. You can sit back and pull the petals off a water lily . . ."

"Oh, yes, giving you coy, flirtatious glances from the shade of my wide-brimmed hat, its big blue ribbons billowing in the breeze, and my parasol ready to ford off your lusty but much-desired advances."

"There you go. Let's head back in now. We've experienced it all. And we might get wet if we actually go out."

Irene untied the rowboat from its place. "What do you say we take the chance anyway." She hopped into the boat and held it steady against the dock as Bob stepped in.

Bob picked up the oars and set them in the locks. They were heavier than he remembered, clumsier to maneuver. He had trouble synchronizing them. Gradually he got the boat moving in the right direction, but not without splashing Irene several times. "Where are we going?" he asked.

"I'm not sure how to answer that," Irene said, shrugging. "It's your lake."

"No, the lake we don't own. But even if I had an idea where I'd like to go, I'm not sure we'd ever make it."

Bob pulled the oars out of the water and held them in the air, dripping. "I never said I was a gondola operator."

"No one would ever mistake you for one, don't worry."

"I guess I can't claim to be much of a rower."

"Well, I love to row. Let's switch."

As they changed positions, Bob gave her a quick kiss on the cheek. "That's about as romantic as I can be in a boat," he said.

"That's just fine. You have nothing to prove on the water. Save it for land." She took the oars and began rowing steadily, keeping close to the shoreline.

"There aren't many houses in this direction," Irene said. "I like rowing around here. You get a sense of what the place might have been like a few hundred years ago."

The stand of spruce went right to the water's edge. They grew from a clutter of large boulders that were the size of a garage, and from fallen trees and old stumps. The forest was too dense to see more than a few yards inland. Rocks and boulders lined the shore. There was almost no sand at the bottom. Outcrops of ledge ran from the shore in places straight into the lake, disappearing in the dark of deeper water. Schools of small fish hugged the shoreline. Larger ones were nowhere in sight. The rhythm of her rowing and the water lulled Bob into a calm, which broke when she began chuckling.

"What is it?" Bob asked.

"Nothing, really," she said. "Just that image of me with a big-brimmed hat and a whalebone corset trying to row a boat when my beau couldn't."

"We're so liberated."

"That's the whole point, though. We're not, are we?"

Bob shrugged. "Maybe. Sure, I guess."

Irene rested for a moment. She lifted the oars and held them out of the water. "I'm sure you would be the one to row if you could have been."

"But I couldn't."

"Right. But that didn't stop you from trying, did it? Even though you knew nothing about it."

"So what? Where does this all wind up?"

Irene resumed rowing. "Nowhere. It's just an observation."

"And what good is it?"

"What good is any observation? I would observe it's odd that you're going to work for a drugstore chain."

"Some of us need the money."

Irene spit into the water. "That's not what I meant. If I were a snob I wouldn't be here with you. But sometimes I feel like you're always pushing at things, expecting them to give way to some underlying machinery. There is none."

Irene had rowed them into a cove with a small, stony island at its center. The surface of the water was smooth, reflecting the white clouds moving quickly across the sky. When he squinted against the bright surface of the water, he could see all the way to the stony bottom of the shallows. He had spent a lot of time talking himself into feeling good about accepting the job with P&V. He didn't like confronting accusations that he wasn't the person someone thought he would be. That somehow it made no sense to find him working for such a business. That was simple-minded, idealistic. He had a life to live and debts to pay. Those were the facts. Not trust funds. Not grad school. Just his own facts.

Irene nudged him with her foot. "Hey, wake up," she said. "This is my hideout." She rowed the boat toward the island. "I used to come here when I was a girl. To get away from everyone. You want to land?"

"You're the captain. I wouldn't mind."

Irene maneuvered the boat alongside a flat rock and steadied the boat against it with her hand. She gave Bob a rope. "Hop out and tie us onto something, will you."

The island was an extension of ledge that submerged at the shore and popped back up a hundred yards out. There were a few spruce, an old log, and several loose boulders. Irene took a seat on one of the boulders.

They sat side by side for a while. Bob felt pressured to break the silence. But she seemed preoccupied. "I guess you're right," he said at last.

"About what?"

"About me and that job. At least as it seems to me. A year ago, if you would have told me I would choose a job like this, I would have said you were nuts."

"So why did you take it?"

"Grad school? Was that for me?"

Irene shrugged. "Only you know the answer to that. I could see you there."

"Not unless I wanted a job teaching English as a second language at Miami Dade Junior College."

"What about law school?"

"And racking up more debt? I would be compelled to take a job at the very kind of firm I despise. And before that, to be one of those barracuda nerds for good grades just to graduate near the top. I don't want to be like that. Not now. Not ever."

Irene tossed a piece of bark into the water. She shrugged. "Why do you have to make up your mind immediately? You could give yourself a year to goof off. Take a trip around the country. Go to Europe."

"With what?"

"With enough to get you over there. Do it on a shoestring." She looked Bob in the eyes. "It isn't that hard."

"Look, I've accepted the job . . ."

"Quit."

"I haven't started yet. Besides, at least it's something . . ."

"As opposed to?"

"Nothing. As opposed to sitting around with nothing to do."

"I can't imagine you sitting around doing nothing. You would write if nothing else. Ask your parents for some help."

"That's great. I tell my folks to send me rent and meal money so I can write the Great American Novel. And while you're writing checks, Dad, take care of my college loan. I'll make it good to you with the money from the movie contract. You have no idea about my family. They'd think I was a bum. There's nothing noble about it."

Irene slid closer and put her arm around his shoulder. "You're right—I don't know your family. I don't mean to sound like I'm cross-examining you. I'm curious. Maybe surprised at the thought of you doing what you'll be doing." She paused as if she were going to say something else, but reconsidered. Bob looked at the sky in the water until a fish stirred the surface and broke the illusion.

Irene kissed him on the cheek. "Hey," she said. "Loosen up."

Bob stood and walked to the water's edge. He watched a minnow dart back and forth in a shallow pool, unable to find its way into deeper water. When the sun emerged from behind a cloud, the pool became a mirror and he saw his face there. He looked too serious.

"I guess I'm superstitious," Bob said. "It happened so easily. I didn't even apply for the job."

"The drugstore thing?"

"Yeah. The guy—the recruiter—visited campus. I was in the interview room at the campus center. Nobody was using it, and then he walked in. I was reading *Revolutionary Road*. He noticed and started asking me what I thought of it. About the way Yates describes American business. We got into a little argument. He called Yates a poet with a grudge about business. I thought he was a poet with a sharp insight on the world of work."

"A condition you're familiar with?" She smiled.

"Do you want to hear this or not?"

Irene nodded. "Go on."

"Anyway, there's some nerd hanging around the door in a three-piece you can tell he just bought. He's leaving sweaty palm prints on everything he touches. And finally the guy excuses himself so he could get on with the interviews. That was it."

"And?"

"And the next week I got a letter offering me the job: twenty thousand with a company car and a chance for a bonus. He must have seen my name on the book."

"You should have told him Yates was right-on about business. You might have gotten twenty-five grand and a sports car."

Bob paused a moment. "You know, my father has worked in a small factory for thirty years. A tiny place, and he has zip. No retirement. Nothing. And I'm reading a book in a room at the end of my senior year in college, having passed the whole spring without even putting together a résumé, and some guy offers me a job right out of school for the same money my father makes? It would rock the foundations of my parents' universe if I didn't take it. It's the fairy tale they always thought college would be."

"Apparently your fairy tale, too. Your destiny." She gave the word *destiny* a sarcastic emphasis. It stung.

Bob grinned and shook his head. Irene retreated.

"I suppose I'm being obnoxious," she said. "But you make it sound like you have no choice. Do you really want to do what you're going to do? Be honest."

"Sure."

"You don't sound sure. No guessing. This is a blank slate. Suppose you could do anything. Would you do this?"

"No, of course not. I'd rather do nothing and get paid for it. Do you know of any jobs like that?"

"Awwww, come on. You sound sorry for yourself about having to take this job. You should sound happy. You should sound like you reached for it, but you say it fell into your lap and you don't know how to get rid of it. Listen to yourself."

Bob grew weary of talking. He lapsed into a daze that gave him some distance—a numbing field between him and Irene. He didn't want to talk about his life and his choices any more. He wanted to get on with it. The great twenty-two-year party of possibilities had come to an end for him. The possibility of being a pro basketball player, of being a genius, of being a writer, of being anything he ever daydreamed about—all that was fading. Or, rather, being forced to fade. Forced by a growing sense that there was a price for possibilities, and that there was a little charge account somewhere on which each possibility was tallied meticulously until, unfulfilled, they all came due. All of his possibilities seemed to have come due that afternoon in the interview room. And he was old enough now to understand that. Mature enough, too.

Irene slid closer. They sat in silence, staring into the water. He could feel the warmth of her shoulder and he sensed a softening in her presence. She wasn't his adversary. Just someone who could still afford possibilities. And of course she was right. There was nothing necessary about this job. Not necessary in an absolute sense. He could imagine taking a year or two off, traveling, doing whatever he wished. He could make ends meet. A job here or there for a few weeks, and then on the road again. He knew where to find the menial jobs—the gas stations, kitchens, farms of the world. Places where people came and went. The places he had worked since he was fifteen. And that's why he wouldn't turn down this job. It was better than those jobs. And besides, it had fallen into his lap.

To turn it down would go against everything he had ever been told. The closest thing to the gospel in his house: Someone offers you a decent job, take it. As long as you're getting paid for honest work, you're doing all a man has to on this planet. Everything else is sweetener. The car, the insurance, the prospect of a bonus—if all that weren't sweetener, nothing was.

The sun had dipped below the mountain, and in the shade the air chilled quickly. Irene had goose bumps on her arm.

"You ready to head back?" Bob asked, putting his arm around her shoulder and rubbing her arm with his hand.

She nodded.

"How about I try to row this time," Bob said. "Practice." Bob stepped into the boat and put the oars in place. When Irene sat down facing him, she looked like another person. Smaller, more fragile than she had seemed earlier. As he pushed off, he tried to catch her eye, but couldn't. Her eyes were glazed, focused on some inner place.

"Why do people say," Bob said, "a penny for your thoughts?"

Irene smiled, coming to. "Guess thoughts were cheaper once than they are today."

"Maybe not. Seems most of the big ones have been around for at least a couple of thousand years. The cheap ones I know are all contemporary."

"Drugstores, for example." Her voice had softened. There was no irony in it. She wasn't interrogating him.

"I wonder if that's even a thought," he said.

Bob picked up the pace of his rowing. He had the rhythm down now. He had watched her and learned. The boat glided easily round a pier of rocks at the far end of the cove and out into the main part of the lake. The rowing invigorated him. His breathing deepened. He sped up.

"You're a fast learner," Irene said.

"Yeah. Fast enough to believe you're just as uncertain about what you're doing as I am. Maybe more so."

"Don't go sailing yet," Irene said. "You're just getting the oars right."

"Okay—but you tell me, what's the difference between doing something because of debt and doing it because of family tradition."

"Easy," she said. "You can pay off a debt. That's what I've been trying to tell you."

"But the point is, you don't have any more options than I do. You're every bit as prescribed."

"That's not true. I want to be a lawyer."

"Then go to Stanford. Go to Harvard."

"Why? To assert some silly version of my independence? I get good training at Michigan, and going there means a lot to my father. I don't need to say, 'See, I'm different from you.' "

"But you are different. You're not a man. There's no father-son stuff going on here."

"How would you know? My father has talked to me about being a lawyer since I was a girl. I went with him to the office on weekends when we lived in Manhattan. I've read some of his law books. I know what it's like, and more important, I know I like it."

"Somehow you sound like you're trying to convince yourself."

Irene shook her head. "I know what I want. I'm not sure you could say the same."

"Forget me for a second. We've already done that tune." Bob stopped talking to catch his breath. The sweat on his forehead was cold. Rowing in the open water was harder. The breeze pushed against the boat, constantly skewing their course into the shore. His right arm ached from overcompensating. "You're saying your father really wants you to go to law school, and always has, right?"

"Absolutely. He has never felt otherwise. He has said a hundred times he thinks women make better lawyers than men. They read judges and juries better, can be more empathetic when they need to be, and tougher if necessary. Less likely to fall into the clubby sloppiness of big firms."

"So you're your father's girl."

"Of course I am. What of it?"

"Look—you started the inquisition on my choices. This is turnabout time."

"I didn't question your choices. I don't think you've made any. You said yourself the job just fell into your lap. I'm suggesting you should start making choices."

"And I'm suggesting you haven't made any choices either.

Not really. You've been bred and raised to be a lawyer. That's not choosing—that's thoroughbred brainwashing.''

"If it is, I have no way of knowing, do I?"

Bob looked away into the dark water as he rowed. He felt like saying, poor little rich girl. But he checked himself. He felt then that money didn't make the difference. That the entanglements of family life were the same everywhere—for the rich and the poor and those in between. An insight. But what good were they, insights? They never made anything easier.

"No," Bob said calmly. "You don't."

"Don't what?"

"You don't have any way of knowing," he said as he angled into the boathouse. "And neither do I."

CHAPTER

4

The weekend before Independence Day, Irene announced that a visit to her parents was in order. Himmel had reported seeing Bob. Her parents were curious to meet him. They had liked Brent.

Despite Irene's assurances, Bob suspected no good could come of the trip. The best he hoped for was tolerance. She said her parents were open-minded. He wanted to believe her. He had begun liking the way things were with Irene, and wanted it to continue. The affair wasn't on the scale of Antony and Cleopatra, but it wasn't a lark either. He looked forward to the time he spent with her every day, to waking in the night and finding his arm over her.

The night before they left, Bob let Irene fall asleep first. When she was off, he got out of bed without waking her and sat on the large ledge of the windowsill, looking out back. He couldn't see much in the light of a fingernail-shaped moon, but he knew what was there and imagined it: a wall of juniper down the slope, two pillars next to an opening in the wall, other emblems of past civilizations, blocks of granite, a bust of some illustrious alumnus. Irene's touch startled him.

"You're worried about the trip home," Irene said. "Aren't you?" She rubbed his shoulders. You're being silly, she seemed to say, although if she had said that he would have snapped at her. That too was a good sign. The fact that each of them permitted the other gestures instead of words. Gestures which meant something specific but which through an intuited rule remained unstated.

As Irene drove down the Taconic, Bob set his seat lower and lower until he focused on the interior light of the BMW. While Irene tried to calm him with small talk, he passed the time imagining what kinds of tests BMW engineers devised for the interior light. The manual switch test—conducted by a mechanical hand, over and over. The lumens test—until the bulb's brightness was nothing short of a street lamp, capable of illuminating the most detailed map of Berlin. The bump test—in case the BMW was to be driven routinely over small boulders. The translucency test—in which hundreds of plastic covers for the lamp varying only by degrees of translucence were considered until the one most like a high overcast in the Black Forest was found. Men in white coats with steel wills walking with purpose down the shiny hallways at the BMW test center. All of them devising new tests to verify the validity of other tests. An infinite regress of tests. The interior light of a BMW could not be taken lightly.

"Bob, wake up," Irene said. She sounded annoyed.
"I am awake," he said, bringing the seat upright.
"You were snoring."
"Sorry," Bob said. The windshield wipers whapped away at a light mist. His neck ached. The engineers had some work to do on the seats. It hurt to turn his head either way, but he didn't want to miss anything. The houses were set back from the road, landscaped to provide privacy without preventing a glimpse of an exotic front yard sculpture or a child's playhouse styled in the manner of Frank Lloyd Wright.
"How far to home?" Bob asked.
"Soon," Irene said.
Irene had both hands on the wheel—the first Bob had seen her driving like that since the Adirondacks. "Nervous?" he asked.
"A bit—I had a few things I wanted to talk about on the way down."

"Sorry," Bob said, yawning. Irene swerved onto a side road, skidding into the turn. Bob patted her on the leg. "If there's something you want to say, I'll listen. Otherwise, I'll let you concentrate on the road."

"Probably a good idea," she said, returning the pat.

They passed the rest of the trip in silence. Stretches of road bordered by trees gave way first to horse farms, and then to clusters of large houses. One more turn onto a street lighted by imitation gas lamps, and Irene swung into a gravel driveway notched between a barrier of trees and a white-slat fence.

After the Adirondacks, Bob had been expecting a palatial residence. But in the dim light of the Friday dusk what he saw instead was an ivy-covered brick-and-clapboard two-story house that zigzagged into a drumlin in back. A golden retriever ambled lamely off the front steps, wagging his tail. Irene rolled down her window as she slowed the car.

"Topper, I'm home," she said.

"Topper?"

"Isn't that a stitch?" Irene threw open the door and the dog climbed into her lap, licking her face. Bob got out and stood by the trunk until Irene popped it open. He took out the bags and was about to carry them to the front door when a short man with a white cotton sweater appeared at his side.

"I'll get those," he said, extending his hand for a shake. "Bob, I assume."

"Mr. Bradley?" Bob said.

"Oh, no," the man said. "He won't be home for a while yet. I'm Harry."

"Harry," Irene said, giving him a hug. "How are you?"

"Good, sweetheart," he said, kissing her on the cheek. "So, you've thrown everyone into tizzy with this decision to take a year off. What a rebel."

"I know," Irene said. "And I'll be making bombs in the basement next, right?"

"No jokes around your father," Harry said. "He's still suspicious of your motives. Gave me an earful this morning." Harry turned to Bob. "But he's got a good report on you. Himmel told him how you helped to clean up some fallen tree. He likes a worker." Harry picked up the bags and headed in.

"What's this about a year off?" Bob asked.

"One of the things I wanted to talk to you about."

"When did you do that?"

"Yesterday—the law school is allowing me a deferral."

"Why?"

"I'm not sure, exactly. I guess I didn't feel ready to dive back into the books yet. I need some time to sort things out."

"Are you going to travel?"

"Let's talk later," Irene said, nodding toward the door. "Right now is a bad time, especially since my folks don't understand. I plan to go out there. I might take a few graduate classes in government after Christmas."

Irene led Bob upstairs to a large room divided into two areas—one with a double bed, dresser, and bedside chair; the other with a desk, two wingback chairs, and a settee. Irene opened another door which led to a bathroom.

"All yours," she said.

As Bob scanned the room again he saw that Harry had already brought his bags up. "Very nice," he said.

"I'm going to find my mother," Irene said. "I'll be back in a while. I'd say take a rest, but you shouldn't need one."

"Yeah, right."

Irene waved her fingers good-bye to Bob and shut his door. He was grateful for a moment alone. He opened two windows, pausing at the second to get his bearings in relation to the rest of the house. The lawn out back extended like a small park along the hillside. Through some trees he could make out the surface of a pond and the white latticework of a gazebo. He sat on the bed and leaned against the headboard. When he shut his eyes, he could still see the lawn. Cutting it had to be a full-time job.

Mrs. Bradley set a silver serving tray of fish on the table. "Is it Robert or Bob?" she asked, giving him the full polite smile. Irene inherited the perfect teeth from her.

"Bob will do fine," he said.

Mr. Bradley appeared tired and bored. Bob guessed he was much older than his wife. His crewcut hair was white and his well-tanned face, loose-skinned. He might have been sixty.

"Blackened bluefish," he said to Bob. "May I serve you some?"

Bob nodded. Irene walked around the table serving wine.

"What's the name of the company you'll be working for?" Mrs. Bradley asked. "Irene told me not an hour ago, but I can't remember."

"P&V, dear," Mr. Bradley said. "There's one in the village, I think."

"Is there?" she said. "Is that a fact, Robert?"

"I don't know," Bob said.

"It's Bob, Mother," Irene said.

"Of course," she said. "And what will you be doing with them?"

"The job's still a little fuzzy—I'll be checking up on inventories for a district of about twenty stores. I start training some time this month, and then it's on to my district."

"Whereabouts?"

"They haven't decided yet."

"You'll have to let us know when you find out," Mrs. Bradley said. "We like to keep track of Irene's friends. Brent dropped us a card from Europe. He's cycling there."

"How thoughtful of him," Irene said.

"Sounds a little thankless if you ask me," Mr. Bradley said.

There was a pause in the conversation. The sound of silverware tapping china. Irene opened another bottle of wine.

"I don't know, dear," Mrs. Bradley said. "I thought it was rather nice of him myself."

"Not Brent, Lucy," Mr. Bradley said. "Bob's work. The job he's got. I bet there will be a lot of traveling."

Irene grinned at Bob to let him know everything was going okay. He didn't believe it for a second. Cocktails had been awkward. At one point, after introductions, Irene's mother and father had huddled to one side of the room whispering to each other. Bob thought he heard Mr. Bradley mutter something about "damned reassessors." But he still couldn't help feeling they were also discussing him. After a little talk about the acid rain problem in the Adirondacks and Mr. Bradley's second silver bullet, it was time for dinner. By then, Bob felt glazed. He'd stuck to club soda, so it wasn't booze. It was a feeling that there was another person inside him monitoring everything he did and said in front of the Bradleys.

"So, Bob, tell me about your father," Mr. Bradley said. "What's his line of work?"

"He works in a factory."

"Good. What's he do in there?"

"It's a small place. He does a little of everything. He even packs the skids for shipping." Bob watched Mr. Bradley's face closely for a clue as to what he was thinking. To his surprise, it seemed to lighten.

"Now there's an art," he said.

"What's that?" Mrs. Bradley asked.

"Packing a skid," he said.

"A what?" Mrs. Bradley said.

"A skid, dear. You know, a platform for stacking boxes. I watched a bunch of Greeks preparing them at a plant in Astoria."

"What were you doing there?"

"You know Burt," Mr. Bradley said. "Never knows what to do with his money. Wanted to buy a plant that makes electrical plugs. He asked me to look it over with him. It was a dirty business, but I marveled at those Greeks. Stacking the boxes high as this." He held up his hand above his head and jiggled it. "Tall as a man they stacked those boxes. Like masons, fitting them in like blocks of granite. And then winding the metal straps up and over, all around . . ." He swirled his hand to show how this was done. He glanced at his wife. "You know me. I can talk with any man. So I got these Greek boys talking about their work, and this little fellow who ran the place kept saying, 'No shrink-wrapping for this plant. Just steel straps.' " Mr. Bradley chuckled. "It's a shabby business, that shrink-wrapping, isn't it?"

"The boxes slide," Bob said.

"Precisely," Mr. Bradley said emphatically. "And I'll bet your father's the kind of man who'll have nothing to do with it."

"It sounds dreadful," Mrs. Bradley said.

Bob gave Irene an imploring look to change the subject. She shrugged at him.

"What is it they put in those boxes?" Mrs. Bradley asked.

Bob decided that if they wanted to talk about this, he'd

humor them. "They manufacture circuit breaker boxes for mobile homes."

"In Connecticut?" Mrs. Bradley said. "I would have thought there was no demand for such things there."

"I suspect they ship them all over the country," Mr. Bradley said. "Isn't that right?" He paused for Bob to nod in agreement. "You see mobile homes everywhere today. They're affordable housing. We'll probably see a few when we go out to Michigan to visit Irene, dear."

"I'll have to keep my eyes open," Mrs. Bradley said. "Perhaps we'll even see a few of your father's boxes there. Would you care for any dessert?"

"I'm all set, thanks," Bob said. He'd just finished the last of his salad. It was as if Mrs. Bradley wanted to conclude dinner immediately. He couldn't imagine why it should continue. Irene appeared amused by the conversation. But he was in agony.

Mr. Bradley poured himself another glass of wine, finishing the bottle. "Irene, could you see if there's another chilled?" When she left the room, he turned to Bob. "You'll be joining us for the pageant tomorrow, won't you?"

Bob put the last forkful of bluefish into his mouth while trying to think of what to say. When Irene returned with another bottle, he swallowed the fish, and said, "What pageant is that?"

"Oh, a little tradition of ours," Mr. Bradley said. "A costume party of sorts."

"Father, I thought we'd stopped that," Irene said.

"Stopped?" Mrs. Bradley said. "Not stopped, dear. Suspended for a few years, perhaps." She turned to Bob as if he were due an explanation. "A neighbor of ours, Elihu Spur, fell into the pond and nearly drowned. It shook everyone up. But that's forgotten now, and Elihu has sequestered himself year-round in Palm Springs. We thought this year we'd resume."

"But you haven't set anything up," Irene said.

"That's because your mother finally came to her senses," Mr. Bradley said. "She's having a caterer take care of that. The tent, the trappings, the banners, and the whirligigs."

"I simply didn't have time this year," Mrs. Bradley said. "The flower show took all May and half of June to organize."

"Of course it did, dear," Mr. Bradley said. He sipped his wine. "You shouldn't involve yourself in those details anyway."

"You could have told us ahead of time," Irene said. "We would have come another weekend."

"That's precisely why we didn't tell you," Mr. Bradley said. "Don't worry. We have costumes for both of you."

"Costumes?" Bob said.

"We'll leave tonight," Irene said. "This is ridiculous."

"It all starts with a grand breakfast, including lots of pancakes . . ." Mrs. Bradley began.

"And lots of champagne," Irene said. "Everyone drinks until there's no question of foolishness. It's like white on white."

"That's the point of the pancakes. So no one falls into the pond again. We dress up, you know." Mr. Bradley poured Bob another glass of wine. "All the legends. Franklin, Hamilton, Jefferson . . ."

"Betsy Ross, and the wives, of course," Mrs. Bradley said. "No one gives credit to the wives of the legends."

"That's as liberated as Mother gets," Irene said, rolling her eyes.

"Who's Benedict Arnold?" Bob asked.

"A sense of humor," Mr. Bradley said, patting the back of Bob's hand. "Very pointed."

"And who am I to be?" Irene said.

"A fun-loving lady of society," Mrs. Bradley said. Her speech had become slightly slurred. "There for the occasion."

"And me?" Bob asked.

"One of my sergeants at arms," Mr. Bradley said, gazing into the opaque white of the wall. "I'm Washington."

"Bob, we don't have to do this," Irene said. "We can leave."

Bob watched Mrs. Bradley dab her lips with the cloth napkin. Mr. Bradley remained preoccupied with the wall. Neither appeared to have heard Irene. "I don't mind," he said.

"A sensible indulgence," Mr. Bradley said, hoisting his glass into the air as if about to propose a toast. Instead he held it there, examining it. Bob wondered whether he'd found an imperfection. But it seemed more likely that he'd forgotten what he intended to say.

"I propose Bob join me in the study for an after-dinner chat," Mr. Bradley said. "You two ladies can tidy up."

Irene sighed. "If it's brandy and cigars for you two, I'd love some myself."

"The brandy or the cigar?" Mr. Bradley said.

"Both," Irene said.

"Really, Irene," Mrs. Bradley said. "Let's leave the men to their talk. I've got a new section of garden underway out back that I've been wanting to show you."

"I'll see you in a few minutes," Irene said. "We'll take a walk around the grounds. The fish jump in the pond this time of night."

"You've probably seen a few fish jump in your time, haven't you, Bob?" Mr. Bradley said.

"Yes," he said. "But never Elihu Spur."

"He'd have to have made quite a migration to be in the pond tonight," Mr. Bradley said, leading Bob to the study. "But take a look after we've had our brandy."

Law books lined the walls. Several lay open on his desk. He clicked on a small desktop lamp and shut the door behind Bob. "Let's see," he said. "You have a preference in brandy?"

"Whatever you're drinking," Bob said. He'd never had brandy.

"A little Courvoisier will suit me," he said, opening the door to a built-in cabinet. He pulled out the bottle and two snifters, filling each about halfway.

Bob took a mouthful right away and had to fight himself to stop from gagging.

"Oh, goodness, Bob," Mr. Bradley said, slapping him on the back. "Warm that up, first. Like this." He rotated his tumbler, swirling it in his hand.

"I haven't drunk brandy before," Bob said. He figured straight talk was the order of this room.

"Well, this is an occasion for celebration then," Mr. Bradley said. "You'll find it's a drink that grows on you." He walked over to his desk. "I am going to have a cigar, if you don't object."

"Go ahead," Bob said. "My father smokes them."

"Ahh," Mr. Bradley said. He slid open a wooden box and pulled out a cigar wrapped in white paper. "You probably don't want to try one?" He slid the top back without waiting for Bob's reply. "I just wanted a chance to get to know you better."

Bob took a deep breath and let it out slowly. "I've never gone to the study for brandy and cigars after dinner. For conversation, you'll have to lead the way."

"I'll do that, too," Mr. Bradley said. "Very good. I think Irene was right to bring you down. We were curious. She's an impulsive girl—a woman now. I'm against her taking time off before law school. But she'll do what she wants regardless of our concerns." He paused, swirling his brandy and raising the snifter to his nose. "And I think I can say she's very fond of you. She made that clear to us earlier."

"I'm fond of her," Bob said.

"I'll bet you are," he said, lighting his cigar. "But this isn't a heavy talk about how I expect you to treat her. She can take care of herself, don't you think?"

Bob smiled. For the first time, he felt at ease. "I have a hard time imagining a situation in which she couldn't," he said.

"To be honest," Mr. Bradley said, blowing out smoke as he spoke, "I'm more curious about you. You're bright, I assume that. And I'm curious why a boy like you would do what you're going to do."

"How so?"

"Let me get to the point. I believe you're an ambitious young man—and I consider ambition an attribute. But this job of yours—inventory checking—it's the slow path. I'm not talking about anything but you here. I was thinking about this during dinner—why inventory coordination, or whatever you called it? Why that?"

"What do you mean?" Bob asked.

"Let me illustrate. I used to run track. Did the four-forty. And I learned there are two factors that determine speed: length of stride and stride frequency. It's common sense. What I'd suggest to you is finding a job that gives you a greater financial stride at an increased frequency. You can flail around in a position like yours for years before you start to make money. You can work like a pack mule and get absolutely nowhere. One bitchy boss, one silly office intrigue, and your career could be sidetracked for years. I'm talking about real money. The kind of money that enables you to enjoy life.''

"I'm satisfied with the job I've got lined up. I'd like to do that for a while first. Besides, they're expecting me.''

"That's admirable. But let me give you something to think about. Never hesitate to leave one job for something better. Just consider what I'm about to say. Every day, I work with bankers and other people involved in international financial dealings. A young man like you can make a lot of money very quickly by working in the currency business. It's a hellish pace. But if you can stand it, you can retire in ten years. It's just something I think you should consider, that's all.''

"But it's not something I'm interested in right now, thanks,'' Bob said. "I'm satisfied with my choice.''

"Of course you should be.'' He inhaled through the cigar for a moment and continued: "But it's an odd choice for—what was it?—an English major. A command of language, I presume?''

"No one knows these days.''

"Surely some love of it?''

Bob nodded. He supposed there was that. He couldn't quite figure where Mr. Bradley was headed.

"And you haven't thought about advertising? People who are clever with words make good money in that line of work. Some of our neighbors started as copywriters at agencies in Manhattan. They never lack.''

"It's not just the money—''

"Isn't it, though?'' Mr. Bradley interrupted. "When we decide on a job, we of course want to like it—but don't we also want to make good money? As much as we can with the training we've got?''

"I suppose.''

"Understand me, now, I know I'm putting you on a spot— but I can't resist trying to fathom your reasoning here. I want to play the devil's advocate.''

"It comes down to this—I accepted the job, I said I'd do it, and I follow through on things, that's all.''

"Yes, of course.'' Mr. Bradley said this without sounding patronizing. He circled his desk, pausing to glance at the bookcase, almost theatrical in his motions. The brandy in one hand, cigar in the other, his props. Bob could imagine him addressing a jury, although he suspected Mr. Bradley was the kind of lawyer who never went to court. "You know, this is a business unknown to most of America. But believe me, this is what the world is all about. Not ideologies. Not democracy versus communism, East versus West, but the ebb and flow of capital, the trading of currencies. It bankrupts one nation and leads another into prosperity. Where the currencies flow, there's harvest in the midst of drought. But where the capital has dried up, there's famine in the most fertile basin. Managing those currencies, trading them, that's the heart of what the real business world is all about. Marketing, inventory control—superficial responses, far-removed symptoms of the real forces, the real economic tides and currents. If you're interested, I could open a door for you. From there, you're on your own. All you've to do is give me the sign."

Bob finished his brandy and set the glass on Mr. Bradley's desk. The man was being avuncular, not the devil's advocate. He felt a tug of curiosity about what was being proposed.

"Well, Bob?"

"I'm going to think about it," he said.

"Take some time," Bradley said. "See how it feels to you in a few days. Based on what Irene's told me, I'm willing to bet you've got the kind of mind that's right for that business. And I want to see Irene's friends do well. It's as simple as that."

Bob found Irene waiting for him on the back patio. "How'd it go?" she asked.

"Okay, I guess."

"That doesn't tell me anything."

"I think that your father wouldn't mind seeing me get into the currency business."

"Oh, God. Not the 'tides of currency' talk."

"The very one."

"He didn't look drunk at dinner."

"He didn't act drunk in there. Somehow, though, I think he would rather see us living a little farther apart than it looks like we will."

"He's worried," Irene said. "He doesn't want me distracted during law school and he's already concerned that I'm not starting immediately. As if I could change my mind. It's not you specifically. It's anybody, any possible distraction. He was delighted when Brent and I broke up. He threw a party. Mother may have felt otherwise. She's more of a snob than he is and thought Brent came from the right people. She said, 'He's *our* kind of people.' "

They walked away from the house, into the dark of the garden and beyond, down stone steps and onto the lawn. It was misting still.

"They're not bad parents," Irene said. "They let me do as I please. At least most of the time."

"It's clear your father knows you'll do what you want," Bob said.

"I'm glad of that."

They took a seat on the gazebo steps. The mist felt good on Bob's arms and face. Good the way a familiar sight or sound feels inside. The mist fell alike everywhere, in Westchester County and in rural Connecticut, on Volkswagens and Volvos.

Irene leaned her head on his shoulder. "How are you taking all this?"

Bob didn't answer for a long time. He looked at the lights of the house through the trees. He saw a light where he thought his room was, although he couldn't be sure. He didn't remember leaving one on. "I think everything's making me uncomfortable these days. Some of it's good, some I can't tell about yet. There's a lot going on."

"Yeah, it's an odd time," Irene said. She exhaled slowly. Bob concentrated on synchronizing his breathing with hers. "Do you want to leave?" she asked.

Bob shook his head. "I'm half-curious about the party."

Bob woke in a glare of sun. Someone knocked at his door. He could hear Mrs. Bradley's voice.

"You awake, Bob?" she said. "Guests will be here soon."

"Getting up," Bob said.

"I'm leaving your costume here in the hall. It should fit."

When he was sure she had left, Bob rolled out of bed and opened the door. In a neat pile, Bob found a pair of long white socks, a white shirt with flared sleeves, a russet jacket with brass buttons, and a pair of pants that looked something like knickers. He carried the pile into the room and looked out the window. Two men in gray uniforms were pitching a large candy-striped tent on the lawn. Red, white, and blue banners were festooned from the ornamental trees on the patio, where a large grill had been set up. Mrs. Bradley appeared wearing a shiny blue dress and holding a white wig in one hand. She was greeted by another woman wearing a gray dress. The woman pointed to the tent and said something. Mrs. Bradley waved the wig as she replied, emphatic. Another man appeared in a blue jacket and blue pants and wearing a white wig. It took Bob a second to realize it was Mr. Bradley. He interceded in stately fashion between his wife and the other woman, but in a moment, he too began gesturing emphatically toward the tent.

Bob glanced at the pile of clothes on the bed. He wished now that he hadn't agreed to do this. After he showered, he dressed in the costume. He felt preposterous. The coat was too snug. He couldn't raise his arms higher than his shoulders. Just as long as he could drink, he thought. It would take a lot of champagne to loosen him up today.

Sunday night, Bob drove back. Irene was too tired. Mr. Bradley invited Bob to the study for more brandy, but he declined. He used the drive as an excuse. Before they left, Mr. Bradley handed Bob his card. "Call me at the office anytime," he said. "This is my direct line."

The costume party had been a frolic. After several glasses of champagne, Bob had lost his self-consciousness. He felt as if he was an invisible bystander who could, at his discretion, participate with the revelers. He enjoyed seeing a colorful carnival of Westchester's best playing grab-ass in the name of patriotism. A grass-stained Ben Franklin and Betsy Ross, with dirt and dry grass stuck to their outfits, emerged from the hedges. It was downright Elizabethan—but with a twist—because this frolic in the forest led no one to a new identity, only to satyrian excesses, with the confidence that no matter who was deflowered yet again, it would still be by one of the good neighbors who affirmed your values anyway. On seeing Bob, and as Betsy brushed the grass off him, the man dressed as Franklin said,

"Abstinence, like rust, consumes faster than labor wears; while the used key is always bright."

As they headed out of Westchester County Bob thought of his encounter with Mr. Bradley during the pageant.

Mr. Bradley had led three men—a drummer, piccolo player, and flag bearer—a re-creation of the famous image of Revolutionary patriotism—to the main patio to start his speech— an edited version of Washington's Farewell Address, on the importance of neutrality. He paused with Bob, asking, "Enjoying yourself?"

"You bet," he said.

"Well, throw yourself into it. Let go. Enjoy. And avoid the pond."

"I'll try."

"Good," Mr. Bradley said. Or was it George Washington? "You'll find yourself asked to perform many fairly absurd roles as an adult, especially in business. All having nothing to do with your self, whatever that is. But it's the flourish, the élan you muster for the effort that determines success. Trust me."

"I do," Bob said.

"Good boy," he said, patting Bob on the back. To his triumvirate, with a wave: "Onward!"

Irene had tilted back the seat and had her eyes closed. He wanted to talk to her. But he kept his thoughts to himself. He thought about how his father had passed the day—with burgers and a ball game probably. And did his mother have holiday duty at the hospital? The Fourth had never been a big deal in his house. And he thought about her father's proposition and asked himself whether he was being a fool to ignore it. After all, it appeared to be the great get-rich scheme. The one everyone in his family had been looking for ever since he'd been a boy.

The voice Bob heard as he thought this made him uneasy. Something was out of alignment if he had to force himself to consider the option. The people who made money the way Mr. Bradley described didn't think about it. About whether or not it was the right thing for them. They just did it. And they were born knowing how. Every driveway he passed, every well-lighted tennis court and pool, every BMW, Jaguar, Mercedes, or Volvo, every large house in the county, was filled with people who knew that world in a way he felt he never could. The sheer scope of it overran any question of whether it was justified. Obviously it was. How could it exist otherwise? In one house, the son of the inventor of Speedy Alka-Seltzer, himself the marketer of Ultrasuede. In the next, the scion of a plywood fortune. Then, the descendant of someone who traded baubles for an island and whose fortune now multiplied exponentially on its own, mysteriously removed from all labor other than that of some ex-Ivy League jock in a three-piece suit manipulating its movement from dollars to yen to deutsche marks to pounds minute by minute on a computer screen, a process halted only for lunch at the club and a game or two of squash. In this, the best of all worlds, the best players were those whose fortunes grew steadily, underwriting imaginative family vacations to the South Pole, philanthropic one-upsmanship, and weekend excursions to resorts and inns whose names were secrets shared among their select clientele and passed from one generation to the next. There were shades of gray, of course. That knowledge imparted from parent to child through casual gestures, intentional oversights and silences as carefully conceived as the instructions to a maid. That knowledge he could never possess, which Irene knew—as surely as she knew her own name—never having to give it a second thought.

CHAPTER

5

B ob Bodewicz squinted to read his watch: 5:30. He rolled over to find out why his training session roommate was up so early.

"Did I wake you?" Scott asked. "Sorry. Going for my run."

"How far is that?" Bob asked, his tongue sticking to the roof of his mouth.

"Five miles."

"Every day?"

"Yeah, except when I do ten."

Bob had gone drinking with Scott and two other trainees after they checked into their hotel somewhere outside of Boston. Bob had no idea of its exact location. They were picked up by a P&V employee who shuttled them to the hotel in a company van. Bob spotted him first, standing by the baggage claim with a sign: P&V Trainees.

Bob had already forgotten Scott's last name. So when Scott left the room Bob checked his luggage. Ryan. He had just graduated from the University of Washington with a degree in marketing. He got the job because he was related to an executive, or so he claimed after a few drinks. "I think I'm qualified anyway," he added.

The other two trainees for the session, Rick de Assis and

Adam Clack, were Northeastern graduates. They seemed to have the same attitude as Bob did. It was a job. Good pay and a car. With a chance for a decent bonus if everything worked out. Adam had majored in political science, Rick in psychology.

As the evening wore on it became clear that only Scott was deadly serious about the training program. He fidgeted as Bob, Rick, and Adam tried to imagine what inventory coordination would involve for a drugstore—counting prophylactics? Birth control pills? Candy bars? Rick suggested that the week of office Christmas parties would be a good time to have displays of Santa donning a rubber and urging all customers to be prepared to enjoy the holidays.

Scott drained a beer and set the glass down with a thump. "Guys," he said, "we've had some laughs about this—but don't you think we should give the job a chance? I mean, why are we here if we don't want to do it?"

"Hey," Rick said. "Relax. I'm not knocking the job—although I can't say I see myself doing it in ten years."

"Of course not," Scott said. "If you're not an executive by then, you should change careers."

"That wasn't quite what I had in mind," Rick said.

Adam snickered. Bob sipped his beer and looked at Scott as if he were seeing him for the first time. The guy was too serious. Scott sounded like the little engine that could with a college degree. And he seemed to assume no one knew as much about business as he did. But just because Bob's father worked in a factory didn't mean he was ignorant of marketing. One of his uncles was a corporate consultant who had escaped the minimum security prison of Litchfield and gone to college. Bob looked to him as a model. Bart wore custom-tailored suits, but he didn't lose his sense of humor about it. It wasn't his religion.

Bob flagged the waitress and ordered a round of schnapps—a drink he had never tried until his brother, who was still in Germany after a junior year abroad, wrote him about it. "Let's have a toast to our jobs," Bob said, trying to lighten things up.

"Go ahead, but excuse me," Scott said as he rose. "Don't want to start the job with a hangover."

*   *   *

Scott was asleep when Bob got back to the room. He moved with the exaggerated caution he adopted after drinking, undressed, and skipped brushing his teeth and washing his face to avoid waking Scott. As he pulled the covers of his bed back and lay down his stomach felt queasy. At first he suspected the drinking. But it wasn't that kind of queasiness. No, it was nerves. The way he used to feel on the first day of school. He tried to calm himself by remembering the mantra he used when he meditated regularly—but that tape seemed damaged by neglect and didn't work. He had forgotten to call Irene. But she would understand. He had to meet the guys he would work with. Lying flat on his back, his hands folded across his stomach, he listened to the traffic outside above the hum of the air conditioner. At last he realized his eyes were shut and he was dreaming. A dream of moving from room to empty room in a large house. He was looking for something and couldn't find it. There didn't seem to be anything at all in this house.

Over breakfast, Scott confided in Bob that his primary goal in working for P&V was to gain background for applying to a graduate business school. "A year or two in the trenches," he said, slicing up a grapefruit, "and I'll be a much more appealing candidate. What about you? What are your goals?"

"I don't know," Bob said. "Get rid of my college loans."

"And then what?"

Bob had to admit he hadn't thought about it. This seemed to drop Scott into silence. He kept glancing at Bob, as if there was food on his tweed jacket—the only decent one he owned. Each time he glanced, Bob checked. He hadn't spilled anything. Scott wore a three-piece blue suit with gray pinstripes. He looked like a boy dressed up for a funeral, but his formality and pose of self-assurance kept Bob off-balance.

At 7:45, Scott was ready, briefcase in hand, for Lester, the chauffeur. Bob had a yellow legal pad to take notes. When the van showed up, Bob climbed in behind Scott, taking a back seat.

"Where are those other two loafers," Lester said to no one in particular.

Just then, Rick and Adam emerged from the elevator and

ran across the lobby. Adam wore a blue blazer and gray pants; Rick a tweed jacket and corduroys like Bob's. Bob wasn't usually as conscious of clothes, but Scott's suit made him feel underdressed. The sight of Rick and Adam relieved him. If they were all underdressed, it would take a paycheck or two to correct the problem.

"You boys out late last night?" Lester asked.

"Too late," Adam said. Rick said nothing and leaned his head against the window as the van pulled away.

Lester weaved in and out of traffic on a three-lane highway where cars jammed at every intersection. Zigzags of telephone wires and high power lines disappeared into a brown haze of exhaust. Lester swung across two lanes of traffic and bounced into a semicircular driveway marked by a modest sign: P&V Corporate Headquarters.

"Is this it?" Bob asked.

"It looks like a grammar school," Rick said.

"Very good," Lester said. "It was before this whole sprawl was rezoned commercial. But wait until you see the inside." Lester pulled the station wagon up to the main entrance. "Here you go, boys. Good luck! I'll see you later this afternoon."

Scott led the way through the doors. "I suppose we should report to the principal's office," he said.

Bob was surprised to hear Scott say something like that— maybe there was hope for him after all. Scott immediately went to the receptionist, whose desk sat squarely in the middle of the main hallway. Instead of linoleum or tile, the hallway was carpeted in a dark blue, the color of the letters on the company's store signs. The school lockers had been pulled out and replaced with files that stretched up and down the hallway on either side of the receptionist desk.

"Our trainees are here," the receptionist said into a tiny microphone in front of her lips. Her voice had the practiced monotone of all efficient receptionists: "Good morning, P&V, will you hold please . . . Mr. Prescott is out of the office today, would you like to leave a message?"

The drone of her voice lulled Bob. The grammar school character of the building, its low ceilings and large glass windows, unsettled him. He hadn't enjoyed grammar school, or high school for that matter. Now he found himself drifting into

that stupor he always adopted in school to avoid being con-
sciously bored. He couldn't hear what Rick and Adam were
saying to each other and could barely make out the sound of
Scott drumming his fingers on his briefcase.

"Welcome to P&V."

Bob jumped. In front of him stood a tall woman in a
peach-colored blouse and long denim skirt. Her brown hair was
cut short, and the sharp angles of her face were softened only
by the large circular earrings that she wore. "I'm J. C. Greene,
personnel director."

Ushered into a conference room, they were each given a
series of forms that took the remainder of the day to complete.
Tax, health, benefits information, driving history, company history, facility tour, company policies—it was dull and anticli-
mactic. The week went further downhill from there. There were
binders to take home and review each night. Corporate philos-
ophies to review, job descriptions, and a detailed explanation
of responsibilities. But the forms bothered him the most. There
were fifteen samples in his binder, at least six of which had to
be filled out routinely: a Call Report, Inventory Evaluation,
Merchandising Evaluation, A.S.A.P. (Appearance of Store and
Personnel), Traffic Estimates for Location and Store, and
Weekly Special Mix (Impulse) Recommendations. Worst of all
were the "Quad" forms. Each P&V store had ten basic quadrants dedicated to certain types of products and merchandise.
Household products was one quadrant. Over-the-counter remedies another. From the pharmacy to the checkout counters, coordinators were required to inspect each quadrant and note
anything of significance. Bob hated workbooks in grammar
school. The forms reminded him of those days. Especially when
he learned the company initials originally stood for "Price &
Value." How goofy could business get?

All week, the themes of one brochure entitled "P&V: A
New Retailing Concept for a New Age" were repeated in the
lectures and briefings. "P&V," Ms. Greene said, "addresses a
whole new niche in retailing—that of convenience, price, and
variety. We sell everything from Twinkies to motor oil, jogging
suits to books on civil suits, maps to raps. It's what America
wants—and as district inventory coordinators, you'll constantly
be fine-tuning the inventory of your stores to address those

special needs. And the key to meeting those needs is under-standing your quadrants and making sure that what our cus-tomers want, they find.''

"I'm not sure I like it," Bob told Irene when he called her on Wednesday. Scott was in the shower, and it seemed like the only private moment he'd have to talk to her. "So much pa-perwork. It makes me sick. You drive around day and night, get somewhere, and look around at the store, chat with the people there, and then roast 'em in the reports. They want to know the good, the bad, and the ugly, and then they follow up. People lose their jobs. It's vicious."

"You didn't think a job like that was summer camp, did you?" Irene said.

Bob cringed. She was right. But where or how did she come up with a better sense of real work than he had. "Yeah, I guess," he said. That was as much as he could say.

"Have they told you where you're going?"

"Not yet. We haven't even met any of the vice presi-dents—they're at some kind of management retreat on Nan-tucket."

"Yeah, I'm sure. Lots of solemn heart-to-hearts with one another. Boozey philosophizing about the future of the com-pany. A round or two of golf, a little fishing, and maybe, if there are enough women there, a little grab-ass. That's what management does at retreats."

"My, aren't we worldly," Bob said, who for the first time began to imagine himself as a manager.

"I'm sorry—I shouldn't say that." There was a pause. Bob could hear the faint, unintelligible intimacies of other people talking to one another. "I miss you," she said.

"Ditto," Bob said. "It was—" He stopped himself.

"What?"

"It was an odd time to have this job start."

"Odd? How about rotten?"

"Yeah, shitty."

"Fucked."

"Scummy."

"A crow fart of a time."

"Oh, stop, Irene," Bob said. "You arouse me when you talk like that." Bob looked up and saw Scott grinning at him.

"Be back in a minute," he said, going back into the bathroom and shutting the door.

"Who was that?"

"My roommate," Bob whispered. "A serious guy. He reads everything they give us and wants to get an M.B.A. some day."

"Where was he?"

"He was in the shower—I didn't hear him come out."

"Where's he now?"

"I think I embarrassed him. He's back in the bathroom."

"Maybe we should bring all this to a halt for now."

"Aww."

"Yes. It's best. Call again. They pay, right?"

"Yeah."

"Hey?"

"What?"

Bob heard a kissing sound in his ear. He kissed back, and said good-bye.

Scott knocked at the bathroom door from the inside. "Okay to come out?" he shouted.

"Yeah, I've lost my hard on," Bob said.

"Do you need a towel?" he asked, opening the door and giving Bob a big grin.

"I used a Call Report form," Bob said.

On Friday, they had their first role-playing session: They were given expense account situations and asked how they would respond to certain questionable items. Scott relished the challenge and shined. He knew just what to itemize and what to exclude, and he persuaded his partner—Adam—to be more scrupulous in his itemizations. Bob and Rick agreed it was okay to write off dinner with a competitor who was a friend, even if no business was discussed. They maintained there was no way to anticipate with certainty that business wouldn't be brought up during dinner. For that they got demerit points against winning a gift certificate good at the company's test market store. Scott won it going away.

"He'll buy another notepad," Rick said. "Wait and see."

Afterward, Greene handed them a thick binder of photo-copied Call Reports for review over the weekend. There had to be at least six hundred pages of them. It crushed Bob. He could see that they were expected to stay in their rooms reading this stuff rather than touring Boston. As they headed back to the hotel Rick and Adam made no secret they wouldn't bother with the stuff. Bob knew that Scott would read all of them, and that he would at least make an attempt. He didn't like being shown up. It was a jock sort of attitude—but one that seemed to work in business.

Sunday night Bob was looking through the binder of re-ports and came upon a special insert: Store Layout as a Func-tion of Maslow's Hierarchy of Needs. There was a graphic de-piction of a pyramid with five layers labeled in ascending order: Physiological survival—the need for oxygen, food, water; Safety—the need for security, protection, order; Belongingness and love—wanting acceptance by others; Esteem and status—the desire for reputation; and Self-actualization—the desire to know and understand. These categories, which the report claimed to be absolutes about human nature, governed the ten quadrants of the P&V stores. From food to the latest inspirational mes-sages from evangelical preachers, P&V sold it. Each quadrant offered at least something for one of the layers in the pyramid of human needs. Computers at the headquarters monitored ac-tivity in all quadrants by data gathered at the point of sale through the scanning of bar codes. The slightest downward variation in a quadrant's sales was assumed to indicate that the product mix there no longer fully satisfied a needs level. While needs remained constant, the ways in which they were satis-fied changed constantly. New products and new services con-stantly redefined how needs were satisfied. New quadrants could be introduced, provided they were demonstrated to sat-isfy needs. "This is," the report concluded, "the only justifi-cation for new products, new layouts, new quadrants. Without demonstrable appeal to a specific need as defined by Maslow, there is no reason to add or subtract what already has been es-tablished as successful. On the other hand, it should be noted that P&V has survived, grown, and flourished by continual re-sponse to changing consumer definitions of how these needs are to be fulfilled. This is the key to success." The report was signed by Warner Prescott, President and Founder.

Bob stood up and walked over to the window of the room. He didn't disagree with Maslow or Warner. Actually, the whole analysis seemed extremely simple. All of the business did. The trouble came from making it complex. What bothered him was the idea that people were as predictable as that. But it had to be so. The company made money on that assumption. He looked out at the lights of cars traveling this way and that. So many lights, their movement so random in appearance. But if he believed this, the people behind those lights were all driven by the same pyramid of needs. Know them, respond to them, exploit them. And who, he wondered, exploited his.

The second week involved tours of actual store sites. Oliver Connor, Vice President, Store Site Development, sat up front in the P&V van as Lester steered in and out of traffic. "It still blows me away," Connor was saying, "that Warner opened his first store where he did. Not in a million years would you find a P&V in a site like this. It defies all logic, but we don't keep it open for nostalgic reasons, let me tell you."

Lester turned the van into the crowded parking lot of a small plaza. They were somewhere in Somerville. There were six or seven storefronts, and at first Bob couldn't find the P&V sign.

"You'll notice this is the only site with unique store signage," Connor said, as if anticipating the question Bob was about to ask. "A concession to the requirements of the plaza."

"So this is where it all began," Scott said, sliding the van door open.

"You make it sound like an act of obeisance is called for," Adam said.

Scott tapped Adam on the shoulder. "I don't care if you're not serious about this—but I am. And at least cut me that much."

"You sure as hell aren't my boss," Adam said.

"It's a good thing for you, too," Scott said. "Otherwise . . ."

"C'mon guys, knock it off," Bob said. "We'll all be out of

one another's hair soon enough. We ought to be able to put on a show of civility until then."

Adam and Scott gave him frowns that told him to mind his own business. The phrase struck him as curious. "Minding his own business." Here at last he had a job, a real job, and it seemed to him he was minding his own business by asking them to knock off the bull. After all, if two or three of them were bickering all week, it would be difficult to remain uninvolved. Ultimately, that would make everyone look bad.

Rick nudged Bob to move on. Scott had already entered the store, and Adam waited by the door for Rick. "It sounds like the poles have been established—Adam and Scott—cynical and serious," Rick said.

Bob nodded. He liked Rick. There was something different about him. He was older, but it wasn't just that. When they had gone drinking the first night, Rick mentioned taking a couple of years off from college and living on an island in the Caribbean. "All I did was spear fish and eat red bananas," he said.

"Yum," Scott said.

"You should try some time off," Rick said. "Some time away."

Rick said this without sounding self-consciously worldly—which made him sound all the more worldly. During the lectures, the talks, the play-acting, he maintained a demeanor of poised concentration without becoming eager to display how much of the day's lessons he retained. At the same time, he didn't take any of it very seriously.

Bob followed Rick inside. Rick grabbed Bob by the sleeve and pointed to Scott, who was by himself and saying to no one in particular, "It's remarkable the number of facings this store actually permits. And the low-level lighting system keeps even that merchandise near the floor easy to see, and, of course, appealing to the customer."

"Think he is saying all that into a little tape recorder?" Bob asked.

"I think he is a tape recorder," Rick said. "He will probably do well here if he doesn't make everyone sick first."

Bob didn't mistake Scott's intensity—he was a competitor. Someone who would say, since this is for bucks, let's get serious. Let the Adams snicker, Scott would play the game for keeps. If this were a cross-country race, Bob would rather go against Adam than against Scott.

Bob recalled his Uncle Bart stating that every recommendation made in business should start with careful observations recorded on a pad. "Record everything you notice, even if you don't yet have an opinion about its significance. Put all observations into sentences without caring about progression. Later, sort through them—find the patterns, the symptoms, and draw conclusions." Bob tried to imagine the way Bart would view the store: bins of candy and sale-priced cassettes along with cheap lighters and batteries were featured in the impulse zone; toward the back of the store were the more expensive items— cameras behind a locked case, assorted houseware. Even if he hadn't read up on the organizing principle of Maslow for each quadrant, he could see how careful observation would lead him to a similar hypothesis, and how that could guide him when recommending changes.

"Okay, guys," Connor said. "This is Howie Storch, the manager of Somerville Store One. I was just telling these gentlemen that nostalgia has nothing to do with why we keep this site open. Maybe you could elaborate on that."

Howie brought his hands together in front of his chest, a man with a big secret to tell. "Boys," he said. "Nostalgia doesn't contribute to the bottom line—and so if the place don't pay, it don't stay. What does count, however, is a little barometer of profitability we call sales per square foot. And this little store, thirty feet by fifty-five feet deep, is the top grosser in sales per square foot for the entire chain."

"It's a gold mine," Connor said. "And there seems to be no limit to how much we could gross here. We've even considered buying out the entire plaza and making it a super P&V similar to the ones we're planning for Chicago."

Howie stepped forward. "But Warner said, 'No, I don't want to alter the character of the neighborhood.' "

"That's the kind of man Warner is," Connor said. "He told us, 'I know you're right, but let's leave it as is and make our megabucks elsewhere.' "

"Not that this store doesn't pull its weight, mind you," Howie added. "It's organized on a six-quadrant system—and that was Warner's brainchild, too. I was just a clerk when I started here and I thought—I'll be honest with you—I thought Warner was a nut. Some know-it-all guy from Harvard. Oh, God, when I think about the late nights we put in here organizing the quadrants. Seasonal goods and specials, impulse purchase, food items, houseware, cosmetics, health- and multi-remedies, and, of course, pharmaceuticals.''

"Some nights we'd work 'til three getting things fine-tuned only to open up at nine the next morning and find the rubbers in the impulse purchase quadrant.'' Howie leered at each of them.

Only Scott guffawed.

"That's a manager's joke, that one,'' Howie said.

Connor stepped forward. "Today, our stores have a minimum of ten quadrants, one of which is dedicated to experimental mixes. Guy Boyer, our vice president for research, constantly monitors the action in Quadrant J—that's what we call it. He test-markets the mix based on research from our model store at headquarters.''

"But, I'll tell you,'' Howie said. "You never know what will work for sure until you've seen it work in the field. Stuff that moved out of the test store could stall over here.''

"Howie makes a good point—and this isn't really my area so I'll just touch on it before Buck Remer briefs you on marketing—but we can't possibly account for the market differences in geography through the testing in our model store. All we get is a general idea—a clue.''

"That's where Quadrant J comes in,'' Howie said.

"Exactly,'' Connor said. "It allows us to fine-tune each store. Pretty soon, you get a customer base that comes in the door the minute you unlock it.''

"You ever seen tropical fish when you shake the food out on top of the water?'' Howie asked, and grinned. "Just like that.''

Bob glanced at Scott. He was taking notes on a small pad.

Connor next took them outside. He gave them a quick overview of customer and traffic census taking. "Our site selection process today takes into account government census data, transportation department studies, market analyses, and, of course, gut intuition,'' he said. "We feed it all into the hopper—a special computer program that spits out the parameters we have to deal with if we're going to open a store.''

Connor took them to stores every day that week. To suburban stores, city stores, ghetto stores—even to a couple of stores in old mill towns. It was eight o'clock when they got back to the P&V headquarters on Friday. Ms. Greene left packets of information for all of them at the front desk. A cover note said: "Review these prior to your marketing and merchandising role-playing sessions, which start Monday."

Bob opened his packet and inspected the contents. There was a handwritten note on top:

> Bob: Glad you're aboard. Look forward to meeting you. You join me in the Midwest territory, District 3—based in Ann Arbor.
>
> Byron Cutter, Regional Manager

Beneath the note were several documents easily totaling over one hundred pages. Bob was ecstatic at being based in Ann Arbor, but groaned at the sight of the reading. Scott shuffled through his papers.

"I guess I won't have much time for swimming this weekend," he said.

No one asked him where he was going.

Lipton answered the hall phone at the fraternity house. "Tell me all about it," he said. "I'm dying to know what your training's like."

Bob cleared his throat. "C'mon, Lipton. Not now. I want to talk to Irene."

"Oh, fair enough," he said. "But promise to tell me when you get back."

Bob promised. Then he heard Lipton talking excitedly to Irene.

"Hello, Bob?" Irene said.

"Sounds like you need some bug spray," Bob said.

"Yeah. Maybe a six-foot ant trap with an M.B.A. degree as bait."

"Perfect. I could use it here, too."

"Is it bad?"

"Just my roommate. He's a little serious."

"Other than that? Do you like it?"

"I guess. It's strange. It's simple yet demanding. Like weeding a garden. You can't stop concentrating; you can't take shortcuts. But I've got some good news."

Irene took a second to ask. "What's that?"

"They're sending me to Ann Arbor. It's definite."

"Oh, great," she said, sounding relieved. There was a pause. Through the static, Bob could hear the inflections of another conversation.

"Irene, you there?"

"Well, yeah. Sort of."

"What do you mean?"

"I was thinking, that's all. Since you've been gone, I've been thinking about not living in Ann Arbor."

"What are you talking about? I thought you were happy about this."

"I am. I am happy. I mean, I was thinking about living just outside Ann Arbor. You know, a small town. Some place far away from school and students. I could dull out a bit. Relax."

"Live wherever you want. We . . ."

"How would you like that?"

Bob paused now. "You mean live together?"

"Aren't we just about doing that now?"

"Sort of, I guess. It seems different, that's all."

"You don't have to if you don't want to. It seemed like something to consider."

Bob was grateful they were speaking over the phone. He didn't want to see the expression on her face during this conversation. Nor did he want her to see his. He watched himself in the mirror over the desk, feet on the bed, knees to his chest, phone receiver pressed to his ear. "It's such a big change when you do that outside of school. I'm going to be on the road practically every week. At least for a few days."

"See, you can get away anytime you want."

"It's not that. I'm surprised. You're not the clingy type." He regretted saying this immediately.

"This isn't clinging, Bob. It's a suggestion. I thought we were having a good time. Maybe you didn't."

"No, no. I didn't mean it like that. Not at all. I . . ."

"Look, think it over. If it appeals to you, let's try it. But don't make it out to have life-long ramifications.''

"Irene, I'm sorry I said what I said. Let me think about it. I like the idea. And as far as living outside of Ann Arbor, that's fine with me. I grew up in the country. I don't need a college town.''

"When will you be back?''

"Saturday—a week from tomorrow.''

Irene kissed into the phone. "I miss you.''

"Miss you too,'' Bob said. "Bye.'' He put down the receiver and looked at the square plastic overlay that fit over the phone's push buttons giving the numbers for various hotel services: Housekeeping—211, Room Service—215, Valet—212. He wished there was one for advice—he could use it. He had hoped he would be based in Ann Arbor. But he had never considered the possibility of living with Irene. Now that she proposed the idea, though, he couldn't imagine why he hadn't thought of it. After all, why pay for two places to live? And it wasn't as if they would be married. He would be away plenty. At conventions. On the road. The weekends would be their time together. So, sure, it made sense.

But then again, staying at her place or having her at his for the weekend seemed a whole lot different from living together. There was no place to retreat. No place where you could refuse to open the door. His former girlfriend had proposed several times that they live together for a summer on Nantucket. They could go there and get jobs, she said. Each time, Bob backed out by claiming he needed to live rent-free at home to raise as much money as he could for college. And he believed that. But now he had no such excuse. So what did it matter? Only it did matter. What if the company wanted him somewhere at a moment's notice? What then? If he lived alone it would be no problem. But living with Irene, he could imagine all sorts of complications. Broken promises, messed-up weekends, upsets. Especially if she was looking forward to the next year as a time to relax and have fun before immersing herself in the grind of law school.

At the same time, he cared for her. Living together seemed like a good way to find out what was in store for them. Only he wished all of this had unfolded at its own pace, not Irene's. She had been the instigator throughout. She had made the first move by inviting him for a weekend in the Adirondacks. Now she was making the first move about living together. She seemed to like making things happen rather than letting them happen. Maybe that was his problem: this assumption that things just happened. Like the way his job had happened. Maybe he needed to recognize that there was a time for letting things happen and a time to make them happen. That was the message for people who wanted to get ahead in business. Maybe it was also true for—God how he hated the word—relationships.

Bob tried to look at it another way. What was the risk? What was the downside? They could split up? Have bad feelings? Somehow the whole thing with Irene seemed too easy from the start. He remembered running in a state cross-country championship when he had been a junior in high school. He went through the first mile of a three-mile course in 4:34, a step behind the three leaders. He'd said to himself, There's no way I should be going this fast, I can't sustain it. And he dropped back, way back, until he was out of contention. He had talked himself into a mediocre showing when he might well have been able to stay at the front. No one sustained that pace. With Irene, he felt as if he had gone out fast and that everything was great. He didn't trust things that came that easily. But maybe it was time to begin.

There was no way to know if this was what he wanted for himself until he experienced it. He could either remain restless and passive, or he could move in with Irene and try to make things fun. At least the time would go faster. When his eyes focused on the mirror above the bureau on the opposite wall, he saw himself there—an adult in years, but no less certain of himself than a child. Perhaps that was it. Perhaps he wasn't ready for the transition into business, into living with someone. Perhaps he still wanted college, its classes and parties, reading and fun. He didn't feel ready to be serious about life yet. Not like Scott was. He stared at himself as if he were a stranger: his shirt untucked, tie loosened, his blond hair too long and shaggy for business. His last haircut was in May—given by the girlfriend of a friend. He looked like a kid playing dress-up. Dress-up for success.

CHAPTER

6

On Monday, J. C. Greene escorted them to a room called The Pit, where they would meet management and commence role playing. As the group walked down one hallway, then another, Bob noticed that despite all the modifications that had been made to the grammar school, the drinking fountains remained knee high. Rick stopped at a drinking fountain, kneeling to get closer.

Greene paused. "Nothing in this building is without a point," she said. "Warner could have changed all those drinking fountains along with everything else, but he left them."

Rick wiped his chin. "I wish he hadn't," he said. "Makes me feel like a clutzy little kid."

"And that's precisely why he didn't change them," Greene said. "Warner says we should never be so satisfied with our success that we forget tomorrow's markets are drinking from one of these right now."

The Pit was an amphitheater without seats. The room angled upward from the speaker's podium in steep, concentric semicircular terraces. Except for the walls, a single shade of P&V blue carpet covered the entire expanse. The walls were vertically ribbed with P&V red fabric rectangles. Bob touched one; it was soft.

"Sound deadening," Greene said.

Bob turned to look at her. She stood by the podium.

"The Pit is a multi-purpose facility," Greene said. "We can have lectures in here—just sit on the terraces—role playing, and, simply by opening these blinders . . ." She pressed a button at the podium, and the wall behind her slid slowly to one side, revealing a bank of wall-to-ceiling plate glass windows. The lights dimmed suddenly, and behind the windows was a brightly lit P&V store. "Simply by opening these blinders," Greene continued, "we can look out on our test store and actually observe consumers without being seen. Almost every market experiment is first developed and evaluated at the test store. There's nothing going on today, but later we'll take you through the store and show you the types of things we can do. It's a remarkable facility. No other drugstore chain fine-tunes its inventory to the extent we do. That's why each of you, as monitors and troubleshooters, are so critical to the successful implementation of market tests and inventory recommendations."

The door opened and a tall man dressed in a dark, three-piece suit walked in.

"Good morning, Buck," Greene said. "Gentlemen, this is—"

"I'll handle the introductions," he said. "Boys, I'm Ted Remer, vice president of marketing. The folks call me Buck."

Buck shook hands with each of the new DICs. He paused with each person to add something personal. When he got to Bob, he said, "You're the English major? Well, if I make any grammar mistakes, I can ask you how to fix them."

Bob surprised himself by responding without thinking. "To be honest," he said, "I don't see that grammar has much to do with this business."

Buck stared at Bob for a moment. Bob kept his eyes right on Buck's. You couldn't back down from a guy with a nickname like Buck.

"You got that right, buddy," he said. "If you can do it with good grammar, though, all the better. No one wants to get the school marms upset. Heck, they're customers, too."

Buck cleared his throat and made a sound as if he were about to sing. "Up to this point, you've learned a little bit about P&V," he said. "You've seen some stores, done some book-work. But now it's time to get on your feet. Because ultimately, this job is about you—you represent the company.''

Remer told them that if they worked hard, and more importantly, that if they worked intelligently, they could count on building a career at P&V. He said there was no denying that the job of district inventory coordinator involved a lot of paperwork. But the minute a DIC started thinking that the job was just paperwork, he was doomed. Because the guys who got ahead at P&V did more than fill out forms. They innovated. Came up with new ideas. Made things better. The thing that separated P&V from the competition had nothing to do with storefronts or locations or dollars per square foot. It had to do with gray matter. Brains.

Remer emphasized this point by tapping his head. He continued by emphasizing that each of the new recruits was ''selected based on brains.'' That was Prescott's philosophy for hiring, and it had brought the company success. As excellent students, you could learn how to read the marketplace. But this required a new alphabet. He introduced this alphabet with slides. The first was titled ''Buck's Vowels.''

''You can't spell success without them,'' Remer said.

They were:

    A - nticipate trends
    E - veryone is a potential customer
    I - nnovation is the key
    O - pen minds open doors to new markets
    U - nderstand your competitors

Remer illustrated each of these rules with a case history involving a P&V DIC. How a guy just like one of them anticipated, innovated, understood. How a simple addition to standard inventory took a store from average to stellar performance. He spoke of bundling services and products, an idea Bob had never heard described. Wrapping presents was a simple example. But when a terrible hailstorm broke hundreds of windows near Toledo, an alert DIC recommended bundling putty knives with putty cans and window points to build extra dollars into every sale. Remer said it was a service to the customer and a bonus for the DIC. These were small examples to illustrate a big concept, Remer said. Altering the entire makeup of a store would be the ultimate example. It had been done, and that too meant a bonus for the DIC who made it work.

Remer grew increasingly animated as he talked, one hand pounding the other, or one hand pounding the podium. He covered the P&V philosophy on storming a market, on anticipating and responding to trends, on customizing inventory within markets to appeal to different demographic characteristics, and on tactical responses to competitive countermeasures.

Bob's mind began to drift. He thought of Irene's father telling him that this job dealt with just the symptoms of economics, that tides of currency were the real force at work. Putty and putty knives, hair spray and Hula Hoops, what did they matter next to currency? No sooner had he framed this question than he realized that the distinction wasn't so new. It was another way of posing the one and the many problem, as old as the pre-Socratics.

Bob expanded on the thought, Remer's voice now little more than a faint drone, his gestures as obscure as hieroglyphics, the images and words on the screen remote. He could come closer to the god of the marketplace through the Many of P&V or through the One of currency. He could rise up transcendently by meditating on the unifying power of arbitrage or by immersing himself in the glittering and transient debris of discount consumerism. For the first time, he had the feeling that he'd rather deal with the particulars of the consumer world than acknowledge that currency was the prime force in the world. There was something too deterministic about it. He would rather work in a world that permitted at least the illusion of choice.

Remer was asking a question. The realization that it was his name being called flushed Bob with embarrassment.

"Excuse me, could you repeat the question?"

"Nod off?" Remer said. "Very well. What I asked you was, based on what we've seen and discussed so far, how would you recommend responding to the cocooning trend as it's been defined thus far?"

Bob blinked at the screen, looking for a clue. There was a photo with a caption "The new cocooners" that showed a man and a woman sitting on a couch in the glow of a TV.

"Maybe I could take a crack at that," Scott said.

But just then Remer clicked off the projector and turned up the lights. "Gentlemen," he said, "I'd like to introduce you to Warner Prescott, our president, founder, and guiding light."

"Okay, okay, Buck," Prescott said. "Lay it on any thicker and they'll begin to think there's something evangelical about all this."

Prescott didn't look anything like what Bob expected, although now that Prescott stood before him, he didn't know why he'd expected anything else. Tall and thin, Prescott wore jeans and a tan jacket. His tie was pencil thin, a sliver of purple down his blue shirt. He had a soft leather shoulder bag, which he left at the door before making the round of introductions. When he stood before them at the podium, he pulled a pack of cigarettes from his jacket and lit one, inhaling deeply before speaking.

"I'm glad you're with us," he said. "I don't like speeches, and I was never a jock, so I can't give inspirational pep talks à la the locker room. What I can say, however, is that you and your job are the most important link in this company. Despite the fact that one P&V store can be as different from another as night and day—believe me, the folks who run our computers never let me hear the end of that—"

Remer chuckled.

"Despite that"—Prescott took another drag on the cigarette—"there is something they all have in common." He paused, as if he was expecting someone to say what that was. Slowly he took a pad from the pocket of his jacket and jotted down a note. "And that is, a commitment to good service and to offering quality merchandise at an excellent price."

"There it is," Remer said, nodding. "That's it."

"You're the link from store to store," Prescott said. "You make sure this mission is carried out—is implemented. You adjust things when it's not. You make sure our store personnel appear as they should and respond to customers as we insist they must. You recommend modifications in the mix, you evaluate the effectiveness of special promotions. Most of all, you keep things focused at the point closest to the customer. You tell us back here at the office whether our research, our ideas, and our decisions are relevant to moving merchandise on the street. Without your diligence, without your candor, without your ideas, we cannot succeed, and most definitely we cannot grow.''

Prescott's head turned slowly toward the door as if he had heard something Bob didn't. Without looking at them, he spoke again. ''What I noticed when I inherited a drugstore fifteen years ago was that the traditional pharmacy simply surrendered customers to supermarkets, department stores, and the other large retailers. The traditional pharmacy was more oriented to service, and its customer base was being eroded by the mass-marketing retailers. My idea was to make a hybrid—a service-retailing operation. Only, instead of offering everything all the time''—he paused, looking to see if anyone picked up on the allusion—''I chose to offer the right thing at the right time, and to change that as the variables changed. The problem with the big retailers is, when the going's good, they do great. But when it's bad, they lose. You know, when the air is filled with birds, all you need in order to be a good hunter is to point a gun overhead and pull the trigger. Something's bound to fall. But tomorrow's customer won't fly in a flock. That's why businesses that don't know how to aim won't be here in ten years. And those of you who will be here in ten years, and who will share in the success we will create, will be the ones who join me in aiming this company, one customer at a time.'' Prescott's head turned back toward the group, and he looked at each one of them, as if he could read minds. ''Gentlemen, I have to catch a plane. But I leave you in good hands. It's been a pleasure to meet you, and I'm glad you're with us.''

During coffee break, they were joined by Billie Coleman, vice president for store operations. He took a seat in back. Remer called the group together at the front of the room and explained the importance of role playing. It was, he said, a way of evaluating their progress and identifying areas that they all needed to work on. There were no grades, everyone passed, and they shouldn't be too concerned about it other than to try hard when they were assigned a role. Some would be simple, some difficult. He decided to illustrate.

''Billie, would you come down here and pretend you're a disgruntled customer,'' Remer said. ''I'll be the manager.'' Remer turned to them. ''There are, of course, right and wrong ways to handle such situations. First I'll illustrate the wrong way.''

Coleman sauntered across the floor, holding an imaginary object in his hand. He wore a tan suit and a Hawaiian tie. ''Excuse me,'' he said to Remer, ''are you the store manager?'' By the tone of his voice, Coleman was pretending to be a woman.

''Why, yes I am,'' Remer said. ''How can I help you.''

''Well, I thought P&V stood for price and value,'' Coleman said. ''But when I got this conditioner home, I discovered it had shampoo in it. I can't tell you how this upsets me. I mean, here I am thinking I'm putting conditioner in my hair, and actually I'm shampooing it again. Do you know what that does to my hair?''

''Now just a second, ma'am,'' Remer said. ''You're telling me you bought a bottle of conditioner and found there was shampoo in it?''

Bob recognized Remer's tack from the handout entitled ''Sales Tips.'' Always repeat a customer's objection to show that you heard it correctly. This establishes a human link with the customer.

''Yes, that's what I'm saying,'' Coleman said. ''That's why I'm here, dammit. Do I have to repeat myself?'' Coleman folded his arms across his chest and tapped his foot.

''Frankly, ma'am, I find all this a little hard to believe,'' Remer said. ''In all the years—''

''Are you calling me a liar?'' Coleman demanded.

''Not a liar, ma'am,'' Remer said. ''Simply that I've never heard—''

''I'm telling you it's the truth and I can't believe you won't investigate this,'' Coleman said. ''I'll call the TV station and the consumer affairs office right now.''

''Now wait a second, ma'am,'' Remer said. ''You're getting hysterical here.''

''Hysterical?'' Coleman screeched. ''You call this hysterical? You want to see hysterical? No wonder you call *shampoo* conditioner. It's obvious no one in this store knows the English language.''

Adam was beside himself. Remer broke the acting and approached him. ''I appreciate that this can appear amusing, especially at first,'' he said. ''But this is serious. Try to pay attention." He turned to Rick. "Why don't you step into the manager's role."

Rick faced Coleman, who appeared small and old next to him.

"What seems to be the problem?" Rick said.

"Do I have to repeat myself?" Coleman screamed. "Why can't anyone solve my problem?"

Rick took a step back, as if knocked back by the force of Coleman's voice. He appeared stunned. "Look, lady," Rick said. "No one has to shout to get service here. And as for your problem, whatever that is, I'm not sure we sell anything powerful enough to get rid of that."

Adam roared. Somehow Bob kept from a similar outburst. This proved fortunate, because Remer became incensed.

"You guys aren't in college anymore," he said. "This is for real. If you don't want to treat it seriously, I'd just as soon know about it now. The door's right there—what's it going to be?"

Adam bit his lower lip and sat up straight. Rick shrugged his shoulders. "I'm sorry," Rick said. "I didn't think you had to surrender your dignity just to satisfy a customer."

Remer walked up to Rick and stared him straight in the eyes. "You don't," he said. "Scott, why don't you show Rick how to do it."

Scott set his notebook on top of his briefcase and walked quickly over to Coleman. "I understand you've had a problem with the conditioner we sell, ma'am," he said. "Our policy is to make good any problems you experience here. Would you accept a refund, or should we simply substitute another bottle of conditioner?"

Coleman slipped back into the character of the customer. "Well, since I can't have both, I guess I'll just get another bottle of conditioner."

"And let's check this one before you leave to make sure it's the real thing," Scott said. "By the way, if you feel your hair has been damaged by a double shampooing, would you accept a gift of a trial size of our premium conditioners? There are several herbal formulations that might quickly return your hair to its natural body."

"My, you are helpful," Coleman said. "I will take one of those. And take a substitute bottle of conditioner."

Scott turned toward Rick. "Please accept my apologies for the mix-up. I'll personally check into this situation to make sure it doesn't happen again. And as for our help, some aren't fully trained yet. But when they are, they'll represent the highest level of courteous and knowledgeable service. That's just as important as price and value at P&V."

Coleman smiled quickly. Remer chuckled. Rick fiddled with a pen, as if he hadn't heard Scott.

Remer concluded the morning session with a summary of the key traits by which managers and employees were to be evaluated. One of the forms DICs were expected to fill out was called an Employee Conduct Report. Each month for each store, overall employee performance had to be evaluated. Mishandled complaints, sloppy dress, poor service, and poor initiative were all grounds for write-ups.

"Doesn't that make us something of a snitch?" Adam asked.

Remer turned the floor over to Coleman, explaining that employee conduct came under sales.

"When it comes to providing a uniformly excellent level of service in our stores," Coleman said, "snitching doesn't enter into it. These people are hired and trained to provide that kind of service. When they don't, it's up to the manager to upgrade them. And if the manager doesn't do it, you do."

"We'd all like to have managers who look after their stores a little better," Remer said. "But some do and some don't. When you expand as rapidly as we have, you can't always find the perfect manager. But we're getting there."

"With the guidelines presented in these handouts," Scott said, "I feel we're properly informed to judge good as well as bad performances. I would think it's equally important to single out extraordinary performances."

"Only when you want one of the employees beholden to you," Remer said. "Make 'em work for it." He walked toward Scott and stared him in the eyes. "You know what I mean?"

Scott appeared confused, as if he'd forgotten something he was supposed to remember. Suddenly Coleman hooted at the podium.

"Of course we want to hear the good," Coleman said after he stopped hooting. "Believe me, we need to hear it."

There was a burst of laughter from Remer, the kind that sounded like a lawn mower failing to start. Bob found himself laughing too, and could hear his laugh everywhere else. Because it wasn't his laugh. It was *the* laugh. He'd been hearing it since he first arrived at the hotel. It was in hallways, muffled by the carpet; at the elevators, punctuated by the blue ticks of static electricity; in the lobby, amplified by the atrium glass and the tile floor; and always at the bars and restaurants, rising above the sharp clanking of plates and silverware. Wherever men in suits congregated. It was everywhere at P&V. The laugh of fraternal conviviality, a we're-all-chums-in-this-crazy-business chuckle.

After lunch, Remer set the stage for the next session of role playing. Rick was to be the manager of a store that had recently experienced a drop in impulse zone sales, a critical barometer of profitability. Remer gave a demographic profile of the neighborhoods within trading distance of the store: ethnic white, blue collar, and loyal. Adam was assigned the role of the DIC. His task was to find out why the specials weren't moving, and what should be done.

"How are you this week, Rick?" Adam said, grinning as he sauntered across the front of the room with his hand extended.

Rick kept his arms folded. "The name's Bill. When are you going to remember that?"

Adam suppressed his laughter. "I understand sales in the impulse zone are down. Have you noticed that?"

"Of course I have," Rick said. "I'm the manager, right?"

"Yes, Bill, you are the manager," Adam said. "That's why I was wondering if you had any ideas about what's causing this."

"Easy. It's the stuff. It's all wrong. Nobody wants it. Those guys back in Boston have to get their act together."

"So you're saying that the merchandise mix for the impulse zone isn't right," Adam said.

"Excellent," Remer said from the side, jotting a note on a small pad.

Rick took a second to get back in character. "Yeah, precisely. The wrong stuff."

"As you know, Bill, the mix of specials is carefully assembled to appeal to customers with the demographic profiles of your trading area. The formula never failed in the past."

"Look, I don't care what kind of numbers you've got," Rick said. "I'm saying the stuff is wrong."

Adam arched his eyebrow melodramatically and, imitating Mr. Spock, said, "A most illogical opinion, given the evidence."

Bob laughed to himself. Rick smiled and, in the tone of Bones, said, "We're talking about human beings here. Flesh and blood, not some pile of statistics and impulses on a circuit board. But I suppose some kid like you, still wet behind the ears with all your numbers and your forms, wouldn't understand that."

Adam laughed so hard he lost concentration. After a moment, he regained his composure. "All right," he said, "I'm ready to go again."

"Too late," Remer said calmly. "You blew it. Scott, take his place."

Scott smiled and stepped forward. "Let me assume for a moment," he said, "that you're interested in making your store more profitable. That would be good for you, wouldn't it?"

Rick stared at Scott as if this were a trick question. "Yeah. I want the store to do good."

"Of course you do. And if I can show you a way to make your store more successful, you'd be interested in it, wouldn't you?"

"That depends."

"It depends on whether or not you believe it would, right?"

"Yeah. Exactly."

"Good," Scott said. "Then let's take a look at the facts."

"What facts?"

"The facts pertaining to stores such as yours."

"You don't need to show me that. I know what the facts are about this store, and they start with the fact that you guys in Boston don't know what the hell you're doing."

Scott stammered for a second before regaining momentum. "So you're suggesting that the reason your specials aren't moving is due to the fact that the mix is incorrect."

"Exactly."

"Well, let's take a look at these statistics, and I think you'll find they indicate that the impulse mix for your demographic trading area has been successful almost anywhere—"

"Stop right there."

"What do you mean?"

"I mean halt. Cease and desist. Stuff it. Or do you need numbers to understand English?"

"I can see we're going nowhere. Of course I'll have to—"

"Write me up? Go ahead."

"That wasn't quite what I meant."

"What did you mean, Mister Nibbitz?"

"Hold on a second," Scott said, now openly annoyed. "Where do you get off calling me names."

"I get off anyway I can, Mister Nibbitz."

Bob glanced around the room. Remer and Coleman appeared engrossed.

Scott stuck a finger in Rick's chest. "Look, I'll lay it on the line, pal. Your attitude stinks. The facts prove you're wrong. You can't argue with case after case. If you promote your mix, display it properly, and direct customers to it, it will sell. That's indisputable."

"Hold on, social science breath," Rick said. "You don't even understand the rhetoric you peddle. Your statistics prove nothing. They just indicate trends. There's nothing absolute you can conclude from them. Trends change all the time."

"And so do managers," Scott said.

"What are you going to do? Write me up? Go ahead. File your report. Get me fired. I'll have another job in a week, and you'll be back in a month trying to figure out why sales are still down."

"I give up," Scott said, turning to Remer. "There's no way to deal with a situation like this. He's completely irrational."

Remer cleared his throat to speak. From the side of the room, Coleman cut him off.

"He's not completely irrational," he said. "He's right, for one thing, about statistics. They don't *prove* anything."

"Yeah," Remer said. "But we live and die by them, don't we?"

"And that's wrong," Coleman said. "They're guides, not prescriptions."

"Let's save the philosophy for later," Remer said. "Right now, I want to see how Bob would handle this."

"There's plenty to be said about this," Coleman continued. "I don't want our DICs beating up on managers by misusing research."

"Later," Remer said.

Bob took a slow deep breath and exhaled. He felt a sensation in his legs that hadn't been there in years. Race legs, he called them. A rubbery feel he got just before races in high school.

"Since you have the advantage of watching Scott hammer on some basic points, let's give this edition a little twist," Remer said. "Let's assume we know for a fact that our manager here, Mr. Rick, hasn't been giving the impulse mix adequate aisle presence through dumps, stacks, and bins. We don't know what he's doing, actually, with the presorted merchandise we ship him. It's just not getting out there. You got that, Rick?"

Rick nodded.

Bob had no idea what he was going to say. When he stood before Rick, though, he knew he couldn't be academic. "Hey, Bill, it looks like you've put on a few pounds since I was here last."

"What is this?" Rick said. "Weight watchers? I've got a job to do, so if you're here to shoot the breeze, why don't you pull someone else aside. But make sure it isn't a customer."

Bob hesitated, unable to think of a response. Then he recalled that according to the sales tips given them, silence was the best response to objections or obnoxious rejoinders from prospects. So Bob emphasized it, staring straight into Rick's eyes. Rick fidgeted uneasily.

"Well?" he asked.

Bob said nothing, just stared.

"Hey, look," Rick said. "I'm on edge. Things haven't been going well. The impulse mix has been a disaster."

"I'd like to see what I can do to help figure out what the problem is."

"I know what the problem is—the stuff is all wrong for the market."

"You know, Bill, this used to be one of the most profitable stores in District Five. The same methods used then are used now—"

"Only we're not getting the same results, are we?"

"Yes, sales have slipped. But I noticed when I was walking around the store a few minutes ago that the impulse mix isn't well displayed. A lot of it is squeezed in a corner back near the pharmacy."

"And you could find an inch to put it anywhere else?"

"Well, you're right about that. This store is cramped." Bob paused and inadvertently glanced toward the audience. He saw Coleman smile and give him a thumbs up. "You know, I've actually got two stores smaller than this in very similar trading areas, and the managers there tell me they've got the same damn problems as you."

"Yeah?" Rick said, trying to sound as recalcitrant as possible.

"What I'm thinking is, since you all share similar trading areas and similar store space problems, maybe we could all spend a week together visiting one another's stores and brainstorming some ways to compensate for the space problems."

"You can't squeeze any more out of this space, I'll tell you right now."

"And if that's what we all conclude, then dammit, let's get management in here and see what we can do to change everything. But first, let's see if we can come up with an answer on our own. If there is no practical answer, then we'll have three managers and a DIC in agreement about it, and that will count for more. Now how about it? Should I schedule it for two weeks from now, or would it be better to get going next week?"

Remer was on his feet clapping. "That was fantastic," he said. "I didn't have a clue as to how to handle him. And, Rick, you were a son of a bitch, just perfect."

Coleman patted Rick on the back. "You were a slippery little mother. Absolutely perfect."

Bob felt a surge of exhilaration. If success in business was as easy as this, he could get into it. He knew that now for the first time.

Coleman patted Bob on the back as he passed. "You were stunning," he said.

Scott had already disappeared around the corner. Rick and Adam dawdled at the door, waiting for Bob.

"After watching you, I know I'm not cut out for this job," he said.

"C'mon," Bob said. "It was one day."

"One day? I've been getting those looks for almost three weeks." He laughed nervously.

"What about Coleman? How serious do you think he is, wearing that Hawaiian tie?"

"I think he's serious enough to know he can't look as macho as Remer, so he comes on looking goofy," Adam said. "He can't possibly be a jerk. All that femmy behavior—it's a disguise."

Bob hadn't thought about it until that instant, but he knew Adam had to be right. It was that little "bit," that tiny flash of something extra. Bob remembered his Uncle Bart saying that a lot of people do jobs well. "What gets you promoted, though," he had said, "is something that gives routine good performance a special style. Look like a flake, but act like a shark."

Bob wasn't paying attention and missed the stop Coleman told him to take. When he emerged from the subway, he was at the corner of Boylston and Tremont streets, on the edge of the Boston Common. It was the heart of Boston, and he felt like backtracking on foot rather than waiting for another subway. By the time he got to the other side of the Common, though, he was sweating and wished he had waited for an air-conditioned train.

Coleman's directions were easy to follow. Bob soon found himself in a neighborhood of attractive brick townhouses and cobblestone streets. Coleman's apartment building was on a corner. The two sides that faced streets had balconies with wrought-iron railings. A doorman wanted to know if Bob was expected. When he said he was, he was pointed toward the elevator.

Bob looked for a button to push, but there was none. He

realized the elevator wasn't down. After a minute, it appeared, its door sliding open. An old man in a uniform beckoned him in. "Who are you visiting, sir?" he asked. As soon as Bob told him, he nodded and shut the door behind. There were no buttons inside the elevator, either. Only a circular control with a handle coming out of it. When the operator pushed it forward, the elevator rose. It reminded Bob of something that would be on the bridge of a ship—at least as depicted in the movies.

At the third floor the operator opened the door and motioned Bob out into a lobby with a highly polished parquet floor and an oriental carpet. There were two apartment doors. Coleman's was open a crack. Bob knocked. When no one answered he pushed it farther open without entering. "Billie? Anyone here?" He decided to walk in.

The living room was large and felt empty. There was a black leather couch and two matching chairs positioned around a glass coffee table. A lamp the size of a silver basketball was turned on above the table, attached by a long silver rod to a pedestal at the side of the couch. "Billie?" Bob called again. No answer.

There was a fake wall—a facade—cantilevered to the floor and dividing the living room from the dining room. As Bob walked around it he realized it was a huge section of a billboard for the movie *Bonnie and Clyde*. There were two other sections on either wall. Read in proper succession: "They were young . . . in love . . . and they were killers." Bob moved backward toward the windows and the balcony, trying to get a full perspective. One of the boards had a huge faded pink stripe across it. He realized there had to be pieces missing because the pink stripe was part of Faye Dunaway's leg. Bob's eyes moved back and forth from the sections, and then to the couch and chairs, and across the expanse of carpet in the living room, which was splotched with dark brown squares and rectangles. At first he thought these were stains, but then he realized it was the carpet's true color and that all the rest had faded. The patches were where other furniture had been.

Off in the apartment a toilet flushed. Its sound snapped Bob from his inspection and made him self-conscious, as if he had intruded on Coleman's private affairs. He quickly moved back toward the door. "Billie?"

Coleman popped into view down the hallway. "Bob," he said. "Some host I am." He had taken off his tie and jacket, and his yellow shirt ballooned out. Until that moment, Bob hadn't realized how thin his arms were.

"I just walked in . . ." Bob motioned to the door. "It was open."

"Of course, of course." Coleman walked into the kitchen. "You were great today," he continued as Bob followed. "A marvel. Pour yourself a drink." He popped open a cabinet over the sink. "Here are the glasses. The stuff's in the fridge."

Coleman handed Bob a glass that looked like a small goldfish bowl. The idea of drinking anything but beer in that quantity made Bob nervous. But he didn't feel he could refuse to drink. Not without sounding like a prude. He opened the refrigerator door and didn't take a second to find the booze. There was a glass pitcher of martinis on the milk shelf, flanked by two bottles each of Tanqueray gin and dry vermouth. Below that were two uncovered trays of partially eaten TV dinners and several slices of pizza covered loosely by plastic wrap. There was a lime on the bottom shelf.

"Just move in?" Bob asked.

"Oh, heavens no," Billie said. "I've lived here, let me see . . . fourteen years now. But the way the place looks, I might as well have just moved in. The place seems as big as a warehouse without . . ." Coleman paused. "Aww, there's no sense in talking about that. Let's just say some of us choose between work and a relationship. I chose work, and you can see what I lost—my twenty-dollar-a-square-foot carpet tells it all. If this were a movie, I would sniffle and say, 'You see where the furniture was, but not the man who went with it.' "

Bob started to pour his drink when Coleman reached over and tapped the back of his hand with the glass rod in mock punishment.

"No, no, no, my pup," he said. "Stir, then pour." He cocked his head back and laughed. "Apologies to James Bond, but that's how I insist on them—stirred, not shaken."

Bob eyed the door, still open a crack, hoping Rick and Adam would show up. Scott had said he couldn't make it. For the first time, Bob was envious of Scott. "Nice billboard," he said.

"Isn't it terrible?" he said. "The minute they put that up in Cambridge, I said to myself, Your leg belongs to me, Faye. I hired some ambitious young students to saw it off and cart it up here. That's the way Cambridge is—anything for a laugh and a buck. Have you ever been over there?"

Bob shook his head, sipping his martini. It was so cold it was almost without taste.

"Well, it's a pity you're heading out tomorrow—I'd show you the night life here. There are lots of troublemakers like myself who hoot and holler all night long. Would you be up for that?"

Bob was spared having to answer by the arrival of Adam and Rick. They were laughing as they entered.

"There you two are," Coleman said. "What? Off partying? You should have saved yourselves for me." Coleman picked up the phone and ordered two large pizzas.

Bob sank into one side of the couch, drink in hand, while Coleman poured for the newcomers. The prospect of eating pizza and drinking martinis seemed like a formula for at least embarrassment, if not humiliation. He tried to imagine a way to excuse himself gracefully, but any option he could imagine seemed to risk insulting Coleman's hospitality—if that was the right word for it. He decided he would stick the night out, switching to water when the pizza arrived. That seemed the diplomatic thing to do.

"What a jackass you made out of Scott," Adam said to Bob.

Bob raised his eyebrows. "He'll adapt."

"With a scar. You wounded his ego for sure." Adam raised his glass. "Here's to Bob, slayer of the marketing nerd from the West Coast."

Bob checked the expression on Coleman's face. It was blank.

"I'm not going to drink to wounding his ego," Bob said, conscious of how cautious he was. He couldn't get Bart's words out of his mind. Look like a flake, but act like a shark. Coleman looked too much like a flake. The invitation for drinks and pizza could be one more official act of surveillance in the disguise of a party. It wasn't inconceivable. It wasn't even unlikely.

"That's the spirit, Bob," Coleman said. "Leave work behind and have fun. I wanted to get to know you boys better, and I wish Scott were here, wounded ego and all. I'd consider it a challenge to get that mind of his clogged with marketing data off of business for a few minutes.''

If Bob had to guess, he suspected people in management were more like Scott than not. They all worked long hours. Even if they were out to have fun, the note taking never stopped. Coleman's words made Bob more aware of the need to avoid getting drunk. Rick and Adam didn't seem much concerned about this possibility. As the night wore on they became tipsy and loose with their comments. They made fun of the training, of Scott, of Remer, and of Prescott. Bob contradicted them several times and he knew Coleman noticed that. He wasn't being a company cheerleader. Nothing as simple as that. He was looking after his own ass. When it came down to it, Coleman was too friendly. Too willing to invite opinions to be trusted. Every once in a while he would cock his head back and laugh, adding a beige comment such as, ''You're taking this too seriously.'' But Bob wasn't sure who was being serious. All he knew was he had taken the job this far—far enough to read the material, to study, to think about it, and to try to do his best. And he wasn't about to blow it all in one night in the disguise of a good time. Rick and Adam could do as they chose. If Coleman was on the level, then all Bob seemed was a little square. If he were taking notes, Bob came off great. His biggest challenge of the night came from keeping his glass away from the swooping pitcher of martinis, which moved almost independently of Coleman's hand, refilling glasses before they were half empty. As Adam and Rick slipped into states of incoherence, Coleman emerged as the main storyteller, laughing at his own jokes, feigning camaraderie at the difficulties of adjusting to the corporate world.

By eleven, Bob said he had to get back. He was the only one who could lead the other two.

Coleman threw his arm around Bob and hugged him. ''You're an angel of mercy for these two wayward sailors,'' he said. ''Go then, take them back to their beds, and I'll see you at breakfast tomorrow.''

Bob thanked him for the evening, which had been as desolate as any he could remember. Adam needed Bob's assistance to stand while waiting for the elevator. He noticed the elevator man didn't seem surprised by their states.

"Down," he asked.

"Oh, God yes, get us down," Rick said, slurring his words.

When they got off at the last subway stop, Adam threw up. Rick sang "Yellow Submarine," repeating the line, "We all live in a yellow submarine, a yellow submarine." He paused only to laugh.

Saturday night, as Bob sat wedged between two large businessmen on the flight to Syracuse, he mulled over the events of the past week, which had culminated at a breakfast that morning in the Atrium. It was intended as a congratulatory send-off. Adam was missing, and his absence preoccupied Bob. He whispered across the table to Rick. But Rick refused to answer any questions. "Later," he whispered back.

When Rick was able to talk alone to Bob, he told him it turned out Remer and Coleman had met with Adam and him before breakfast. They told Adam that they didn't feel P&V was the right place for him. They gave him a month's salary and wished him luck in finding a career better suited to his temperament. Adam, already packed, had left immediately. They told Rick they didn't believe he was yet ready for the road, but that they thought he had excellent promise. They offered him a rotation of jobs beginning with a stint as an assistant to the director of research. In six months or a year they would re-evaluate him for a district job, if he still wanted one.

"Was Adam upset?" Bob asked.

Rick gave him the dumb-question look. "You know how important he thought all this was—like it was a dumb game—and then to be told he was no good at it? He didn't even say good-bye to me."

"How do you feel about it?"

"They made the right decision."

As the plane took off, Bob could still hear the matter-of-fact tone in Rick's voice. Without caring for Adam, he felt numbed by the news. It had happened so quickly, so surgically. And he doubted the decision had been made that morning. Coleman must have known the night before. The whole evening was probably one last look. And Adam had spent the entire night cutting up on Scott and corporate procedures—with Coleman acting entertained throughout, all the while confirming the decision to get rid of him.

What made the morning further troubling for Bob was Remer's doting. "You made a name for yourself here this week," he told Bob.

"Thanks," Bob said. "I guess you mean that in a good way."

"You bet," Remer said, squeezing his shoulder. "You displayed some real cunning in the role playing. And though you don't have Scott's business background, you've got street instincts. You'll work hard out there, and the way the company is expanding, you'll have a promotion in no time. The opportunity is there. And I'm betting you're the kind of guy who'll go for it. You know, I was an English major. I even taught high school in Plattsburgh, New York, before realizing there was no money in reading Robert Frost to teen-agers. That took me three years. But I can tell you already know it."

Bob stammered out a response of thanks, but held back an odd mix of emotions that made him feel simultaneously resentful and excited. He wanted to be good at things, to do well, to get ahead. What was the point of work otherwise? But why was he good at something he cared so little about? Why did he want to win the respect of men like Remer? Men he wouldn't have taken seriously just two months before?

Bob didn't have a chance to ask Scott how he felt about Adam. But he knew Scott would respond with an expression of stoic acceptance and likely produce a moral. It seemed the lore of business was filled with basically cynical tales ending in morals that explained success or failure. Bob didn't feel intimidated by Scott anymore. He knew he had done well over the past week, and he knew Scott knew that too. Scott had even come to respect him, so much so that he cut out the talk about the importance of marketing and the genius of Warner Prescott, as well as the condescending speeches on what to do in the field. Scott's respect signaled to him that, although Scott didn't like him, he could see that Bob would be good at the job, perhaps a serious competitor for advancement. People didn't have to like each other in business. They just had to do things right.

It might be difficult to imagine Remer and Coleman spending Saturday afternoon together anywhere but in the office. But, as far as Bob could tell, they didn't care if they got along anywhere else but at work.

Bob found Irene waiting for him in the main lounge. They hugged and kissed. On the way to the car, Irene said she wanted to hear all about the session. She had made reservations at a restaurant so they could talk over dinner.

Bob tried to imagine how he would tell her "all about it." Now that he thought about what had taken place in The Pit and in preparing for The Pit, it seemed faraway and silly. Almost difficult to recall. The less effort he put into remembering it, the more relaxed he got. By the time they got to the restaurant, Bob felt ready for sleep.

"I don't know if I'll be good company," Bob said. "I'm kind of drifting away."

"I bet a good drink and some wine will get you going," Irene said.

The waiters wore tuxedos, not exactly what he expected in Syracuse. "Irene, I'm not certain I have that much cash left. The check for this week's work is in the mail."

"This is on me," she said.

"Wait a second. I'm the one with the job. I ought to be paying."

"You get the next dinner. Right now, I'm the one with the money."

The wine proved unsuccessful in reviving Bob. His descriptions of the training session were uninteresting to him, let alone Irene. The kind of visceral intensity he had summoned for role playing seemed to have sprung from some source unavailable to him now. He wondered if he'd ever find it again.

At one point, Irene asked, "Is that it? Just that? And that's what they call training?"

"I guess you had to be there," Bob said. "It's different in the context of the place. When you're there, everyone believes it's important, and somehow it becomes important."

"It all seems so trivial. Or just common sense."

"C'mon," Bob said. "Did your father talk to you about the details of his work? I mean the real mundane details? My father never did. Only the arguments with foremen or strange stuff. Nothing on the day-to-day. It was a good day or a bad day. A long day or time flew. That was the extent of it."

Irene conceded that was true. "Take away his 'tides of currency' speech, and he never had much to say about work. I knew what he was working on—say a merger—but not the paperwork side of it."

"I guess it's not so hard to imagine that I'm not that excited about the prospect of customer census taking and training high school dropouts to look and act in a uniformly positive manner according to P&V guidelines."

Irene lit a cigarette. "Why bother with it then? Why not find a job that does excite you?"

"I guess I believe a job is a job. And maybe I like the idea that I'm considered good at this one."

"But you would be good at whatever job you did. Whether it was teaching or scraping turds off the floor of a vet's dog cages. The question is, what do you want to *do*?"

"I guess I want to do what I'm good at. I don't want to be a lawyer if I'm only average. I want to be better than average. And I want to be successful. Not an also-ran."

"A what?"

"A guy who finishes the race behind the pack of leaders."

"Leaders in what kind of race?"

"In any race."

"The race in drugstore inventory control?"

"That will do for now. What difference does one job make. In ten years, I'll be doing something else."

"A lot of people believe that and wake up in ten years and find themselves so entrenched in the routine they've made for themselves, so comfortable and so secure, they can't change."

"Yeah, of course. But I'm not like that."

"No one ever is. But you wake up one morning . . ."

"And find you're a bug? A pod person? Come on, Irene, I get the feeling you don't like what I'm doing, that's all."

Irene reached across the table and took his hand. "And I get the feeling you don't like it, at least not the way someone says that's what I want to do for the rest of my life."

"I have no idea what I want to do for the rest of my life. And I don't know anyone I respect who does."

"If you think I'm looking down my nose at you, you're wrong. But if you want to know whether I think you're better than this job, the answer is yes."

"What's 'better'?"

"Better is being happy with your choices. I don't think you are. Not the way you represent them."

"I haven't made that many choices in my life."

"If you don't start now, when will you?"

"What are you? My conscience?"

"No, I'm not. But if we're going to live together, I don't want to be there with someone who's miserable all the time. What do you want?"

Bob reached across the table and held Irene's hand. "Look, I'm tired. I'm not making sense. Today, they fired one of the guys I trained with. Just like that. He's gone. Maybe he should have been fired. But still, it's hard for me to accept that I'm in a world like that. Right now, for the near future, I am."

"You still haven't said anything about us."

Bob rubbed his eyes. They were dry and stung from the smoke of Irene's cigarette. When he finished he looked at her. He thought for a second he saw a flicker of doubt in her face. It was the first time he had seen it there. Or maybe it was just shadow. It had been there and gone. Now she was recomposed and staring at him.

"I've thought about this whole thing . . . ," he said.

"And?"

"And I wonder what's up with you. I like you. I like the things we do. But this—living together—it's a change."

"Yeah?"

"Why me?"

Irene laughed and coughed smoke into the air. "Why you? Because you're there. What do you mean, why you?"

Bob put his head in his hands and stared at her, elbows propped against the table. "I'm sorry, Irene, but some times this all seems a little strange to me. I want to pinch myself and ask if you're really that interested in me. There's a part of me that wants to believe it. And there's another part saying, 'Don't be a jerk, you're just a diversion. She just broke up with Mr. Swifty and you're a temporary replacement.' "

Irene snuffed her cigarette out. "I don't want to live with

temporary diversions. So tell that part of yourself to go fuck himself. The part of you I want to talk to hasn't answered yet.''

Bob felt a sudden release of tension. A surrender of sorts. And it gave him the kind of calm he remembered from the pure exhaustion of a long run. ''Yeah,'' he said. ''I want to live with you.''

Irene rubbed the back of his hand and smiled. ''Good. That's good. I'm happy.''

After the hour's drive back to the fraternity house, it was past midnight. By the time they got to bed, they were both too tired to make love. Irene fell asleep on Bob's shoulder. As her breathing deepened, he drifted off too. But it was a light, fitful sleep, marred by sudden twitches. On the last jerk, Irene moaned and rolled away from him.

Bob pushed himself up quietly and sat at the edge of the bed. He put on his pants and went to the bathroom. The light of the hallway was harsh, and he noticed how tattered and soiled the carpet was, how the walls were stained and pocked. Much dingier than he remembered things. The bathroom was in worse shape. Wads of toilet paper collected at the base of an overflowing waste basket. One of the sinks was stopped up with brown water. As he stood at the urinal he read a line of graffiti written in red marker: ''Sometimes you get the bear, and sometimes the bear gets you.''

When Bob flushed—the sound an eruption in the stillness of the night—he suddenly felt possessed of a new conviction for his job. He had no apologies to make to anyone. He had only to do it. To throw himself into it, to do it better than anyone else. Because nothing appealed for long unless you immersed yourself in it. It was so simple. Why hadn't he thought of it before. He could do that much. And more.

Bob crawled into bed and put his arm around Irene. She shifted closer to him, pulling his arm tighter to her breasts. He kissed the nape of her neck and settled into a warmer part of the mattress. Slowly he felt the return of sleep, this time a deeper, thicker sleep than he had known in weeks.

CHAPTER

7

That Tuesday Bob got a call from his new regional manager, Byron Cutter, announcing that it was time to start. Bob had been told to expect a three-week break between training and field orientation, but Cutter said he hadn't heard a word about it.

"You don't want to forget everything you've just learned, do you?" Cutter asked.

"I won't forget it," Bob said.

"And I'm not about to forget I've got a fifteen-store district here with no DIC during the back-to-school rush. It's our second most busy time of the year and that makes it extra good for orientation."

Cutter told Bob to meet him Thursday in Ann Arbor at a motel just off the thruway. "Get yourself a plane to Detroit and take a shuttle bus to town," Cutter said. "They make a stop right at the motel. I'll have a room there."

If Bob could have thought of a way to stall, he would have. He was sick, his mother was dying, he was having an operation. None of it would have come off right. At least he didn't feel adept enough at fabrications to try one. He and Irene had only begun to plan what to bring with them and to figure out the logistics of setting up an apartment together. They were going to go out together. Now all that was out the window.

Bob wanted to tell Irene immediately, but he couldn't find

her. The car wasn't in the parking lot. Bob guessed she had
gone grocery shopping. While he waited for her to return, he
grew nervous. He tried to think of what to say, rehearsing several possibilities. Then he gave up and decided to pack his bag
to avoid thinking about whether or not Irene would be angry.
When he heard her voice downstairs, he left the suitcase on the
bed and went to the bathroom. It worked better than words.

When Bob returned to the room, Irene was sitting on the
bed, her hand on the suitcase. She had a what's this? expression on her face.

Bob nodded. "That manager, Cutter, called. He wants me
out there on Thursday. I have an eight A.M. flight that morning."

"Refuse to go. How are we going to move our stuff?"

"I can't refuse. That's my boss." Just what he had feared.
They weren't even in an apartment yet, and already the job was
at odds with Irene.

"It's unreasonable. You have no place to live. You don't
even have a bed to sleep on."

"He wants me out there during the back-to-school rush.
He's going to take me to a few stores and then cut me loose."

"When do we look for an apartment?"

"Later. I'll live in motels. You can't come out right away.
Not until the orientation is done."

"I could come out and look while you're working."

"I think we should look together, don't you?"

Irene grinned. "The only one I'd worry about looking for
an apartment alone is you. That you'd take some basement better suited for potatoes than us."

"Nice. Lots of confidence."

"Left to your own devices, you eat sardines out of a can.
I can only conjecture about the implications of that for apartment hunting. That's why I have to be there with you."

"All right, you win that round. But what about all the stuff
we were going to bring."

"Sell it."

"Not my books."

"You need that copy of *The Scarlet Letter* for your work?"

Bob knew she was right. But he could not bring himself to
sell his books. He drew the line there. During training, when

the idea that he would be living in motels at least a couple of nights a week sunk in, he had this image of himself using the time at night to read some of the lesser works by writers he admired. All of Faulkner's stories. *Pierre.* Cooper's novels. But now he could see what a joke that was. There were the forms to think about. He spent a week learning them—and just when had he imagined he would be filling them in? He never thought about it. Not seriously, anyway. But now he knew. Instead of rounding out his knowledge of American literature, he would be commenting on the appearances of high school dropouts, counting customers, monitoring the impulse purchases. He had been presented a vision of his future, a future in which he was much reduced from what he had always intended for himself.

"I can't give up the books," Bob said. "We've got to bring them."

"You could send them home. That's what I'll do with mine."

Bob shook his head. "I want them."

"Okay. We'll make arrangements with Lipton to ship them out once we find a place. It's not that big a deal."

Bob agreed. It was a small concession to a part of his life he was otherwise about to leave behind.

Bob's orientation consisted of eight straight days on the road. Cutter drove the company car Bob would inherit the day he put Cutter on a plane for Cleveland. It was impossible to make a complete circuit of the fifteen stores in Bob's territory, so Cutter took those in a straight line south from Ann Arbor—Toledo, Bowling Green, Findlay—and then west to Fort Wayne. The stores in South Bend, Niles, Adrian, Jackson, Westland, and Lansing Bob would visit on his own.

Cutter was a short, paunchy man with oily, receding hair and a ruddy, pocked face. He didn't look healthy, but he walked and talked fast, and that combination made Bob feel he was always racing to keep up with Cutter no matter how unfit the man appeared.

At the stores, Cutter stressed checking displays, talking with managers, and sorting out problems in quadrant and impulse sales. The company's impulse sales were especially important. "Most companies use this junk as loss leaders just to lure people in the door,'' Cutter said, elaborating on information that had been skimmed over during training. ''But Prescott had a better idea. He fine-tunes the impulse merchandise store by store according to the demographic profile of the trading area, and then he gets incredible prices on the stuff. The names change, but you'll find the items are the same within limits. When the impulse sales go down, take a look at the stuff and the customer base. Something's out of whack.''

On drives between stores, Cutter frequently tantalized him with the prospect of promotion and bonuses, reiterating that Bob was on a management track position. ''You come up with some ideas of your own, and they work, you'll be on your way,'' Cutter said.

At night, Bob had dinner with Cutter, and after one beer, left him bivouacked at the bar to return to his room, where he filled out the forms required for each store. His concentration waned by eleven, and he sometimes fell asleep sitting on top of the bed, listening to the local newscasters' nightly reports of fires and grain prices. He would wake at the sound of the national anthem, turn the TV off, and ask for a wake-up call at 6:30. That gave him time to shower, and to watch the beginning of the ''Today'' show, which provided something to talk about over breakfast.

Bob began to wonder what Cutter regarded as training. He never asked to see his reports. Bob had no idea that he was doing anything right. They worked through Sunday, and by Monday Bob was ready for a break. But Cutter wasn't about to stop.

''Sounds like it's sink or swim,'' Bob's father said one night. After failing to get hold of Irene, Bob called home just to hear a familiar voice.

''What do you mean?''

''He's letting you make your own bed.''

''But it's supposed to be a training session. Why doesn't he give me more help.''

''Look, he said he needed you on board during the school rush, right? It's going to be a pain in the ass for him if you don't work out.''

''So?''

"So he's satisfied, or he would say something. Was there a guy there before you? In your position?"

"It's not clear. Either Cutter did it himself, or in combination with a couple of other guys who went out of their regular districts. Most of the stores weren't properly serviced. The whole district is underperforming."

"See, they've given you a chance to turn a place around. I bet the big shots in Boston are watching. So do your job and relax about Cutter. I know when I break somebody in at the factory I can't worry every second about him. I've got twenty other people to watch, too. Setups to do. Inventory to check, production schedules to coordinate, material to order. I can't hold the guy's hand all day."

Bob thanked his father for his advice. It was always this way. Simple and direct. Sink or swim. Make your bed. No hand holding. Maybe all business was like that—even for guys with graduate degrees. A cut-to-the-quick attitude. Fast walk, fast talk.

"Have you heard from Carl?" Bob asked.

"One letter. We've tried to call him a few times, but he's never in. I guess his roommates don't leave messages. I guess he's all set to stay on for one more semester. Have you heard?"

"Yeah, one letter. He's got some translations he wants to do. And an independent study idea. He seemed puzzled by my job."

"Yours?" his father said. "What's he got to be puzzled about?" Bob recognized his father's tone: mock indignation. He used it for situations like this one, when Bob's or Carl's intellectual pursuits overshadowed practical concerns. It was a pose on his part, a kind of head scratching, I'm-just-a-simple-guy-who-puts-food-on-the-table attitude. When in fact he took a vicarious pleasure in watching Bob and Carl attend college—something he never got around to doing. Of course, when you graduated, everything changed. You put away the toys you played with for four years and did just what Bob had done: get on with earning money.

"I guess he was surprised I would work for a drugstore chain, that's all."

"And what were you supposed to do? Part-time at a hamburger joint?"

"I guess he thought I would go to graduate school. Or teach a little while."

"I don't know a professor with a company car."

"Yeah, but I don't think he cares about that. He probably wants to go to graduate school himself."

"That's all well and good. But he's also got to buckle down a little harder with his courses to do that. He's got four incompletes he needs to make up to graduate. Four papers he'll have to finish his last semester. All because he goes off on crazy tangents."

"He'll get them done."

"Let's hope so." There was a pause in the conversation. Bob heard the static-muffled chatter of another conversation. Since he would often be on the road, it was a sound he would have to get used to. His father spoke again, hesitantly: "How's that girlfriend of yours?"

"Okay," Bob said. To his own surprise, he continued: "We're going to try living together."

"Living together?"

"She doesn't start law school until next year now. She delayed it."

"And what will she do?"

"She'll take a few graduate courses in government next semester."

"And what else?"

Bob could tell what was next. She's living off of you? He had never said much about Irene to his parents. "She doesn't have to do anything else, Dad. She's pretty well off."

"Oh. Well, we'd sure like to meet her."

"Maybe some time in the spring. I don't think we'll get back east before that."

"Get back any time you can. But don't compromise the job."

Bob glanced at the pile of paperwork on his bedside table. "It's so much bullshit paperwork."

"That's information. You gather it, write it up, and ship it back in a timely fashion. That's what counts. But don't become a robot, for chrissake. Use your head. Make suggestions."

"Yeah, right." What did his father know about a job like

this, working in a factory for thirty years. What was worse, how come his advice sounded so similar to Remer's.

Bob's father cleared his throat. "I could have done a lot more with my life than I did. But I was missing something. Not just a degree. Something else. Self-confidence or concentration, I don't know. Maybe just someone to come along and kick me in the ass. To say, get on with it. But that's not the case with you. Your biggest problem is walking around feeling dirty about taking a job with a drugstore. I can tell. But knock it off. You've always worked your butt off for whatever you wanted. Now it's time to make yourself a career. So focus on all this grunt stuff and get it done. They won't keep someone like you out there forever."

"I hope you're right."

"I am right about this. About you. And about me."

After Bob hung up, he tried to throw himself into the paperwork. But it didn't go easily. It was so menial. So repetitious. He felt like he needed downers to get it done. Something that would make filling in the blanks much more of a challenge.

By Friday, Bob found the only way he could get through the paperwork was by using the General Observations sheet to write a brief description of the town and its happenings. Sometimes he transcribed a letter he saw in the local paper. Or, he included fragments of conversation overheard in restaurants. And at other times he recorded his own observations. Then he sent the whole package back to the office in Boston. One package per store location. Two or three hours of typing per night.

He sometimes wondered whether they read anything he sent. Or whether they just weighed it and figured it was okay if it totaled a pound or two each. His fingers smelled from the chemicals on the triplicate forms. He couldn't believe college grads were paid to do work like this when anyone with an eighth-grade education and a driver's license could do the same. He mentioned this to Cutter on the last night. They were having a beer at the Fort Wayne Holiday Inn. Cutter nodded solemnly and then launched into a pep talk Bob wished he had anticipated before complaining.

"When you start in the trenches, you learn the dirty side

of any business,'' Byron Cutter said. ''You become a real soldier. Not one of those academy officers. But someone who
works his way up through the ranks, decorated for bravery under fire all the way. Somebody who knows the business better
than any M.B.A. from Harvard. Christ, one of those wafflers
couldn't get the pen out of his briefcase before the competition
had him surrounded and suckin' inventory up his rear. That's
because this whole business is brand new. No one has fought
a marketing war like this. There are no case histories. You're
part of my platoon, and the chief is giving us all the leeway we
need to redefine this business from the minute a customer
walks through the door. Hang on, buddy. Hang on.'' He
rubbed Bob's shoulder with his hand, and raised his beer with
the other.

''Barkeep, get us a pitcher,'' Cutter said.

Bob cringed inwardly. He had no tolerance for foxhole
chatter, and now it looked as if Cutter would be serving it up
for at least as long as it took to drink a pitcher. That and the
shake-the-weaklings-out-of-the-ranks lecture. He had become
painfully aware that his reports could doom a manager. Every
time a manager was written up for procedural problems, he was
said to be ''dicked.''

An hour later, Bob reached Irene back at the frat house.
She was ready to drive out the next day. When she asked how
things had been going, he told her how his reports could be
used to terminate people.

''If the guys are no good,'' she said, ''why cover for
them?''

''Yeah,'' Bob said. ''But it's not that simple. They always
have excuses. There's always another side to it. But when you
write up the report, it comes out black and white, not gray.
And according to Cutter, management in Boston acts overnight. The guy is gone—poof!''

''That sounds awful,'' Irene said. ''Don't they get due
course?''

''What's that?''

''A warning, verbally, then in writing?''

''I guess not. I don't know.''

''In any case, how can you change it?''

''I can't,'' Bob said. But knowing this didn't make him feel better about writing up a manager. Especially if the guy had a family. Those were the cases that hurt. Bob would see photos of their kids taped to the metal panels of their elevated offices. But the company had trained Bob to look for certain slipups he found with disturbing regularity. The average P&V manager was the kind of guy who had tried one or two careers before and failed. Some weren't meant for retailing; others were incapable of responsibility.

"We need to drum those losers out of the P&V corps," Cutter said over breakfast the last morning. "Coleman told me yesterday that your reports are excellent. You've got a head for details, which makes management decisions easy."

As Cutter said this, Bob imagined himself as a corporate angel of death. By his reports, his observations, and checklists, the fate of managers was determined. He recalled Buck Remer's final words of advice: "We want the red and blue colors of the P&V sign to offer the same assurance of quality in Louisville as it does in Chicago. . . . You're going to write things that ultimately cost some folks their jobs. But that is the nature of this world—the weak limbs get pruned. . . . Remember, at P&V, it's not how long you've been in the race, it's how fast you're moving."

Bob knew bullshit when he heard it. What he didn't know until he got on the road, however, was that the company lived by its bullshit. By the end of the orientation, Bob found he had developed a tolerance to it. Enough so that he could stare at the corporate acronym without the mental equivalent of a dry heave and mouth the corporate mottoes to managers and employees without suppressing a laugh. He was ready to write reports, note problems, and play the role of corporate tattletale. He would give the job a chance. He could hold his former self in abeyance for the time being. The self who would snicker or rebel. Because there was money involved, the kind he had never seen before. If he could turn his district around, there would be a bonus for him, perhaps as much as his starting salary. Even if he got half of that, it would be more money than anyone in his family had ever held in hand before. He and Irene could go to Europe. There would be money enough for a lot of things, and it would be his money.

CHAPTER

8

Bob and Irene moved into the apartment in Sterne the last week in August. He had asked Cutter for a week to get settled, so Cutter suggested day trips: Adrian, Findlay, Bowling Green, and back to Toledo.

As soon as they got their phone connected, Bob called the home office to give his new address and was told Coleman wanted to speak with him. Coleman wasn't at his office, though, and his secretary indicated the message had something to do with the Toledo four store. Bob tried calling Cutter to get more information, but got his answering machine.

Irene wanted to get as much as possible done during the first week they were in the apartment. At night he shuttled Irene between Sterne and Ann Arbor to buy the accoutrements of living with someone: bath mat, dish drainer, bathroom and kitchen towels—things he would never have gotten if he lived by himself. It seemed she thought of something different every day.

By Wednesday, Bob was exhausted. He had taken a three-day break between training and orientation and, if he counted the weekend of apartment hunting, had been working ever since. Now he drove all day and evening. He had a briefcase full of weekly order forms and a ream of sales figures that he had to wade through each night to assess what was happening in Toledo four by himself. It looked like Sherman Hite, the manager there, hadn't come close to selling his inventory of impulse mix items for three straight months. Plus, when he and Cutter had visited the store during orientation, there had been several dress code violations by the staff noted in the report. Bob hadn't even done a complete evaluation of the store. Now he suspected that a thorough going over would amount to a death sentence for the guy, especially if Bob could identify what was wrong with the impulse mix. Everything was happening too fast. He wanted a little more space between the move, the apartment, living together, and the underside of the job. Just a little breathing room.

"I'm beginning to wish," Bob said, "that we lived in Ann Arbor. It seems we head in there every day as it is. Besides, what the hell is there to do in this town."

Irene was dusting off the few books she had brought out with her and putting them on the built-in bookshelf. "I know this is a bad week," she said. "But it will get better. Sterne's greatest asset is its utter lack of appeal. You understand what I'm saying?"

"Yeah, you're saying this is a jerkwater town."

Irene set a book on the shelf. "Exactly. Think for a second. You're on the road five days a week. So really all you have to put up with is a weekend of boredom. In January, I'll be taking courses in constitutional history, federalism, and public administration—that's a full graduate load. I need a cell. Sterne is my cell. And living here this fall will give me a nice bland stretch before I throw myself into all that."

"What am I then? The perfect partner to have in a dull town?"

Irene dropped the dust cloth. "Don't be like that. It's a good chance for us to get used to living together. If I were studying on top of what you're doing, we'd be no better than strangers."

"I just want to have some fun once in a while, that's all."

Irene put her arm around Bob's shoulder. "Oh, get off it. You make it sound like you're out there in the big bad war earning big bucks and what you deserve is a warm, fun-lovin' gal to be at the door when you get home. Isn't that what you're saying?''

Bob sat at the edge of the bed and exhaled slowly. She was right. He was tired and wondering what preconceptions he had had about living together. He knew it was different from living together at college, but he wasn't sure in what way.

"Bear with me," Bob said. "I'm trying to get used to everything at once."

Irene sat beside him. "We both are. Law school won't be a picnic. And neither will the graduate courses. I've never worked hard—I mean *really* hard—in my life. School has been easy up 'til now. Everything has been easy. I could party all weekend and still get my work done. But I don't want to try that this time. I want this to be for keeps."

Irene said "for keeps" staring into the window as if she saw something. Bob followed her gaze but found only a reflection of them sitting on the bed. He got up and closed the curtains. He sensed a serious gap between them. Not the money gap, which he had felt from the beginning and tried to ignore. This was a gap of intentions. He realized he didn't have anything he felt like doing "for keeps." He couldn't imagine being a district inventory coordinator for keeps, or, for that matter, being anything at P&V for keeps. Sure, he could throw himself into the job—week by week, but not for keeps. Her sense of purpose was unsettling. She seemed to know more about living than he did. At least about the way she wanted to live. Did that come from money, or was it hers alone? He sat back on the bed and put his arm around her. Her shoulder was cold and he felt as if he were touching her for the first time.

"Let's call it a night," she said. "Don't forget your uncle."

"Right. Where did he say he would be?"

"I wrote it down. Some place near the Toledo airport. He wanted me to come along but I told him I was tied up. I'm not ready to start traveling around with you. I mean, after lunch, what would I do, sit in your car while you visit the store?"

Bob patted her on the back. "And this is the person who wanted to dull out?" He stood. "I think I've got to do some paperwork before I can come to bed."

"It'll wait," she said. "Get in there." She pulled Bob down onto the bed.

Bob lay there, his eyes almost shut, too tired to move. Irene went to the bathroom to wash up. Finally he undressed and crawled under the covers. After a while, Irene returned. He was almost asleep. He held still as she crawled into bed, not wanting to lose his descent. But when she snuggled up next to him, molding her body against his back, he suddenly found himself thinking about their living together. About how many nights there could be like this one, if they lived together for a lifetime. And that seemed too much to consider. Overwhelming in a way nothing had been that day.

Irene's breathing deepened into a clear, clean rhythm. He tried to focus on it and let it lead him into sleep. But that didn't work. He rolled over, and Irene reversed her position, her shirt creeping up her side as she shifted. He stroked her flesh there, below the ribs. He meant it to be a reassuring stroke. But the idea of him reassuring her felt like a joke. He rolled away from her and tried to remain still. But he couldn't. Finally he got out of bed and dressed quietly, thinking he would go for a walk.

Bob made it from the porch to the corner before he lost his interest in a walk. From where he stood, he could see a truck idling at a traffic light, revving its engine before continuing. For a moment, he thought about being that driver, with nothing more to worry about than finding a good place to stop later in the night for a strong cup of coffee. It was a simple fantasy, and comforted him the way a fantasy should. But only for a moment. Because as soon as he imagined drinking that coffee, he thought of a schedule. Surely the driver had one. Something that dictated where he would be at what time. Then he wondered if the driver had his house in hock to pay for the rig. There was no avoiding schedules and money.

After sitting on the porch steps for a minute, Bob decided he would carry a chair into the backyard. Charlie and Rita had a pleasant backyard. A flower and vegetable garden along the sides, and a flagstone path down the middle, which encircled a tree at the center.

Bob had been sitting for a few minutes before he heard the sounds of other breathing. He turned and saw Charlie and Rita on the back porch, still as sculptures in their lawn chairs, watching him.

"You two have a fight or something?" Rita asked.

Bob glanced up at the second-floor window. It was shut. "No."

"Sometimes a move will make young people fight."

"Young people!" Charlie said. "Ha! What about old people?"

"Okay, everyone fights after a move. What of it?"

"We're not fighting," Bob said. He scrambled within himself to change the subject. "This is quite a backyard."

"Isn't it?" Rita said. "It was in terrible shape after we bought the house. But we brought it back."

"A lot of work," Charlie said. "Would you like a beer?"

"Sure." Bob moved his chair closer.

"Folks in Sterne used to call this place Randolph's Castle—that was the doctor who built it."

Bob compared the house to others in the neighborhood. It didn't seem much larger.

"We bought it while we were still living in Detroit and renovated the whole thing. You know those hardwood floors upstairs?"

The way she asked the question made Bob wonder whether she meant something other than what he had been walking on.

"From an old schoolhouse. Every board."

"That was work," Charlie said, emerging from the house with a Stroh's for Bob. "Man, every weekend, down on my hands and knees fitting those boards, cutting, fitting, and nailing."

"We got it down," Rita said. "That and the woodwork— brought it all back."

"There were four years when I worked on the line at Chrysler five days a week and rebuilt this house on weekends," Charlie said. "Back and forth, back and forth." Charlie moved his beer back and forth as he said this, slopping a little out of the top.

Rita lurched from her chair with a napkin. "Will you watch out. Look at this."

"It's only a porch, dammit," Charlie said.

The floor of the back porch was covered with artificial grass. Rita got down on her hands and knees to rub the turf with the napkin, which immediately shredded into smaller pieces. "Now look at this," she said. "A mess." She picked up a few of the pieces and went inside, letting the screen door slap shut. She returned with a brush and a bucket of hot water smelling of pine cleaner. "You can't let beer soak into this stuff. It never goes. That's why they don't let major league ball players spit on it."

"Is that true?" Charlie asked.

"Well, I don't know for sure," Rita said, "since you're the one who told me."

Charlie ran his thick hand across his scalp. "It was a labor of love, this place."

"For our retirement," Rita said.

"Couldn't live in Detroit anymore. Too much going on."

"There," Rita said, rising. She dropped the brush into the bucket and set it next to her chair. "We were broken into four times in two years. We saw an ad for this place in the paper and thought it would get us closer to our daughter."

"Yep," Charlie said, as if this needed to be confirmed. "She's married to a farmer out here."

"At least he calls himself a farmer," Rita said. "He doesn't seem to make any money. We keep bailing him out."

"Figures soy beans are the ticket this year, but I don't know," Charlie said. "He sure works hard."

"He works like a jackass," Rita said. "And I'll you what else: no more! If beans go bust, he goes with them. She can come live with us. That's why we've got that room up there."

Charlie gave a single, emphatic nod. There was a pause in the conversation. Bob felt awkward, as if he were privy to information he shouldn't know. He always felt that way when he heard speculation about a family member's marriage breaking up. But the older he got, the more he heard it. He guessed that was the way it would be all his life, since he had read in the Toledo paper that one out of every two marriages ended in divorce. The headline for the article was "Divorce Today: Easier and More Popular Than Ever." It went on to suggest that no-contest divorces were about as easy to get as gasoline credit cards. You filled out a form, waited a few months, and bingo.

"We thought you and Irene could join us for a picnic here the weekend after next. If you don't have other plans."

"Thanks," Bob said. "Irene probably will. I think I'm supposed to be in Columbus at a convention."

"You work weeks and weekends?" Charlie said. "What kind of company is that? Don't you have a union?"

"It's the nature of the business. All major conventions fall on holidays or weekends."

"Geez," Charlie said, crunching his beer can. His hands said a lot about his life. The pinky and ring fingers were bent outward at the last knuckle, as if they had been caught in a door. His index finger was missing its tip. "You must be getting good overtime pay, that's all I can say."

"Charlie!" Rita said. "Mind your business."

"That's okay," Bob said. He knew this game. They tell him about their daughter's ne'er-do-well husband, he tells them something personal like how much he's making. He wouldn't bite. It was getting completely dark and he felt again like walking. "I think I'm going to head out. All that driving I do makes it a pleasure to take walks."

"You should try a sauna once in a while," Charlie said. "We built one over at the farm. It kept me alive while we worked on the house."

Bob took the path at the center of the backyard and stopped when he came to the tree. He hadn't noticed anything unusual about it before. But now that he was closer, he saw that its bark was smooth up to a specific point. Above that it became rippled and knotty, as if traumatized long ago. The limbs and branches twisted up and down, snarling together like a pile of unraveled yarn. The leaves were something like an elm's, only smaller and too irregular for him to be certain.

"This tree is an experiment," Rita said.

Bob jumped. He hadn't heard her walk up from behind. "What happened?"

"A gardener's curiosity. An elm altered as a sapling by cutting it in half and grafting the top to the bottom. The limbs can't figure out whether they're roots or branches. They go up and down at the same time."

Bob thought about the elm as he walked around the block. It seemed like an odd thing to do to a tree, or for that matter, to have thought of doing in the first place. What did it prove? That nature could be confused? As he watched the curtains to a ranch house's picture window drawn shut, he believed that if it was possible for a tree to be pained, then that tree surely was. Not knowing whether it was supposed to grow roots or limbs, so doing both poorly, what kind of existence was that? If the tree was in his backyard, he would cut it down.

When Bob woke, the pale glow of street lights illuminated their bed. He had been dreaming, but he couldn't remember what. His hand again rested on the soft spot below Irene's ribs. Without a thought, he slid it down along her hip, his fingers stroking at her panties. Her breathing became throatier and faster, and she rolled toward him, moving her tongue across her dry lips, her nipples hardening to his touch. As he closed his eyes he heard the slap, the slow slap of cold water in the Adirondacks, and he saw the water moving against that stone boathouse year after year, through all the seasons. He held onto this image throughout. He was surprised to find himself wondering how many other couples in Sterne had wound themselves together at the same moment. Five? Ten? No, not in such a small town. Not in Sterne.

As Bob opened the door to leave the next morning, Irene called to him.

"I almost forgot," she said. "I'm sorry." She held a blue piece of paper in her hand. "A letter from your brother. It came just before I left the college and I packed it away. I found it again yesterday."

Bob glanced at the envelope. His name was written in his brother's familiar scrawl. When Bob had written last, he asked Carl not to send any more letters to the college address, but Carl evidently never got the letter or ignored it. He tucked it in his briefcase and kissed Irene good-bye. He had a long day in front of him. He would read it when he stopped somewhere for coffee.

Uncle Bart was halfway through a dark drink when Bob got to the Bull's Pen, a stable-styled restaurant for young executives located a few miles from the Toledo airport. Ticker tapes churned away at either end of the bar, each surrounded by a small but loud crowd. It was 11:30 A.M.

"Hi, buddy," Bart said, rising to shake Bob's hand. "How's life in the trenches?"

"How did you know they call it that?" Bob asked.

"Oh, that's what everyone calls it. A tough way to make a living, but let me tell you, there's no better way to learn the business from the ground up."

"Yeah, so I've heard."

A cocktail waitress swung by. She wore a bright green apron imprinted with a bull on one pocket and a bear on the other. "Good morning, gentlemen. The Dow's at 1738, up thirty. Can I get you something to drink?"

"Another Rob Roy," Bart said. "And one for you?"

Bob shook his head. "Got another call to make after lunch. A real problem spot. I'll have a coffee."

Bart drained his glass and set it on the waitress's tray. She disappeared into the crowd around the bar.

"How did you get my phone number so soon?" Bob asked.

"I just happened to call your mother after you gave it to her. I wanted to see about driving up from the city to visit your folks tomorrow."

"How are they?"

"Same as usual. They sound real excited about your job."

"Yeah," Bob said. Driving down from Ann Arbor that morning, there had been something about the slant of light that made Bob think of autumn. He thought about how Bart would come up from New York each Labor Day weekend and take Bob and Carl to the fair in Goshen, and how Bart would scream louder than they did on the rides.

"So you have a girlfriend you live with?"

"You heard that too?"

"Sure did. Irene, is it? Tell me, what's she going to do up there in . . . What's that town?"

"Sterne."

"Sterne?"

"It's outside Ann Arbor. Irene will take classes there in January. And she's starting law school a year from now."

Bart raised his eyebrows. They dropped slowly back into

place. Bob appreciated the refinement of the expression, no doubt perfected in thousands of business meetings.

"Just what the world needs," Bart said. "Another gal lawyer."

Bob shook his head. "She comes from a long line of lawyers. Some firm in New York was started by her grandfather. It's all banking, takeovers, and international finance."

"I'd say you've got yourself a tall order in her."

"What do you mean?"

"Most guys on the road have a hard enough time with a girlfriend. But a lawyer's daughter to boot—watch yourself."

"I don't know what you mean, Bart."

"I mean, Bobby, that every time you want a little trim you'll have to plead your case before the bench."

"Cut the shit," Bob said. "That isn't funny."

Bart reached over and patted the back of Bob's hand. "I was only trying to keep things light. You know I don't mean it bad. A girl like that takes dough for granted. And then there's law school. That changes the way people feel and think. It's a great discipline. But you don't get much warmth from a lawyer. They beat it out of them in law school. Especially at one as good as Michigan."

"What do you suggest instead? A bimmy?"

Bart cocked his head and looked at Bob clownishly. "Don't knock a bimmy if you haven't tried one. They're nice to come home to."

Bob laughed. "You're a piece of work. If you were a car, you'd be a collector's item. You're always the same old cowboy, and yet you never stop surprising me."

"I admit *you* surprised me," Bart said, tapping a swizzle stick on the table.

"How's that?"

"I had you figured for grad school. Something frivolous. A Ph.D. in literature."

Bob didn't feel like talking about that. "Well, here I am. Down here to figure out why some store is screwing up. Write a report, do the whole investigation thing."

"And I'll toast that," Bart said, lifting his glass.

"You come here often?"

"About once a month—I've been serving as a consultant

to the newspaper owner here. He's looking to buy some TV stations.''

"So you get to come and go. But these guys live here."

"Nothing beats New York, that's true. But as long as you've got some smart businessmen and the makings for Rob Roys, any town's tolerable."

Bob wasn't sure about that. When he swung through with Cutter, all he could see was a wasteland of miracle miles, power lines, smog, and rusting plants. Hard times had come to Toledo. But hard times were good times for P&V drugstores, where, in the words of the company's advertising jingle, "Your dollar takes a joy ride, 'cause P&V's on your side."

"As long as you're the guy advising everyone else," Bob said.

Bart smiled. He was a large man with a ruddy, drinker's face. His teeth seemed oddly small for the size of his head, sharply pointed and askew from one another, as if they'd bitten onto something very strong that had pulled them out of line. They reminded Bob of the teeth of a pike, perfect for a corporate consultant. "All right," Bart said. "But what about yourself? Why are you out here?"

Bob wasn't up to this game just now. "The job. That's it. I'd never be here except for it."

"That's right. And you're in the fastest growing segment of retailing. You're working with a bunch of pros, learning the business from the floor up. You're right where you should be. But your next goal should be back to business school for an M.B.A."

"I hadn't thought about that."

"Well, start thinking about it. Business schools are sick of kids right out of college. They're looking for guys with some commonsense experience. Get yourself an M.B.A. after two years on the road and you'll start knocking down megageeters."

The waitress came and took their orders for burgers. Bob watched Bart's eyes follow the swivel of the waitress's hips as she left. "I can't believe this job counts for all that much. I mean, it isn't much more than a lot of paperwork."

"Ahh, but what does it take to do that paperwork?"

"As far I can tell, mostly patience."

Bart shook his head. "Observation. Observation, and the ability to translate perceptions into descriptions that yield conclusions." He swallowed the remains of his drink. "It's Aristotelian."

"I think you elevate it too much."

Bart shook his head again. "Don't ignore the value of learning to be a skilled observer. It's not that different from being a skilled reader. Both lead to an appreciation of details. And both require you to use language that is anchored in details. A language that produces verifiable description and logical conclusions. Ultimately, that's a powerful language. But learning that language the way you are now will give you one heck of a living, as opposed to what you'd get after graduate school."

"I guess," Bob said. "Still, all the paper seems a little absurd."

"Not really. A few minutes ago, you said you had a problem account to deal with this afternoon. That's what it's all about. Give me the details. Let's brainstorm it now."

Bob described the store in question. It was located in a plaza in a middle-class neighborhood. Sales were excellent for the first six months of operation, in fact almost unusually so. Then, without explanation, they began slipping. The decline was serious now, a year after opening. There was no competition within the typical two-mile radius P&V considered as the critical trading area.

Bart listened attentively while sipping his drink. When Bob finished, he turned over his paper place mat, took out his gold Cross pen, and jotted down the facts as Bob had given them.

"Any time you're stumped by a business problem, simply pretend you're a physician called in to diagnose an unknown illness. What are the symptoms? What areas of the body in question does the disease affect? What are the possible mechanisms within the body that would have to malfunction to account for this?"

Bart wrote down these questions below the facts. He folded the place mat and gave it back to Bob. "I could go on like this for hours, but you get the idea," he said. "Check to see whether the decline is uniform across all product categories or whether there are a few areas in the store especially hard hit. Then check the attitudes of employees. Are they treating customers properly? Ask the store manager what he thinks. If he doesn't have a plausible explanation and a possible solution, get rid of him.''

"I can't get rid of him. That's not my job.''

"You can write a report that instigates his dismissal.''

"You sound so cold about it.''

"You have to be cold about it. You're not in the charity business.''

"You know what I mean. It doesn't feel right to be collecting information that gets guys fired.''

"Nonsense. Believe me, sometimes being fired is the best thing that can happen to a guy. I've served as a hatchet man for several companies, getting rid of whole departments. Neutron Bart, they called me. Only the buildings were left. And you know what? Some of the people actually thanked me.''

On the drive back to Ann Arbor that evening Bob realized his uncle was right. Sherman Hite couldn't cut it. A chubby ex–junior high math teacher who didn't know algebra well enough to get rehired and who couldn't understand how a thousand-person layoff at the nearby auto parts plant could have caused such a drop in sales.

"They're on unemployment,'' Sherman said, tucking in his blue shirt at the back. Its tail popped out again when he bent over to pick up his pen. "Christ, they make more from unemployment than I do here.''

"That's not the point,'' Bob said. "People feel different when they're unemployed. They're depressed.''

"Tell me about it,'' Sherman said. "I ate and ate and ate. I watched TV all night in the dark and ate potato chips. I looked down one night and saw my gut squeezing up through my pajamas. Twenty pounds I gained. On unemployment. And the God's truth is, I never got it all off, either.''

Bob could hear Bart's voice inside saying, Get rid of the jerk. He's useless. He's the disease all by himself. "Sherman, think about what you just said. We've got to get some snack food in these aisles. You should have been recommending a change in the impulse mix. The layoff is the reason. It's right in front of your eyes and you never told anyone.''

"I suppose that means you're going to put that in one of your little reports, doesn't it."

Bob raised his hands as if to say, How can I not?

"You might as well kick my ass out the door right now if you do. I'm asking you to think about it. Please."

Bob did think about it. He knew he wasn't a creep. And there was nothing creepy about writing down what he saw. But it still felt cold. Then he thought about the bonus. He knew his recommendations to alter the store's product mix would be acted on. More canned foods, fewer radios and midget TVs. More candy. Candy always sold well in low-income store locations. Or wherever people drank too much and were generally depressed. Calculators would be replaced by tool kits from Taiwan, and the TVs with cheap Walkmans, one manager with another, hopefully one who owned a shirt that fit.

"They're not as ruthless as all that," Bob said, trying to avoid a confrontation. His words rang false. He would have to work on his tone.

"What do you know? How long have you been on the job?"

"Sherman, I've got to do my job, and you've got to do yours, right? Now if you don't mind, I've got to look over the store."

"Be my guest," Sherman said. "And when you come across the Drano, pour me a cup. I'll drink it right now."

Bob laughed. The sound of his laughter also sounded false. He could only guess how awful it sounded to Hite. "Oh, come on. It isn't all that bad, is it?"

Hite stared at him. "Just do your job and shut up. I've got stuff in my office." He wheeled around and went into his metal cubicle, shutting the door behind. Through the top layer of frosted glass, Bob could see his dim form standing there.

Bob turned off Route 23 at the Michigan border and headed west into the countryside. As he passed a series of huge grain silos he came into a town called Blissfield. There wasn't much more to it than a couple of bars, a supermarket, and a few houses with cornfields for backyards. A faint gray dust covered everything, muting from red to pink the barroom's "Stroh's is spoken here" neon sign.

A gray mutt darted across the road in front of the Blissfield Post Office. As Bob braked, his briefcase fell off the front
seat, spilling the pages of information that he would fashion
into a report of sufficient insight to precipitate Hite's dismissal
and gain the attention of top management. The thought of it
suddenly deflated him. He had never imagined driving through
a town called Blissfield, zigzagging at right angles across a flat
landscape, carrying everything he needed to screw up one
man's life and to turn around a store that preyed on people's
weaknesses, all in pursuit of twenty grand, money that the
woman he lived with could get just by calling home.

Bob pulled the car over and sat looking at the sun, almost
level with the horizon. It had to be the land that made him feel
this way. Flat as a countertop. All of it had once been part of
the lake. He was probably no more than fifteen feet above Erie
at this point, ten miles inland. He had never been at the shore
of Lake Erie. Anytime he drove near it, swamp brush obscured
the view. It was like pubic hair, that swamp brush. And as a
traveler, that made him something on the scale of a louse. What
had happened to the big adventure he always imagined his life
would be?

Bob bent over to pick up the papers from his briefcase. He
found Carl's letter there, still unopened. He looked at the
stamp, a German stamp depicting the face of Immanuel Kant.
Carl had drawn a balloon from Kant's lips and written something in it. The postal stamp obscured the words, but after staring a bit, Bob was able to make them out: ''I used to contem-
plate everything, but now I'm dead.''

Good old Carl, Bob thought. He still nails me even when
he's not trying. At least Kant critiqued pure reason. I'm busy
critiquing Sherman Hite. With some reluctance, he opened the
envelope and pulled out the blue pages of the letter. There was
no telling what to expect. He began reading:

Dear Bob:

    In your last letter you ask if I think there is a sadistic
streak to the German psyche and I say absolutely there is.
In the short time I've been here, I've noticed that my German flows as smoothly and warmly as blood every time I'm
inclined to violence. When I kicked out at the dog that

snarled at me the other day, I said, "Get away, you shitty dog," in the best German I've mustered yet. The dog made a hasty retreat, no doubt convinced I was a native. There is a monster inside every German, and their writers have known it since the turn of the century. Maybe there is a nationalistic monster in everyone, although it's generally the blind spot for that country's citizens.

You saw *The Coca-Cola Kid*, didn't you? That might well be our blind spot—the great international commitment to penetrating new markets. Didn't he say something like, "Money is God's way of expressing his approval of man's actions." Do you consider yourself on the order of the Coca-Cola Kid? Do you possess an unshakable belief in the will of God and P&V to solve any consumer's problem? Or, do you find that spirit in anyone else at the company? I'm curious. I'd like to know. Write me.

Right now, all I'm certain about is the fact that this job has won you big points with Dad and Mom. I'm getting those vibes in letters and through the one phone call we've connected on, so the feelings must be pretty potent. I'm sure they now expect some similar stroke of good luck and hard work from me. Really, if I had known that taking the front seat when I was a kid would have caused you to create these kinds of parental expectations for me, I would have said, Hey, Bob, you sit up here between Mom and Dad, and I'll get in back where they won't notice me. I suppose I'll have to make sure to study in some room where a recruiter has scheduled interviews, only instead of *Revolutionary Road*, I'll talk about *The Metamorphosis*. When was the last time you delved into Kafka's work? I think that, as a whole, it is one fabulous depiction of the paranoia and self-doubt we (our family that is) suffer from. Actually, I suppose no recruiter in his right mind would hire somebody who liked the writings of Kafka. Maybe I'll find another writer. Céline?

To be honest, hearing about your job depresses me in at least two ways, not that any of this is your fault. First, imagining you actually doing it—because that implies I could come to take a job like yours. Second, as a signal that my formal education is nearing an end and that I find myself knowing no more about what I'd like to be when I grow up than when I began. It seems my fate is to be a grown-up who wonders what it means to be grown up. It's ridiculous, but somehow your example gives me anxiety about what I'll do when I get back for the last semester at college, and worse, what I will do after that.

Could you tear yourself away from paperwork one night to give me an accounting of what's going on with you? Maybe I don't understand the least of it. And any news of Irene you feel up to discussing. I think I've got to find a girlfriend or I'm going to take a Kafkaesque plunge into depression with none of the creative justification. Take care,

Y.L.B., Carl

Bob folded up the letter and slid it back into the envelope. The line Carl added to Kant's head now seemed a little darker than it had before, especially when Bob imagined Carl writing it after the letter. He would write Carl a serious letter. Soon. But he would have to be careful. There were so many points in the letter that bordered on bitterness. He had hoped that being in Germany would soften Carl's feelings toward him. To the extent Carl cared to write letters, he supposed it had. Still, Bob opened Carl's letters as if they were capable of exploding at the slightest jostling. Bob's confidence that he understood his brother had been intact since childhood until it had been destroyed over the Christmas break during Bob's junior year in college. They had argued every day that vacation. Bob was at a disadvantage, physically and psychologically. He had blown out his knee in a pickup basketball game during finals week, and it was operated on two days before Christmas. The injury depressed him to the point that he did poorly on his exams, further intensifying his malaise. When Carl arrived on Christmas Eve, he found Bob on the couch with a soft cast from ankle to hip. Bob could move around, but it hurt. So except for trips to the bathroom and a little exercise, he stayed put on the couch, allowing his parents to shuttle in sandwiches and beers, and when the pain became intense, a few drinks.

Shortly after getting back home, Carl prodded the Ace bandages. "Let me see the scar," he said.

Bob wasn't about to unwrap the bandages. Before he could understand how it happened, they were arguing. With their parents off at a factory Christmas party, there was no one to referee. The argument grew increasingly intense. Not simply over seeing the scar, but about everything right back to childhood. Carl kept invoking the authority of his new girlfriend, Amy, a psychology major.

"Amy says you're always trying to dominate me," he said one time after another, illustrating the assertion with numerous examples, each trivial as an isolated incident, but cumulatively significant and all of a single nature. "You've almost ruined me, and now I'm not going to take it."

Bob felt defenseless. If he had been able to walk around, he might have left the house. Or, possibly have taken a swing at Carl. Instead, he began to believe him. It hurt to think of himself as such a tyrant. It hurt to imagine the frustration and anger his brother had held in over the years. How else could Carl be so bitter about things that happened years ago?

When Carl offered to get him a beer, Bob was surprised and said, "Yeah, I feel like I need one." Carl obliged by pouring it over Bob's head. Bob grabbed one of his crutches and swung feebly at Carl, who sidestepped it with ease. Lurching, Bob swung again and fell off the couch, his knee twisting beneath him. The pain was so intense he saw spots. Carl refused to help him up.

"How does it feel?" Carl said. "How does it feel to be the weak one?"

When Bob got back to Sterne, it was dark. Irene greeted him at the apartment door with a kiss. "So, tell me all about the trip to Toledo," she said.

"You must have had a slow day to want to hear this," Bob said.

"How about Bart?"

"Can I save it for tomorrow?" he asked. "I've got some things to get down on paper before I forget them." He wanted to get an immediate start on the paperwork for Toledo four. But when he tried to step around Irene toward his desk, she blocked him with another kiss.

"How about a trip into Ann Arbor? We could go to a bar. I'll drive."

"I've got some work to do," Bob said. "And really . . ."

"It's just that I've been in the apartment all day. I don't feel like looking at the walls and ceilings for another minute."

"I know you want to get out, but this situation is a mess and I think I've got to write a report that's going to get somebody canned. I knew this would happen sooner or later. I just didn't expect it would be this quick. And I don't want to slapdash off something like that."

Irene plopped down in a chair and exhaled. "I'm sorry," she said. "I'm feeling cooped up. Maybe the countryside wasn't such a hot idea. I just wish we could go somewhere. It doesn't have to be a bar. A movie. Something."

Bob looked at her and hesitated. "Like what?"

"Like anywhere. What do you say? I'll get you up tomorrow at dawn with hot coffee and pancakes and let you work all day." She smiled at him.

What a smile, Bob thought. He hadn't seen it enough to get tired of it. And right then, he didn't believe he would ever tire of it. He wanted to believe anything was possible when he saw that smile. A smile like that could get her out of any mess, could get her almost anything she wanted.

"All right," he said. "Let's go."

Irene jumped up and hugged him. "Good. I made a cold supper for us—in the fridge."

Bob walked into the kitchen and reached for the refrigerator door when he noticed a note stuck to it. It said "Brent," and had a Cambridge street address with a phone number.

"What's this?" he asked.

"Oh," she said, smiling again. "Brent called. My parents must have given him my number."

"It's our number. Does he understand that? Why is he calling?"

"You're such a caveman," she said. "He knows all about you. He even remembers you from school. He'd like to meet you, and he's happy for us."

"What's the point?"

"What do you mean? He's trying to keep in touch, that's all. We were together for nearly four years. Isn't that reason enough? We didn't part as enemies, you know."

"The guy makes me sick, that's all."

"If that's all, why don't you take a couple of aspirin and

go to bed. Let's skip Ann Arbor. Honestly, you're in such a pissy mood when you get back. Father has commuted an hour each way for years and never acted like this.''

''Well maybe I'm not as tough as your father. But at least give me a month to get that way.'' Bob felt like taking a walk. He didn't say what he was doing. He turned and left the kitchen, picking up his briefcase on the way. He could get a start on his paperwork at a coffee shop.

''What are you doing?'' she asked.

''Going out.''

''Where?''

''Anywhere.'' He shut the door behind him.

Irene opened it but did not follow. ''Why are you like this?'' she said. ''Bob? Dammit, answer me.''

Bob left the house quickly. As he rounded the corner at the main block of Sterne, he walked right into a large woman in a blue pants suit backing out of a storefront with a box in her arms. The box fell, rupturing and spilling a dozen small bottles onto the sidewalk.

''I'm sorry,'' Bob said, stooping to pick up a couple of bottles rolling toward the street.

''My fault, my fault,'' the woman said. When she saw him retrieving the bottles, she waved him off. ''Forget it. Let 'em go. What's the use?''

Bob noticed she had emerged from Bessie's Beauty Shop. ''You Bessie?'' he asked.

''That's right.'' She tossed the remains of the box and several bottles into the backseat of a rusted Olds 88. ''Bessie ex-of-the-Beauty-Shop. We've gone tits up. No one cares anymore.'' She stood up and smacked her hands against her thighs. ''Goddamn sticky stuff. Who are you, anyway.''

Bob told her.

''Oh, yeah. Rita told me about you two. Well, good luck. It's a hell of a time to be getting married. If I were you, I'd hold off on kids as long as you can. And whatever you do, don't get carried away with the nightlife here.''

Bessie laughed at her own joke, got into the car, and revved the engine to life. She pulled a beer from the plastic netting of a six-pack on the seat beside her and drove off, clearing the tracks just before the train signal began flashing.

Bob regretted the lie about being married. He decided to take his paperwork to the Trackside Bar and Grill, where he could order a burger and watch the freight train rumble into town. He ordered a draft from the female bartender, who sported a roll of flesh that hung over her belt beneath a tight T-shirt. The place was dark and empty except for an old man at a table in the back and a young woman at the bar who swapped whispered words with the bartender. The woman had taken off her wedding band and was twirling it on the bartop. When it spun off and landed somewhere on the floor, she didn't bother looking for it.

Two men in gray work suits jumped off the engine of the train and came inside. There were two shots waiting for them by the time they got to the bar. They tossed the drinks down and left as abruptly as they had come. The old man tapped his empty beer glass for a refill.

"What's on the train?" Bob asked. The bartender looked at him as if he were weird. After an awkward silence, she ran a rag along the top of the bar and stopped in front of Bob.

"You ready for another?"

Bob shook his head. He clicked open his briefcase and took out the form entitled "General Observations."

"Stuff for Kwik Kake, I guess."

"What?" Bob asked.

"What's on the train. Stuff for Kwik Kake."

"Oh, yeah?" He looked at the train. Nothing appeared to be going on. He looked down at the blank form. If it wasn't for this one form, he wouldn't be able to stand all the paperwork. He pulled a pen from his pocket and began writing.

As a college boy you probably never imagined yourself in a city like Toledo on business. At least not any business you thought yourself intended for. But you are here, and what you remember is passing through neighborhood after neighborhood of look-alike small white houses on your way to Store 4. Houses that appear undersize next to the enormous Oldsmobiles and Electras and Impalas parked in the small driveways glistening uniformly with new coats of black sealer. So uniformly you wonder if driveway sealing is a public service or a regulation in Toledo. Many of the garage doors are open with lawn chairs at their fronts, as if for reviewing a parade that is to come, or that has preceded your drive down this street—was it Talmadge or Maple?

The urgency of this trip springs from things unsold, especially unsold impulse mixes in Store 4. You would like to close your eyes to these houses and allow your company car to carry you to the destination guided by an automatic pilot of troubleshooting instinct, but instead you examine them as if there is a clue to the store's problems encoded in the perfectly tended lawns and the lamps centered on tables at each picture window. You have a suspicion that if all the men and women and their children had had a chance to, they would have moved away a year or two ago, would never have bought such large cars or small houses or big boats, would have left the driveways unsealed, the windows dirty, the carpeting uncleaned, and moved somewhere else. South probably. But swiftly and silently fortunes changed, pivoted on that invisible axis of shifting economic trends, and now they are all trapped here, bunkered in for a siege they don't understand and never expected to endure. Without serious adjustments, it will be a war of spiritual attrition, its major casualty the firmest of American traits, the otherwise unshakable urge to define one's self and to express one's love through purchasing. You're thinking all this as you turn into the plaza where Store 4 is located, its parking lot pocked with potholes, the asphalt crumbling, small balls of litter tumbling across its empty expanse, past still-emptier storefronts. This is the frontline of a battleground, the red and blue of the P&V sign a beacon of hope. You are undaunted in your conviction that analysis can turn the tide of ruin here. Surely symptoms can be cataloged, causes identified, remedies proposed, and administered. Surely some solutions, some answers are at hand.

Bob read over what he had written. It was good enough for tonight. Maybe too good for Sherman Hite. He would finish off Sherman in the morning, but in the corporately more acceptable staccato of facts and figures, a barrage from which no one could emerge with their job intact. He finished his beer and ordered a burger.

CHAPTER

9

Bob woke to the smell of bacon and eggs. He and Irene hadn't had any serious arguments before. He didn't consider the scene of the previous evening to have much gravity to it. But it was a skirmish. And she obviously knew it.

Bob rolled out of bed and walked into the kitchen. "Truce?"

"And we don't have to discuss Brent?"

"Please. Not a word."

"Good. Then we can have a nice breakfast and do something together today. Like go to Ann Arbor and find a restaurant with fresh shrimp on the menu. I have such a craving for shrimp."

"Sure." He looked into her eyes. She met his stare straight on. He was looking for a clue, a sign—something behind those eyes that would tell him for certain what she was really thinking. Then she smiled and everything became pleasantly opaque. He shuddered at the thought of how powerful her smile was, how complete its victory over him. She was much more composed at every minute of the day than he could be except in his best moments, those short bursts of self-confidence.

"I have to finish the report first. People back in Boston are expecting it."

"Of course," Irene said. "I shouldn't have been so pushy

last night. I'll make a pot of coffee for you. Get you buzzed so you can do it fast.''

"I won't need that much," he said. "The report will write itself."

"Good. The earlier we get there, the better. I'd like to walk around a bit."

Driving to Ann Arbor, Bob could feel himself unwinding. The muscles in his neck, his back, his legs, all seemed looser than they had in a month. As they drove into town, he recalled the paper he had written in American studies on the campus demonstrations of the sixties. Ann Arbor, a tree with a female's name, a place where the cops let you smoke joints in public, the place where the SDS got started. Tom Hayden, a member of the Chicago 7 and one of the principal writers of the Port Huron Statement—a document Bob ranked with the Declaration of Independence—had gone here. It had seemed like a place where people could live according to their convictions, where for a few years anything had been possible. That was what he felt when he was writing the paper, with no tear gas to sting his eyes and none of the National Guard in riot gear to threaten him. He wondered now whether all the fervor he felt for the sixties had more to do with the hormonal surges of late adolescence than with any political convictions. Because, driving sixty miles an hour in his company car, past fields of sunflowers, he couldn't help feeling he was as far removed from acting upon ideals, any ideal, as one could possibly be.

Bob had only seen Ann Arbor itself from the perspective of the Goodyear Blimp, Curt Gowdy's voice saying, "What a day for football, for these two Goliaths of Big Ten football—Ohio State and Michigan—to meet." Many of the one hundred thousand fans had their faces painted with the school colors; they seemed like Indians. It was that odd mix of memories, football, and radicalism that colored Bob's mood as they drove randomly down one tree-lined street after another.

The houses were so different from those in New England. He didn't know how a student of architecture would describe it—but to him, the houses in Ann Arbor were quainter, smaller, and their porches more important to the activities of children and adults. It was almost cinematically middle class and didn't seem like any place where the SDS could take root. As if Ozzie and Harriet could be inside any one of the houses. Their kids playing hide and seek among trees or riding bikes along the sidewalks. Mothers who didn't work and drove station wagons. And then gradually the transition to student housing, student slums, where towels and confederate flags served as curtains, and the occasional open window provided a glimpse of a room painted bright purple. The throb of a stereo cranked all the way up vibrated the windows of the car.

When they got to campus, Irene showed Bob the law school, which had its own self-enclosed quadrangle. The buildings looked like a huge Jacobean estate that had been set down in a neat rectangle. Their walls were covered with ivy, and the atmosphere was more solemn than the rest of campus, which was a sprawling mishmash of buildings and crosswalks that even on Saturday were packed with students. They reminded Bob of the people he had seen at Kennedy Airport when he had accompanied his mother and father there to put Carl on the plane for Germany: a stew of differing races and languages, with the paradox of appearing chaotic in general while each person was guided by a specific purpose.

As they walked among these students, Bob envied Irene's decision to go to law school. Her options were still open, her life continuing to evolve. His options seemed to be narrowing. Each choice he made limited possibilities further. To accept a job had seemed like a rational thing to do at the time, but as they walked away from the campus, he felt as if he had been swept up by forces—whether money, or chance, or his own tendency to acquiesce to his parents' wishes rather than to ask them to accept his—and that this passivity had led him here, today. The situation seemed an issue of character: his. After all, why acquiesce? Why be the model son who takes the job upon graduation—the good job? Why hadn't he tried out one of his fantasies—writing. Perhaps he, the English major, was more skeptical about art than he admitted to himself. Perhaps inside he believed art was something better left to those who could undertake it without sacrifice. Perhaps he was weak, afraid of risk. Not the risks that businesses took, which could be evaluated through the cold logic of dollars and cents. But risks that had indefinite outcomes, such as attempting a novel. You ran the risk of being regarded as a poseur if you said you were working on a novel. Worse, you risked finding out you were a lousy writer. He had avoided all of these risks and many others. He had never hitchhiked across the country, although he had always wanted to. Never gone to Europe with or without money. Never left home for a summer to find work in Maine or Block Island or Nantucket. Instead he worked at menial jobs. Now he would see a little of the country—parts of three states— the smart way, as his father would say. He was getting paid for it. He had run his life like a little business, shaped it by work, measured the worth of his time by the standard of the minimum wage. Such an industrious lad! And for all his good works a payoff: this fine job! One where he got to use all those verbal skills describing deficiencies in repetitious shelf displays. Such a more practical way to engage his talents. It made him feel sick.

Irene prodded him in the chest. "A penny for your thoughts."

At the sound of her voice, his other self propped in: Get your head out of your ass. Give the job a chance. You need something to eat? Is that the problem? Self-pity is too easy on an empty stomach. Eat. And look at Irene, not yourself. Have a good time with her.

"It was nothing," Bob said. He put his arm around her shoulder and hugged her.

They walked for what seemed miles that day, past bars, coffee shops, bookstores, ice cream parlors, and junk food shops. They hopped from one place to the next, caught up in a chain of movement that created a feeling of directed activity. They stopped for dinner at a restaurant that was in the old train station, and a bottle of wine and shrimp scampi gave the day a sense of closure. On the way back to Sterne that evening, while Irene turned the radio dial from left to right and back again, Bob realized he had not thought about himself or his work for several hours. He had let himself be carried along by Irene without resisting or asking why. Somewhere along the way he had lost that dull ache of self-consciousness. For the better part of the day, he had been aware of himself only as part of a couple. It was odd and exhilarating. To not be obsessed with his own decisions, his own problems. He couldn't remember feeling that way before. At least not in a long time.

"Aren't there any decent stations in Michigan?" Irene said, clicking off the radio.

"I like the quiet better anyway," Bob said. With his free hand he took one of Irene's and squeezed it gently. She leaned toward him, and he felt expanded and tranquil, as if at last he felt at ease enough to comfort someone else.

The woman sitting on the porch introduced herself and her husband as Esther and Webb, Charlie and Rita's daughter and son-in-law.

Webb stood and shook Bob's hand. "Charlie tells me you've got a job that makes you work on weekends. Isn't that odd for a college grad?"

Irene tugged at Bob's hand to keep him moving. But he resisted. It would be rude to leave, despite how much he wanted to get upstairs. "It's just the way the job is," Bob said. "I can take time off during the week if I want."

"That so?" Webb said. He was one of those men who was smaller from the rear up, his shoulders narrower than his waist. He had a tiny head, with a monk's bald spot on top.

"It's not that bad," Bob said. Irene tugged at his hand again.

"Tough way to break in a new wife," Esther said. She had thick hair, cut close, like Gertrude Stein's. She was bigger than Webb, and in a denim jacket and jeans looked a good deal more formidable.

"It's tough being a new wife any way you look at it," Bob said to Irene.

"Tougher than I can understand," Irene said and smiled at Bob.

"I told Rita to get her over to the grange," Esther said. "That way she could meet some young wives."

"And I'll do that this week," Rita said, emerging from the house with a pitcher of lemonade and glasses on a tray. She set the tray down. "Now that you two are back I'll get more glasses."

"Not for me, thanks," Irene said. "We ate some shrimp in Ann Arbor and I don't think they're settling right."

"Seafood's about the only thing that isn't reliable in this state," Rita said. "That and American Motors."

"Go ahead," Irene said when Bob looked at her. "Have some lemonade. I've always wanted to have a glass while sitting on a porch in the evening. If I felt better I would now."

Bob felt a shift inside. He was self-conscious again. He nodded to Irene as she shut the door behind her. "Where's Charlie?" he asked, turning to Rita.

"In the cellar fixing a drain," Rita said as she handed Bob a glass.

"The man works himself ragged," Webb said. "There's got to be an easier way."

Esther gave Webb a nudge. "God knows if there is, you'll be the first to find it."

Rita rolled her eyes and Bob sensed he was now in the middle of an ongoing topic. He took a chair next to Webb, wondering whether he should drink up and leave.

"Now how am I going to make a soybean plant grow when it don't rain?" Webb said. "Christ, I'm ready to quit the farming business. Nothin' in it." He slapped his hand on Bob's knee, as if he were making a point at a podium. "I'll tell you, don't ever get any ideas about being a farmer. Lots of people get those ideas. About how nice the land is and everything. Forget it. The land doesn't give a shit, the weather you can't predict, and the price is fixed by cigar smokers in Chicago."

"Let's not get morose," Rita said. "You'll give Bob a bad idea about Michigan."

"Besides," Esther said, "it wasn't half the weather's fault when you didn't get the seed in until late May."

Webb turned to Bob. "The damn planter was busted . . ."

"Cause you didn't fix it over winter," Esther said.

"Cause I was working at Kroger's to make ends meet."

"Will you two lighten up," Rita said. "You sound like two old crows bitching in a tree."

There was a pause. Webb shifted in his seat. "I'll tell you what I think," he said. "I think Charlie's still got all this energy because of that sauna. That's what does it."

"It's fifty steps from our back door," Esther said. "Why don't you try it?"

"Of course I could. When I wasn't fixin' the planter or cuttin' pork chops at Kroger's."

"Or sleeping on the couch after lunch."

"Give me a break," Webb said. "I was only making an observation about Charlie." He rubbed Bob's knee. "Do as I say, not as I do, you know."

Charlie swung open the door and let it slam behind.

"You fix it?" Rita said without looking at him.

"Yeah," Charlie said. "Can I relax now?"

"Why, certainly," Rita said. "Here." She held out a glass for Charlie, but he waved it off.

"What is this? A lady's club? I'm getting a beer. You want one, Bob? Webb?"

Webb was about to accept, but Esther glared at him. "All set, Dad," she said.

Bob held up his glass of lemonade to signal that he was all set, too.

"So you're from Connecticut," Esther said. "Is it true everybody's rich there?"

"Sometimes it seems everybody except my folks."

"And what do they do? Work in New York?"

Bob laughed. "My mother's a nurse. My dad works in a small factory."

"You must find Michigan pretty different," Esther said.

"The land's flatter," Bob said. "The people aren't as snobby."

"You're right there," Rita said. "And if we could ever bring Detroit back, you'd find that Michigan is probably the best state in the union. It's flat around here, but up north it's got mountains and forests. It's as wild as you could ask. And minerals—you name it. Iron ore, nickel, gold. Oil and gas. Why, we could secede from the union and survive without an import. It's a great state to be a smart young man in. There's all kinds of opportunities."

"The colleges are good, too," Webb said. "I just wish I had gone to one."

"They're good enough to have rejected you," Esther said.

"I'm not saying you have to go to school to succeed. Geez, look at those mink farmers. They've got it made. But you know, I hear chinchillas can make money. With that barn, I'm thinking of giving them a shot.''

"A shot at what?'' Esther said. "A shot at proving you can't do that, either?''

Bob cringed for Webb, who looked as if he was ready to respond, when Charlie came back out with a six-pack.

"You need your ears checked?'' Rita said. "Webb and Bob don't want a beer.''

"I know,'' Charlie said, slamming the six-pack on the porch floor. He popped open the first and let the foam spill to the floor.

"You did that on purpose,'' Rita said, wiping spray from her dress.

Bob decided it was time to head upstairs. He drained his glass and excused himself. The bickering got under his skin, reminding him of the worst days at home: continuous minor skirmishes between his mother and father, and sniperlike asides which, left to fester, turned into full-blown arguments later. If that was what love was all about, he didn't want it. He wondered if he was really in love with Irene, or with the idea of living with a woman whose numbingly beautiful smile and knowledge of faraway places enabled him to forget all the lawns he had mowed just to attend college. As if touching her somehow transformed him into a classier and more interesting person. The well-being of their day together had changed again into another, more self-conscious state. He was aware again of how the routine of work was not what he had expected it to be, and of how it placed a strain on things. The summer at college now seemed unreal, divorced from the demands of making money and living together. Of course things could flourish for a while here and there with an intensity that passed for "love.'' But what then? He didn't know. He needed some rest before another morning of paperwork. Inside, the smell of pork roast was thick in the short hall to the stairs. It was a smothering, oily smell. But he lingered on the second-floor landing, forcing himself to believe it was a good smell, forcing himself to believe he could smell it every day for the rest of his life, as if it weren't food at all, but the scent of routine, of lives lived together for many years.

CHAPTER

10

The Belvedere Motor Lodge wasn't the place where Bob would have preferred to stay in Fort Wayne. The building had a facade that seemed like an abandoned Ethan Allen store: paint peeled from pillars at the main entrance, green shutters hung askew at the windows.

Inside, an old black man in a porter's uniform attempted to pry his bag from his hand. When Bob insisted on carrying it by himself, the man waved his hand in disgust and returned to a Naugahyde couch that might once have been blue. The lobby rug was bald in spots. Bob had made the reservation over the phone, sight unseen. He thought about turning around and leaving, but instead walked up to the main desk, where the balding attendant asked him if he had any luggage. When he held up the bag, the attendant asked if he was traveling on business, in which case he could qualify for the Business Traveler's Special, a room with two double beds for $17.50 plus tax per night, and a coupon good for a complimentary cocktail at Ye Old Gent's Lounge, right off the lobby. Bob accepted the special rate. But the idea of anyone's staying there on business amused him. Its location, superseded by several generations of urban development and a new highway, made it inappropriate by any criteria save two: It was cheap and he was practically broke.

Expense account checks for his first three weeks would take three more weeks to arrive. He had received his first paycheck since Boston only the past weekend and blew a large chunk of it on the trip to Ann Arbor.

Bob tried to count his blessings. There were places worse than the Belvedere, including one called "The Dapper Bungalow Park" on the same side of the street separated only by a vacant soda stand. The bungalows, with exterior walls of pocked concrete, looked more like fallout shelters that had been excavated. The highway—two lanes in either direction divided by a WPA-era grass median and called Commerce Boulevard—was a snarl of power lines and monolithic neon signs, which he heard sputtering defectively each time he brought his car to a standstill at the frequent traffic lights. Most of the businesses on the strip were discount toy and furniture stores, used car lots, and fast-food restaurants, places built during the heady days of the early sixties when concrete, neon, and aluminum facades were used to give hamburger and root beer joints a space-age appearance. Brick weathered so much more gracefully than these "modern" materials of this slapped-together expressionist era of American commerce. Bob liked looking at all this more than he cared to admit. It reminded him of what business was capable of thrusting upon the public in the name of progress and then leaving behind in a rush of economic amnesia induced by corporate goals.

Bob went to his room, washed his face to rid it of the film he seemed to have picked up since checking in, and headed back to the lobby with his coupon for Ye Old Gent's Lounge. The hallway was lit by small lights designed to appear as candles, their night-light–size bulbs tapered to resemble flames. There was barely enough light for Bob to evade a tray of partially eaten chicken wings that had been placed in the middle of the rug since he had gone to his room.

Bob had been with Byron Cutter to these lounges during the orientation week. For the most part, they were dimly lit and stale, the tables usually covered with plaid plastic. Located to one side were stainless-steel pans, warmed by Sterno pots, holding deep-fried breaded cauliflower, zucchini, and mushrooms, or chicken wings drenched in rust-colored hot sauce.

Ye Old Gent's Lounge was no exception. If anything, it

was less appealing: There was nothing to eat except salad bowls of Rice Chex and Wheat Chex mixed with midget pretzel sticks. A handwritten sign over the cash register read: Monday Night is Lady's Night: 2-Fers on Bar-Mixed Drinks. As he surveyed the room, which appeared too large for the other two sitting at the bar, he noticed there was an elevated dance floor and a disc jockey's booth above that. Once his eyes adjusted to the light, he saw that the floor had holes in it and that the disc jockey's equipment had been removed. Several wires dangled from the turntable stand, moving like a spider's legs in the sporadic gasps from the lounge's air-conditioning system.

Bob took a seat near a man at the bar, and after a few minutes asked the guy if he would pass the bowl of party food.

"Yeah, sure," the guy said. "Sorry." He said this while staring straight ahead. He had on an army-green jacket, and jeans that sagged below his paunch. When he turned to hand Bob the bowl, a patch on his chest flashed. Bob leaned forward, trying to read the words on it backward in the bar's mirror. They were written on each side of a triangle: "Silent Swift Deadly." Below this: "1st Recon BN."

Bob became aware of how his jacket and tie must have appeared to the man. But where men drank together, regardless of race, color, or creed, camaraderie was always possible. So the beer commercials promised.

"You were in the army?" Bob asked.

The man looked at Bob stoically. "Oh, this . . ." He pointed to the jacket. "My brother's."

Bob waved to the bartender for another beer, suddenly feeling like Studs Terkel on a great American expedition. Why was this man wearing his brother's jacket and drinking at Ye Old Gent's Lounge at the Fort Wayne Belvedere Motor Lodge?

"Where'd he serve?" Bob asked.

"Nam," the guy said. "He's disabled now . . . mentally."

"Gee," Bob said. "That's awful." He introduced himself. The man's name was Hank Armas.

"There's usually no one over here," Armas said. "I like that."

"You drink alone?"

"Not like old George Thorogood. I stick to beer." He

leaned back from the bar and grabbed a roll of flesh from his belly. "And beer sticks to me."

"So where does your brother live?" Bob asked.

"At home. With me. Between his pension and my check, we make it happen."

"I guess that war was rough on the guys who went there."

"Tell me about it. How old are you anyway?"

"Just out of college."

"You're a kid. You don't know shit. You even have a wet dream by the time of Tet Offensive?"

"What's the problem?" Bob said, beginning to suspect for the first time that being Studs Terkel had its downside. "I don't like much of what I've heard about Nam."

Armas grabbed Bob by the lapels of his jacket. "Don't call it Nam. You haven't earned that right."

Bob grabbed the man's hands and then pushed them away gently. "You're right. I don't know."

Armas patted him on the shoulder. "Sorry," he said. "You're just a kid." He finished his beer in a gulp and called for another. "Here," he said, and waved his glass. The bartender ignored him. "You know, none of you guys know. Nobody in your whole fuckin' generation knows. You think it's all Schwarzenegger and Stallone. And that's why you can't call it Nam. You earn the right to call it that when you've been there or have some nut for a brother who's been there. It should rhyme with *jam*. How come it doesn't? Can you tell me that, mister college guy?"

Bob shook his head, more certain than ever that he didn't know the language.

Armas picked up his beer glass and slammed it on the bar. "Can't I get any service here?" he shouted.

The bartender waved him off, continuing to talk to a woman in a pink pant suit. The words "Mary Kay" punctuated her responses.

"Goddamnit," Armas said, sliding his glass toward the couple. It fell off the bar.

The bartender walked down the length of the bar, wiping his hands with a towel. "I told you the last time you were in here," he said, "that if you made yourself a pain in the ass ever again, that was it . . ."

Armas waved his hand in protest. "Okay, I shouldn't have dropped the glass, but—"

"No buts. You aren't getting served."

Armas flipped the bird at the bartender, wheeled, and left.

The bartender lurched forward as if thinking about going after Armas, but caught himself. He glared at Bob. "What's your problem? You a friend of that dipshit?"

Bob shook his head. "Just met him now. I'm a guest."

"In that case, what'll it be?"

"I already got my complimentary drink."

"Then have another on me. I'll join you. We can wash the taste of the guy out of our mouths."

Bob nodded, thinking he would make it a point to avoid the lounge. Aside from his store calls, he would remain in his room.

By Thursday the scrambled eggs tinted brown with pan grease, the mildew-scented hallways, and the rust-stained toilet bowl had his spirits sagging as much as the mattress. He tried giving himself a break at fast-food places, but the wafer-thin burgers and unfrozen buns held more appeal when he didn't have to eat them. The only meal he could afford at a diner was liver. It was always the cheapest item on the menu. Liver with bacon and onions. Breaded liver with mashed potatoes. Chicken livers. Calves' liver. Goose liver.

Bob had applied for credit cards—American Express, Visa, and MasterCard. How he wished he had one piece of plastic in his pocket now—even a Gulf card with its almost magical power to give him a bed, his car gas, and his belly food. Food other than liver. How he looked forward to handing the card to a waitress in a Holiday Inn restaurant and asking her to fill him up.

After his Wednesday liver supper, Bob returned to his room and flicked on the black and white TV to watch the local news as he figured his expenses. The mayor of Fort Wayne was unveiling a new plan to promote the city nationally: "Fort Wayne is Going Places." The city was undergoing a renaissance, putting a new shine on its rust-belt past, rebuilding, rejuvenating, responding to its latest flood. Did anyone know, for instance, that Fort Wayne had an average of 49.3 dentists per 1,000 residents? Bob turned the news off. The city was a good one for P&V, which had a proven approach to cities on the underside of their best times. Cities where workers who had made fifteen dollars an hour in manufacturing were suddenly taking jobs for five dollars an hour in a mall store and asking their wives to work, too. (Convenience foods—one-can meals—were big sellers in the impulse area.) As long as the mayor talked about how many dentists the city had, Fort Wayne would be going places—primarily to the five P&V stores. Although Bob needed three full days in the city to go through all of the stores, he knew already that of all the areas within his district, this one was closest to being on automatic pilot. He spent the better part of his days offering employees tips on cross-selling customers, on ways to generate multiple sales and improve display appearance. He gave a set spiel to employees at a special meeting. Little things that he hoped would, in the long run, lead to a bonus. Money that, as he figured his expenses, he wished he could get a loan against. As he suspected, nothing added up right.

Starting cash:	*$117* and change
Gas:	$12.00
Lodging:	$52.50 + tax
Meals w/receipts:	$27.56
Parking:	$1.75
2 6-packs beer:	$6.50
Total Accounted for:	$100.31

The problem: Bob had only $9.73 left. If he bought a donut and a cup of coffee, he might have enough money left for the gas it would take to get back to Sterne. He wished he had borrowed money from Irene, but he couldn't bring himself to ask. He had to make this happen on his own. Otherwise, why the hell was he working? If he had to, he could chew on his belt to live. Watch more motel TV. He flicked it on again. The mayor was gone. Yeah, he would tough it out. Learn the ropes. Survive in the trenches. He started to laugh at his own posturing when the phone rang.

A man's voice: "Bob?"

He didn't respond, unable to identify it.

"Hello?"

"Yes," Bob said at last.

"How you doing out there?"

"Good enough. Who is this?"

"It's me, Rick."

"Rick back east?"

"Aww, cut it, man. Don't give me this 'I've been in the desert too long' line. Yeah, the back-at-the-headquarters Rick."

"Isn't it a little late for you guys to be working?" He glanced at the TV. The network news was coming on. Six-thirty and another kidnapping in Beirut. Where would Preparation H be without terrorists? And where would the broadcast news be without Preparation H. The burning itch, the pain—an insurgent guerrilla war all by itself in which soothing intervention was the only answer.

"Oh, yeah," Rick said. "The place is deserted. But I had to stay late to finish a management summary on the research we did on nostalgia. It looks like we're going to make it a quadrant all by itself. Call it The Classic Corner. So I finished and I called. To check in."

"Groovy."

"Hey, that's nostalgic."

"I'm running with you on this one." Bob stretched out on the bed, his head propped against the wall. A train of chemical cars was on fire in Tennessee. "So how did you find me?"

"Your itinerary."

"Doesn't say where I'm staying."

"Irene does."

"I didn't know you knew about her."

"Cutter told me. Said from the sounds of it, she was good-looking and smart. Everything a guy on the road should avoid."

"Cutter's full of advice. I only wish I could get ahold of him to hear it."

"I've heard he's something of a mystery man. People at the office don't know what to make of him."

"Neither do I. He's nice enough when I'm with him. But I can't seem to reach him when I have a question. And I'm not about to call Remer or Coleman with a bunch of silly-assed stuff.''

"Maybe you should . . .'' Rick's voice trailed off. "I had to look around before I say anymore. I'll tell you this: Cutter has written rave reports about you. He's backing you hard. More than his other DICs. He really likes you.''

"Good.'' Bob made up his mind not to be modest about praise. Not when money was on the line. "So what else?''

"Not much beyond that. Isn't that good enough?''

"Sure, it's nice to hear. Any word from Adam?''

"Yeah, he's teaching remedial English to the basketball team at Cambridge Latin.''

"And liking it?''

"I guess.''

"How about you? How do you like the research stuff?''

"Up to now, I love it. I've asked to stay in research permanently. I might go to grad school for social psychology. There's a program at B.U. the company will pay for if I maintain a three-point average.''

"That goes for everyone?''

"Once personnel clears it.''

"Why didn't I hear about this earlier? I might have tried to stay in the office.''

"I don't know that they broadcast it. It might be an unofficial perk to people they think will stay on board.''

"And that's you?''

"As far as I've led them to believe. I'll figure out what's next once I get the degree. But I don't mind what I'm doing, either. It's fun.''

Fun. Bob wasn't sure he would say the same for his work. Charles Kuralt waved to Bob from the back of an old caboose moving into the sunset on a flat expanse of western Montana. "I guess I couldn't say the same for what I do,'' Bob said.

"Yeah,'' Rick said quietly. "I'm glad I didn't get sent out there now. I probably would have quit.''

Dan Rather nodded to Bob and signed off for the night. "Entertainment Tonight'' was up next. Bob decided to change the subject before he checked out of the Belvedere and the job simultaneously. "So how's our pal Scott?''

"Oh—great. I almost forgot. He's such a jerk. Can you believe he has written three—count 'em—three ten-page memos already with full-of-crap ideas about where the company should go next."

"I thought Prescott welcomes ideas."

"He does. His door *is* always open. But it's the tone of these things."

"Yeah?"

"A salad bar? A P&V money market account? Give me a break. He knows all the trends but he can't translate them into practical actions. You know, the type who knows exactly what's hot and what's not, but can't for the life of him convert that knowledge into a single doable idea. And then there's the story about how he lectured his regional manager, Seth Kaplan, between stores during orientation. Kaplan wants nothing to do with him. But Remer held back. Remer thinks a year or two on the road will bring him back to earth."

"It might land me in an asylum."

"Hang in there," Rick said. "You're scoring the points. Keep writing reports like that one on Toledo. Everyone was talking about it."

"I guess it could cost some guy his job."

"You bet it did. They've been trying to get rid of that guy for a year, but never had good-enough information. Cutter let the store slide without analyzing why. I haven't seen it yet, but my boss Boyer said he could get it. Hey, I've got to get going."

Bob felt a surge of excitement at this news. People were noticing after all. "Yeah, thanks for calling. I've got more reports to write."

"Take care—and by the way, a little present is winging its way to you."

Bob's spirits lifted again. A raise? A partial bonus? "Oh," he said, trying to sound calm.

"Prescott's latest kick: *The Art of War*."

"What's that?"

"Some Chinese classic by Sun Tzu. Full of oriental wisdom. Supposedly there are six different Japanese commentaries on it floating around the business schools in Japan. All interpretations of its marketing applications."

''I can imagine. The yen for change and other marketing loans from abroad.''

''I think it's a little strange. But, listen, figure out a way to weave it into a report. You'll knock everyone over.''

Bob woke to money anxiety and the sound of his phone at six. ''Good morning, it's fifty-seven degrees and Fort Wayne is going places,'' the operator said. He decided in the shower that he would hold off buying gas until the last possible minute. Maybe someone somewhere would take a check. As he dressed he pulled aside the curtains and looked at the back parking lot. Beyond a wire fence, dimmed by the film of soot covering the window, was a development of aging bungalows that looked as if they were built in the forties. He slid open the side window for fresh air. A woman in a blue bathrobe was hanging laundry from her back stoop. Underwear, bras, and white socks dangled as she yanked the squeaky clothesline forward. He could hear the distant moan of a train. A dog barking. The whine of a car whose engine would not turn over. Trucks downshifting at the traffic lights on Commerce Boulevard. Fort Wayne, going places.

Bob stopped for a cup of coffee and corn muffin on his way out. He got lost looking for the road that would take him west out of this decaying area of the city and onto Interstate 69. After stopping for directions at a gas station, though, he got redirected and turned around. He hoped that his meandering hadn't used up the exact amount of gas he would need to get home.

As he hopped from light to light Bob reviewed his work for the week. At each store, he gave the thirty-minute audiovisual presentation on service quality entitled ''You Make the Difference.'' It was right out of one of the training notebooks, recommended for all new employees and for general review once a year. Bob rehearsed it in his room and gave it to groups of yawning and whispering men and women, many of whom were older than he. Neither their ages nor attitudes put Bob off. He'd seen Cutter deal with them, and it amazed him how motivated the employees could get if you simply acted like you knew what you were talking about and memorized their names. The rehearsing helped create this impression. And practice made perfect. Bob learned little tricks to keep their names straight. Snickers and wisecracks subsided, then vanished, to be replaced with shouted responses to his questions and a general fervor. The presentation itself was divided into five sections, each of which asked the employees to put themselves into the shoes of the customer. The sections came under the headings, Care, Listen, Observe, Suggest, and Exit, the first letters of which spelled the word CLOSE. The underlying message was that each employee was responsible for sales, as in "close" the sale. Only by committing to excellence in each category would the employee and the company be successful.

With heavy emphasis on the "you," Bob summarized, "*You* are the only one who can *care*—care about store appearance, care to help that mother find what she is looking for, care about checking the backroom for missing merchandise. *You* are the only one who can *listen*, listen to the customer's questions, his complaints, his needs. *You* are the only one who can *observe*, observe the person shopping, his dress, his habits, his patterns. *You* are the only one who can use all this information to *suggest*, suggest purchases above and beyond what the customer might originally have intended—but not to force this, either—remember, to suggest is not to order. Last, *you* are the only one who can tell when the customer is ready to buy, and therefore, you are the only one who can *exit* the customer, exit him to the cash register before he reconsiders his purchase."

By this time, the employees were attentive. In conjunction with the slides shown on a bare wall in the backroom, his words gave them a unified method of approaching their work and their careers—at least the illusion of their careers. He concluded with a slide that showed simply the acronym CLOSE.

Bob read the letters aloud to the group, "C-L-O-S-E." He circled around front to the wall and stared toward the audience, pretending he could look into each person's eyes. Actually the light from the projector blinded him. But he knew they couldn't tell. The silence became a device. Something he could use to control the audience. His job was more than information gathering and paperwork. It was acting. Now he had them. He raised his hand, palm toward the audience as if signaling them to halt, and spoke, "What am I saying? . . ." and then, as he spoke he turned the gesture into a pointed finger that he moved across the audience. "I'm saying you make the difference. You, John. And you, Betty. And you, Rachel," until he named everyone. "But remember, to close, you've got to get close. Get close to your customer to close him. That's the key to success, that's what gives you the difference. And that's what makes for a career at P&V. This company promotes from within, and we want you to build your careers here." He swallowed hard before continuing. "Some of you sitting in this room right now will become managers. That's what I want to see, that's what everyone at P&V wants. And that's what the CLOSE approach helps make possible."

Theater of the marketplace, that's what it was. Acting. He had been in plays in high school and college. He could do it. In fact, he enjoyed it. Getting existential, playing the role of motivator, becoming the motivator—that made the time go faster. But toward what? School had started. Everywhere, Bob saw buses and kids and police with radar guns. For the first time since before he had been in kindergarten he wasn't in school. Seventeen years of education. The sense of time was different. In school, the passage of time led somewhere—to the next grade, to culminating exams and insights, to a mastery of subjects. Here, time was cyclical, repetitive. His route, his district would not change. It would only be repeated. Traveled again and again, the way his father and mother traveled from home to work, work to store, store to home. Circuits of monotony. Repeated anecdotes. Paths of arguing as worn as shortcuts to the beach. Only the prospect of praise and promotion and, most of all, the bonus enabled him to concentrate.

Just before Bob reached the interstate entrance ramp, he saw a college-aged boy hitchhiking and holding a sign that read, Ann Arbor? He pulled over and opened the door. The boy stuck in his head.

"Thanks a lot. Ann Arbor?"

"Sure," Bob said. The guy looked no older than a freshman in college: short red hair, freckles, a faint mustache, blue jeans, and a T-shirt. He tossed his knapsack into the backseat and climbed in. "Wow," he said. "I was waiting an hour. I thought I'd have to walk." He held out his hand for Bob to shake. They swapped names and shook.

"You go to Michigan?" Bob asked.

"My girlfriend. She started this year."

"Look, what do you think about splitting gas. I'm almost out of cash."

Steve appeared surprised. "Sure, I guess. I don't have a whole lot either, or I would have taken a bus. How about . . ." He straightened his legs and dug down into his pockets, pulling out several crumpled bills and odd change. "How about four dollars and fifty cents?"

"Perfect," Bob said. It was perfect. Just enough. Bob drove past the entrance ramp to a discount gas station, filled his tank with as much gas as he could buy for eleven dollars and fifty cents, and looped back to the freeway. It was a stroke of luck.

After an hour in which Steve did nothing other than listen to his Walkman, Bob was surprised to see him pull a joint from his pocket.

"You mind?" he asked Bob.

Bob smiled and shook his head. A second stroke of luck in one morning. For the first time, he felt as if there was hope for his life on the road.

CHAPTER

11

The Buckeye Convention Center was, according to a brochure Bob received as he entered, big enough to hold three Ohio State football fields with room to spare. The Congress of American Retailing Pharmacies (CARP, as everyone called it) was the biggest expo of the year, and this year, it was held near Bob's territory, otherwise he wouldn't have been asked to attend. Exhibit booths stretched as far as Bob could see, an orgy of neon, flashing lights, and chrome. Every manufacturer with a product that could conceivably be sold in a P&V store had a booth, as did P&V and its competitors. He would be there until Wednesday night.

Bob checked in with Byron Cutter, received his identity badge, and was told to wander around and get the feel of things.

"It's a great spectacle," Byron said. "The enormity is overwhelming. Makes you proud to be in the business. Let me tell you something else you'll find here, too—respect! Some guy from Kroger's told me we were redefining the market. How 'bout that? 'Redefining the market.' "

"That's good," Bob said. Byron's voice sounded far off, as if Bob had cotton in his ears. He guessed that the brilliance of the lights had overloaded his senses.

"I can tell you're soaking up the enormity of all this," Byron said. "So head off and do some exploring. Let me know what you think. And by the way, your report on Toledo four was a winner. Coleman and Remer took action on it. All of your reports produce action. You get a fix on a target and—" Cutter pursed his lips together and made the sound of incoming artillery, his arms swooping through the air. "Ba-boom. Every time. You're one hell of a DIC. You light a fire under my ass anyway."

Bob smiled at Cutter. "Thanks," he said. He disliked the man. But in business, if someone you dislike happens to be a superior, you don't wear your dislike in front of him. At least that was how he read Sun Tzu. "Practice dissimulation and you will succeed." He had no idea of how to relate that to a P&V store, but it made sense at times when dealing with superiors.

Bob wished he had mastered the art of dissimulation for dealing with Irene. When he got back from Fort Wayne, her first words to him were an announcement that she had taken a job on a weekly newspaper in Sterne. Her decision made no sense to him, and he said so. What could be worse than working for the pathetic little gossip sheet he saw littering the drugstore newsstand and the town's two coffee shops?

"What do you mean?" she said, angry for the first time he could recall.

"I thought you wanted to relax before January," Bob said. "Sometimes a job like this can be a bigger pain in the ass than you expect."

"Oh, come on," she said. "Do you really think writing one article a week is going to be taxing? The guy—Art Poindexter's his name—wants me to write one article a week on someone turning his life around. A farmer finding a new line of work, a laid-off factory worker who gets a new job. That kind of stuff. Really, what's wrong with that?"

"Nothing is *wrong* with that. It seems silly, that's all."

"You tell me what I should do while you're gone all week. Pine away?"

"Isn't dulling out what you had in mind?"

Irene smiled at him—a chilling smile that made him feel small and foolish. It was one more variation of her repertoire. "Maybe it would be easier if you were around a bit more."

Bob couldn't remember exactly what he said next. Only that it was sharp and quick. Something about her being mean and manipulative. In retrospect, a dumb thing to say. She went into the bathroom and shut the door, her decision intact, his spirits sunk. Though they apologized to each other later, there was a chill between them that lasted until he left for Columbus.

Saturday night, there was little more than maintenance talk going on between them. Talk such as: "Did you order the pizza?" and "Are you taking a shower tonight or in the morning?" He took a walk to get away from the confines of the apartment.

Bob had noticed most people in Sterne didn't bother closing their curtains at night, as if everyone knew everything there was to know about everyone else. Bob didn't try to be furtive about staring into these houses. He didn't consider it peeping. At worst, he was nosy, looking the way a schoolboy glances at classmates' graded tests to see if he did better or worse.

Bob couldn't say what the test was, only that he felt he didn't have any answers. He walked away from the main street, the streetlights fewer and the shadows deeper as he headed toward the cornfields at the edge of town. Overhead he could see the constellations, although he had forgotten their names. There was a chill in the air, and a slight breeze rustling the leaves in the trees. They had not turned yet, but when a slight breeze blew, you could hear them. They were drying out, slowly.

Just before the fields began, he turned onto a side street to begin his way back into town. In the house on the corner he could see a man at the head of a table being waited on by a woman. The man hunched over a steaming bowl of soup, which he spooned up rapidly, the woman at his side. The man wore a blue short-sleeved sport shirt, like a golfer's. It stuck out, because the standard uniform for men in Sterne was a Dickies green or blue workshirt, the type that gas station attendants wore in Connecticut, minus the emblem. Something about the scene held him still and watching. The woman—his wife?—standing dully by the man's side as he gulped down the soup. When he finished, he handed the bowl to the woman and she disappeared into another room.

Bob started to walk again, and stopped. The nature of the

test was now clear to him. It was a test on domestic life. Not on lost school days. Not on childhood. Rather, this was the one for the rest of his life. The one he always felt his parents had failed. Surely there was more than a bowl of soup and a shared bed to domestic life.

The man at the table yawned. Bob yawned, an unseen companion in boredom and fatigue. The man pulled a muffin from a basket. He buttered it and leaned back in his chair, eating the muffin in small bites, chewing slowly. Apparently there were no great adventures in store for this man tonight. No Mozart to listen to, no Picasso to view, no Melville to read. And with the new fall line-up for prime time still a week or two away, no new shows to watch. It was a muffin kind of Saturday.

Bob began snickering at his own thoughts when he noticed another movement in the house. His eyes swung across several dark windows to a lighted one near the rear. There the woman stood, staring straight out the window toward him while she washed dishes. He immediately continued walking, worried that she had noticed him. But when he glanced at the woman again, he noticed her gaze was fixed at a point straight ahead. Of course—she could not possibly see out the window of a lighted room into a pitch dark street.

During the drive to Columbus, the image of that house and its man and woman kept coming back to him. But as indelible as the image seemed to be, he could not assign a single meaning to it. Until he understood it, he felt he had not completed the test. He didn't know what his grade was. Nor did he know theirs.

As he passed Marion, there were signs for Harding's tomb, where the remains of the small-town boy catapulted into a job he should never have held were interred. And he wondered— on his way to CARP, driving a car he could never have afforded on his own, trying to understand why two people he didn't know were leading a life that made no sense when seen from the outside—how was he different? What sense did his life make at the moment? How successful had he been at mediating the demands of a job and living together? The constant shifting of gears. There were so many little reasons he had now. Reasons for things he never thought about a year ago. Reasons why he took a job with a drugstore chain. Reasons why he was in Michigan and why he lived with Irene. Except that when he thought about himself one year ago and himself now, passing a barnside billboard for Bucyrus Popcorn, version-A self and version-B self, the gap was absurd. Not in any horrifying way, but in a quietly comical one. What were they doing—he and Irene? Nesting? Going through some free-enterprise rite of passage into adulthood? And to what end? To sit at a table some Saturday evening with a bowl of soup.

Bob calmly carried this thought onward until he concluded that he had two choices: living in comfort with compromised ideals, or living in discomfort with ideals intact. It wasn't a hard choice to make. He preferred being comfortable. And to be comfortable, he needed money. To get money, he needed a promotion. To get the promotion, he needed to concentrate on his job more. He needed to get selfish. He needed to dissimulate, conceal, dissemble. More important: He needed to stop beating himself up over the job and begin going about it without apologizing to himself all the time. All this analysis and self-reflection he could flush right now.

Bob circulated among the booths for the rest of the afternoon, taking in the "enormity" of this spectacle, although he suspected that Byron hadn't chosen that word deliberately. As he walked from booth to booth he was overwhelmed. He never knew there were so many consumer product companies. Even in checking the displays and inventory of the P&V stores in his district, he had never paused to tally just how many different brands and companies and display ideas there were. At one display, a woman with cheeks heavily rouged talked about the potential "sales per square foot" with a voice that Bob imagined would be perfect for telephone sex.

"Once your lady customers become active purchasers of the Windsilk face prep," she was saying, "the Buckbuilder Display System takes them one step at a time through the entire Lady Winston Beauty Pact—your promise to them that they can look and feel younger by adhering to the four-tiered program— in the process turning each and every one of them into the most valued customer of all, the repeat customer . . ."

Each booth, each display, had its variation. Some aimed at

men, some at women, some at parents, and some at children. An entire convention center filled with proven methods of lifting money from consumer pockets into the corporate till. Of course, Bob had grown up with it: with the pimple creams and deodorants, the dandruff shampoos and the teeth whiteners. He had made his share of impulse purchases with all the imagined freedom of the next guy. But to witness the money and intelligence behind all of the shiny, illuminated innocence of the store layouts and product displays sent a shudder through him. Cutter was right, whether he knew it or not; it was an enormity—of creativity, of talent.

Bob saw for the first time that somewhere long ago this culture had made sacrosanct the sale itself. It was the only true American religion. The transfer of money from one hand to another in the belief that better things would come about. If you had money to spend, the state of your home, body, and soul could be buffed and shined, with no waxy buildup. Wouldn't neighbors, your boss, your loved ones, be glad to know you cared enough to buy the very best. That you cared enough to hand over the money with which God had expressed his satisfaction in your works to another person's pocket, or that your economic soul was in such fine standing with the elders of this institution that you were able to say, "Charge it." So go on, America, expiate the sin of dandelions on the lawn, of pimples on the face, and save the damned from being unloved, unliked, or unattractive. Unclog the bowels, arrest their unmitigated movements, sanitize the basin of their reception. Be a good daddy and get your kid a treat—then scrub his molars with liquids, powders, and pastes approved by dental societies. Get something for your loved one, get something for yourself, or do-it-yourself the way Thoreau would with everything you'll ever need to be a home handyman. It was all here, on every dollar bill, on every cent we spent—In God We Trust. Keep it moving, keep it changing hands, and you express the fervor of your devotion. You express your trust in "independence" and "freedom of choice."

It was much bigger than Bob. The Buckeye Convention Center was only a minor star in a small galaxy, a pinpoint of light in an infinite universe of transactions. He began filling his bag with the brochures being handed out at each booth. Soon the plastic CARP EXPO bag stretched from the weight of brochures promising bigger profits, faster turnovers, greater inventory control, more eye-catching displays. All the hot topics for people in business—the business of the business. The transactions beneath the transactions. One layer after another. And the research! Everything so documented, so thoroughly tested, so established in focus groups. Backed by cable TV test marketing, by couponing, by ten or twenty or thirty years of market leadership. His arm ached from carrying them all. But he took more, switching the bag from hand to hand until at last the day was done and the highly varnished desktop in his hotel room was covered with stacks of papers and brochures and samples. Their bathroom would be stocked with soaps and shampoos, aftershaves, and colognes until January.

Bob showered, and sitting at the edge of his bed, he dried himself as he surveyed the room. A cable TV which, in addition to a spectrum of offerings available immediately, offered "play for pay" extras, including adult movies, great moments in boxing, and highlights of the World Series, from 1950 to 1980. There was a radio by his bedside with a key to local stations, a card on the table by the dresser with today's menu specials, and, of course, the plastic facing over the phone with the three-digit codes for everything a businessman or woman could want—laundry, valet, food, information—making each hotel, to varying degrees of success, the corporate world's version of the royal palace. Anything he wanted, they would bring to his room. And Bob didn't doubt that with the right call, that could mean *anything*. The only difference would be in the size of the tip, in the type of transaction.

The next day's drive back was difficult. Bob hadn't slept well, and the monotony of the drive back was broken only by billboards asking, Isn't It Time You Tried One of Those New, High-Energy Hog Feeds?, or stating, Hayes Starter Pellets: Early to Market, Early to the Bank. The corn tassels had begun darkening, and the harvesters had come out of the machinery sheds and stood at the edges of the fields. The corn fields stretched in all directions and stopped abruptly at Findlay, where the snarled pipework of a refinery began. And then the last leg of the drive, past Bowling Green and Toledo and up over the border to Michigan. Each mile north, the sky toward Detroit took on a darker tint of metallic brown.

Bob had become conscious of a change in his sense of distance. He could see that five-hour drives would become a matter of routine. Perhaps only once had he ever been on a five-hour car trip as a child—and then only because his father got lost trying to follow his mother's instructions as she read a map. Five hours from northwest Connecticut could have put him in the middle of the Maine woods—another world. Here you were either in a town or city not unlike the one at the start of the trip—except that the high school and college football teams wore different-colored uniforms—or you were in another cornfield. So much distance, so little difference. When at last he turned off Route 23 and passed again through Blissfield, the straight road ahead seemed to confirm his choice of the previous day: He would rather be practical and comfortable, even if his ideals would be compromised. Whenever he felt that dark little cartoon cloud of self-doubt over his head, he would know he was being immature and unrealistic. Something to be recognized as a bad mood that would soon pass with a good night's sleep or a nice meal out. That was all it had ever had been. Nothing more than that.

With all this settled, Bob set his mind on Irene. He looked forward to seeing her. They would have a good time this week—what was left of it. He would work out of the apartment, get his paperwork done promptly, and head into Ann Arbor each night if she wanted. The only major business preoccupation was breaking in the new manager at Toledo four and helping him to develop a new impulse mix there. One that got the laid-off folks spending their money again.

Irene was due back with a six-pack of beer and cigarettes when the phone rang. Bob picked it up, and a voice asked simply, "May I speak to Irene."

At that moment he heard Irene opening the apartment door and setting a bag on the chair while she relocked it. "Sure," he said without thinking. He set the phone on top of the refrigerator and told Irene there was a call for her. He had taken a seat on the couch, his eyes shut and his head resting on the back, before he realized it had to be Brent. He hadn't heard Brent's voice on the phone before, but he was sure that no one in Sterne had a preppy inflection. When she began talking in a hushed voice, he was certain. She wasn't being as secretive as a whisper would make her, but she certainly didn't want to be heard, either. When he heard her ask, "What flight?" he began to feel angry. Dammit, hadn't he driven all the way back from Columbus that day? Hadn't he resolved not to pout about his little job anymore? Why should he share his private life with her old boyfriend? And then it just happened. Like slipping. Like missing a step on a stairway in the dark. He was crazy. He ran into the kitchen and yanked the phone from her hand.

"Brent," he said, "this is Bob, the guy who lives with Irene now. Get it?"

"Wa-wa-wait a sec, Bob," Brent said. "It's not what you think—"

"Don't tell me what I think," Bob yelled. "I don't want you calling here again."

Brent didn't say a word.

"Get it right, pal," Bob said. Then he slammed the receiver back on the phone.

"Jesus, what's your problem?" Irene screamed.

"I'll tell you what it is," he said. "It's this thing, right here." He began clubbing the wall phone until it loosened, and then he yanked it off, leaving only four wires dangling from a hole in the wall.

"You're nuts." She stood up and started poking Bob in the ribs. "When are you going to stop lugging around all this poor-little-sensitive-me shit. I'm sick of it. Knock it off. Grow up."

Didn't she know he was trying to grow up? Didn't she? He wanted to hit her. He raised his hand and held it cocked back, trembling. She stared him in the eyes, almost daring him to do it. She kept staring at him after he dropped his hand to his side.

"You don't have any guts, do you?" she said. And she left the room calmly.

Bob sank into a chair at the kitchen table and began to weep. He wept like a child, his lower lip stuck out, his chest heaving, his nose clogging. And the more he cried, the more he could imagine someone seeing him through a window. How pathetic. And that made him cry harder.

When Bob woke the next morning, Irene was gone. He stumbled into the kitchen and saw that it was ten-thirty. He had promised Cutter before leaving Columbus that he would call on Toledo four that day. But as soon as he opened his eyes he knew he wasn't up to it.

There was a note for him on the kitchen table:

Dear Bob:
Maybe it's a mistake for you and me to live together. I blame myself, not you. I think we needed more time to know each other first. Living together seemed like a good idea before we were doing it for real. Now I don't know. Brent called to say he had a layover in Detroit on a flight to Indianapolis. He wanted to meet you and me there. That was the reason he called. You were so rude. I can't forgive the part of you I saw. I'm going to see him anyway. And to find somewhere else to live. Maybe we can try to see each other later. Please try to understand.

Bob pulled the kitchen curtain to the side and confirmed that the BMW was gone. A check of the main closet revealed that she had left her belongings behind. Maybe she would return for those. But, on the other hand, she could afford to leave all that behind.

At first Bob couldn't think what to do. He made himself a cup of instant coffee and sat at the table, rereading Sunday's sports pages. The results were the same as he remembered, the losers still the losers. Only his game had changed. He reread the note. "Please try to understand." That phrase hurt most. Yes, he was trying to understand. He hoped all along that she would understand. The place. His job. The choices he made. There was no shortage of things to understand. He could accept everything else she said. She probably made a mistake with him. He was wrong to have fallen into it so easily.

Toledo four didn't concern him now. Cutter would take an excuse. Bob would say he was hung over. That would do fine. The fire under Cutter's ass wouldn't be quite so hot.

Bob showered for a long time and dressed slowly. Another

walk was in order. But on the way out, he knocked at Charlie and Rita's door. Charlie opened it.

"Did you notice when Irene left this morning?" he asked.

"Naw," Charlie said, his breath smelling of beer. "She took off early. Shopping is it?"

"I guess," Bob said. "I was conked."

"Me too. Rita's gone shopping somewhere. Let 'em. C'mon in."

Bob didn't think yes or no, he simply followed Charlie. He hadn't been in their half of the house before. Everything was golden oak—the trim, the wainscoting, the furniture. Except for the TV, it looked like a nice midwestern antique shop.

Charlie was watching "Let's Make a Deal." There was a six-pack of beer opened on the floor in front of his seat. He pulled a beer out for Bob.

"Yep, Rita's shopping for a rug to give Esther. May as well get good and drunk, because I'm going to pay for it either way."

On TV, a man dressed as a bunch of celery jumped up and down to get Monty's attention. "All right," Monty said to the man. "I've got five hundred dollars in my pocket. You can have that right now or whatever is behind door number one." The man chose the door. It slid open to reveal a hundred dollars' worth of potting soil. The audience moaned. "Look at the bright side," Monty said, tapping the man's costume of stalks and leaves. "Maybe you can grow yourself some companions."

"Always take what you've got in hand," Charlie said. "You never know what's behind the door."

Bob nodded. That was one message of the show. But another was, take a risk if you want big results. He wasn't sure what he would have done in the celery-man's place. He sipped from the beer and watched the show further. After a while, Charlie began talking. It became a monologue, both of them watching the TV.

"Took my first job at Ford because I was told I'd be building autos. But when I got on the other side of the door they said the only work was digging a sewer tunnel. I was a kid who needed a job, and no one else wanted what they had. The pay was good, real good at the time. Two bucks an hour. They gave me a little shovel and said, 'Do it.' Day after day this way and that, turning when I hit a boulder, going down, way down, the boys propping up all the way with two-by-fours. When I got to the banks of the Rouge, I had finished. Two months it took me. Ten hours a day of digging and one after that scrubbing the dirt off. And my fingers"—Charlie waved his hand in front of Bob's face. It was an old man's hand, spotted. Some of the fingers were bent at the last joint. Despite Charlie's age, the hand was still strong—"my fingers were swollen for five years after that. They got crooked from holding that shovel. But the men respected me. I gave them a way to shit into the river. When the union came, they wanted me in there. I threw a Pinkerton over the fence and would do it again today if God gave me the strength. He was bustin' heads, so I grabbed him around the chest, lifted him like a bag of dirt, and he was gone."

Charlie laughed and shook his head. Then he paused as if he had forgotten what he intended to say. "All that diggin' made me strong as an ox. But there's no work like that today. No one would have it. The jigs don't give a damn. The company doesn't. The union is rotten to the core. The members don't give a damn." Charlie took a sip from his beer and exhaled slowly. "And I don't give a damn. Long as they send me my check each month. Rita can buy all the rugs from here to China." He paused again and reached behind his chair, pulling out a bottle of Canadian whiskey. "Here, stick a little of this in there."

Bob held out his beer can and Charlie topped it with whiskey.

"What the fuck," he toasted.

"What the fuck," Bob said and tossed down the beer. It hit him right away. He had forgotten breakfast. Charlie got him another beer, and after Bob had taken a couple of swallows, he topped it again.

"I'll tell you another story," Charlie said. "I ran away from home in Sweden when I was fourteen. Came over as a stowaway and heard there were Swedes in northern Michigan, so I got up there and took a job on a farm. Roan workhorses this high . . ." Charlie raised his hand above his head. "They raised them. I rode one bareback into Superior in the middle of July and the water was still so cold my nuts shrunk into peas. It's a cold place up there, but a man can make it if he tries.

You find a house—a small one—and call it your own. Grow a few things in a short summer, and if you're any good with your hands, you make do. That's all that counts, right?"

Bob nodded.

"How do you make do?"

Sunlight spilled in through the windows. His head was swirling. "Bullshit. Just bullshit. The same as every college grad."

"Ha. You tell the truth at least."

"Is there still work up there?" Bob asked.

"Up north?" Charlie said, handing another topped can of beer to Bob. "Sure. In the quarries. The mines. On the water. If you're not fussy and don't mind real work, there's always a job up there."

"I'm not fussy," Bob said.

Just then the door swung open and Rita strode in. "What the bejesus are you two doing here?"

"Not one goddamned thing," Charlie said. "We're taking the day off."

Bob stood, wavering. He couldn't add anything to that.

"And whose idea was this?" Rita said. "Never mind, I know. You should have a little decency to think about your friend's life here." She patted him on the back. "He can barely stand."

"I'm fine," Bob said, and left the apartment, shutting the door behind him. As he climbed the stairs he heard Rita yelling at Charlie. He couldn't make out the words.

The sight of his briefcase set inside the door of his apartment nearly gave him the heaves. How much had changed since the night before. With the same mindless movement of someone doodling, he reached for the briefcase and unsnapped its latches. Its top flipped open like the jaws of a mechanical, amusement park monster. He attempted to position it on his lap as he sat on the couch, but it slid to the side, several half-completed reports falling to the floor. The printed typeface of the forms now seemed pretentious and self-important, like the official documents of a small and insignificant nation—the kind of place in which the Marx Brothers would find themselves mired. Inventory, impulse mix, census, customer, C-L-O-S-E, words from some patriotic chant in that faraway place. Say 'em right, or it's off to the dungeon. Unless you're willing to marry the president's overweight, ugly daughter.

Bob leaned back and shut his eyes. A mistake. The sensation of spinning set in. He forced himself to concentrate on something, anything, and he began thinking about things up north. Where a man never went long without work, so long as he had a rusty white pickup with a snowplow up front and a tool box in back. There would be firewood to sell, driveways to plow, and in the spring, repairs on summer places for the rich. He would live in a trailer, although he didn't care for them. But up north, near Superior, you took what you could find. You learned to live with less. So, sure, he could live in a trailer at first. But he would look for a small house, too. Two or three rooms, not much bigger than a garage. When you walked in the front door, you'd find yourself in a main room with a wood stove. A couple of chairs and a folding table. A secondhand couch covered with a bedspread, a kitchen sink on the back wall. The bedroom would be off to the side. No bureau. His clothes, all of them, in a green army duffel bag. He would hear the sound of the lake out back, the waves slapping off rocks night and day, the wind blowing down right out of the North Pole. There'd be onions hanging from twine on the front porch. That was it. That was the place he'd have.

The lock of the door clicked, and Bob opened his eyes for a second, the late sun slanting through the windows. It gave an orange tint to the white walls of the apartment. He had no idea what time it was or why Irene stood before him, frowning. His mouth wouldn't open. He felt dry and hot.

"Are you okay?" Irene asked softly.

Bob summoned his concentration. "I got drunk."

"I know," she said. "I saw Rita on the way up. She told me. We'll talk later. I'm not leaving. I'm back. Here, let me help you." She gave Bob a hand and led him to the bed. He fell onto it, and she covered him with a blanket.

"Try to relax," she said. "Forget about last night. And forget about my note. Let yourself drift off."

He was drifting off. He could feel it in his legs. They were limp. And he could see those onions hanging from the porch ceiling, their skins dry and loose. So loose they would burn if he put a match to them. The flame would singe the onions, the brown skins crackling as they caught fire, the flame moving up the twine to the ceiling. He'd smell the burning onions as the ceiling caught, its old paint peeling back in the heat like the scales of a dead fish, giving off a smoke thick enough to sting his eyes. He would have to be quick. Move to the bedroom and gather up the few things he would need. Because the fire would be in the main room by then, falling in from above and spreading across the linoleum as if it had been spilled. He would toss everything out the window and jump after it. Then pick himself up, grab the duffel bag, and toss it in the front seat of his pickup. The fire would be going full force, popping out the glass and sucking in the air. It would be beautiful, the way things burned up north. A sound he would hear all the way to the shore, where he would wash his face in the icy water before moving on. A sound that would stay with him for a long time.

CHAPTER

12

The next day, there was no probing for or picking at motives for Bob's actions. There was no questioning what Irene and Brent had discussed. In the future, Bob would be less mistrustful of her and she more open with him. No whispering, no ripping the telephone off the wall.

Bob's job required that he get down to Toledo four. Before he left, he was able to rewire the phone. It didn't fit on its wall mounting as snugly as before, but it worked.

The progression of that fall could be measured by the descent of the daily high temperature: a degree or two lower every twenty-four hours. There were no spells of Indian summer. Bob began to envisage the circuit of his territory as a giant clock. Sterne was at the center, his stores, towns, and cities the markings on the dial, the route he traveled again and again. As he drove, he would imagine himself as the minute hand moving to the next point on the dial.

Bob worked hard each night on the road to clear up the bulk of his paperwork before heading home, perhaps leaving space only for him to check something against the reference materials he kept out of his cluttered trunk. Rather than becoming a burden, this dedication to punctuality seemed to make time pass more quickly. And he knew that Boston appreciated having his reports by Monday or Tuesday of the next week. This also left the weekend open for doing whatever Irene and he felt like doing—more often than not, heading into Ann Arbor for a day of browsing, with dinner capped by a concert or a movie.

Gradually, as Bob sat in one motel room or another listening to the TV while he marched through the paperwork, he began to think that there had been a fundamental change in both him and Irene. That somehow the sharp contrast between his routine of road and work and home and Irene had slowly altered them. As much as he looked forward to returning home each time, he was also preparing for how he would respond to any number of possible things she could do or say during the weekend. He never wanted to be out of control again.

In a similar way, it seemed that Irene accepted his road work as being dreary, and that he looked forward to the weekends as a time to have fun—or if he was still tired, to lounge around the apartment and watch old movies. Their lives together existed in forty-eight hours of congenial neutral ground, a space of vanilla-like goodwill and predictable lusts that adequately served each of them for the time being. It was convenient. Somehow, this knowledge didn't panic Bob. Not as it might have had he been a teen-ager, when love and passion were thought to be great gusts of feeling. This was a practical love: She had her reasons for being in Michigan, he had his. And they were happy together.

The job suffused him with a set of principles, guidelines, and goals. Bob's sense of time, in this system, became a chain of causal relations. If the present state of sales wasn't acceptable, something had happened in the past that needed to be identified and corrected to bring the future into conformity with goals. He had a set of tools—research and a trained eye—which could detect problems and their causes as well as provide a well-established strategy for fixing them. It was a routine to bolster one's self-confidence in the world, which became a surprisingly predictable place when understood as an algebra of Maslow's needs and Prescott's principles.

It was inevitable that Bob would carry this business view of the world into his life with Irene. One weekend in Ann Arbor, her mood had turned sour. He set about asking a series of questions that he later realized was simply a variation on proper sales techniques. "Was it something I said?" (Open probe) No response. "Did the pizza upset your stomach?" (Closed probe) Without intending to be manipulative, he channeled her actions by getting her to commit to hypothetical situations. "If we stopped for a soda, do you think you would feel better?" And finally, he closed the evening with a restatement of benefits and a request for action. "I agree it has been a long day and we're both a little tired. Should we head back home after the movie, or would you rather go now?" Irene opted for a soda and the movie, and felt much better.

If Irene was aware of how the stratagems of Bob's work had infiltrated their lives, she didn't acknowledge it. Now he could consider this comically. As he stood before the small bathroom mirror of a motel in Bowling Green he recalled an episode of thwarted passion (Irene: "Jesus, can't you keep that thing down for one night?") and realized that he hadn't employed the right preparatory techniques. Instead he had rolled over and waited for his horniness to subside. Now, his mouth full of toothpaste, he knew he could have easily applied his business training. And what a new meaning "probing" took on! He'd probe to find out the objection, commit her to the prospect of some benefit through a hypothetical conditional, and close by convincing her to embrace a cleverly stated set of benefits posing as foreplay, thus opening her to the possibilities he had originally intended.

As humorously as he rehearsed this salesmanship before the bathroom mirror (later wondering whether he could be heard through the wall), he had to acknowledge how much his consciousness had been colored by the performance and conditions of his job. The evidence made him defensive at first. How could this have happened? Was he at fault for allowing it? But then again, how could it be otherwise. Hadn't any of his father's world view been affected by the assembly line? Didn't the NFL's greatest coaches and players pass the off-season lecturing to businessmen on how to improve, using the metaphors of the playing field? And wouldn't Irene change, too, when she finally began law school?

Bob remembered Becky Warner, a girl in his dorm, weeping one Sunday evening after her boyfriend, who was in law school, had left. She sat in Bob's room complaining about his reaction to a trivial incident. "He actually said there was no precedent for me to be upset with him," she said. He would begin preparing himself for that now. He would pick up one of those pocket dictionaries of legal terms and begin reading it.

The Bowling Green store had become a pet project for Bob. Everything about it appealed to him. Now he even enjoyed the ride over the flat farmland south from Toledo, a trip he first found painfully monotonous. The town center was little more than five commercial blocks in all directions east and west, north and south, with houses clustered around this axis. There was a movie theater, a hardware store, two motels, two farm-supply stores, tractor dealers, and a state university where the well-to-do from Cleveland and the farmers from the surrounding countryside sent their sons and daughters for a good time and a little learning. Set in the midst of corn and soybean fields, the town seemed like the last outpost of provisions before a nonstop expanse, the tedium of the horizon broken only by a few trees, TV antennas on thirty-foot towers, and the squat circular cones of corn silos.

The store had been a borderline proposition. Locked in a row of shops at the center of town, its location was considered problematic. Not enough parking. Not enough random walk-in business. The company was ready to close it; its sales per square foot were the lowest in his territory. But when Bob noticed that next door was the town's favorite lunch and supper place—a cafeteria-style restaurant specializing in beef raised by the owner—he figured there was plenty of walk-by traffic waiting to be lured into the store.

Lyle Swift, the manager, claimed he had seen Cutter only twice in the year the store had been open. A thin, nervous man of forty, with prematurely gray hair slicked straight back, Lyle didn't know what the problem was and admitted to Bob that, as a family man, he couldn't afford to wait for the store to turn around. A lifelong citizen of Bowling Green and a member of the Rotary Club, he had seen businesses come and go and wasn't about to stay with this one as it sank.

"I'll be honest with you, son," Lyle said. "I've got my oar in the water and friends from one end of this town to the other.

I'm a manager's manager, and when P&V came here, I said, 'Why fight the future.' So I left Falcon's Lawn and Garden to hop aboard a chain operation. But the people here don't accept outsiders, other than students, and the company is too rigid in its plans. It just isn't responsive to what we need for merchandise.''

Bob told Lyle he appreciated his honesty and asked what changes he would recommend. Lyle replied that it was hard to say. Folks in Bowling Green were set in their ways. Everyone knew the pharmacist at the town's other drugstore—heck, they had grown up getting everything from cough remedies to their first rubbers there—and people weren't going to change. At least that's what Lyle supposed.

Bob didn't bother developing a lengthy analysis of the store's problems. He wrote down what Lyle told him, and in two weeks, Lyle was set adrift to find his new ship. The store's assistant manager, a forty-eight-year-old widow named Dorothy Plank, was appointed interim manager until the store was closed.

Plank was an earnest, hard-working woman who knew nothing about retailing. Her husband had been a farmhand who died of a heart attack, leaving her no insurance money and no means of support. The store was important to her. Bob spent three days in Bowling Green at the start of Dorothy's reign as manager. On the first day, he reviewed the basics of inventory management and indoctrinated the employees with the principles of CLOSE. As he went through this routine he became conscious of being looked at as a slick easterner who wasn't worth trusting.

"I don't get it," one teen-aged boy said. "You get folks to buy more than they meant to buy? Now why should we do that?"

Bob stumbled a moment. "That's a good question and I'm glad you brought it up," he said, trying to think of what to say. "But let me ask you one. Have you ever gone into a store, say a supermarket, and got something you didn't have on the list?"

The boy nodded.

"It wasn't something you didn't need, was it? You could use it?"

The boy nodded.

"Well that's what this is all about, right? All you do by following these steps is help folks remember what they truly needed without knowing it."

"Oh, I get it," the boy said.

After leaving the store that night, Bob found a diner on the west side of town where he ordered the liver and bacon special. Eavesdropping on the families in the adjoining booths, he decided he would return to the diner for breakfast, lunch, and dinner, and use whatever he heard there for his report and proposal. In the chatter between brother and sister, parents and children, husband and wife, he found a prescription for what ailed P&V in Bowling Green.

> It's easy to imagine you've been to a town like Bowling Green. It's like something you've seen in the movies. The sort of place where people pick up litter on the sidewalks and put it in trash baskets. Where almost everyone who's been here ten years knows everyone else. Where teen-aged couples hold hands and—can you believe it— smooch. And when the town isn't packed in the Bowling Green State Falcon's windy stadium (the top row of which is probably the highest vantage point in the area) on a fall afternoon, they're watching the local boys do their best on the football field, all the while resenting the spoiled rich kids from Cleveland who drive Nissan 300 ZXs down Main Street and into the countryside, past row after row of soybeans and corn, each seed of which costs more money to put in the ground than its perfect growth can possibly yield.
>
> But the bankers here aren't styled after Capra's Mr. Potter. They're just pathetic local guys who got degrees at the college and have no idea why their farm loans are going bad. There are two thriving businesses in town: both casket factories—one that builds caskets for adults, and the other that builds them for children and pets. There's a job there now and then. But otherwise, everyone is scrambling to find a buck or two pumping gas and raking leaves, working the grounds for the college, or as clerks—whoever saw more part-time clerks?—in the town's two supermarkets and assorted farm and dime stores, where all of them wash the

windows once a day, as if anyone needed a better view of bare shelves and dwindling prospects.

Of course the college gives the town a proverbial shot in the arm with every change of semester, especially with the first wave of students in September. But after that, what hope?

What to do? Close up and move on—chalk it up to an overzealous expansion plan? Or, can it be turned around?

I say, sit in a diner here one night—any night—and listen. What you hear is talk of what was bought—a car, a planter, a dishwasher for the wife—and why is that, with the muffled booms of foreclosure sounding almost daily?

The fact is, these folks are dying to buy—and they just need a reason why. That and a few bucks to get the merry-go-round of prosperity moving again. We can give them that, but it's going to take a little more than the standard dog and pony show to get them in the door. What's more, we have to recognize that these people sense things in America aren't the way they were ten years ago. They look around and see genuine Swiss in the dairy case of their supermarket costing less than domestic Swiss, they see imported cars beating up on Detroit, they see famine around the world with no one buying their crops, and then they see the rich kids from Cleveland—not exactly the garden spot of economic rejuvenation but a far sight better off than this place—not giving a damn about anything and confident of their futures, and they want to know what's rotten in Denmark.

What will it take to get store traffic up? I have a hunch we can have a store that caters to both groups in this town—students and townsfolk alike—but it's going to take some cleverness. What I see as a possible answer will need to be implemented without the standard testing procedures—because we don't have time for research. At the present rate of sales per square foot—consistently dismal for two straight years—Dorothy Plank will be walking the plank in six months and it won't be one iota of her own doing.

We need to stop ignoring the psychic battleline here and begin catering to it. Here's what I suggest: On one side of the impulse zone—"Born in the USA—and good as gold." This is merchandise made in America, or at least by American companies (I doubt we could find enough stuff actually made in America), from TVs to candy bars, jogging suits to small tool sets, the "gold" reference designed to appeal to these folks, who, I'll bet, still believe we should be on the gold standard. On the other side, "Valueville—where your dollar gets you more." This would be imported merchandise selected to appeal to rich kids and professors, a standard well-off suburban mix.

We promote the store as the place of choice—implying it's where you control your destiny with your own purchasing power. That's exactly what none of the town's folks feel right now—and P&V can create that illusion. "From stars and stripes to the rising sun, P&V gives you the world of choice." Like it? It's not too corny—excuse the expression—for this town. We've already got the stuff, it just needs to be reconfigured. I'll personally put it together. The inventory is there or available. We just need to shake it up to get things popping. If Lee Iacocca can do it for Chrysler, believe me, Dorothy Plank can do it for P&V in Bowling Green.

I don't want to stretch my point too far, but if this works here, I don't see why it wouldn't work in any midwestern college town, except where the school is based on ag. We'd be the new kid on the block everywhere, giving people just what they don't get anywhere else in life—choice, and the surge of optimism that only buying merchandise can give an American.

One parting note: There is a Department of Popular Culture here at Bowling Green U., an academic enterprise where it's possible to get credit analyzing anything from weather reports to rodeos. If we do a bang-up job on this, we could probably get noted not only in the Harvard Biz Review, but also the department's own little journal. Just something to mull over.

Bob read over his report. The cheery tone of the ending bothered him, but he figured it would strike the right note with the Remers of the world back East. He nailed down his observations by selecting an inventory mix for the impulse zone. It seemed this was the kind of effort Cutter said was needed to earn a bonus. And if he was putting up with all of this, if he had read and reread the sales and retailing materials given him in Boston, and all the management theories and acronym gimmicks for training service workers, if he'd done all that just to be a route man for a couple of years before finding himself, then all he was doing was running laps. He'd had enough of that in high school. Besides, if his recommendations succeeded, what had he done except to direct the attention and interests of the company toward a little town that obviously needed a shot in the arm. There was nothing wrong with that kind of scrutiny. It would enable Dorothy Plank and everyone else to keep their jobs.

The evening was cold. A drizzle fell as he headed back from Bowling Green. The smell of wet fallen leaves, the dull gray light of late afternoon, reminded him of cross-country practice.

Training with his brother, Carl, had been tough from the start because they were training against each other too. Both of them were good distance runners. That's the way it had been from the beginning. The very first run they ever took—and this only with the news that there would be, for the first time, a cross-country team at their high school—was five miles in the ninety-five degree heat of late August. The next morning they got up and ran the same course again. By the start of the season, they were competitive with most of the better runners in the area. The next year, they were virtually unbeatable.

Their coach, a Dartmouth graduate and a former runner, increased the sense of competition between them. Carl was better on long, flat courses. In races over three miles on a flat course he would beat Bob. But on hilly, short courses of up to two-and-a-half miles, Bob would win, and there were more of those in the area. The coach picked up on this quickly and would stagger them in practice runs against their strengths and weaknesses. On hillwork over a mile, he would send Carl first, twenty to thirty seconds ahead of Bob. And if Bob didn't beat Carl, he would give Bob "dessert." That was an extra hill or two to run, in under a certain time, after the regular practice was finished. It was brutal. On long, flat runs, he would send Bob first and expect Carl to win. If Carl didn't, he got dessert—also hills, because they hurt the most.

The result was that even when they went for a ten-mile jog on the weekend, they couldn't stop feeling competitive.

One or the other would have to alleviate the tension by saying, "I'm not going to push today—you go ahead."

The tension became so intense that Bob's hands used to sweat, beginning around one in the afternoon on practice days. He would linger in the hallway between afternoon classes to catch the coach, an English teacher who thought *A Separate Peace* was the greatest book ever written, to find out what the workout would be. "Distance," he would say. Or, "Speed." Or, worst of all, "Dessert."

Race days the first year were calm by comparison. Bob and Carl knew one or the other of them would win, and neither really cared. They chatted as they ran ahead of the pack, sometimes electing to tie at the finish line by holding hands as they crossed. But, during the second year of running, the dynamics changed. Carl beat Bob on a hilly course, and, for the first time, was considered the team's top runner for the upcoming meet. That was at a race in Thomaston—one of the hillier courses in the region.

Overall, Bob had won more races than Carl. But Carl had proven himself the better runner at that point and won the place alongside the best runner of the other team. Bob could not accept being superseded by Carl. Many times since then he tried to excuse what had happened on the grounds of the intense rivalry the coach had provoked between Carl and him. Maybe that did have something to do with it. But the facts were what they were.

Some time during the middle of the race, with no one behind them, Bob and Carl were side by side. They were on pace for a course record, Bob could feel it. And he wanted to win. It was his kind of course. But Carl started to pull away more than a mile from the finish line. Bob tried to go with him, but couldn't. It was possible Carl would fade later, but Bob felt that sudden lack of confidence that colors the psychology of running like a dye. He knew if he let Carl go, he would lose contact and finish behind him, though, still well ahead of anyone else. "Let's tie," he said. Carl looked at him. "Okay," he said. "But pick it up." Carl wanted the record. Bob tried to pick it up, but instead Carl had to hold back.

As he drove from town to town, he compared the time on the dashboard's digital clock against the mileage signs and his speed, attempting to maintain a constant sixty miles per hour. Slow for a truck on a hill, compensate on the downgrade. Interval training all over again. Measure your speed. Make your move. Never let them hear you breathing hard as you pass. Take them. Coach Medina's words kept going through his mind as he brooded about what he had done to Carl.

When they had come to the last hill, perhaps a half mile from the finish, Bob kicked. He knew that Carl couldn't keep pace with him for a half mile uphill. As he pulled away, Bob told himself Carl was slowing. But he knew now Carl had not slowed, except earlier in the race, when he let Bob keep up with him. Bob won, and Carl didn't speak to him for a week. They never discussed the race. But it was there all the time. It ruined the rest of the season. Carl never won again and Bob couldn't forgive himself. At the state meet, something snapped inside. He began jogging at the two-mile mark, where he had been fourth at the time. When Carl ran past, Bob yelled to him, "Go get them." Carl didn't respond. Later Bob found out Carl had stalled and gradually dropped back in the standings as one by one less-talented but more competitive runners passed him by. It didn't seem fair. Still, Bob knew anything else was too much to hope for. Especially after what had happened between them, after what he had done to Carl. That fact stuck with him as he drove back, every mile of the way.

CHAPTER

13

Bob found a note from Irene on the door saying she had run into Ann Arbor on an errand and would be back for dinner, with good news to boot. There was mail, she said. Inside he found two expense checks and an unmarked first-class envelope. He ripped it open and found a brand-new Gulf card, his name, Robert Bodewicz, stamped in neat, computer-type black letters. He popped a can of Stroh's in celebration: good-bye Belvedere Motor Lodges of the world. Then he noticed the blue airmail letter from Germany. He sat down with his beer and opened it.

Dear Bob:

Thanks for your two letters, and especially for the lovely stationery of the Findlay Oilman's Motor Lodge, whose broken script logo provides all I need to know about the quality of accommodations you went on to describe. I can tell you're on the way up, because it doesn't sound like things can get any lower.

I have been on the road myself lately, leaving the cozy confines of Bonn for a cultural excursion to Berlin, west and east, and if Isherwood can lay claim to being a camera, I can say I felt like an infertile sperm passing down the smelly channel between this city's two sides, a split between the buttocks of politics, where all travelers are participants in an international sodomy. I am kumera. If there is a navel of the world, then surely Berlin is its rectum.

Where West Berlin isn't gray or a vacant lot of weeds, it is one of the most gross hyperboles of consumerism. All storefronts, price tags, flashing arrows, and strobe-lit signs. All in reaction to the East. The city is like a big ugly whore of commerce, made up in motley neon clothes, purple eye shadow, and a chartreuse wig, trying to seduce the East, to lure it over the wall and give it everything the great woman of State cannot provide, including meat every night and the salacious thrill of passing warm coins and bills softened with the pocket sweat of consumers. Does P&V have plans for a store in Berlin? Price and value are erotic words here. Propose it and become a tumescent DIC.

If West Berlin is garish, East Berlin is worse. And since I've used all my metaphors on the West, I'll leave it at that. Happened by an East German bookstore, and it reminded me of a religious bookstore in America. It had one section only: Classics. I looked, expecting Holderlin, Goethe, Schiller, etc. But all I found was individual or boxed sets of Marx and Engels, and, can you believe it, Jack London.

The sign of a young bourgeois European Marxist is the forty-five-volume hardcover set of Marx and Engels, printed in DDR and set by the stereo or on top of a preposterously large TV, which is tuned into a show called "The Goal of the Week," reviewing a German's outstanding soccer play.

If this letter sounds somewhat cynical, consider that my time here is winding down and that my return is imminent. My German hasn't improved nearly as much as I had hoped, and I'm wondering sometimes why I bothered to come over here, given the fact that I haven't gotten laid, didn't travel as much as I wanted, and spent too much time with ear infections. It makes me wonder what the hell is in store for me after college. I don't mean this as a slam, but your path isn't for me.

I'll probably be back a few days before Christmas. Do you and Irene plan to come East? I would like to meet her. Let me know.

> Yours in fraternity,
> Carl

Bob got another beer and sat at the kitchen table. He could see out the back window and would know when Irene got back. The idea of returning at Christmas to see Carl seemed odd. He wondered if Carl was aware of the anniversary of their argument. Still, there was nothing in his letter to make him believe that Carl was continuing that dispute. Rather, he seemed confused but not snotty about Bob's job decision. Of course there were plenty of asides about business, but Bob had made those too as an undergraduate. It also seemed that no one stopped making them, even after accepting the fate of having to work.

Only then did Bob notice he had been using a copy of *The Sterne Tattler* as a coaster for his beer. He lifted the can, its wet marks making rings like cartoon eyeglasses across the headline, The Loomis Family: Down But Not Out, and On the Rebound. It was by Irene, her first feature after three weeks of obituaries and announcements.

> Ask anyone about the way Art Loomis handles a Kenworth, and you'll hear he was one of the best, always on time and capable of backing a 4,000-gallon milk hauler through the smallest gate opening without so much as scraping a tick of paint off the posts. But when farmers quit the dairy business because of low prices, there wasn't as much demand for milk truck drivers, no matter what a man's skills. So Art Loomis lost a job on seniority to another driver. After thirteen years of providing for his wife and four children, Art Loomis became another statistic in the monthly unemployment reports.

The story went on about how Loomis, a devoted family man, looked for work as a driver everywhere, but got only one job offer as a short-route freight handler.

> It meant commuting to Inkster each day and running a route that took me through some real tough neighborhoods in Detroit. The pay was less, the commute awful, and being a country boy, I couldn't see myself doing it.

Loomis tried to pass himself off as a carpenter at a gravel pit. "I had built the addition to my house with a little help," Loomis said. "But I guess this job was too demanding for that. They let me go after a month."

Then Irene brought in the wife's point of view, a nice

touch for the *Tattler*'s readers. "We thought we would have to sell our house," Becky Loomis said. "Art was drinking too much beer and watching TV—that wasn't like him—and we were arguing all the time."

Then Irene revealed that Art had found a job in the new booming segment of the American economy, the service sector. He applied for and was accepted as the assistant manager of a new Q-Mart and Fill-up station. The job paid only a little better than half of what he had made, but it was a job. Besides, as an employee of a major oil company, the health insurance and other benefits were excellent.

Becky helped make ends meet by learning several new inexpensive dishes to make for dinner. (Irene included the recipe for a complete-protein brown rice goulash, as a sidebar to the article.) The kids helped by starting a garage-cleaning business, which they advertised through the *Tattler*. Irene brought the story to a fine moralistic close by quoting Loomis. "No man gets a break who doesn't keep looking." Irene then concluded, "For Art Loomis and family, that break came after six months of unemployment and anguish, just one mile from where he and Becky had made their home for ten years."

"What do you think?"

Bob looked up at Irene. He hadn't heard her come in. "It's good," he said. "Probably perfect for your readers."

"You know what? I did it all in two days. It blew Poindexter away. He loved it and ran an extra five hundred copies. They sold out already. And he sent one to his friend at *The Detroit Free Press*, and they said they might run it in their Sunday 'Lifestyles' section. I could get five hundred dollars for it. That's more than enough for all my government textbooks and a semester's snacks."

Bob managed to say that was great. But her words, like the article, seemed to him exploitive. Then again, after his Bowling Green recommendations, he was no one to talk.

"Poindexter has a lead on some guy who lost his job at the Chrysler proving grounds after they started importing all those Japanese cars." Irene lit a cigarette. Bob hadn't seen her smoke in a few weeks, but apparently the role of feature writer for the *Tattler* had gotten her going again. She blew smoke toward the ceiling. "He got a new job after taking a state-funded skills redevelopment course. Now he reads meters for the utility company. He's also in AA. It sounds good.''

"Sounds like you might be able to buy a few law books with that one.''

"Bob, don't be like that.'' Irene tried to frown but couldn't hold the expression. She started laughing. "I guess it does, doesn't it.''

"And at four cents a word, it's a good thing Poindexter isn't a tough editor.''

Irene gave him a kiss on the cheek. "He thought the recipe idea was great, and the only reason I included it was for the words.''

Bob glanced at Irene's BMW. "You didn't drive that to the interviews, did you?''

"No. Poindexter thought I should use his beat-up station wagon.''

They decided to head into Ann Arbor for the evening. Irene drove. For the first time since the Adirondacks, Bob noticed she was using two hands.

"Okay, what's up?'' he asked, not sounding too sympathetic.

"Nothing, really.'' She ran her hand through her hair and put it back on the wheel. "It's just these two guys I met today when I priced the government books. They told me about the constitutional history professor. He's a tough one, they said. Performs as a sifter for the program.''

"Maybe you shouldn't bother with it. You'll have enough of those professors next fall.''

"I know,'' she said and hit the wheel with her hand. "It's just that . . .'' She turned on the radio, then turned it off. "It's just that I would feel better if I do run into one of these types before law school. And then there are these guys.''

"What guys?''

"The guys I met. They were sizing me up, I could tell.''

"For a date?''

"No, as a student. As a competitor. Thirty seconds after meeting them, they had gotten me to tell them I was going to law school. And then it was, 'Why are you taking this class' and 'Where else did you apply for law.' That kind of thing. The 'how-smart-are-you' routine.''

"They can't all be like that.''

"I don't know. They said probably half the class in con history has either gone or is about to go to law school. That's real competitive.''

"Why bother then? You'll have enough pressure next year. Take a gut.''

"I don't want a gut. I want something to help me make the transition. Something like an interim step.''

"The way you describe it, it sounds every bit as hard.''

"Yeah, maybe.'' Irene loosened her grip on the wheel and then tightened it. "I feel like I need to do this, though. It's important. I know my father wants me to do well, and I want to do well. There's no cruising here. It's not like undergraduate courses. Everyone is out for blood. For money. My father was second in his class. I'd like to show my father I can rise to that level.''

Bob didn't say a word. He stared at a farmhouse they were approaching, listening to the thud-thud-thud of the radials moving over the spaces between blocks of pavement. What did it matter, this jousting between generations? But as he thought this, he knew he was lying to himself. It did matter. He was supposed to do better than his father. But if his father had been a stellar student, what then? He might be feeling what Irene did.

Bob massaged one of Irene's shoulders as she drove. "Why would your father expect as much of you? Especially since the school is probably so much more competitive today than it was then.''

"He doesn't. I do. I'm the one that decides that.'' Irene slowed the car as they approached a trailer truck on a hill. "For me, it's a way of respecting my family. A way of nodding to them. I guess I never knew that until now. I guess that's it.''

After dinner and a movie, they made their way to the Michigan Union. Irene stayed calm as long as they kept moving. Whenever she had a moment to herself, though, he could see her start to tense up. Based on how easily things must have come to her as an undergraduate, he hadn't expected that of her. But there was some other element at work here. The family thing. He hoped a few beers and some jazz would help her put it aside for the rest of the night.

The Union's club was packed. Waitresses with trays of beer hovered around tables. A dreamy haze of smoke drifted upward. A quartet played at the far end. After they finished a set, Bob hugged Irene. "How did you like it?"

"Huh?"

Bob realized she hadn't been listening. "You okay?"

"Yeah, sure," she said and smiled at him. He had seen enough of her smiles now to recognize the difference between appeasing and pleasing turns of mouth. If an Eskimo could discern fifty or so shades of white, he now knew the dozen or more smiles that Irene had mastered.

"Do you want to stay?" he asked.

"Why not?" She sipped on her glass of beer.

"You seem a little spacy, that's all."

"If you can't space out on jazz, what can you space on?"

Bob took a swallow of beer. It was cool and fresh. He took Irene's hand and squeezed it. "Hey, you going to open up or are we going to be alone together for the rest of the night."

"I'm sorry," Irene said. "I guess I'm not good company. It's school, that's all. It's only a few weeks away and I can't get those guys out of my mind."

"You make it sound like a prison sentence."

"It is, sort of. I mean, for the next three and a half years, I'll be becoming a lawyer. And at the end, I'll be a lawyer. That's it. That's what I'll be for the rest of my life."

"And this is just occurring to you now? Irene, this is your choice."

"I know. But it seems so final."

"You can always be an ex-lawyer."

"No one is ever an ex-lawyer. Your brain never loses that training. All you can be is a lawyer who doesn't practice."

"I don't want to be a troublemaker, but why do it if you're so afraid of the consequences."

"Come on," Irene said. "You can want to learn to swim but be nervous about your first dip. This is a much bigger dip than that. Maybe the full extent of it is hitting me all at once."

"How bad is it? Really? Your dad doesn't seem like some

vampire of logic. Christ, he's even capable of metaphor—'tides of currency.' Finishing second didn't finish that part of his brain.''

Irene sat back and lit a cigarette. ''I know you're right,'' she said. ''But it was those guys. They were Machiavellian, I swear.''

''Sure, I can believe that. But why let them wreck you? Nothing is that serious.''

''That's easy for you to say. When soapsuds don't sell, put drain cleaners in their place. TVs or candy bars, what's the difference? Tastes change, demographics shift, everything is in flux. And when you finally get sick of working for a drugstore, you can do something else. You're not much different. But this is the law. It takes you over. That much I *have* seen. Even in the way my father talks to the dog. Everything has the tint of legal thinking. Everything follows inductively from precedents, deductively from principles.''

Bob waved his hand at Irene and laughed. ''Cut the crap. The law is just a big bog floating on nothing. It changes all the time. One thing is the law one decade, and you know damn well if another president has his way with the Supreme Court, something else will be the law before he is out of office. Abortion's in, but it could be out. The law is as whimsical as the Church. It does whatever people in power want it to do. Dictators make it bend to justify torture, democrats to reflect the mood of the mob. Even the Constitution gets mulched up with amendments that get appealed and repealed, depending on the temperature of the body politic. The law is just like soapsuds, only the brand changes take a little longer to see. Every decade has its favorite brand of my rights and yours. So don't make your career sound so deadly serious next to mine. It's every bit as whimsical. You don't need to be a Marxist to see that.''

Irene smiled at Bob. ''Phew,'' she said. ''There's the guy I knew from Melville class.''

Bob shrugged and asked the waitress for another glass of beer. The quartet had started up again. By the time the next break came, it was close to midnight and Bob felt tired. Irene put her arm around his shoulders and hugged him.

''You're so contrary,'' she said, as if there hadn't been a

gap of thirty minutes since they last spoke. "I mean, I saw what's on my mind. You ask. And then you turn it into a major production."

"Yeah, I know." He wished he was better at listening.

"I suppose I don't feel all that different from anyone else about to make a big change. But knowing that doesn't make it easier. We see ourselves changing and want to read more into that change, to understand its consequences, when in fact there's nothing to be understood. There's only the experience."

Bob nodded.

"All I ask for is some encouragement. That's all. Can you do that?"

"Sure I can," Bob said. He wanted to be that kind of person.

"I don't think this is all in my head. Law school will be a total grind. And with real creeps competing constantly for their rank."

Bob nodded again. He was trying to imagine what that would be like. But how could he really understand? All he needed to get ahead was mastery of a few rules of the marketplace and a few instances of their clever application. There was none of the open competition that Irene was anticipating. At least none he knew of. Each person was free to work as hard as he wanted. If he had business instincts, no one would stop him. It was competitive, sure. But he feigned innocence about that competition. Sure he wanted a big bonus, a promotion. But without appearing to be anything but an earnest, bright guy who wasn't falling over himself to earn it. And so what? What was wrong with that?

But if he were to go to a law school like Michigan, he knew he would get sucked up into the open competition that existed among the students there. The stakes were high—perhaps higher than his paltry bonus. For the top students, a position in a major firm. A starting salary close to six figures. Those were big bucks, the kind that made things raw between people. If he were there, he would be studying all the time. And if, under scrutiny, he didn't measure up to the best and the brightest, what tack could he take to diminish it all, to make it small, to say none of it matters one fuck to me? He couldn't imagine what he would say to justify being less than the best. It was win or don't play the game. The game was easier to win in business.

CHAPTER

14

By mid-November, Bob had graduated from the Belvedere Motor Lodges of the Midwest to Holiday Inns, thanks to his Gulf card. With his checking account primed with expense checks, Bob allowed himself some of the more expensive menu items at dinner, although he had come to enjoy liver. He looked forward to the beige pleasantry of Holiday Inns, to being treated with abstract courtesy by desk attendants and with deferential obedience by waitresses. He had two new jackets and two new dress slacks. He permitted himself the small vanity of feeling he looked successful for his age. The store managers had become comfortable with him, quick to adopt his suggestions, willing to share their problems with a candor that made solutions easier to formulate. Bob took care to emphasize this cooperation in his reports, attempting to dispel the home office's impression of DICs and managers as adversaries. Sure enough, there had been some bad apples at Bowling Green and Toledo four, but there were capable replacements installed now. Things were looking up. By and large, the rest of the managers were a competent, if unimaginative group. But he felt anything but an assassin as he strode into stores unannounced, giving a fraternal wave to employees and managers. They were—it was corny but true—a team.

Bob had made an effort, a determined one he liked to think, to put aside his self-doubts about the job and his future.

For the time being, he threw himself into his job with a single-minded energy he hadn't mustered for anything since high school cross-country and track. Whatever management, his coaches, asked for, they got. Motivating him was the belief that if he maintained his concentration and was consistent, thorough, and prompt in all he did, things would work out. The invisible hand would tap him on the shoulder, would give him a goose upward.

There was also a sense in which much of this effort was for Irene's benefit. With each new week, her government courses, and beyond that law school, drew closer. He hoped his example would set the right tone for her. While he could still joke about getting taken over by his job, he knew Irene would eventually need to do the same. The would-be professionals in love: he with his career, she with school and a career in the offing.

Cutter remained out of touch. Bob left message after message on his machine and continued to forward copies of paperwork with an additional cover letter of additional observations that did not get sent east. Bob had tried to reach Cutter three times over the weekend prior to leaving for South Bend. When he checked in at the front desk of his motel, there was a message for him. He assumed that Cutter had finally returned a call. But it was Rick.

Bob first called the manager of the South Bend store to let him know he would be there that afternoon. To certain hardworking managers, Bob extended this courtesy. There was no sense in witnessing an aberration of procedures, especially if the manager had gone out of his way to correct problems noted by Bob.

With that done, he called Rick direct.

"Boy, have I got some news for you," Rick said after Bob asked what was up. "Cutter is gone."

"Split?"

"Fired. Kaput."

"What did he do?"

"Nothing. I mean, he wasn't doing anything at all. Supposedly Remer got sick of not being able to get hold of him and flew out to see him face-to-face."

"Did he?"

"Well, what I heard, and this is just what is going around in the halls, is that Remer knocked on Cutter's front door for about five minutes. He heard a TV on inside. No answer though, and he's getting pissed. Then he hears a shot in the backyard. So he walks around the side of the house and there's Cutter in a lawn chair, wearing only pajamas, with a bottle of Scotch in one hand and a pistol on his lap. He's shooting at the birds that land on his bird feeder."

"What else?"

"I don't know. But I doubt you tell a man to his face that he's fired when he's got a pistol in one hand and a bottle of Scotch in the other."

Bob laughed. But his heart sank at the thought of how strung out Cutter had become.

"I would have loved to have seen that," Rick said.

"I'm not so sure I would. Not that scene anyway. He didn't get a chance to say, Take this job and shove it. He fell off the edge."

"Yeah, maybe," Rick said. "Just a sec."

Bob heard Rick cup the receiver and mumble something.

"Sorry," Rick said. "Someone looking for nostalgia research. That's a go for the quadrants, by the way. Where was I? Oh, yeah, I don't mean Cutter isn't pathetic. It's just back here, you don't see much of these guys and they remain kind of abstract. So when you hear a story like that, it borders on farce."

"None of us is too far from that."

"I'll say."

"So what will they do about the position?" Bob asked. "Cutter's?"

"Leave it open."

"Great. It's not like I don't need some help now and then. In effect, he hasn't been on the job for months. I could use some guidance."

"Cut it, Bob. You're doing better than anyone and you know it. Your reports are the only ones circulated here. Everyone reads them. That proposal on Bowling Green went right to the top. Prescott reviewed it personally."

"You're kidding? I mean, I knew one or two of them circulated. But every one?"

"Every one," Rick said. "You're the reason they won't hire a new regional manager. Remer and Coleman asked whether I would be interested in your district. They said there was no sense in hiring a new regional manager when you would be ready for the job in another six months. They want to send you to the Oxy Institute for managerial training. Theory Y. The Japanese stuff. Quality circles. All the new stuff."

"When?" Bob said, his voice sounding distant to his ears. Rick's news had caught him off guard again.

"I don't know. I told them I wanted to stay where I was. I'm starting classes in January, and I like this. They'll contact you soon. I think they're going to hire a DIC in Chicago and let you orient him there."

"Me?"

"They will bring him in for training, too. But they figure you would show the guy the ropes in the field."

Bob thanked Rick for the call and said he had to get going. He didn't want to discuss all this a moment longer, as if too much talk would make it disappear.

"Aren't you going to celebrate?"

"When it's official," Bob said.

After he hung up, he felt odd and listless. He didn't know how to act over the news. Exuberant? Or buttoned up and professional. He didn't feel capable of either extreme. He felt like spending the afternoon in bed, eating pizza and watching soap operas. But it was close to two, and he barely had time for a slice at a roadside stand if he was going to wrap things up in South Bend that day. He had a lot to tell Irene.

"What do you expect?"

"I don't know exactly. It seems they should have let me know. If they were serious."

"Maybe," Bart said and finished his soda. "Hit me again," he said as the waitress passed. "I might die if I have to drink this diet stuff for the rest of my life. I think I'll fall off the wagon around Christmas just for fun."

Bob emptied his beer and handed the glass to the waitress. It had been two weeks since Rick called him, and not a word from Coleman or Remer. He hoped Bart might have some way of putting it in the right perspective. But after a half hour of listening to his uncle, who was now on the wagon, he felt frustrated. Bart's advice was often as cryptic as it had been when he was drinking. Still, Bob wanted to hear more. Usually there was one idea in his rambling monologues that sank in, that Bob could use. That's why he had driven down from his last stop at Westland, speeding the entire trip, to catch Bart before he left Toledo.

"What's the big deal with all this Japanese stuff anyway?" Bob asked. "What have they got?"

"Productive, quality-conscious workers and paternalistic corporations."

"But what has that got to do with management? Isn't that a cultural thing?"

"To some extent, sure," Bart said. He wiped his mouth with a napkin. "There's a lot to be learned from their management techniques. Especially in manufacturing and a retailing-service business like yours. Right now the Oxy Institute has the market cornered on this training. It's the best place you could go."

"If they send me."

"That's right. All you know is your buddy back east said he heard something about it. Maybe they're waiting and watching you a little more closely. Those seminars aren't cheap."

"Since they haven't replaced my regional manager, they could look at his unused salary as paying for it."

"They probably do."

Bob scanned the room. Everyone engaged in being happy. Backs slapped. Hands shaken. Business cards swapped. Appointments registered in pocket calendars. The up-scale tavern as the archetypal business environment. "How did your trip go?"

Bart's eyebrows jumped upward a notch, and he nodded to the waitress as she brought them their drinks. "It was a breeze."

"Oh?"

"A meeting with the board of directors. A presentation of four possible acquisition opportunities and a couple of marketing ideas. They seemed quite satisfied."

"Do you get nervous about big presentations?"

"Not if I'm prepared. And for me, preparation means channeling expectations. If I told you Thanksgiving week was the warmest time of the year and you saw the flurries falling today, you would be disappointed."

"In the weather, not you."

"Unless I was the weatherman. There's a way that consultants act like weathermen. I make forecasts, and if things turn out the way I forecast, or more important, better than I forecast, I'm guru of the day."

"So don't be wrong."

Bart shook his head. "So don't create expectations you can't fulfill. It's a question of backtracking logically from what you know can be done. Say you're sure you can analyze a company's problems and provide solutions. Tell them up front that every company is unique and that a benchmark study is called for before answers can be developed. Then when you come in with the analysis, plus the solutions, you exceed expectations. Of course your fees will exceed expectations, too. If they expect the answers though, and you come back with weak stuff, you lose. Before I make a presentation, I create expectations I know I can meet."

"How can I apply this to the job?"

"You already have. You were an English major who grasped marketing—that's a surprise—and your reports exceed expectations. You're in a great position. A power position where you can leverage your career when you get the chance."

"Yeah, but how often does a chance like that come along?"

"I would guess it already has, based on what you told me about the Toledo and Bowling Green stores. And now they want you to train a guy in Chicago?"

"Only because the regional guy is gone. And besides, it's between Christmas and New Year."

"Hey, buddy, they're giving you a chance to orient a new guy. That's a helluva compliment."

Bob finished his beer. "That's what I tell Irene. She doesn't see it that way. Thinks the trip to Chicago during Christmas week is unforgivable."

Bart lit a cigarette and blew the smoke overhead. He put

his elbows on the table, cupped his hands together, the cigarette extending upward like an artificial middle finger. "It was Ted Williams," he began, "at least I believe it was Ted Williams who once was asked how he could hit with such power and still have a high average. He said something like, 'Most of the time, I swing to make contact. I suppose I'm better than most at that. But once a game, I get my home run pitch to hit—everyone gets his once a game—only I don't miss it as much as they do.'" Bart drew on his cigarette and blew the smoke upward. "You have the same opportunity," he went on. "Each week, you make contact. But once or twice a year, you get your pitch. It looks to me like this Chicago trip is the third for you in five months. Three fat home run balls. You connected on the first two. The third is Chicago. Don't miss it."

"I won't. I've got to go."

"Do you *want* to go?"

"Yeah, sure."

"Say it. Say, I *want* a chance for a promotion."

"Of course I want a promotion. It's a bad time of year, that's all. She starts grad classes in a week."

"Some unsolicited advice?" Bart snuffed his cigarette. "Don't look at the calendar, look inside yourself. Ask yourself, What do *I* want. That will keep you on the right path."

Bob slid his beer glass toward the center of the table and pulled it back, tracing the path of condensation.

"She's a girlfriend," Bart said. "And you're her boyfriend. One year from now she'll be in law school, and you can bet you won't be able to get in the way of that."

"Why does it feel like it's Irene or the job?"

"It's not. That's a false dilemma. You need to make her aware of that. That this is a special case. A special opportunity."

"I wish I could believe that. But I keep thinking they haven't gotten around to hiring a regional manager—and that's the only reason."

"That might be. But you don't know for sure. And the one thing you *do* know is that the Chicago business is important. You've got a clear shot to show them what you can do as a manager. Don't think like such a kid. Most people would drool to land a job like yours. Christ, log a year and a half with this company, fluff yourself up with an M.B.A., and you'll be knocking down a hundred grand in no time.''

Bob shrugged. ''What can I say? I feel like I can do more than I'm doing, and I don't feel like waiting.''

''That's good. You're ambitious. Anyone who isn't ambitious isn't worth a tinker's damn. But don't stop appearing patient. And most of all, don't look like you aren't enjoying yourself. That's the most successful combination in business. You look like, golly I'm having a blast at what I do, all the while wanting more.''

Bob remembered a technique he used for passing runners during cross-country and track. He held his breath and ran by them fast, fifty yards of sustained effort, as if he weren't straining at all. It broke them. The appearance of effortless, unlimited strength. He liked the idea of applying that to business, only he didn't know who he could pass.

''What are you thinking?'' Bart asked.

''I think I need to shut up and do the job. I was okay with that attitude until I heard about all this. Then I got antsy. It doesn't help that Irene seems to feel as if she wants me to spend more time with her right now.''

''Have a heart-to-heart with her. Tell her what this means in the big picture.''

Bob grinned. The big picture. That was the one he had so much trouble with himself. It was only by focusing on the little picture that he could keep his mind on work.

''Even if she doesn't understand, relax,'' Bart continued. ''You haven't made a mistake.'' He leaned over and patted the back of Bob's hand. ''I'm not trying to be too much of an intruder about this. But if a trip to Chicago Christmas week is going to wreck a relationship, something else would have anyway. Take it from me. I've messed up one myself.'' Bart finished his soda and checked his watch. ''Oh, boy,'' he said. ''Got to catch the stage coach.''

There was something at the core of Bart's advice. Something undeniable. If he was going to advance, sacrifices had to be made. Sacrifices like time together with Irene. Time for talk. Time for fun. If he didn't make those sacrifices, advancing would be much more difficult. And if he wasn't going to advance, why bother with all the bullshit in the first place. You either played to get ahead, or you didn't get in the game. He wasn't going to use his job as a holding pattern, circling law school for three years until Irene was ready to get on with her career. He had to make it happen for himself. Maybe she would come along. Maybe they would split up. Maybe she would bend to his schedule for the time being. Although, once she was in law school, that didn't seem likely.

Bart rose. "A last thought: It occurs to me that *The Art of War* could be read for advice on love. Deception, strength, the high ground—I'd say it's all there, wouldn't you?"

"Yeah," Bob said. "All there."

As Bob drove back that evening, he made up his mind to take a low-key approach to the trip. He had over a month to prepare her. Little by little, he would make her sense how important it was. Little by little, the way the flurries gathered in the rows of corn stubble stretching off on either side of Route 75. Little by little, he would make her believe it was the best thing for him.

CHAPTER

15

The low-key approach didn't develop as Bob had planned. He figured he could lay the groundwork for the Christmas trip by blaming Cutter's screwup. If he hadn't gotten himself fired, there would be no need for Bob to train a new DIC in Chicago. But Irene continued to balk.

"If it's that important," she asked, "why doesn't somebody from Boston handle it?"

Bob didn't have an answer. He heard himself say, "It's my big break, don't you see?"

"No, I don't," she said.

"If I take care of this assignment, it will make a big difference."

"For you? A big difference in the job? I'm not denying it. I'm surprised, that's all."

Bob hesitated before asking why.

"You can't be serious, can you? About this job? It's . . . it's beneath you. You're better than it."

"What should I do while you get your head together for law school? The 'tides of currency' kick? I prefer it out here. Rubbing elbows with Brent's preppy peers doesn't appeal to me. I'm good at this job. Maybe that's all I needed to know about myself. I might have been afraid at first I couldn't cut it. But I can, and I can whip almost anyone's ass at this stuff."

"Amen, and who cares."

"You ought to care. Because I can tell you almost to a dollar what you'll be blowing your big law bucks on in five years. I can read you like a clock. This business isn't trivial. It's everything. It tells me more about people than I ever got from reading literature."

"And literature tells me more about you than I ever needed to find out in person."

They sat facing each other without speaking for a long time. The room grew dark. Once it became difficult to see her eyes, he let his anger slip away and walked across the room to sit beside her.

Bob put his feet on the coffee table, his hands behind his head, and leaned back on the couch. "I'm not saying I'm searching for the cure to cancer. But this is the job I accepted, and I'm obligated to do what they ask me to do as long as I hold it. Beyond that, it's no fun if I don't try to do it well. That's what all this effort is about. For me. And if it's not for you, then I'm sorry. But how could I have known that I would throw myself into this? How does anyone know what it's going to be like when you get into something totally different from school? Nobody gives a shit about what college I went to as long as I went to one, or whether I got an *A* in some class. So everything you've spent all this time thinking is important becomes meaningless overnight. And if all you ever got praise for, or cared about getting praise for, was the way you read and wrote about books, you don't have any way to measure yourself except by a pay stub, and if that's the level I'm at, I'm barely passing. I either get better, or I'll be a Cutter in ten years."

Irene said nothing. She lit another cigarette. Bob put an arm around her shoulder and pulled her toward him. She didn't resist. "You understand me?" he asked.

"I'm afraid so," she said softly.

Christmas Day, Irene was still angry with him for leaving, despite what Bob felt was a full month of preparation. Before they opened their presents, they had breakfast together, finishing a bottle of champagne with an omelet Bob made. They called their families. By the time the champagne was gone and

the phone calls over, Irene looked gloomier than Bob had seen
her all day.

"It's not that bad," Bob said. "Lots of people work on
Christmas Day."

"Sure. Firemen. Cops. Nurses. People with something at
stake in their work. But not people like you."

"People like me travel on Christmas Day," Bob said. "Especially when there's no way to get to Chicago before eight the
next morning."

"I can't help feeling I won't have any time to see you after
the start of school," she said. "I wanted some quiet time together."

"So did I," Bob said. He had bought both of them ice
skates for Christmas. They were going to spend some time at
a lake nearby. She'd gotten him a copy of *Moby Dick* with
Rockwell Kent engravings. It had been one of his favorite books
in college. The self-destructive pursuit of transcendent truth, the
ambiguity of language. He loved thinking about that stuff back
then. But he'd spent the entire fall trying to forget it all. The
gift surprised him.

"It's beautiful," he said. "But I'm not going to grad
school, you know."

"Believe me, I know," she said. "That's why I got it.
Everything you need to know about business is in there. You've
got to go where the customers are. You've got to be efficient in
processing them. To hell with *The Art of War*. Just read *Moby
Dick* if you want to learn how to run a business. It's all in there.
It's the best thing ever written on American business. Druck-
er's a waste of time."

As they drove along Route 12, Bob gazed into the stubble
of corn and sunflower fields. This year, there was no white
Christmas. He hadn't noticed until then. He remembered seeing
snow a month before, when he saw Bart. That he wasn't disappointed felt odd suddenly. When he was young, no snow
had been a major disappointment. Now, away from family and
tree and presents, Christmas was no different from any other
day, full of its own weather, its own highs and lows, its sky
and barometric pressure, but little else. He wasn't sure he liked

that change in himself. Then again, maybe that was just another thing to get used to feeling.

They passed farm after farm, each house lighted warmly in one room, the family room. There was ice over the puddles by the side of the road. It looked cold enough. And the sun would be setting in another few minutes. Bob had forgotten how early the dark came on Christmas Day.

"Right there," Irene said, pointing straight ahead. The road dipped. Off to the side, there was a small farm pond that appeared frozen over. Bob pulled the car over and got out. He walked along the pond's edge, trying to gauge the thickness of the ice. Irene was bolder. She walked out on the ice, testing it a few feet from shore by rocking up and down. When she satisfied herself that the ice was safe, she crossed the pond quickly, sliding to a halt at the opposite shore.

"Let's try it," she said. "If we fall through, how deep can it be?"

Bob looked around. Venus shone overhead next to a sliver of the moon. The sky was still light, but not for long. "We've probably got twenty minutes to blow. You still up for it?"

Irene answered by taking off her shoes and putting on the skates. She took to her feet unsteadily and began skating. Bob went back to the car and fetched his skates. They were black hockey skates, the leather stiff and the metal runners sharp and shiny.

"How long has it been?" he asked as she skated past. "You look good."

"Once or twice in college. That's all." She wobbled and sank to a full body-skidding slide as she said this, laughing all the way down. "Not often enough."

"Wait 'til you see me," he said. "I haven't been on skates since high school."

Bob felt like a beginner. The ice was bumpy and pocked. But gradually he found the rhythm and glided cautiously toward Irene, who was trying to skate backward. She lost her footing and slid along her bottom toward the far shoreline. Bob tried to anticipate where her slide would come to a halt, cutting over the middle of the pond. He could see the water below the ice, dark, its depth unknown. He passed over a fish frozen solid. Irene wrapped her arms around her knees and waited for him.

Bob was picking up speed when his skate caught on a pocked section of ice and sent him face first down. In summer, it might have been a belly flop. The cracks appeared ahead, zigzagging in a pattern that would have been pretty if it weren't heading toward him. He turned, trying to avoid placing additional pressure on the ice, and looked behind. Sliver-like cracks were slowly moving toward him from behind, too.

"What's taking you?" Irene said. She stood up to skate toward him, but he waved her off.

"The ice. It's cracking."

She took several steps toward him and stopped. "Roll," she said. "Don't stand. Keep your skates from banging."

Bob rolled once and listened. The ice sounded as if it were wheezing faintly. He rolled again. Sky, shore, ice. Sky, shore, ice. He was within a few feet of what was certainly shallow water. He got to his knees and then stood. The ice held. He walked to shore, where Irene waited.

"Hey," he said. "Great idea, this pond."

Irene smiled and kissed him. "What are you complaining about? You lived."

"Lived to miss my plane if we don't get going."

"I hoped you wouldn't notice."

Irene was quiet the rest of the way to the airport. She kept flicking the radio, trying to find a rock station that wasn't playing "Jingle Bell Rock." When they got to the airport, Bob suggested she head back home rather than waiting with him.

"I'll call when I get there. And I'll let you know when to expect me back. It won't be bad."

Irene shook her head quickly. "I think you've got to find an easier way to make a living," she said. "There ought to be some limits in your life."

A car in back of them beeped. Bob kissed her quickly on the cheek, grabbed his suitcase, and shut the door. "I'll call, sweetheart," he said through the glass. She nodded and drove off.

Bob tried to put that nod out of his mind as he headed toward his flight gate. He didn't need to ask a lot of questions, to wonder about what was going on. He needed to be more mechanical for once. All he needed to know was that he had received a vote of confidence that would be envied by any other DIC. Every time he recalled Irene's words, "afraid so," and how he let it go, how he didn't say a word, not even so much as a vague question, every time he started to rip himself up with what she might have meant, he reminded himself how glad anyone he worked with would be to hop on this plane in his place. He was the lucky one. Don't blow their confidence, he told himself. Do it well, don't gripe, and look ahead to a promotion, even if it took a year to get. His own thoughts were a pale imitation of the flatter locker-room speeches he had heard in high school. But it worked. Stanislavsky said, "Find the art in yourself, not yourself in art." This was a role he could perform.

At the very least, management would be even more aware of him. Billie Coleman was flying in the last day to monitor the field training. And Bob wanted to make sure that he took a report of his good work back with him to Boston.

CHAPTER

16

It didn't feel like the opportunity of a lifetime. Four days in Chicago, and the snow hadn't stopped since Bob stepped off the plane Christmas afternoon. Riding the El out to Evanston with Mike Wong, the Loyola graduate he was training as a district inventory coordinator, Bob couldn't ignore the squat old bag lady sitting next to them. "I told them it was coming," she began saying. "They didn't pay any attention, but look now. I told 'em and look at it now." She repeated this until Bob nodded to Wong that it was time to change seats.

"You're not used to Chicago, are you?" Wong asked.

According to Wong's résumé, he had grown up in Chicago, the son of Chinese immigrants. Management back east loved the idea of hiring a minority. Bob didn't understand why Chinese were considered a minority when there were more of them in the world than anyone else. Wong's parents owned four restaurants in the Chicago area.

"There are hundreds of old ladies like her in this town," Wong was saying. "You pretend they don't exist. That's what everyone does."

When he and Wong got off at Evanston, Bob looked around for a cab, and, seeing none, cursed. "I'm sick about your car," he said.

"Don't think about it," Wong said. "What you did was

probably a damn sight better than I would have done if I'd been trying to drive."

After a long night of drinking, Bob had scraped and dented the right side of Wong's Rabbit on a parked flower delivery truck. The roads were slick. In four days, he'd seen only one truck with a plow, and that one didn't appear to be operating. With six inches of fluffy snow falling daily, the accumulation was substantial, and along the streets it compressed into tiny glacieresque obstacles and deep slippery ruts. The body shops where they took the car that morning estimated the damage at six hundred dollars.

Mike stood on the El platform, catching a few of the larger flakes and dabbing them in his eyes. Bob took this as a sign that a short break was in order.

"Let's grab a coffee before we find out where the hell store five is," Bob said.

"And a seltzer," Mike said. "I feel like a leprechaun has been urinating in my mouth all night."

"*Lucky Jim*, right?" Bob said. Mike nodded. He was the first person that Bob had met in the company who was well read and enjoyed talking about books. They passed the time driving between stores, talking about novels or stories. The night of the fender bender and paint scrapes, they had gone drinking after a staged reading of *A Child's Christmas in Wales* by a group of actors in a bar near the Loyola campus.

Bob found a message from the office when he got back from the bar: Coleman was coming in the next day. That surprised Bob. And then he got angry. Why? To take over the training? To take away the chance he had to prove what he could do? But after a minute, he calmed down. Coleman wouldn't bother with the trivia of training. This would be perfect. He was there to watch Bob, not to train Wong.

Bob let Wong know that Coleman would be in town earlier than expected.

"Don't let Billie fool you," Bob advised him. "All the gestures, all the silly talk, ignore it and concentrate on business."

"I still don't understand how a guy with the title of national sales manager could spell his name like that."

"You will when you meet him," Bob said.

Mike pressed Bob to tell him more about Coleman. But Bob decided it would be wiser to let Mike define his own relationship with Coleman. There was only one fair thing he could say: "Just don't try to drink with the guy. You won't be able to keep up. And for all you know, he's looking to see whether you'll make a fool of yourself. Managers play strange games sometimes. Never drink with one."

"I can't keep up with you. I wouldn't even try to keep up with him if you couldn't."

They finished their coffee, called a taxi, and found their way to the storefront that P&V had rented in downtown Evanston. Their job was to give the P&V PROVE lecture to the new employees. This was something Bob had thought of himself, and management loved it. They had asked every DIC in the company for a theme for their Chicago media blitz. Bob wrote a twenty-page memo (dangerously long, but, following a suggestion from Bart, Bob gave the memo the impressive title White Paper, making it immune to rejection by the company M.B.A.s). First he proposed that they run music from the song "Chicago Is My Kind of Town," changing the "my" to "our" and finishing up with the P&V logo turning into PROVE. The jingle went, "Chicago is our kind of town, we'll PROVE it. Your kind of price, we'll PROVE it. Your kind of value, we'll PROVE it." Then the music went under and there was a donut for the weekly specials, finishing up with a booming, "Chicago, Chicago, our kind of town!" P&V logo up and fade out. He concluded, "There will be a synergy of promotion and training, learning and pride that will give this group the skills and enthusiasm to make an unforgettable impression on our first Chicago customers."

What really sold management on the idea was using PROVE as an acronym to train the new employees into the P&V system. Mike and he met with groups of the new employees and drilled them on the fundamentals of interaction with customers: First, P-robe to find out what they're looking for; R-espond to those needs; O-vercome any objections to the merchandise recommended; V-erify that the customer has made a smart choice by citing other satisfied customers or the quality of the product; E-xit the customer into the checkout line before he can put the merchandise back.

Mike couldn't believe that people made a living thinking up such nonsense. Bob assured him that they not only did, but that they also put themselves in line for promotion.

"If you say so," Mike said. "Still, I didn't think I went to college just to earn a living psyching up a bunch of high school dropouts."

"I know," Bob said. "But try to think of it as giving these people remedial job training."

"You don't believe that."

Bob smiled without answering. Of course he didn't *believe* it. But he knew it worked. For him and in the eyes of management. The fact that it worked went against many of the things he had always believed were true or wanted to hold as values. *Lucky Jim* wasn't any help in straightening out store inventory problems or in rallying new employees behind the neon aegis of P&V's corporate philosophy.

"You can't tell me everyone in corporate America is obsessed with this," Mike continued. "I was thinking about getting an M.B.A. There's got to be more to it."

"What exactly were you expecting?" Bob said. "Most M.B.A. programs would jump at an applicant with this kind of experience. You've been in the trenches. You're a soldier. Not some novice." He almost gagged at the sound of his voice.

"Well, right now, it's making my headache worse," he said, draining a glass of Bromo Seltzer. "I can't imagine Coleman getting into this, from the little I've spoken with him."

"Are you kidding?" Bob said. "He sent a letter congratulating me for the PROVE training concept."

By the time they finished their coffee and flagged down a cab, Bob's head hurt. He watched Mike, who had his eyes shut and his head leaning against the window. The back of Mike's hand still bore the orange stamp of the bar they'd been at the night before.

Bob leaned his head back and shut his eyes, trying to relax. There was music coming from the speakers at the back of the cab. An ad came on: The voice of a man introduced himself as vice president of retail sales for Biggy Value. "We're committed to parents with younger children," he said. "That's why we're holding our annual Teddy Bear Fair this winter. Teddy

Bear Fair is a way that Biggy Savings shows you that you save in a biggy way when you shop at Biggy Savings. . . .''

Bob thought of Bart's advice: think of business problems as a disease to diagnose and treat. What are its symptoms? Everywhere Bob drove in his territory, he felt there was a more fundamental disease, which he couldn't begin to identify. One that made all the other diseases possible. Teddy Bear Fair was a symptom. So was PROVE. The symptoms were everywhere he looked. Only two things were certain: that he was a carrier of the disease and that his career could easily reach a new level of reward if he simply developed more ideas as well-received as PROVE. There was a big payoff for ignoring the disease. Because people, as the P&V management continually hammered into its DICs, were the key to success in the service business. Figure out how to keep underpaid, undereducated people highly motivated without the prospect of being promoted beyond the confines of their small workplaces, and there was plenty of money to be made. That was the secret of success in the fast-food business. And it was true of the legions of computer screen operators at the end of every toll-free phone number, or in every bank and insurance company. Once you engendered a sense of mission in each person charged with repeating menial tasks all day, you were ready for all the laurels America could bestow. Prescott had made the front cover of *Business Week* as one of America's top-compensated executives, and his philosophy of business (that decision making should be ''cascaded'' to the lowest level of responsibility) received a special sidebar presentation.

Bob saw how he was of two minds about it. Take the money if it were there and live as well as you could in a disease-ridden system, or draw the line for yourself, no matter how pointless moral stands had become. Irene favored the latter. But at the moment, he was taking it, if only to prove he could do it. How he had come to love the sound of that indefinite pronoun. If you've got it, flaunt it. Do it. Make it. Go for it. You could project anything into an indefinite pronoun. ''It'' was the American Dream. You name it, it's yours. All you've got to do is work for it. If you've got it, it'll show. Bob believed he had it, even if he wasn't so sure he liked it. That's the way it was.

*   *   *

When Bob unlocked and swung open the door to his room at The Palmer House that night, he felt as if he'd opened an oven. He kept the door to the hallway open, assuming the temperature would even out, but it didn't. Waves of dry heat swelled around him. So he opened the window, which offered a horizon of other rooms and a dark air shaft that he was cheered to assume opened at some point to the sky overhead, since the space was filled with oversized, fluffy flakes. He stuck his head out the window and tried to catch a glimpse of the sky overhead, but saw nothing except other windows, some lighted, others dark. Below, the view was equally opaque. He cleared his throat and spit, listening to the night sounds of Chicago going on outside the perimeter of this odd space. He spit again, half-expecting to hear someone below shout in anger. But all he could hear were the beeps of cars and cabs, the wail of a siren, and an odd swishing that seemed to underlay all other sounds. It might have been the El, or the wind, or somewhere to the east, the dark waters of Lake Michigan. It was lulling, and reminded him of being somewhere else, although he couldn't say where. He pulled his head back in and walked over to the door. He looked up and down the hallway. It was empty. He chained the door, leaving it open a crack to permit the cold air to blow through the room, sucking in a few flakes along the way.

As Bob turned from the door to call house maintenance about the thermostat he noticed that the message light on the phone was blinking. He hoped that Irene had called. He'd spoken with her only once since he'd been in Chicago. While he waited for the desk to retrieve the message, he considered what he might say to her.

"Your message, sir," the clerk said, "is from Mr. Coleman, who asks that you make appropriate reservations for dinner at Lawry's and for later at Rick's Cafe."

"What is Rick's Cafe?" Bob asked.

"It's a jazz club in the Holiday Inn on Lake Shore Drive. Pretty nice, really. Would you like me to call in your reservations?"

Bob waited for the clerk to call back. When the phone rang, he asked, "We all set?"

There was a silence.

"Who were you expecting?" It was Irene.

Bob stammered through an explanation about the reservations. He paused between thoughts, listening for some clue to her mood. There was none. He finished up by saying, "So, you see, that's all it was."

"You sound like a guilty little kid," she said. "What have you been doing in Chicago?"

"It's too boring to describe. Typical company stuff." Hearing himself say this, Bob imagined saying these words for the rest of his life. It would be his refrain to his wife, whether or not she was Irene.

"When are you coming back?"

"The day after tomorrow. When Coleman leaves. He'll tour the stores quickly and be gone. That's it."

"You promise? We have a lot to talk about. Plans to make . . ."

She paused, waiting, he suspected, for him to ask what plans she had in mind. He wouldn't bite.

"You know my situation," he said.

"I don't like living with a traveling salesman. You're not the person you were."

Bob cupped the receiver and exhaled slowly. "I'm not a salesman, dammit, Irene. I've told you that. And every time you talk to one of your friends, that's what you call me."

"You're playing word games. Okay, you're not *a* salesman. All I know is you're on the road all the time and I'm in a stupid little town in this stupid little apartment."

Bob ground the earphone of the receiver against his ear. Whenever they argued, this was the path they took. What he couldn't understand was why she chose to move to the countryside in the first place. If she wanted peace and quiet in the country, what did she think that felt like after a little while? Of course it was lonesome.

"Bob? . . ."

"What."

"I feel like I need to talk with you about everything. I need to know where you stand."

"Stand on what?"

"Not over the phone. No more of this on the phone. Our

bills are high enough, and all we do is argue. I need to talk with you in person.''

"Yeah, okay," Bob said. "But what's so big about this that we can't talk over the phone."

"You don't understand, do you? You talk about my life like it was an inventory problem." The tone of her voice shifted into sarcasm. "Not sold on Sterne? Let's check the mix of emotions and see if any adjustments are necessary. Let's try a new facade. Let's make an effort to PROVE what this town can do.''

Bob was no longer angry. He was cold. The air from the open window had cooled down the room. He could see his breath.

"Okay, Irene," he said, moving his free hand through the vortex of his own breath. "In person, you got it."

"I've 'got it.' Right? Bingo, another score for the big DIC . . .''

"Knock it off. Who do you think you're talking to? One of those machines from an M.B.A. program? Who am I to you?"

"I don't know who you are. A voice on the phone. Someone who comes and goes. A presence. Not a person."

"All right, all right. So what's the bottom line here?''

"There is no 'bottom line.' Just this: We talk when you get home the day after tomorrow."

"I don't like ultimatums," Bob said.

"It's not an ultimatum," she said. "It's just to let you know I don't want to spend the weekend going to movies and eating dinner at nice restaurants and having Monday roll around before we realize we haven't said a single serious word to each other all weekend."

"Irene, can't we talk now?''

"No, Bob, no more negotiating on this. I need to talk with you in person, okay?''

"Okay, Irene."

"Bye."

"Don't hang up."

"I hope everything goes well for you. Really."

A click and the phone went dead. Bob sat there, watching the small plumes of breath emerging from his mouth. He hung up the phone and got under the covers. His tie hung over a chair. It looked like a schoolboy's tie. He turned off the light and listened. Cold air moved in and out of the room, pushing the door against the jamb and then sucking it back until the chain stopped it. In-out, in-out. The rhythmical breathing of some great beast. A man passing the door complained of the cold air to a woman who giggled and said, "I'll warm you up."

Bob sat in the dark for a long time before he noticed that the message light was still blinking. He assumed the clerk had forgotten to turn it off. He called down.

"Did you forget to turn off the message light to room six twenty-three?"

"No, sir," the clerk said. "Wanted to let you know your reservations are confirmed. That's all. Rick's Cafe at eleven, the start of the second show."

"Who's playing?"

"Can't say. I could call and find out if you wish."

Bob told him not to bother. When he hung up the phone, he left his clothes in a heap by the bed, lowered the window partway and shut the door to the hallway. He would go to sleep listening to the swishing sound still coming from the dark of the shaft. But when he lay down, he couldn't get to sleep. He picked up the phone. He wanted to call someone. Anyone. He needed to talk. He dialed his father's number. It would be ten in Connecticut.

After a few rings, his father answered.

"Dad? It's Bob."

"Hey, how are you?"

"All right. I'm in Chicago."

"Chicago? Not bad. Guess what? Your little brother made it back finally on Christmas Day night."

"I bet you're having fun."

"Chicago can't be that tough. You can have a heck of a time there, I bet."

Bob's father loved the idea that his job permitted him to travel. To him, it was like the army with none of the problems of the army. Paid meals at fancy restaurants. Good hotels. Interesting sights. "Yeah, I've been having a good time. I'm training a new guy and we're opening five new stores. It's busy."

"Don't forget to smell the roses," he said. "Don't work all night."

Bob thought about Mike's car. "Naw, I'm getting out around the town, too."

"That's the spirit. Enjoy yourself. You're young enough."

"I think Irene wishes I weren't out so much."

"She's got to understand. When you're on the road there's nothing else to do."

"No, I meant being out on the road itself. The job."

"Yeah, exactly. It's the job. She's got to understand that. That's where your money comes from. We can't all have it from the family."

"She's not like that. She'd just rather see a little more of me."

"Sure, that's sweet. But you've got to do what you've got to do, right?"

Everything was so simple. There wasn't any use in trying to talk about it. "I guess."

"Don't guess. It's a fact." From somewhere in his father's room, Bob heard his mother saying, "Merry Christmas, sweetie." And then Carl urging his father to turn the phone over to him.

"A fact?"

"You bet it is."

"Yeah," Bob said. "I suppose you're right."

"Hey, you son of a bitch," his father said to Carl. "Get your hands out of my pockets. I'll swat you. I'm giving him the phone, Bob, before he rapes me."

Bob couldn't think of what to say on the spot. When he did speak, he sounded as though he was talking to someone presumed dead. "Carl?"

"Hi."

"Hi? How about 'how are you?' "

"I'm sure you're doing great," Carl said. "You usually do."

If Bob could have punched the phone and had Carl feel it, he would have. "Don't be that way," he said.

"I didn't mean it the way it came out. I meant I've heard a lot about you since I've been back. It sounds like things are going great."

"Yeah, they're good."

"I'm glad for you. Maybe you'll turn out to be some marketing maven. Who-da-thunk-it?"

Bob wrapped the cord around his wrist as if he planned to use the receiver like a cop's club. He tapped the side of his head with it. "I never cease to amaze myself," he said in feigned boredom. "I admit I like the job."

"Good. I hope I'm lucky enough to find something I like doing."

"Get an early start if you're talking about a job."

"Naw," Carl said. "I'm going to steer clear of that for a while. I want to try a few other things first."

Bob wanted to ask, Like what? But he didn't ask. Because he didn't want to know. That might make things sour a bit for him. "Hey," he said. "I don't want to cut you off, but I have a long day tomorrow. The VP for sales is coming in and wants to see what I've been up to."

"The VP? Better get some shut-eye."

Bob tried to read more into Carl's reply than he knew he should. "Yeah, it's late." He had Carl say good-bye to everyone and hung up.

"Lawry's," Coleman said and laughed, pausing only long enough to take his first sip from the extra-dry Tanqueray martini he'd ordered. " 'Don't they make seasoned salt?' Oh, Bob, you are a stitch. That's good. Really good."

Coleman's squealing laughter attracted the attention of people sitting nearby. Just before he laughed, Coleman cocked his head back, as if he had something caught in his throat. His mouth opened, and after another pause, his laugh began, his head dropping in a series of measured hitches until he ran out of breath.

Coleman made the waiter return his martini, saying, "That's not *dry*, my dear man, D-R-Y as in desert dry." He turned to Bob and said, "You can't get a decent martini west of the Mississippi, can you?"

"Actually, the Mississippi is farther west," Bob said quietly. He wasn't trying to show up Coleman.

Coleman cocked his head back and screeched. "Is that so? I thought it went right through Chicago. Oh, dear, just imagine

what a martini's like farther west. Probably tastes like Kool-
Aid.''

Mike looked at Bob as if to say, What have you gotten me
into? Bob wasn't so sure he could answer that question. By the
time Coleman had arrived at the lobby of The Palmer House,
he was obviously half-drunk. Bob tried to see Coleman as he
imagined Mike saw him: a small, almost petite balding man
wearing a pink Brooks Brothers shirt that appeared so large it
looked as if someone had squeezed it inside his jacket. His
monogrammed cuff links clacked on the tabletop each time he
reached for his drink, as if dragging his arms down. His hands,
tiny as birds' feet, almost seemed too small to grasp the glass.
He palmed it to his mouth in a quick, agile movement, obviously well practiced, the drink swishing to the edge but never
spilling.

Coleman chuckled to himself as he started in on his extra-
rare prime rib, a piece of meat so large it overlapped his plate.
Bob and Mike had finished their entrées half an hour ago while
Coleman filled them in on his career.

"I made my reputation at the Coop," he had said between
martinis. "The Harvard Coop, you know." He paused until
Wong nodded, and continued: "Those were the days. Went to
work in cutoffs. In jeans when the weather was nasty. Now
look at me . . ." He held up his arms as if he were a reluctant
but undeniably classy testimonial to corporate fashions. "Anyway, the Coop was still in its Che Guevara phase, as I called
it. Everyone was so ideological in those days. It was good business for a while. But I finally convinced the manager to start
selling some other merchandise—T-shirts with college logos,
mugs, window stickers—I advertised the stuff. Well, first thing
you know, the manager woke up and tore out the left wing—
get it . . ." He cocked his head back for one squeak and went
on. "The whole literal fuckin' left wing was turned over to me.
The Globe covered the change as a sign of the times. And my
name caught the eye of Warner Prescott, and he had only five
Boston-area P&Vs at the time, so I got on board at the right
time. That's who I am—lifestyles of the rich and ripped I call
it.''

Coleman tugged at the waiter's elbow as he passed.

"We're getting closer," he said, waving his empty glass. "Let's try again. Practice, practice, practice."

The waiter stared without expression at Coleman. "Would the gentlemen care for a drink?"

Bob and Mike declined.

"If you're not going to drink with me at least have the good sense to order dessert," Coleman said. "Go ahead. I'm paying. And I'll catch up yet. You've never seen anyone who can eat raw meat as fast as I can."

Coleman said this so loudly that he was overheard by a group of men at the next table. They laughed at him. When the waiter left with their orders, he continued.

"A bunch of tractor salesmen, no doubt," Coleman said. "I'm telling you every time I fly into O'Hare I half expect to see Marshal Dillon greeting visitors and asking them to check in their six-shooters. The town's got a frontier quality to it that horrifies me, yet I keep coming back for more. And I love Lawry's."

"What's the agenda for tomorrow?" Bob asked.

"Always all business, Bob, my boy?" Coleman said. "Lighten up. But, if you insist, there is more to my trip than simply a desire to meet my first DIC of the Oriental persuasion."

Bob watched Mike's eyes for a sign of what he was thinking. They betrayed no contempt for Coleman. He'd succeed in the company. Bob was certain now.

"Bob, you're the experienced one here," Coleman said. "In which aisle do you find men and women's grooming products?"

"Shampoos, face creams, and lotions?"

"Yes, dear, the stuff you obviously avoid."

"Aisle one, of course. That's the company layout."

"Right. It has been the company layout. But that's going to change. We're going to conduct an experiment with our new Chicago stores. A little brainstorm of mine. I call it the gauntlet. You know, after that dreadful Clint Eastwood movie?"

Bob and Mike shook their heads.

"Oh, you must see it. You must." Coleman started on his new martini. "Anyway, my idea is to split our grooming products—men's shampoos on one side, women's on the other. But women's face creams will be beside men's shampoo, and men's shaving stuff next to women's shampoo. Typically, a customer buys toiletries and grooming supplies as multiple purchases—face cream, shampoo, and conditioner. Research tells us that this customer comes to the store not to shop randomly but to get those specific items. By splitting them on opposite sides of the store, I force that customer to take a walk. A walk across my gauntlet: the new impulse zone. Or, as I call it back in Boston, son of impulse zone.'' Coleman hooted and continued. ''Just when you thought it was safe to buy conditioner—bum, bum, bum, bum-bum-bum. You cross a center aisle crammed with the unavoidable discounts that leap into your arms. No shopper will resist. I'm playing a hunch it can boost our sales of specials in a big way. But what I'm asking you to do is re-organize those stores before they open next week. That means opening up the gauntlet aisle—making it wider—and splitting the inventory as I've described it. It's a lot of work, but I'm banking on it being worthwhile. Have to catch a flight tomorrow, but I'll work with you two at the first store and you can handle the others, one day at a time after that.''

Bob must have looked as rotten as he felt. Coleman responded to him.

''Look, Bob, I know you flew out here on Christmas Day and you're undoubtedly sick of Chicago—but for just a few more days I'm asking you to be my tiger.''

''It's that I promised I'd be back the day after tomorrow. My girlfriend will be upset. That's all.''

Coleman waved one hand, as if he were excited, his other palming the martini to his mouth. ''Poor baby,'' he said, but without the usual attendant sarcasm. ''She'll discover all businesses are like that. Long lunches and expensive suits, golf and boating, exotic trips for sales conferences, too much drinking, oversleeping, spending more than you earn. But that's what keeps us going, too. You keep reaching for more just the way I'm asking for you to reach for more now. You'll learn to walk the tightrope with her, you'll see. Because she'll start to love the money. They all do. And you'll find the best moments of all are right out here, watching your good ideas work and watching yourself pull down the loot.'' Coleman cocked his head back and laughed, his highest-pitched, longest laugh of the night. "Oh, God, oh, God. Will you listen to me?" He put his fork and knife down. "If you don't do it for that, do it for the Gipper, right?" He patted the back of Bob's hand. "You'll work it out. The best ones always make the right choices. And I think you're one of the best."

Bob didn't cringe to hear that. He liked how Coleman didn't seem to give orders as if he were in the marines: "Do this or else." Coleman preferred to manage by sharing an idea like the one for his gauntlet and then giving you room to implement it. If you did it well, he gave you credit. If you didn't, he either marked you for firing or let it slide, your prospects for promotion permanently diminished. This was Bob's big test. Chicago was his project, Mike his DIC to train, PROVE his promotional and training idea, and the "gauntlet" his merchandising concept to implement. He felt bad about Irene, but this trip was too loaded with opportunities to be compromised. He felt just as he used to at the start of a cross-country race: nervous in a good way, eager to be tested, confident of success.

On the way to Rick's Cafe, Coleman sat between Bob and Mike in the cab's backseat. "I make no bones about it," he was saying, "I tell all our new people these are the sacrifices you're asked to make once in a while." He patted Bob's shoulder. "But there's money, extra money for the ones that give me that effort. A lot of extra money. Double your salary in bonus. That's what it has been for the inner circle of the best DICs. But enough of the shoptalk. It's the time of night to hoot and holler. And I've got a treat for you at Rick's Cafe. Don't you love the name? You probably know it, don't you, Mike?"

"Not really," he said. "I've never been there."

"It's a fine jazz club. A fine one. And Marian McPartland is playing there tonight."

"Who?" Bob asked.

"Oh, my word, you don't know . . ." Coleman looked at Bob in the dim glow of streetlights and headlights. "You don't know her, do you? She is an angel. An angel on the piano. One of the luminaries of our age. I haven't seen her in years."

Rick's Cafe was right off the lobby of a typical Holiday Inn, but it was classier than the typical lounge. Multileveled, with a modest number of tropical artifacts—palms, sandy gardens, ceiling fans wheeling nostalgically away. Waiters wearing white jackets and bow ties took the drink orders just before Marian McPartland came out for her second show.

"How I love that Frenchman in *Casablanca*," Coleman said. "He makes one of the greatest linguistic faux pas in film history. You know, he says, 'Rick drinking with the clientele? There's another precedent broken.' I mean, of course, one doesn't break precedents. One sets them. I love it." He cocked his head back and laughed, attracting the attention of couples at the neighboring tables.

When McPartland began playing, Coleman sat back, sipping his drink in silence. Between every two or three songs, Coleman ordered fresh drinks. As McPartland finished playing "You Turned the Tables on Me," Coleman turned to Mike and Bob and said, "I just died and went to heaven." After the final number, "I'll Be Around," she stood up and bowed, and Coleman leaned toward them again, opening his mouth to speak but saying nothing. He clapped with a slow, clumsy enthusiasm, finally uttering "On . . . on . . . core. Say it, for godssake."

Bob and Mike clapped and chanted "encore." With the rest of the audience doing the same, they didn't feel foolish. McPartland reappeared. The audience gave her an intense burst of applause. She sat down again and went into a medley of "Yesterdays" and "Yesterday." At its conclusion, Coleman stood, wavering, clapping as loudly as his small hands permitted. "Lady," he said, waving to Marian McPartland, who smiled at him, "I just died and went to heaven." Coleman didn't so much sit as fall back into his chair, his eyes shut, his tiny double chin dropped to his shirt. "She smiled at me," he said.

People at the next table chuckled. Bob nudged him in the shirt, eventually making contact with his arm, but Coleman didn't move.

"What?" Mike asked. "Billie passed out? Another precedent broken?"

"Yeah," Bob said. "Let's go. He'll catch up with us tomorrow."

"I don't know about that. My folks would never leave someone at a bar in one of their restaurants like this."

Bob thought about it for a moment and agreed. As discreetly as they could, they lifted Coleman by the arms until he revived enough to walk. He was quick to recover and soon made his way on his own. "You two are my guardian angels tonight," he said as they took him back to The Palmer House. "But be ready for Billie the Tiger tomorrow."

At the end of the next day, Mike drove Coleman out to the airport. Bob sat in back, listening as Coleman explained why he saw his gauntlet as the idea that would push P&V over the top in Chicago. They had spent the entire morning and part of the afternoon working with a confused, mutinous staff at store one rearranging the inventory to Coleman's satisfaction. Mike and Bob would bring the remaining managers over the next day to show them the changes firsthand and then help with the implementation over the following days. Everything had to be completed by the January second opening. Bob would have to be there until then.

While Mike was double-parked out front, Bob tried the pay phone in the airport lobby to call Irene and tell her he wouldn't be back. It was only four o'clock, but he couldn't get through to her. When a cop began tapping on Mike's car for him to move, Bob hung up.

"My folks want us to eat at their restaurant tonight—on the house," Mike said when Bob got in the car. "I'll get you a fake receipt for the meal."

Bob smiled at Mike. He'd be fun to work with. They joked about Coleman as they drove back into Chicago, but also allowed that he had a kind of genius. The gauntlet was bound to work, Bob told Mike. It had all the characteristics of a successful merchandising concept: simplicity, exposure, consistency, and incentive. Week after week, the gauntlet would prove the undoing of thousands of shoppers for grooming products. At the downtown P&Vs, they'd find themselves impulsively buying three-packs of dish soap, cans of minestrone soup, and combo packs of laundry detergent and fabric softener; at the southside one, it would be cans of okra, three-packs of hair straightener, and repackaged Halloween candies; in Evanston, Redken Mousse With Hair Muscle Number 4, Day-Glo stripes for joggers, miniature TVs from Korea, and eight-packs of cassettes.

After drinks and dinner, Mike suggested they finish off the evening at a piano bar off Michigan Avenue. Bob offered to treat, since he had a receipt worth $73.89 for dinner. The bar was warm and quiet for the first hour. Mike and Bob went over the day's work.

The bar started to fill up. The piano player, an older man with a goatee, invited people to choose songs to sing. He started off by performing several Tom Lehrer songs, including "The Old Dope Peddler." A chubby schoolteacher from Des Moines attending a convention sang "Misty." Her friend sang "Yellow Submarine" and got the rest of the teachers at the table to join in. The scene was amusing but friendly, and Bob was enjoying himself. He and Mike switched to brandy. When the waitress, wearing a scarlet vest, brought a second snifter for each of them, Mike put his hand on Bob's arm.

"Have you been watching the waitress?" he asked.

"No, why?"

"Watch her."

The waitress cleared the glasses from an empty table. She cleared the tray behind the bar, saving herself one unfinished drink, which she then drank quickly, looking around to see if anyone noticed. She didn't see them watching.

"What manner of person is she?" Mike asked slowly.

Bob glanced at Mike to see what kind of question that was before realizing that he was simply well on his way to being drunk.

"I'd say she lives alone above a neighborhood drugstore just north of here," Mike said, as if he intended to find out.

"Naw," Bob said, trying to lighten things up. "Creatures like her are part of a pack—a pack of booze hounds—a special breed."

"I'll have to study up on the sociology of the adult barroom for this job," Mike said, his eyelids drooping. He leaned back in his chair and shut them. Bob was about to suggest they leave when a commotion broke out at the bar.

"Out of my way, back off," an old man was saying.

The crowd parted to let the old man through. He wore a tatty overcoat and thin tie, and looked as if he might be a street person.

"What'll it be tonight, Rex?" the piano player asked.

"Same as always, William," he said, propping himself with one hand on the piano, his other holding a draft high over his head. "Let her go."

The piano player began with a flourish, leading into a melody Bob had heard before but couldn't quite place. The room grew hushed, and as the song came 'round again, the old man sipped on his beer, cleared his throat, and began singing "Good Night, Irene." His voice was surprisingly steady and strong, the way Bob remembered the crooners from his father's old 78s. Bob looked over at Mike to see if he understood the irony of this one song, but he was fast asleep. The old man sang verse after verse. Bob closed his eyes and sipped his brandy, trying to fight the impulse to become maudlin.

As the old man sang the chorus the crowd joined in, filling the room with a uniform reverberation that left Bob feeling completely alone. He was selfish not to have called Irene. A fool. The guilt stung. He hoped, how he hoped, she was still awake. He rubbed his eyes, stood, and cleared his throat. It was a little after midnight, one back in Michigan. He decided to try her.

"Good night, everybody," the old man said, waving as he walked out to the applause of everyone at the bar.

There was a pay phone at the back of the bar. Bob slipped in a quarter and told the operator the information for calling collect. The phone in Michigan began ringing just as the red-vested waitress moved toward their table. He still had half a glass of brandy sitting there. When the phone rang for the third time, Bob hung up.

CHAPTER

17

B ob took the shuttle from the airport and arrived at the Michigan Union in the early afternoon. He had been in Chicago for ten days. Irene had already started school and said she would meet him after her Constitutional history class let out at four. It was now five.

He wasn't good at waiting. He had been to the bookstore, a coffee shop, and read the sports pages of three different newspapers. He had no money left and no book to read. The crisp creases of his dress pants had gone soft, and the blue Oxford shirt, his favorite of the three he brought to Chicago, had taken on an oily shapelessness and pungency. Ordinarily he didn't think his sweat smelled much, and more often than not, didn't bother with deodorants. But after the extended stay, sustained on fatty, rich food, his body signaled its rebellion with odd scents and irregular bowels. Pacing the lobby, his back itching, he wished he had gotten around to laundering his stuff at The Palmer House. It was a legitimate expense. The next time, he would know better.

Bob had tried to anticipate Irene's response. But at last he gave up. Anticipating her different forms of anger became worse than suffering any one of them.

"Well, the company man cometh."

Bob sat upright. He hadn't seen Irene coming. "Hi," he said, and stood to kiss her. She blocked his advance.

"You're going to have to earn these lips."

"I missed you," he said.

"Sure you did," Irene said, leading the way.

"Do we have time for dinner?" Bob asked. "I'm really hungry."

"I can't. Not tonight."

"Maybe a pizza on the way out."

"All right. That's a possibility."

Bob followed, not knowing where she had parked the car. The air was icy cold and still. As she walked the puffs of her breath billowed off to her side until they disappeared. The cold stung his nose and throat. He had been inside heated rooms and heated cars for too long.

When they got to the car Irene started it and sat in the driver's seat, staring straight ahead and not speaking. Today she wasn't going to let Bob drive. That was okay. He just wished she would unlock the passenger-side door. He knocked at the window.

"Oh," she said and leaned across to flip it open.

Bob tossed his suitcase in back. Irene continued to stare. He began to feel uncomfortable. "I was expecting you around four," he said, trying to sound indifferent.

"It's not that easy to wait, is it?"

"No, I guess not."

"There are so many people who are going to law school in this class they treat it the same way. Some of them set up a study group and invited me when they found out I was starting law school in the fall. Today we divided up assignments after class."

The front window began to frost. "How's it going?" he asked.

Irene clicked on the blowers and put the car into gear. "It's going," she said. "I don't know where. The students are very competitive, and there is an awful lot of work. Nothing like undergraduate school."

"How many in the study group?"

"Six, including me. All of them are older. One has a Ph.D. in something."

"Sounds like a good group."

"It seems so. But being a good group means each of us doing lots of work. You know, 'the chain is only as strong' stuff."

Bob scratched the frost off the side window. "Hey, we missed the pizza place."

Irene brought the car to a stop and threw it into reverse, an oncoming car blaring its horn as it passed. She swung quickly into the lot and came to a crunching halt in a snow bank.

"You okay?" Bob asked.

"Fine."

"Do you want me to drive?"

She shook her head. "The pizza."

"I need money."

Irene threw him a twenty-dollar bill. "Something to drink, too."

Bob started to ask if she wanted to come in, too, but she already had a book open on her lap.

Bob sat without talking all the way back to Sterne, the pizza slowly cooling on his legs, the bag with a six-pack propped between his feet. When they pulled into Charlie and Rita's driveway, Bob turned to Irene.

"I'll run this up and stick it in the oven if you bring in my bag."

"I've got books, too."

"Sure, forgot. I'll come back."

Bob jogged up the walk and up the stairs. When he opened the door to the apartment, a gust of cold air rushed across his face. A window must have been left open a crack. He walked quickly to the kitchen in the dark, knowing the way without lights. He turned the oven on to warm and slid in the pizza. Then he flicked on the kitchen light and headed back into the living room. Irene had turned on a lamp, and what he saw turned his stomach. Next to the front door were five or six boxes, stacked and taped. Notes in felt pen on the sides indicated the contents.

"What is this?" Bob asked.

"Why don't you get your stuff, and we'll talk."

Bob couldn't think of anything to say at the moment. So

he went to the car. He tried to imagine another explanation for the boxes other than the obvious one. But there was none. She was leaving. Why hadn't she warned him. A rotten trick. She could have said something, anything on the drive back. He slipped on a patch of ice as he pulled his bag from the back-seat, his pants tearing at the knee on the metal of the car. How could she do this? Just because the company told him to stay in Chicago? Because he tried hard at his job? The whole thing stunk. As he climbed the stairs with the suitcase draped over his shoulder he fought an impulse to yell, and then one to cry. When he opened the door, he summoned his best poker face and sat on the couch opposite the boxes. He would show no weakness. She wouldn't see him buckle. She wouldn't see him so much as waver.

Bob heard Irene in the kitchen. She emerged from the hall with two plates of pizza slices and a beer.

"Didn't you get anything for me to drink?" she asked. "I can't drink beer when I'm studying."

"How can you ask a question like that right now?"

"I'm sorry," she said and sat in a chair on the other side of the room. "I don't mean to sound indifferent about all this." She took a bite of her pizza and chewed slowly. When she swallowed, she continued. "It's not what it appears. Not as bad as you think."

"How do you know what I think?" Bob said, putting the plate on the floor and opening the beer.

"It's all over your face. You're pissed."

"Why didn't you tell me? Why didn't you say something?"

"I didn't want to talk over the phone."

"It's all because of Chicago, right? If I had been here, you wouldn't be doing this."

"Don't be stupid—"

"I'll try not to, Irene, but if I'm a little slow for a swifty like you, bear with me."

"Bob, this isn't a break-up. I've wanted to talk about this for over a month. At least a month. I didn't know whether to move out or not. I wanted to talk—but you were always busy or it didn't seem urgent. But I wanted, I really wanted to get this out in the open before the start of the semester."

"You could have said something. You could have given me a chance."

"How? This has as much to do with me as with anything you've done. Don't you see? So how could you have a chance."

"What do you mean, 'how?' You could have told me what I was doing wrong."

"You weren't doing anything wrong. You were doing what you had to. I don't want to call it quits, Bob. Don't you see? But I can't live out here and go to grad school or law school. It won't work. I know that now. I didn't know it last summer. I have to be close to the library, to classes, to the campus. I lose too much out here. It's more than the drive. It's the distance. It diminishes everything."

"I would have helped. I would do whatever you wanted."

"Stop and listen to what I'm saying. It's not a question of just you. It's not what Bob can or cannot do. You can't be a study group. You can't expect to spend your weekends like a monk just because I need to study all day. It will be better this way. When we get together, it will be right. There won't be the feeling that one of us is accommodating the other."

"So who put you up to this? Brent? Those guys in the bookstore?"

"You're acting like an ass."

"I want to know. You owe me that."

"I told you I've been thinking about this for a month. But I called my father while you were in Chicago—"

"Oh, so you can talk to him about it over the phone, but not me."

Irene took a bite of her pizza. The sound of her chewing made Bob uncomfortable. He wanted to walk out. To go somewhere else. Anywhere would do. The Trackside Bar and Grill. Irene wiped her mouth with a napkin.

"Can I talk?" she asked.

"Go ahead."

"I called my father while you were in Chicago. I was angry at you. But he calmed me down. He said it wasn't your fault. That it was a question of contrary expectations, and that you were only doing your job. But he said I had to follow my instincts about school. That's all I'm doing. I've taken a room in a house full of grad students. It's very quiet. Very serious. No parties, no stereos. And that's what I need. We can still see each other. I don't want to break up. But this is what I need.''

"For now. Four months ago, you needed somewhere to dull out.''

"I told you I was wrong. I wished I knew then what I do now. But I needed to do this to understand how it wouldn't work. I'm not going to compound a mistake—'' Irene caught herself. "I don't mean living with you. I mean thinking I could handle the distance from school and living out here with you. If I'm not there, right there, it won't work for me.''

"We'll move. Find an apartment in Ann Arbor.''

"That won't work. I can see now that I have to get through law school before I start living with anyone. Bob, I've got to be selfish about this. Totally selfish to get through it. And that's all there is to it. Don't tell me you don't understand.''

For the first time, Bob felt his stomach relaxing. There was something right about what she said. He exhaled. "I'm trying to understand,'' he said.

"Have you heard of South Court Place—the graduate student housing for married couples? It's nicknamed Divorce Court Place. It's not you and me, Bob. It's the whole situation. It all has a cost. And if you're not careful, it wrecks good things. That's why I want to protect what we've got. So we don't wind up hating each other, see?'' She got up and sat next to Bob on the couch. Bob took her hand, his eyes moistening, and then hugged her.

"I guess it makes sense,'' he said. The sound of his voice, its tone of reason and conciliation, how he resented it. It was such bullshit, this business of living together. All the little rational decisions that had to be made. Everyone doing exactly what best suited their career objectives rather than their feelings. Of course Irene made sense. He made sense, too. Everybody made sense today. It was the "in'' thing to make.

Irene kissed him, a soft, slow, wet kiss. "I don't want to stop seeing you. I just can't do what I need to do living with you.''

Bob nodded and leaned back on the couch. "Let's reheat the pizza.''

*   *   *

Bob had Friday off. So he followed Irene's BMW into Ann Arbor to help move the boxes and do any other small chores that needed to be done. Irene waved in the mirror at every stop sign and traffic light. After lunch, he headed back. As he opened the door to the apartment he realized it was all his now. He looked around and wondered how that would feel. Right now, it didn't feel bad. He could do whatever he wanted. He collapsed on the couch with the sports page, fatigued not so much by the move as by a night of abundant couplings. Irene seemed pleased that Bob had come around to accepting her move "so maturely" and lavished him with affection. He never got to reheat that pizza. Irene's kisses led them with urgency to the bed. Bob felt angry as well as horny, and the combination proved to be a more potent stimulant for sustained performance than mere lust.

That morning, after loading the cars, they had gone out for breakfast. They sat on the same side of the booth, their bodies pressed together feverishly. All this animal vitality from just his acquiescence to her move was almost too good to be true. As if it were the crazed coupling that went on before soldiers headed off to war, when the sight of a man in uniform (so it seemed in the movies) was courtship enough for any red-blooded American woman. The foreplay consisted of a dinner, a dance, a moonlight walk with a cigarette, and the man mumbling something like, "I might not be back. I guess that's all there is to say." What line ever worked better? The beach was now well prepared for assault; a night of merciless pounding about to begin. He wondered if a woman had ever written one of those screenplays. Maybe someone like Irene could have.

When he finished the sports page he went to the kitchen to finish off the cold pizza. As he sat at the table, he wondered if he needed to write a report on Chicago. Did Wong's performance require a summary? An organized set of perceptions just to keep his own name before management? He stared at the table as he chewed until he noticed a letter from Carl there. Irene's surprise had so occupied him, he had forgotten to ask if there was any mail. Carl's letter was on top of two expense checks and a paycheck.

Bob:

Returned to college early to find an apartment and to see if
I can finesse a better scholarship job than restacking books
in the library. Maybe also to escape the sense that my return
home had become a nonevent: Dad off to factory, Mom to
the hospital, me waking up late and hanging around the
living room with the dog. I felt like I was ten again. The old
TV doesn't even bring in the New York stations.
    So I'm back. Save the address on the envelope. I still
have yet to type up my Trakl translations. I need to write
a twenty-page intro to that to get full credit. I will send you
a copy of the twenty or so poems I translated once I do
type it. Before I hand it in, I would welcome your comments on how the English seems. I mean, this guy's poems
are beautifully bleak and brief. I want that feeling in English, as sharp as it is in the German. If you could judge
the English, that would help. I'm so far into this I'm probably not an objective judge.

Bob put the letter down for a moment. He glanced out the
window at his company car. He could hear Charlie below chipping at the ice on the back steps. Each afternoon water dripped
from the roof and froze overnight. After a couple of days, it
formed thick sheets on the steps.
    He supposed he would have to explain Irene's departure.
Then he thought about reading Trakl's poems. Beautifully bleak
and brief. Why did he need to read something like that? Still,
he was flattered his brother would ask him to look at his translations. A little like the old days, minus the tensions. He continued with the letter.

I really can't imagine what it must be like for you out there,
working each week. Don't you ever miss the feeling you got
from cutting a class or reading something that really sets off
fireworks? Or is the job like that? How did you manage the
transition? From college, that is. If—and at this point it looks
like I won't—if I don't go to grad school, I'll most likely end
up with some job. What I can't decide is whether it should
be a survival job—say here at college—or a real-life thing like
you've got. Obviously Mom and Dad want me to hit the
pavement, résumé printed, ambition fully erect. I could try.
But I was never a good actor. And that doesn't seem like a

part I would want anyway. Then again, I never had you pegged for it either.

Anyway, write me another letter on motel stationery and keep me abreast of your jaunts. Hi to Irene. When I get a telephone, I'll send the number.

Bob heard Rita yelling at Charlie to be careful chipping the ice. "Don't rip the grass," she said. Bob made himself a cup of instant coffee and reread Carl's letter. He hoped things would never get raw between them again. The tone of this letter was promising. He would try to match it in return. But how could he explain anything about his job to Carl? How could he tell him what he knew about himself now? It might be better to resort to simple descriptions of places he had been, things he had seen. That might be the only thing that he could do now. Bob drank his coffee slowly, listening to Charlie stamp his boots on the porch and come inside. Then there was quiet. And then Bob could hear it. The tap, tap, tap of the water landing on the back porch.

CHAPTER

18

B ob first noticed the man behind the counter staring at him when he ordered his Whopper Junior. He nodded to acknowledge the stare, but the man nodded back, as if to say, I know who you are and you've forgotten me. Bob looked more closely at the man's face and recognized, after all these months, Stanley Hite.

"Becky," Stanley said to a teen-aged girl at the cash register, "this one's on me."

"Okay, Mr. Hite," she replied.

"No, Stanley, really," Bob said.

"I insist, Bob. As you can see, I've landed on my feet. In fact, I'd say you did me a favor. I like this a whole lot more than the drugstore. You might say, I can have it *my* way here." Stanley laughed and Bob smiled. Encouraged by Bob's response, Stanley lifted the divider and came out from behind the counter. "I'll keep you company while you eat."

"I was going to have it to go," Bob said.

"You were?" Stanley said. "Why it's not in a bag—here, Becky—this customer wanted it to go."

"Naw, that's all right," Bob said. He resigned himself to the prospect of spending a few minutes with Stanley, all in a show of maturity and goodwill.

"I still see some of the folks from the store," Stanley said as he sat down. "Right here, in fact. Oh, some of them come by four, five times a week—usually for a quick snack, a burger, some fries or onion rings. But we get to chat a bit. And they tell me you did turn the store around. Down in Bowling Green, too."

"I think there was some luck involved."

"Luck? The man calls it luck? Hey, you were meant for the business—and I'll be the first to admit I wasn't. I'm serious, you changed my life by writing that report. I hated getting the call from Remer, but ever since, things have been picking up for this hombre." Stanley leaned back against the wall and spread his arms out on the ledge to either side, striking a pose that seemed to say, Just look at me.

"So I hear you're about to get some special perk," Stanley continued. "What is it? A trip to Arizona?"

"You hear about that?"

"From the regulars. The guys who drop by, I mean."

"Actually, it's not a vacation or anything. It's a seminar. A session on Japanese management methods."

"Oh, I know all about that. We study it here. Quality control circles. The works."

"Oh yeah?"

"Absolutely. It's fascinating stuff. Quality and productivity are big issues for Burger King. As a result, we constantly keep an ear to the ground for the latest on bringing that about. Right now, it's all that 'pursuit of excellence' stuff. And basically, it springs from Japan. Stick to the knitting—so we're not going to sell garden hoses at Burger King—just our basic food products, well prepared, quickly prepared, in and out. That's excellence. And we're going to welcome suggestions from employees, and every once in a while, if there's a good one, we're going to send it down the pipeline to Miami for consideration. And we're going to offer employees the prospect of a full career here at Burger King. You want to be a lifer with us, you got it. That's part of excellence, too."

"Huh."

"Yeah," Stanley said. "You're going to love that stuff. And you'll see a case in point right here—or at any Burger King. The Japs are nuts about us. They've even toured some of our restaurants. You ever been to Arizona?"

Bob shook his head and suppressed a belch.

"Neither have I," Stanley said. "But I've seen it on TV—you know, the football game out there on New Year's Day."

"Fiesta?"

"That's it. The place looks sunny and dry. A nice place to go after the winter we've been having. When you leave?"

"Next week."

"Hey," Stanley said, standing and extending his hand again, "it's been great to see you. Have yourself a good trip."

"Yeah, thanks, Stanley," Bob said, shaking hands again. "And thanks for the burger."

After rumors and a further report from Rick of an imminent announcement, Bob had been informed at last that he was being sent to Arizona for an Oxy Institute seminar entitled "Gung Ho! Adapting Japanese Management Techniques to the American Company."

The announcement came in a package that arrived via Federal Express one Saturday in early March. Charlie greeted the delivery man and, curious to know what it was all about, followed him up to the apartment. Bob opened the package and found a pair of gold running shoes wrapped in a full-size Japanese flag. A card tucked inside one of the shoes read: "It's not how long you've been on the road, but how fast you travel."

"Now what do you suppose that means?" Charlie asked. He took a seat by Bob on the couch.

Rita appeared in the doorway. "Charlie, you leave him to tell us what he got. Can't you keep your nose out of other people's business?"

"Jesus Christ," Charlie said. "It's the first damn time a Federal Express ever delivered something to this house and you want me to pretend it didn't happen? I've been watching them on TV for years."

Rita gave Charlie a look that said, You want to argue? Charlie shook his head and retreated from the apartment, shutting the door as he left. Ever since Irene had moved out, Charlie had been knocking on Bob's door and inviting himself in for a chat. He seemed to feel she had deserted Bob, even though

Bob explained it was only for school that Irene had moved into Ann Arbor.

"It's no way for a wife to act," Charlie said repeatedly.

"Heck, lots of married people live like this today," Bob said, but after a few times, it sounded so false to his ears he let Charlie's remarks slide.

Shortly after Charlie and Rita left, the phone rang. It was Billie Coleman.

"I trust you've gotten our little surprise package," he said. "They assured me it would reach you by noon, even in that wayward-sounding town you call home."

"We can't all live in Boston," Bob said.

"No we can't. But you'll probably be living here sooner than any other DIC, the way you're going. That's a part of what that package is all about."

Coleman proceeded to inform Bob that, yes, his stellar performance hadn't gone unnoticed by management, and by way of giving him some recognition as well as the additional training he'd need to move up the ladder, the company was sending him to Phoenix, or, more properly, to the Camelback Marriott in Scottsdale for a training seminar. Coleman seemed to relish withholding information until the last possible second, pausing at artificial junctures as if he expected Bob to squeal in anticipation of what was being offered. But Bob kept his mouth shut, providing little for Coleman to use in gauging Bob's reaction.

"So what do you think about this? Are you excited?"

"Yeah," Bob said. "I think it's great." Then, surprising himself with his own bravado, he continued, "I think I've earned it."

There was a silence at the other end of the line. "Well, I'm glad to see there's no sparing your modesty," Coleman said. "But you're right. You have earned it. You've done a highly commendable job—better than we imagined, to be honest—and you're the first DIC we've ever honored with something like this."

"I appreciate it. I'm looking forward to the trip. Especially with the winter we've been having here."

"Oh, God, isn't it a beast. I'm not exactly a sun puppy,

but I wouldn't mind going out to that geriatric paradise of Barry
Goldwater's and having my sinuses dry-cleaned. You're lucky.
And by the way, the seminar is Monday through Thursday, but
we're paying for your room through Sunday. Everything is on
the house—whatever you want. Have yourself a great time."

As soon as Coleman hung up Bob telephoned Irene, who
was pleased for him; his father, who was giddy with delight;
and last his brother, who said, "I suppose congratulations are
in order."

"What do you mean?" Bob asked.

"I suppose because that's all I can possibly know about
what you're up to."

"What are you getting at?"

"I guess it's a question of what you're getting at. I haven't
set my goals."

"I only wanted to share the good news with you."

"I've heard it forty times already from Mom and Dad. You
have mentioned this to them for months. What's the real story
here?"

Bob wasn't prepared for this. He tried to think of something to say. Something light. "Come on, Carl, let's recognize
we're not the same."

"But we are the same. We have always been the same except for one thing."

"And that is?"

"The fact that you never give *me* a break."

"What are you talking about?"

"Now you come on. Tell me you're not setting the parents
up to jump on me. When are you going to realize that everything you do has a pure white heat of competitiveness. You've
never forgiven me for being born, Bob. And it's time to start.
I'm not in a race with you any more. I was, in high school, but
it's over now. Over."

"Good," Bob said. "So what's the big deal?"

"There is no *deal*. No trans-ak-ak-shun. Zip. You are and
I am. You know, like the Bible, I am what I am."

"So what do you want me to do?"

"Don't give me that crap. I'm not one of your accounts.
You're not going to probe and find a benefit statement for me,
pal."

"No, I'm serious, Carl. What is it I can do to be your friend? Because I don't want to be your enemy. And I feel like you're putting me into a black or white situation."

"This isn't a situation. It's us. We've met the enemy, you know, and guess who's there?"

Bob momentarily considered hanging up. It was enough of a pause for him to realize he couldn't right the wrongs his brother sensed so immediately but of which he was only dimly aware. "Carl, I can't stop the parents from doing what pisses you off. But you can stop being pissed off by them if you try. You're the one who has to make them recognize your difference. I can do my part to make them realize this, but the rest is up to you. Don't lay this shit on me. It's your life. No one is more in charge of it than you."

"Well said, well said. Right out of your primer of pop advice. You know what really fries me—"

This time Bob had no trouble hanging up. He disconnected the phone to avoid a return call.

Phoenix is the kind of name you don't think about unless you find it in a book. Then it takes on a certain allusive import. It had never occurred to Bob growing up and hearing about "Phoenix, Arizona" that someone once imagined a big bird springing from its ashes when the town was named. As the plane began its descent, all he could see from his window seat was a horizon of dirt. It made sense to him now. What a perk— this conference and a weekend in Phoenix. Maybe he'd find someone interested in chasing after lizards.

The gravelly voiced captain had just informed everyone that the temperature was eighty and, if they hadn't noticed, the skies clear. As the plane banked into the sun Bob closed his eyes and opened them after the bump of landing. He was surprised, he didn't know why, to see palm trees near the main terminal of the airport.

After picking up his bag, Bob fetched a cab and passed the ride to the Camelback thinking about the trip west. In Detroit, it had been fifteen degrees and he'd worn his winter overcoat. He must have looked like a college kid on a flight home. Now it was eighty degrees and he was a management trainee. It wasn't progress, exactly. But it did represent a rite of passage for him. He'd adjusted at last to the real world. After years of despising cheerleaders and class rings, jocks and positive thinkers, he'd at last proved what he knew all along to be true— namely, that he was better than they, not only because he could refuse to play their games, but also, when he chose to, he could beat them at those games.

On the flight Bob watched *The Karate Kid*. Here he was, he thought, on his way to a seminar in Japanese management training methods. What had happened to Henry Luce's American century? To our passion for world dominance? Now we were even surrendering our management methods—the precious bodily fluid of the corporate body—to an Asian nation that was not just a foreign one but a defeated one. What had we come to? John Wayne had given way to Chuck Norris, gunfights to martial arts, and the Protestant Ethic to Far-Eastern philosophy. Japan, the land of zippered-up jump-suited Godzilla, was now master to the world's greatest practitioner of the profit margin? And he, the cynic, the skeptic, had become a disciple in a new age of service-based productivity. Can you say: "Quality control circles"? C'mon, kids, let's make our companies more productive. Let's make things better. Let's make things cheaper. Let's export, import, retort, and contort. His brother despising him, his girlfriend moving out, his parents dumbstruck by his accomplishments—what could be more like the real world?

The Camelback Marriott was a huge place, a series of bungalow-type apartments and a main lodge, set at the base of a rocky, barren mountain in Scottsdale. No one had bothered to take the Santa Claus suit off of the forty-foot saguaro cactus in the front yard, an attire appropriate enough for any management conference, regardless of the season. Bob learned from the front desk attendant that several representatives from *Fortune* 500 companies, including auto, computer, and credit card companies, had sent personnel to the Gung Ho conference. He looked forward to meeting them, these young professionals.

Bob was given a small packet with information about the conference and a key to one of the bungalows, and was taken there on a golf cart by a baggage attendant. When the attendant opened the door and brought the bag in, Bob couldn't believe he had the place to himself. It was nearly as big as his apartment in Sterne.

By the time Bob had showered and walked back to the main lodge for dinner, he felt tired and unsociable. There were, he noticed, clusters of participants in the dining room. They were identifiable by their name tags, which all had the red sun logo of the Oxy Institute. Bob had purposely left his behind. But he wondered, as he watched the earnest conversations going on at the nearby tables, whether he should have worn his and attempted to sit with one of the other groups. His reluctance to join in was probably contrary to the whole intent of the seminar. But until it officially began, he'd keep unofficially to himself.

That night Bob didn't sleep well. He woke from a recurring dream several times. In it, Bob and his brother were going for a jog on a trail up the rocky mountain at the back of the Camelback. At first it was a friendly jog, with each of them pausing to appreciate the desert plants and the odd vistas. Soon though, one or the other started running harder, always when the other wanted to go slower. It became a weird kind of race, with each at one time or another lagging way behind, then running faster and passing, only to slow again and be passed. In the dream, Carl passed him one more time, and Bob yelled for him to slow down. "This is a dream," he told Carl. "Can't you see that?" Carl said, "No way. No more of your tricks."

After four in the morning, Bob did not get back to sleep. He rose at six, dressed, and headed to the main lodge for breakfast. By eight, pumped full of coffee, he arrived at the seminar room and found a table with pastries and juice in the hallway, around which a number of participants had gathered.

A plump, short woman in a blue dress walked briskly over to him and extended her hand, "Lucy Warner," she said, "from the Oxy Institute. Welcome."

Bob shook her hand and fumbled through his pocket for his name tag. For some reason he had trouble getting the pin through the lapel of his jacket.

"Here, Bob," Lucy said. "Let me help you with that." She quickly affixed the tag and gave it a tap with her finger. "There. You're all set. Come over and meet some of the other folks."

A man in a three-piece suit hastily rubbed his hand with a napkin to remove the syrupy remains of a blueberry Danish. "I'm Ross Wilson, Bob, of Lumpkin, Wilson & Fox Advertising and a resident of Old Greenwich, Connecticut." His handshake was very firm, his smile excessively bright.

Just as Bob wondered if anyone else found Ross's volunteering that he lived in Old Greenwich to be absurdly pompous, someone not much older than he stepped forward, hand extended. "Herb Warren, Bob, of Central Medical Supply Corp. and a resident of Old Bayonne, New Jersey." Herb winked at Bob.

Wilson turned his back on them and found a new Danish to attack. "Not exactly the kind of guy I expected to meet here," Bob said, nodding in the direction of Wilson.

"Oh yeah?" Herb said. "What were you expecting?"

Bob shrugged his shoulders. "I guess I just didn't expect someone to feel they had to tell me they lived in Greenwich."

"Old Greenwich," Herb said. "Don't forget the 'Old' part. Have you ever been to Connecticut?"

"Grew up there."

"When was the last time you were back?"

"About a year ago."

"That explains it. You didn't hear about the law. Everybody from Old Greenwich now has to introduce himself with 'Old Greenwich' attached to his name. 'Joe Blow, Old Greenwich, Connecticut.' It's the law. No one who lives there is allowed to hide the fact. They must confess."

"Sounds like only the right thing to do."

"Absolutely," Herb said, slapping Bob on the back. He picked up a blueberry Danish and held it in front of his mouth. "And they won't let anyone from Old Greenwich eat like this anymore." He stuffed the entire Danish into his mouth at once.

"Well, I'm glad they put an end to that, too. Those guys were cleaning out pastry tables at all the conferences everywhere. No one got anything."

"There you go. That's why it's the law." Herb dabbed the blueberry residue from the corner of his mouth. "See you inside. Got to shake the dew off."

The seating in the seminar room was arranged like a horseshoe, with a large movie screen at the open end. Two men at a table to the side counted individual stacks of paper. These were passed out to the people as they took their seats. Pads, pens, and binders were already at each seat. The paper was three-hole punched and fit in the binder, which had the conference name and the Oxy Institute logo on its cover. Bob felt as if he were in grammar school. Herb, who'd taken a seat next to him, seemed equally nonplussed by the proceedings.

By the time everyone was seated and had assembled their binders, the two men stood in front of the screen. The older of them, a white-haired, somewhat portly man with a flabby face and glasses, stepped forward. He introduced himself as Art Lawler, "please call me Buster," of the Oxy Institute, and his fellow presenter as Ron Mikato, a Japanese-American and professor from the USC business school.

"Now the way we like to get things rolling is for each of you to stand and introduce yourself and your company and to explain why you're here," Lawler said.

Bob stared down at his pad and began doodling. He couldn't believe this bull. It was worse than grammar school. But it went on. A woman from the Mantle-Box computer company stood and said, "My name is Martha Poindexter, Mantle-Box, and at our company, we have a watchword—'Maybe . . .' And I think that's why we're all here. Maybe, we said to ourselves, if we learned more about Japanese management methods we could apply them to our work." The contingent from Mantle-Box applauded Martha, and Bob and Buster nodded fatuously. When Herb leaned over and whispered to Bob, "Maybe you could go down on me, baby," the feeling of school days was complete.

Ross Wilson told everyone that at Lumpkin, Wilson & Fox Advertising they have a belief that all their assets went down the elevator each night, because advertising is a people business, and when someone has new ideas about making people more productive and better able to achieve excellence in their work then he, as an owner of this agency, wants to know about it. The Mantle-Box contingent applauded him, too.

When Bob's turn came, he stood and rattled off some facts about P&V and said that he'd been selected to investigate how to apply these methods to that business. He didn't get any applause. Nor did Herb, who said he'd been sent there by his boss to get him out of his hair. Seriously, though, Central Medical had a twelve-state distribution region and relied on superior employee performance for preserving existing business and building new accounts.

With the introductions done, it was time for a break. When the seminar resumed, Buster showed a film about Japan, past and present, entitled "Japan: Land of Tradition, Land of Change." After that, it was time for lunch. At lunch, Herb kept saying he felt he knew Buster from somewhere but couldn't place him. He seemed obsessed by it.

"Why don't you ask him?"

"Naw," Herb said. "Just one of those nagging things. Not worth bringing up."

"Maybe you met him in Old Greenwich."

"Impossible. He would have told us."

The afternoon consisted of a two-hour lecture by Ron on the economic redevelopment of postwar Japan. Bob couldn't help noticing that, even though Ron told everyone that the highlights of his lecture were contained in the handouts, Martha Poindexter scribbled notes at a furious pace.

Buster concluded the afternoon session by clapping his hands at the end of Ron's presentation and standing at the inner center of the horseshoe. "I know," he said, "that I continued to be fascinated by this nation, this Japan, this—and now you might know why we've set this seminar here—this industrial phoenix, emerging from the ruin of World War II and an economy where forty percent of the people earned livings from agriculture to assume a leadership role in the developed world as we know it. Today, just eighteen percent of all Japanese earn a living through agriculture. Think of it. A tremendous swing"—Buster swung his arms slowly to convey some sense of how great the swing had been—"a colossal transition and this Japan, this nation with few raw materials, with no low-cost energy, and with no proximity to the great markets of developed nations, became an economic giant. Tomorrow, we'll begin to understand how they did it . . . how a stimulating, creative blend of the traditional and the new turned the eyes of the world to Japan. There's one word, a key word I want to leave you with today, a word at the heart of all we have to say to you over the next few days. What is this word, this key word . . .'' Buster moved cryptically toward the screen, his back to the group. Then, spreading his arms, the room darkened, the screen lit up, and he turned, bringing his hands together in front of him and holding them there as the click of a slide projector signaled everyone that the answer to his questions was about to be displayed. ''That word, ladies and gentlemen, that word is . . .'' It popped on to the screen in its Japanese character and English translation. ''That word is *ringi*. Tomorrow we'll find out what it means.''

As the group filed out of the seminar room Bob heard the Mantle-Box contingent making plans to go on a sightseeing tour of the desert. Bob had seen Mantle-Box's advertising on TV. Each ad depicted a very well-conditioned man or woman suddenly asking ''Maybe . . .'' and solving some always unclear business problem with a glaze of gibberish—''Maybe if we strapped voice data cables to the back of a midget and had him crawl through the eastern corridor sewer system.'' They could be anywhere—tooling around the desert in a vintage sports car, swimming in a pool, walking with a dog on the beach, taking a shower. Bob especially disliked the ads and their self-serving implication that the entire company was filled with a race of *uber*folks working day and night on their customers' business problems. He didn't fight the impulse to imagine their conversation now. ''Maybe if we went and looked at the plants in the desert. Great? Okay, maybe you should drive. Hey, wonderful. And maybe we'll eat Mexican tonight and get faced on margaritas. Great. And maybe we'll all go swimming and take runs.'' And judging from the way they put their hands all over each other, Herb was probably right. ''Maybe we'll all boff like bunnies tonight.''

Herb came up to Bob and said, ''Hey, let's grab a beer. I'll tell you where I saw Buster last. I remembered.''

They took a table at one of the many small lounges within the Camelback complex. After a few minutes, Herb slid his empty glass to the center of the table.

''It was that bit he gave us about one word,'' Herb said.

''Who gave us?''

''Buster—you know, 'there's one word . . .' ''

''Yeah, *ringi*.''

''Not the word, Bob, the delivery. I was trying to remem-

ber where I heard that line—and not, you know, 'plastics.' "
Herb folded his arms across his chest and rocked his chair back.
He continued: "I was at a seminar on building sales skills about
ten years ago. That was it. And Buster was the presenter. He
said—I'll never forget it, being a kid, it seemed very dramatic—
so Buster said, 'Now I'm going to tell you the most important,
the most absolutely important word to closing a sale, bar
none . . .' and suddenly he looks to the back of the room and
walks out into the audience as if he's seen something, and
everyone is very quiet and wondering what he saw and what
the word is when from out of the blue he screams, 'Shut up.'
And everyone jumps right off their seats thinking he's nailed
some poor bastard for whispering or something, but he marches
right down the aisle and says again, in almost a whisper, 'Shut
up.' That's the word. Keep your mouth shut. More sales are
ruined by saying too much than by any other reason."

"That's two words."

"What is?"

" 'Shut up.' "

"Believe me, if you were there, you'd know what he
meant, wouldn't you?"

"His delivery doesn't work so well with *ringi*, does it?"

"We'll have to see what he does with it. His delivery's
kept him in business for a decade, hasn't it? And I remember
that sales seminar a decade later, don't I? We'll see."

The second day of the seminar consisted of a series of self-
graded tests. ("It makes no sense to cheat, because you're the
only one looking at it," Buster said.) The tests were designed
to reveal autocratic or excessively self-reliant tendencies in managers. Bob scored at a level just below "Caesar" and above
"MacArthur," but well below "Genghis Kahn" and "Custer."
In response to Buster's humorous questioning about how dictatorial they had revealed themselves to be, a quick show of
self-consciously raised hands indicated that nearly everyone had
results similar to Bob's.

"Thirty years ago, when football was still played in the
mud and Levittown was barely built, before free agency and
when the steel industry was still booming," Buster said, walking up and down the horseshoe, "testing like this would have

thrown you up the ladder, made you a management prospect. Today, it might—and notice I say 'might'—it might be telling you that you've got something in common with the dinosaur. Because the day of the dictatorial, I call him the Theory-X manager—who rules because of his subordinates' fear of failure—is drawing to a close. Oh, there might be a job opportunity for him as the head of the military in a Third World country"— Buster held for laughs until a few snickers came and went— "but in America, at the upper levels of management, Theory X is doomed. And Theory Y, the *ringi* system, is moving in its wake."

Buster went on to explain that *ringi*, Theory Y, and a whole passel of other names for the same thing (consultative or cascade management) had been around for years. The Japanese, with their centuries-old emphasis on tradition, loyalty to family, and submission to the group's best interest, had paradoxically used the *ringi* system to move into a new age of high-technology, high productivity, and high growth.

Buster took the leadership role in the presentation. Mikato acted as his foil and provided the "deep background" on more historically or academically detailed subjects such as the influence of Buddhism on the workplace. By downplaying the role of the individual in the spiritual world, Buddhism dovetailed with the basic social principle of family loyalty. Thus, business in Japan offered free transportation, subsidized housing, large bonuses to compensate for low weekly salaries, and, in effect, a tenure system; in return, they got loyal employees who viewed their role within the company in terms of the company's growth rather than of their own advancement.

"While all of these generalizations have certain limitations," Mikato said, "you could say that the traditional post-war Japanese employee sees his tenure at the company not as the road to his personal economic success, but as something akin to the role a leaf fulfills for the tree—as someone who comes, does what he must for the season of his tenure—and eventually retires or moves on to new responsibilities, to be replaced by another, all the while the tree growing larger and stronger."

Herb leaned over to Bob and whispered, "In a nation

raised on the 'Mary Tyler Moore Show' and *Rambo,* I don't see the American worker being quite so altruistic, do you?''

By the third day, everyone learned that there was no way to import the spiritual concepts of an Oriental society into the American workplace. But by adopting certain management techniques, there were possible applications. The notable one was the quality control circle technique, which identified a problem by delegating responsibility to the level where the problem exists and then allowing the workers affected by it to develop a possible solution, to analyze the effectiveness of the proposed solution, and only then to send it on to management.

Bob knew he'd be expected to report on these kinds of possibilities for adoption, and he took extensive notes. At night he ripped off the handouts often verbatim, turning them into another "White Paper" for management.

By the end of the third day, he had become thoroughly disgusted with the Mantle-Box people, who did everything as a group, and became something of the prime example of how the techniques could work. Buster and Ron frequently illustrated "decentralized," "cascaded," and "consultative" management with references to Mantle-Box and praised their group loyalty and team problem-solving skills.

Bob's only real acquaintance, Herb, was sequestered in his room for the better part of Wednesday trying on the phone to solve some big mess back east. So there was no one to share his acerbic feelings about these "Maybe" gung-ho-ers. Nonetheless, he found the approach of the seminar very useful. In fact, he believed he had been using it intuitively in his territory: After all, he made a point of giving each manager every chance to solve problems on a store-by-store basis and consistently asked for and received recommendations from staff.

He had done this to avoid being perceived as a hatchet man. If everyone bought into what he was doing, he had figured, no one was going to reject either his modifications or the occasional necessity of shaking up store management. The thought forming now was that, if he put the right spin on the information gained from this seminar, P&V management would come to this same conclusion. The trick would be not to make his presentation obvious, his ambitions transparent. At last he

was grateful for a liberal arts education. Subtlety would be re-
warded now. And what was wrong with that? Why should he
want to stay on the road any longer than he had to? Why not
get off by getting ahead? The irony of the whole thing was not
lost on him. Here he was plotting how to use team concepts,
the *ringi* system, to promote his own career.

So, too, it seemed, was everyone else. At a poolside cocktail party the night before the seminar came to an end, the
Mantle-Box people, including several good-looking women, began circulating among the fifty or so other participants. Ross
Wilson, too, traveled from group to group, person to person,
and over the deep-fried breaded cauliflower and white wine
spritzers, somehow got you to tell him who was in charge of
advertising and what that person thought of the current agency.
Bob blocked this quickly by explaining he was on the road. But
Martha Poindexter did succeed in getting him to talk about the
company's sophisticated research and test-market systems.

"Sounds ingenious," Martha said, giving her styled hair a
quick flip. "How do they crunch those numbers?"

"I'm not sure I follow?"

"Data base? What do you use?"

When Bob couldn't tell her, Martha offered to get him another white wine. When she returned she talked about the desert for a few minutes. ("It's incredibly beautiful, really.") She
went on to explain that at Mantle-Box, no idea could be rejected at a meeting. "We're not allowed to say 'no.' Only, 'I
don't concur.' " Then, without transition, she asked Bob how
long he'd been with the company and whether anyone he
trained with had wound up in research.

Bob found himself blurting out Rick's name before he even
thought about it.

"I'm not sure Rick doesn't already see one of your Mantle-Box people," Bob said. "Everyone calls on them."

"Quite possibly," Martha said. "But *maybe* not." She
winked at him, and after a few remarks more about the Arizona sunsets, drifted away.

On Friday, with the Oxy Institute seminar over (Bob noticed that the seminar room had been converted for a regional
sales meeting of a door-to-door cosmetics company), he rented

a car and took a shopping trip to Scottsdale. After gawking at small statues of cowboys lassoing horses, which sold for twenty grand apiece, he bought himself a bathing suit and suntan lotion and decided to spend the rest of the weekend by the pool. But as he changed in his room, the phone rang. It was Rick.

"So how is it in the land of sun and fun?" Rick asked.

"It's been terrific," Bob said, beginning to realize that if Rick told other people's secrets to him, he might also be relaying anything Bob said to someone else.

"Great. Hey, I've got a little inside surprise for you."

"And what might that be?"

"The word is, you're DIC of the Year. The top performer."

Bob sat on his bed and wondered why had Rick decided to call him. What was his motive? If this was true, why hadn't Rick waited for proper notification? At the same time, he welcomed the information. Assuming it was true, he could now prepare himself. He would sound cool and collected. Not like some contestant who wins the big prize in a game show. "Are you sure about this," he said. "If you're bullshitting me, I'll never speak to you again."

"Honest, honest," Rick said. "It's the truth. It's done. They're having some plaque made for you now. How's it feel?"

"It feels . . ." Bob stopped. He wanted to say the right thing. But he felt giddy and couldn't think of a political answer. "It feels fucking great."

"You bet it does," Rick said. "And you're my buddy here, aren't you."

"You bet."

"What's amazing to me," Rick continued. "I mean, what's got them stumped, is how much better you did in six months than any other DIC did in twelve. They pored over Cutter's reports and figures to see if he deliberately kept totals low, or if he misreported implementations for some personal reasons. They concluded you did it all on your own."

"This is a great call you've given me."

"It's great news. Of course they have to make sure the other DICs and their regional managers recognize it was legit. You must be in line for some whopper of a bonus."

"Don't say that if you don't know how much it is. Because I can always imagine more."

"More than you make?"

"Don't. Stop this right now. It's too much."

"I don't know. The record for a first-year guy is twelve grand. The way they checked your numbers, it has to be more."

Bob gasped. He didn't mean to sound that out-of-control, but the number, the possibility of that number, made him numb. He knew there was an outside shot. But he also figured it was a lot of rhetoric from the company. Something that happened once in a decade, never more often. Now it seemed he had done it.

"You there?" Rick said.

"No, I'm not here. I'm much higher than this."

"All right," Rick said. "That's the spirit."

"You can't be lying," Bob said. "It would be too cruel."

"I'm not lying," he said. "But do me a favor and don't let anyone know I tipped you off."

Bob assured Rick he wouldn't. Having a source back east was too good a thing to give up for a slip of the tongue. Overwhelmed by the news, he forgot to mention he'd given Rick's name to the Mantle-Box woman. He decided to let it pass. Later. He'd do it later. Right now, all he wanted was to celebrate. But with no one around, how could he? He decided against calling his father. The size of the bonus would overwhelm him. And besides, he hadn't yet gotten it. Irene would be buried with work and the money wouldn't be of any size to impress her. And his brother would loathe such a call. So he decided to celebrate by himself. He punched up a pay movie, *9½ Weeks*, and called room service for champagne.

After drinking half the bottle of champagne, Bob decided to get himself a decent Mexican dinner. Somewhere in Phoenix there ought to be a reasonable Mexican restaurant. Rather than ask a desk attendant for directions, Bob chose to make the trip an exploration. His flight was not until Sunday. No matter how lost he got, he should have time enough to find his way back, pack his suitcase, and drive to the airport.

The farther he got away from Scottsdale and the Camelback Marriott, the bleaker things looked. Car washes and strip bars, trailer parks and the crumbling adobe of retirement ''communities'' built during the sixties. He knew he was heading toward downtown, but allowed himself to take any turn that seemed to promise something worth remembering.

After one such turn, he found himself driving alongside an immense corporate complex, one of those that owns a credit card company, insurance companies, savings banks, and more. He'd forgotten they were headquartered in Phoenix. The building itself was a glass palace, but more striking than the metallic glare of its reflective glass was the corporate lawn, which stretched on as green as a golf course's and, shaded by palms, rolled over the same soil that a few hundred yards to any side was scrub, rock, and dirt.

Later, as Bob nervously made his way out of a destitute Mexican neighborhood—a place of dull gray flat houses, more like bomb shelters than homes, without windows or doors, laundry lines stretching across dirty front yards littered with bottles and tires, baby clothes dangling like surrender flags, dogs lapping at the foul smelling dark water of the ditches along the dirt side streets—he thought of that corporate lawn, that dark green grass with the sprinklers submerged beneath its surface. The image of a sea rose in his mind, a sea of tremendous power, its currents cold, its tides those of currency.

Bob did not find a Mexican restaurant. He gave up after crossing a bridge over a dry riverbed that seemed to make its way right back into the heart of Phoenix. When he got back to his room, he called to move his flight ahead to Saturday and turned out the lights, and for what seemed like a long time sat slouched in the dark against the headboard with his eyes shut.

CHAPTER

19

"Where have you been?" Irene asked. "I've been calling for two weeks."

"I know, I know," Bob said. When he got back from Boston he had listened to his answering machine. Irene had several messages on it.

"Are you seeing someone else? If you are, you need to tell me."

"No, no one. Irene, they sent me to Phoenix, to a seminar on Japanese management techniques. And then to Boston for six days. I tried to call, but you're never in."

"I am too. Every night by ten. You could have tried later."

"I did try. We just missed each other. It wasn't intentional."

"I want to see you. I miss you."

"I miss you, too."

"I need a break from the books."

"And I need a break from the job. It's all I've been doing lately. I delivered the report on Phoenix to management. All the DICs were there. And after I got done, Prescott came up, patted me on the back, and announced I was top DIC of the year. I got a bonus."

"Good for you. You must feel great. I know you worked hard for that."

"Yeah. Hard."

"How much was it?"

"They're not sure yet," he lied. After the meeting, Prescott handed him a check for $18,750. Almost as much as his salary. He didn't want anyone to know how much. And Irene most of all. When he deposited it in his savings account at the Sterne Savings & Loan, the bank's president came out of his office and thanked Bob for thinking of their bank. He couldn't even bring himself to reveal the amount to his father, the person he once thought he would be most proud to tell. He told his father about the award, but stalled concerning the amount by saying that it was still being figured.

"What are you going to do with all that money, whatever it is?"

"Oh, I don't know. Have anything in mind?"

"How about a dinner with me."

"Fine," Bob said.

"Sunday?"

"Can't. I'm going to another convention. In Chicago. How about Saturday?"

"That's a bad night. I've got an outline due for the study group on Sunday. I need that night to get it done."

"How about tomorrow?"

"Tonight?"

"Irene, I just got back fifteen minutes ago. And it's already eight-thirty. I know we're both crazed by lust, but how about tomorrow?"

"There's a lecture I'm planning to hear. It's at seven in the main auditorium. If you don't mind meeting me after . . ."

"Why can't I come along?"

"To a lecture on critical legal studies?"

"Why not?"

"My, you are crazed by lust."

It had been less than a year since Bob's last college class, but he'd forgotten the heady mixture of cigarette smoke and nervous, intelligent muttering that went on in the hallways of academe.

"That's preposterous, that's the whole point of a presidential finding . . ."

"I feel the principles are mutually exclusive . . ."

"I say we get faced after this talk and blow off the weekend . . ."

"Hey, are you here?" Irene asked.

"Yeah, sure, just listening," Bob said. "It's been a while since I've been in a place like this."

"Maybe never," Irene said. "There was no group of people this intense in college. These people are driven."

"To what?"

Irene nudged him in the arm. "Don't be a wise ass tonight, okay? Let's have some fun."

"Good idea. We'll start with this critical legal stuff."

"Bob—"

"I'll stop."

The auditorium was filled. Bob and Irene had to separate to find seats.

"Are these all grad students in government?" Bob asked a balding man sitting next to him.

"Hardly," he said. "I'm from philosophy. What about yourself?"

"Just a spectator."

"Well you're certainly in for a spectacle. Do you know anything about critical legal studies and the law?"

Bob shook his head.

"Don't feel bad. I doubt the crits know anything about the law either."

The keynote speaker was Ricardo Montenegro, a Brazilian who'd been in the United States for several years building up a substantial following for his approach to law and galvanizing an otherwise self-absorbed world of legal scholars into violent anticrits.

"I will not," Montenegro began, "apply the principles of critical legal studies, a label I have refused to use in reference to my thinking, but rather present a program for the development of doctrine, by which the institutional and state apparatus governing the spawning of legal precepts becomes apparent."

The balding man nudged Bob. "I'm going to cut this bastard to ribbons," he said. "I can't wait."

"If it's all the same to you, I'd like to hear what he has to say."

The man stared at Bob, apparently stunned. "Don't waste the energy. I doubt you'll follow it."

For that, Bob made a concerted effort to follow the program Montenegro put forth. But it wasn't easy. He explained the idea that the economic forces generate the conceptual foundations for legal rights.

Bob became convinced he wasn't hearing anything new. His concentration lapsed. He jumped when a burst of laughter broke the drone of Montenegro's voice. He had fallen asleep. He scanned the room to see if Irene had noticed. He didn't find her.

"My critics often say," Montenegro concluded, "that of course legal principles are not in fact neutral. But they ought to be. And we ought to live by and apply them as if they were. To this I say, How can you? You are in a web of prescriptive conceptualization. Your thoughts are not pure, they are not capable of resisting the interconnecting apparatus of mystified principles. And you cannot pretend to know what is beyond the web. You have neither the vocabulary—for that is given by the same forces that proscribe our legal system—nor the imagination to envision anything but an absence of proscription and space along the interstices of competing ideological and economic forces."

After he finished, a large portion of the audience left. Bob saw Irene now, on the far side. She made her way over to him.

"Let's go," she said. "This is a lot of bullshit."

"Wait, I want to hear this guy," he whispered, nodding toward the balding man.

"Mr. Montenegro, if I may, I want to say that for all your radical posturings, I find your program rather reactionary. In your reluctance to posit a new program for admittedly biased legal precepts, you leave the game open to the highest bidders—namely the very institutions that employ critical legal scholars—and the very places with the largest cultural stakes in maintaining a status quo. You're co-opted, and your reasoning is completely self-serving and circular."

After a volley of hoots and a modest round of applause settled down, Montenegro rose again and addressed the speaker. "Of course my reasoning is circular," he said. "All reasoning is. But that doesn't mean it is vicious or empty. Recognizing and utilizing the circle is one way to draw attention to it and eventually to resist it."

"Okay," Bob said. "I've heard enough." And so he had. For months he had troubled himself with whether he'd been self-serving or not; the brief brush with legal scholars had left him convinced he need not worry about such things any more. If the business world was a cold place, the academic one was simply circular. He had two new choices: self-serving ruthlessness or ethical absurdity, in which the only pure act was a passive resistance with not even a bus seat at stake. "Do you go for any of this?"

"They're fools," Irene said. "They've built an elaborate critique of our legal system that purposefully collapses in on itself. They're jargon-ridden, vain, and very active within departments, spawning positions for their brethren. If they ever take over, they'll produce their own orthodoxy."

By the time they finished with dinner, it was midnight. Irene had been very warm throughout, laughing, saying what a good time she was having. Bob relaxed, too, in a way he hadn't for months. On the way out to the car, he stopped Irene and kissed her.

"I have an idea," he said. "Let's spend the night in a hotel."

"I was going to invite you back to my room."

"Naw, this will be more fun. We'll have room service in the morning."

"If you promise to get me back by ten."

"Promise."

After a couple of drinks at the bar, they headed to their room. Irene went into the bathroom and emerged naked, clicking off the light. She took Bob's clothes off, lingering over each new piece of flesh. She devoured him, and everywhere her mouth roamed it felt good. And when they fell onto the sheets, there was an edge to their lovemaking, the way it had been the night she told Bob she wanted to leave. Sleep at last won out. Bob shut his eyes and fell into a stone black night of fatigue, into a deep pool, down, every muscle in his body giving way to the journey.

When Bob woke, Irene was gone. It was still dark. But he could see her coat on the dresser. In the mirror, he noticed a crevice of light coming from the gap under the bathroom door. He rose and tapped at the door lightly.

"Irene, are you okay?"

"Hmmm?"

Bob nudged the door open. There, on the closed toilet, Irene sat naked with a notebook opened on her lap, a pen poised for note taking. She smiled at him.

"What are you doing?" he asked.

"Just a thought or two on something I heard tonight. I wanted to get it down. One of my professors has leanings that way."

"Are you coming back to bed?"

"In a minute. You go ahead." She took a drag from a cigarette and blew the smoke into the ceiling fan overhead. "Honest," she said. Her voice deepened in a poor imitation of Arnold Schwarzenegger, "All ve bak."

Bob shut the door slowly, quietly, and returned to bed. He fluffed up his pillow and lay down, curling his body around a damp part of the sheet. Try as he might, he couldn't get back into the same sleep. Every time he started to, he'd roll onto the wet spot, now cold, and wake. Finally he fell into a light, nervous sleep. When he woke in the morning she was already in the shower.

CHAPTER

20

B ob turned off the lights and engine of his MG and coasted
the last fifty yards of road into the driveway of his parents'
house. In a sequence he'd seen countless times from the inside,
the old Lab rose and barked from the front steps, his father's
head lurched into the picture window, and at the kitchen window, his mother craned her neck in a futile attempt to see through
her own reflection.

The front door swung open, and out came Carl, drink in
hand. He had a Ho Chi Minh beard, which tickled Bob as he
gave him a hug.

"So, how's it feel?" Bob asked. He wished he could think
of something warmer to say.

"No different, as close as I am. Still haven't gotten the diploma, you know. I finished the introduction to those Trakl
translations only last week."

"Then I'll save my official congratulations until later," Bob
said. "How have you been? I know I should have written
more—but . . ."

"Don't worry about it. I didn't write, either. I've just been
trying to dig out from under the semester's work."

"Hey, stranger, you coming inside?"

Bob's father stood in the doorway, beckoning him in with
a wave of his arm. His mother was peering over his father's

shoulder. Bob lifted his suitcase from behind the seat and headed in.

"How long did the drive take?" his father asked.

"Thirteen hours, with two stops."

"Here, let me take your suitcase," his mother said.

"Oh, for chrissake, Ellie, leave it and relax."

But she had already picked it up and was headed down the hallway toward his old bedroom. Carl put his hand on Bob's shoulder as their father waved his arm at her.

"Mom's a little uptight, be warned."

Bob nodded. "I know. 'A house-full-of-visitors-and-no-one-is-helping.' "

"What else is new?" Carl said and then finished his drink.

This was new, to Bob anyway. To be a visitor in his own home. To notice, as he did now, the musty smell that came from the piles of old books that his mother bought at estate sales. The house was cluttered with them.

"Would you like something to eat?" Ellie asked when she returned.

"No thanks. Ate on the way."

"You'll have a drink, though, won't you?" his father said, handing him one.

"Frank, maybe he'd rather quench his thirst with some juice."

"Are you kidding, Mom?" Carl said, sitting down and putting his feet on a mound of old first-aid books.

Ellie shook a gray bang of hair to the side of her forehead and sipped her sherry. "Please, Carl, put your feet somewhere else. Those books are worth something."

"How's business?" Frank asked.

"It's been great. They're expanding all over the place."

"How nice," Ellie said. "Sounds like you hooked on with a winner."

Bob smiled and nodded. He could see how much his parents enjoyed hearing about all this.

"So you were DIC of the Year," Carl said.

"Yeah, the numbers were on my side. The territory was underdeveloped before I got there."

"Good going," Carl said. "And just like a true champ—'I

had a little luck.' But, hey, you're home now, admit it, you were a hero!''

Bob stared at his brother for a second to get a reading. He seemed friendly enough.

"Here's to Bob," Ellie toasted. Everyone joined in.

"Have they figured your bonus out yet?" Carl asked.

"It's out there," Bob said, motioning to the driveway. "That MG." The car actually cost him less than a third of the bonus. The rest was still in the bank.

"And you still love what you do?" Carl asked.

Bob shrugged his shoulders. "What can I say? It's a job. And the pay's real good."

"That's right, it's good," Frank said. "And that's the bottom line out there—what's it pay."

"You've got to like your work, too, hon'," Ellie said. "Otherwise you'll end up like poor old Irwin Corey."

"That's Richard, Mom," Carl said. "Richard Corey."

"You've still got to be happy," she said.

"And there's nothing like a little dough in the wallet to make someone happy," Frank said, banging his glass down on an end table.

"Don't get a water stain on that," Ellie said.

Frank waved her off. Ellie stood and waved back.

"What good does money do if you ruin everything you've got?" she said. "Can I get you some supper while I'm up, Bob?"

"All set, Mom."

"And I'll tell you what good it does," Frank said. There was a tone of challenge in his voice. He waited for her response, but there was none. Bob shook his head at his father, who smiled and shrugged as if to say, How can I help it?

"Enough about me," Bob said. He looked at Carl. "Have you made any plans for next year?"

"That's one topic we shouldn't bring up tonight."

"I've been telling him to get in gear," Frank said. "Every college senior in the country is already looking for work. But not this one."

"And he won't look anywhere I suggest," Ellie said, taking her seat again. "They need someone at the hospital to write the monthly newsletter, but he won't even apply. Too smart for that.''

"Give me a break," Carl said. "This last semester has been a ballbuster. I haven't ruled out anything, yet."

"Pretty soon they'll rule you out if you don't apply," she said.

"Enough!" Frank said. "We'll let it go. You'll get a job when you find out you need one. Right now, Bob, I'd like to take that car of yours down the road. Flip me the keys."

"Not after that drink, you won't," Ellie said. "You stay put."

"Oh, for chrissake. I'm fine." He headed outside.

"No way," Ellie said after him. "You shouldn't be trying to keep up with your sons at your age. I'm not. I'm heading to bed myself. Yep, nighty night." She paused to take a last swallow of sherry. "Nice to have you home, boys. And, Bob, don't forget, there's supper on the stove. Just turn it off before you hit the sack."

Bob went to the front door. He could see Frank inspecting the car in the light from the kitchen window. Frank opened the door and sat on the edge of the front seat, trying to swing his left leg into the cramped driver's compartment.

"Hey, Carl," he shouted, "come on out here and take a look at the benefits of employment."

Carl rolled his eyes as he stood up. "Excuse me," he said, opening the front door. "I believe I'm about to hear all about your car."

"Just look at this cutie," Frank said, still trying to squeeze in his left leg. He gave up and sat there for a moment, flicking on the lights, then starting the engine. "What year is it?"

"Sixty-two. An old lady near Pontiac had it on blocks. It had been her son's. He died in Vietnam. My landlord knew her and told me about it."

"It's in mint condition. You could park it on North Street anytime."

"It looks fine right here," Carl said. "No need to take it there."

Frank opened the trunk and was shuffling a case of samples around. "Even has a little spare. What a cutie." He slammed the trunk shut. "You know, there's a taillight back here that's busted."

"Yeah, some guy in a Winnebago ran into it at a HoJo's parking lot near Pittsburgh. I don't know what I'll do."

"Take it over to Darby's," Carl said. "There's bound to be some MGs wrecked by all the preppies around here."

"Sure, but a sixty-two?"

"I wouldn't be surprised," Frank said. "But if you take this over there tomorrow he'll charge you an arm and a leg. Why not go over tonight and take one. There's bound to be a few of these somewhere in the woods back there." He looked up toward the sky. "Yeah, there's going to be good moonlight. Why pay for it?"

"It's no big deal, Dad. I'll wait 'til tomorrow."

"Hell, if Carl won't go with you tonight, I will. I'll figure out how to fit inside this thing yet."

"Relax, Dad," Carl said. "I'll go with him if he wants to." Carl walked down the driveway toward the fire pond across the street. "I think I heard a fish jump," he said.

"Great," Bob answered.

"Get a pole. There's one with a bass lure on it."

Bob started to open the garage door, but his father put a hand on his shoulder. "Do me a favor and talk to your brother," he said. "See if you can make him think about a job."

"I don't know if I can, Dad. It's his life." Bob didn't feel up to discussing Carl's lack of direction. He wanted to offer any help Carl asked for. But he didn't want to get intense about it. No confrontations. There was some space between them now, and that seemed right to Bob.

"It's too late for that, Carl," Bob said. "Skip the fishing. C'mon."

"C'mon what?" Carl said, walking back up the driveway. "What's wrong with you, passing up some fishing? You sweep in here from the heartland and you don't want to fish? What would Huck Finn say?"

"I've got a better idea," Frank said. "Let's have another drink."

"I guess that does sound better than one of those claustrophobic bass," Carl said.

When Frank returned with their drinks, he said he was tired and heading to bed. "I want to be wide awake for the basketball game tomorrow. Celts need one more to win." He waved good night and headed down the hallway.

The dog scratched at the front door, and Bob let it in. It limped over to the couch and fell into a ball beside Carl, wheezing as it hit the floor.

"You really want to live here next year?" Bob asked.

"No."

"So do you have any plans?"

"Get off my back."

"I'm just asking, that's all. If you want me to shut up, I will."

"You're going to have a hard time avoiding it the way Mom and Dad are acting. They figure you're here to knock some sense into me." He paused to sip from his drink. "Are you doing what you want to do?"

"It's a good job. What do you mean?"

"Driving all over the place, checking up on drugstores, filing reports with a bunch of marketing nerds. Just to become a manager in a drugstore chain?"

"It's not like that. Not that limited."

"Tell me why."

"There are other things to do. Get an M.B.A. Or a job with another company. Lots of things."

"And those options appeal to you?"

"They're options," Bob said. He couldn't understand how Carl could get under his skin, but he did. What did he have to be defensive about?

"All that marketing stuff? Are you really like that now?"

"Everyone has a certain amount of swallowing to do."

"What kind of swallowing?"

"Some of your old ideas. Your old way of thinking."

"You make it sound like a cultural revolution. Old ways of thinking? Out to the Midwest for political realignment. Off to Phoenix for seminars in Oriental management techniques."

Bob stared at the ceiling. He could still see the small, smudged handprint he had put there when he was in sixth grade. He wondered why his father had never repainted. "You act like I'm the biggest spokesman for this job. But I'm not. I never imagined doing this when I was in college. But the salary is good and the work isn't that hard. And I'm good at it. So why should I have a problem looking at myself in the mirror?"

Carl laughed. "I don't know, have you checked lately?"

Bob smiled. "Maybe not. Still, why can't we agree to be different?"

"We can agree. But whether we can leave it that way, I can't say. It always seems to get in the way. Either with the parents, or between us."

"We going to be enemies?"

"I propose a peace pact—a late-night slug-hunting session." Carl stood up. "I'll get the salt. Let's explode a few."

Bob shook his head. It was something he might have done a couple of years ago. But not now.

"Don't worry," Carl said. "I won't let any of those varmints slobber over your dress pants."

"I'd rather have another drink and chat." Bob went into the kitchen to fix one.

"Okay, I'll have another if you fix it," Carl said from the living room. "How's Irene?"

"She's good." Bob poured Carl a strong vodka and tonic. He mixed a milder one for himself. If it was too strong, he would fall asleep after the drive. "She finished with the semester and got all *A*s. Starts law school this fall."

"And what's she doing for the summer?"

"She's gone back home. She'll work in her father's law office." Bob handed the drink to Carl.

"Daddy's law office? What's she do? Give him his pipe and his briefs?"

"Knock it off," Bob said. He felt a flush of anger. "I don't think you've got anything better to do this summer."

"That's the whole point with you, isn't it. You've always got to find something better. Better than the next guy. Better than me. But you can stop trying now, Bob, because I don't care."

"Good. Let's leave it at that."

"That's great—'leave it at that.' You've never left anything between us 'at that.' Not in school. Not in work. Not even when we ran together. You never left it at that in Thomaston."

"That was a bad thing, I know now. But I'm not like that now."

"Not even when you keep plugging your achievements with the parents."

"That's not true. I've tried to keep that down. I've tried to keep you out of it. You don't exactly leave things 'at that' either. Or you wouldn't be dishing out this crap."

"You need a little of it, believe me. This Mister Maturity routine you're pulling with the job is too much. Plus I get the feeling you're laying down the ground rules for another competition between us. This time it's the what-are-you-doing-with-your-life game. And you're doing anything you can to win."

"That's bull. I don't do that."

"Oh, sure you do. You're too hip for the parents to see. It's all submerged. Except where it pops out materially. Like that car."

"The car is fun. If I have to drive five days a week, I want to have fun."

"I want to have fun, too. What do you suggest?" Carl did a somersault off the couch onto the living room floor.

"I suggest we stop talking about this. And I won't let Mom or Dad badger me into any more talk that makes you uneasy. I'll even offer you an olive branch—a six-pack of Heineken if you come with me to Darby's. We'll get it on the way."

Carl paused. "Okay, but don't think I'm selling completely out."

"No, just a tiny sell-out. Everyone sells out a little."

"Right. And some of us more than a little."

"I consider that a violation of the truce."

"Okay," Carl said. "I'll help you look for the taillight to make up for it."

They stopped at a supermarket on the way into town. It was almost too late to buy beer. In this town, everyone bought their drink in the afternoon. If you didn't have enough on hand to get drunk by dark, you'd just have to wait till the next day.

"There's a bottle opener under the seat somewhere," Bob said when he returned. "Sure you're up for this?"

"As long as I have this beer, I'm fine," Carl said.

Darby's was an old family farm that Darby had turned into an auto junkyard. There was a stone farmhouse filled with grills and alternators, seats and radiators, thousands of parts. Darby lived in an Airstream trailer behind the old homestead. The remains of wrecked or abandoned cars dotted acres of woodland and field around the house. It was just far enough out of town for the town board to ignore it. Carl was draining his third beer when Bob pulled the car off to the side of the dirt road leading into the junkyard.

"We'll walk in the rest of the way," Bob said, pulling a screwdriver out of the glove compartment.

"You walk. I'll run in," Carl said, swinging open the door and jogging ahead. He stumbled over a branch.

"You all right? Maybe you should stay here and finish the Heineken."

"Naw, I'm finding you a new taillight. For this little cutie, right?" His voice was getting louder by the minute.

"Try to keep your voice down. You'll wake Darby."

Carl jogged past two wreckers. "See you at the finish line, pal," he said.

"Slow down, you idiot, you'll fall," Bob said in a stage whisper. But it was no use. Carl was already among the wrecks, and in the faint moonlight, almost invisible. "Hey, Darby," he bellowed from somewhere ahead, "I'm pissing on a Studebaker."

Bob had been to Darby's only a couple of times before. It was like a maze even in the daylight. But now, it was far worse. He wondered whether he'd ever find another MG. There were hundreds of cars. Scrub trees grew among them, and there were fallen trees where Darby was clearing a new swath into the woods to make room for more wrecks. He thought he saw Carl just ahead, moving off the main path to the farmhouse. Then he heard a crash of brush and a thump.

"Ouch!" Carl said. "Bushwhacked by a goddamn De-Soto."

Bob tried to speed up, but the footing was poor. Axles, fenders, hub caps, and other rusted body parts were scattered everywhere. He nearly sprained his ankle on a steering wheel. Now, nearer the house, the dogs were barking. He couldn't see Carl at all. Then he heard the creak of a door.

"I've found it," Carl said from somewhere ahead. "Your

next car—Volvo Connecticus—a species that breeds primarily in Greenwich.''

Suddenly there was another voice coming from the direction of the barking dogs. It was Darby's.

"Who's out there?" Darby shouted. Now the dogs barked furiously.

"Shut up, you mutts," he said. There was a yelp.

Bob was worried. There was no telling what Darby would do. Especially if he was as drunk as Carl.

"How about a Rambler?" Carl said. "There's one right here for your rambling ways."

"Shut up, Carl," he hissed, moving slowly toward where he figured Carl to be. Now Darby was shining a light up toward them. It hit the windshield of the car next to Bob, and he ducked down.

"Couple of troublemakers back here, is that what we've got?" Darby said. "Couple of assholes."

Bob's throat was getting tight. He scrambled along hunched over. But he couldn't find the Rambler, and he didn't hear Carl anywhere. Then he heard a belch.

Darby was closer now, crashing along the same path Bob had just traveled. Bob could see him, stooped over, shining the light straight ahead of him, every few steps pausing and swinging its beam to the sides. Bob hid behind a Cadillac as Darby moved past.

"What are you doing, punk," Darby yelled.

"Who, sir? Me, sir?" Carl said.

"Get your drunken ass out of that car," Darby said.

"I'm sure I can explain, officer," Carl was saying. There was the creak of a door and ripping cloth.

"Watch my shirt, you jerk," Carl said.

"Oh, you're going to play rough, huh?" Darby said. There was a slap, and Carl moaned. "You had enough of that, now?"

Bob stood up, ready to charge Darby. Together, he and Carl could beat him to a pulp. But he held still, watching Darby shake something in his hands. It could have been anything. A bag. A scarecrow. But Bob knew it was Carl. He took a short step toward Darby and stopped. Let him get himself out of this mess, he thought. As he listened to them scuffle, he started to breathe hard himself. He felt a mixture of guilt and anger over what was going on. Over what he was doing, standing and watching. But the anger won out. He wanted Carl to get hurt. Not bad. But enough. Enough to learn that things weren't fair. Enough for him to learn what it means to live with an ache.

"Where's your friend, smartie?" Darby said. "Hey, pal, some pal you are. Your buddy here is sick. Puking all over the place."

Darby stooped down and picked up his flashlight. Its beam swept toward Bob's head, and he ducked just in time.

"Nice pal you've got there, smartie." There was a silence, then a thud. Carl cried out and started coughing. Bob stood again, wanting to stop it. If he heard Darby hit him once more, he would charge. But Darby seemed finished.

"That's just a little pat there, boy. Why you so sick? Hey, pal, if you can hear me, I'm leaving your buddy here. And if he isn't gone by morning, I'm calling Red to have him yanked out of here."

Darby walked back along the path, pausing and shining the light around every few steps. Bob ducked again until he was sure Darby was gone. When he heard the tinny slap of a door, he followed the sound of Carl's breathing. The sound of his own movement made it difficult to hear. He paused, listening. He could see the lights of the town by the river below. Darby's junkyard was probably the highest spot in the county. The town was quiet and peaceful in the distance, the kind of place people from the city always imagined New England towns to be. He could remember hitchhiking into town with Carl and sitting around the green. They'd spend the whole afternoon there, just watching the Mercedes, BMWs, and Volvos gliding in and out of the center of town. He remembered how he wanted that life for himself. A nice car, a nice town. It seemed further away than ever now. He listened again for Carl's breathing.

"Carl," he whispered. "Carl?" There was a sour smell in the air. He found the Rambler and Carl under it. He pulled Carl out, and his shirt ripped on a piece of metal.

"Are you all right, Carl?"

Carl moved slowly, trying to sit up. "Where . . ."

"It's okay," Bob said. "Don't say anything. We'll get out of here."

"Where were you?"

"I couldn't find you," Bob said. "I was looking and then Darby came."

"Where?"

"I was lost, dammit. Let's go."

CHAPTER

21

Sunday evening, as Bob drove back to Michigan, it was raining the same rain that had started during the graduation ceremonies. It was a cold rain for May. The college had set up chairs and a stage on the baseball field, and the rain came suddenly, too late to move everything inside. There were umbrellas throughout the audience. Umbrellas with bright candy cane stripes, with the college colors, with paisley prints, and in solid conservative black. But Ellie had forgotten to bring theirs. As speaker after speaker droned on, she got cold and wet.

"I can't stand this," she said, shivering next to Bob. "I'm heading back to Carl's apartment."

Frank and Bob stayed on. But before long, Frank gave in and left. Bob was wet, too. But he felt he had to stay there, that it was important to stay, even though he could not make out Carl's face among the gowns and caps. When Carl's name was finally called, Bob watched him walk quickly across the stage, taking the diploma without bothering to shake the president's hand.

Afterward, there were clusters of graduates and their families milling about. Despite the rain, there was a festive spirit, with the bright buzz of congratulations punctuated by the pop of champagne bottles. Bob looked for Carl, but couldn't find him. So he headed back to the apartment. When he got there, Carl was finishing a drink.

"I had to leave, too," Frank was saying, refilling Carl's glass.

"I stayed, though," Bob said. "I looked for you."

"Thanks," Carl said. "It wasn't necessary."

Bob poured himself a drink and went over to the window and watched the rain run off the roof. The glass steamed from his breath.

"Crazy weather for May," Ellie said.

"Very strange," Frank said. "I hope it doesn't freeze."

"You're not heading back in this, are you?" Carl asked.

Bob thought about staying for a second, then shook his head. "Got to." He raised his glass. "Cheers."

Now, on the thruway near Youngstown, Bob wondered whether Carl had been asking him to stay. He wondered, for a moment, if they could have talked, if they could have managed to have had a good time. But as he glanced at the bright brown glow of a steel mill, he knew there was no chance. Not after Darby's. Bob didn't know whether Carl had an idea that he had stood by as Darby beat on him. He couldn't keep the first image out of his mind—Darby shaking the dark form that was Carl. There were moments when he wished he had been the hero and knocked Darby aside. They could have run out of there together, side-by-side, taunting Darby, making jokes, maybe even ripping off a taillight cover while Darby stumbled after them. They would have told the story to everyone, over and again. Embellishing, making it funnier each time.

But those moments gave way to facts. The fact that there were no heroes when it came to growing up. There were consequences for being a wise ass. The fact that he had to be somewhere tomorrow. The fact that he had reports to make. The fact that if he didn't do his job, someone else would. The fact that everyone did what was required to inch himself along in life. But there was also the fact that the good times between Carl and him were over.

It made him tired to think of all this, but he didn't dare throw another cup of coffee into his stomach. Instead, he pulled off the thruway and found a convenience store where he bought a six-pack of beer. He could nurse these for the remainder of the trip. They would be better than coffee. As he walked back to the car the wind turned colder, straight from the north, and big wet flakes of snow began to fall. They looked like mutant moths.

By the time Bob got back on Route 80, the freakish May snow was sticking to the median, and not long after, to the road. Now that he needed it, the defroster on the damn MG proved weak. The windshield was already a mess of semicircular ice.

By the time Bob saw the last exit sign for Youngstown, he was delighted. He would find a motel and call it a night. As he got off the exit, he noticed an eerie glow in the skyline on the other side of the thruway. He figured it would be a miracle mile and drove toward it. Instead, he found a huge plant, its empty parking lot illuminated by the brown glare of high-intensity streetlamps, the kind designed to fight crime. The plant went on forever, great towers connected by chutes to bulbous metal domes the size of ships. In the light, obscured by the slow-motion fall of sloppy snow, it seemed like a nightmare temple, abandoned, the site of a bygone sect. The sight of such an immense metal building, empty, and the feeling of being so small, kept his eyes transfixed. Only when he felt the gravel through the wheel did he know that he had gone onto the shoulder. But it was too late. He felt the car slide downhill. There was a jolt and he lost consciousness.

White. A white light and stillness. And so this is what death feels like. An absence of everything. A nothingness, he was thinking, when he realized he *was* thinking. But his eyes, or rather, his right eye would not open. The left had been open for some time he knew now. Snow covered the windshield, which had a spider-web crack across it. The edge of a wood post poked in through the snow at the center of the web, and there was glass over him and the seat. He was cold. There was a sour smell in the car, and as he turned his head, he saw the beer bottles broken on the floor. A fine sight for the cops, he thought. He tried the door, but the handle didn't work. He was thrusting his shoulder against it when he noticed the blood on his jacket. He scraped the frost off the rearview mirror and looked at himself. His eye and nose were a mess. He jiggled

the tip of the nose, and the flash of pain told him it was broken. He wished the MG had had a seat belt. He might have
been better off.

Attempting to avoid the glass, he slid across the seat and
tried the other door. It opened without the use of the handle.
He climbed out and looked at the sky. It was just getting light.
The glass cover to his watch was also broken, the hands
stopped at eleven forty-five—he supposed the time of the ac-
cident. It felt like four or five in the morning. Thinking of the
police, he picked up the two unbroken bottles of beer and the
glass from the others that had smashed. He threw them all into
a field beyond the fence that had stopped the car after it had
slid down a bank. The road wasn't in sight. The slope was perhaps thirty yards.

The wind had ceased. The snow was beginning to melt.
The slope was muddy, and he needed to move on all fours to
get up it. He wiped his hands on his pants—what was the difference?—and looked around. He could see now that he had
come into a sharp corner. While looking at the plant, and with
the slick road, he had no chance. In the distance, trucks
groaned along the thruway. Down the road, he saw a diner.

Bob began walking toward it. A truck ignored his thumb
and passed him by. When he got to the diner, he was glad to
see that it was open. As he pushed through the door, he realized he had forgotten what he looked like. The expression on
the waitress's face reminded him.

"What the hell happened to you?"

"My car went off the road up there."

"You need an ambulance?" the waitress asked.

"I don't think so. Just some place to wash up."

"Use the bathroom," she said. "Want some towels?"

"Yeah, and some breakfast, if you don't mind."

"You got money?"

"Yeah, plenty." He tossed his jacket over a stool and
rolled up his sleeves.

The waitress returned from the back and handed him some
towels. They were warm and wet. "This will help," she said.
"How do you take your eggs?"

"Scrambled," he said.

"I should have guessed."

It was a dingy bathroom with peeling paint that might once have been called robin's egg blue. Bob didn't bother looking in the mirror at first. He moistened a towel and dabbed at his eye. It hurt. As the dried blood moistened, it opened. The vision was blurry. Now he looked in the mirror. What he saw was a mess of a person. There were splotches of black dried blood caked to his face. His shirt was stained down the front. It would never come clean. As he realized this, he thought about what Carl must have felt like by the time he sobered up after Darby's. Bob had gotten his mother out of bed, and together they washed his cuts. At first Carl was either too stunned or too drunk to respond. But when he came around, he began to repeat, "I was such an ass. Such an ass." Now, remembering that, Bob started to cry. The tears stung in his cuts and he dabbed at them with fresh water, but they kept coming. His nose was clogged with dried blood, and he started taking short, sharp breaths through his mouth. He was close to sobbing, and he didn't want anyone to hear. He didn't want anyone to know. It hurt enough that he knew. He gave the light's chain a yank and sat on top of the toilet seat in the dark, wiping his tears until at last they had stopped.

When Bob got back to the counter, there was a plate of hash browns, scrambled eggs, and sausage next to the seat with his coat. He ate slowly, out of habit more than hunger. It needed to be done.

"Up by the bend, huh?" the waitress said. She poured him a cup of coffee.

"Yeah."

"It gets three or four every year. Used to be more before the plant closed. Your car a wreck?"

"I guess."

"I'll call a friend for a tow. You got money for that?"

Bob nodded. While she called he thought about that. How he had money for towing. For correcting mistakes and satisfying impulses. In the shiny Art Deco stainless covering behind the counter, he saw himself, warped in the design of the metal. There was a lump the size of an egg above his eye. He ached all over.

"Yeah, he's got money, I said," the waitress went on. "Get over here."

Bob watched her set the receiver back on the cradle. "Help's on the way," she said. "By the way, you got the full special for three twenty-five."

Bob set a fiver on the counter. "That's close enough," he said. She had been good to him. She thanked him and refilled his coffee. While he sat there waiting for the tow, he wanted to call Irene. To wake her up at home and tell her what had happened to him. To say how he had stopped paying attention in a storm and crashed but had managed to live. It was Monday, and she would be up soon if she wasn't already. He could tell her about the crash, about Carl and what happened at Darby's. And he could tell her how he saw it all happen. He didn't know what good it would do to say all that, but he knew he needed to tell someone.

A man with an untucked flannel shirt came into the diner. The waitress poured him a cup of coffee and nodded toward Bob. He took a seat and said, "Is this the guy?"

"Yeah," she said.

"Great," Bob said. "My car is—"

"I know, I saw it."

"Can you get it out? I've got places to be."

"That thing won't get you there. It isn't going to run. It might not even be fixable."

"What do you mean?"

"I took a look on the way over. I'd say it's totaled. It isn't worth any more than the scrap in that plant."

Bob looked at himself again in the metal. If he didn't have blood all over his shirt and his jacket, he would have been overdressed compared to the tow man. But the blood made it seem worse than that. It made him look as if he didn't belong in the clothes in the first place. Like he had stolen them from a corpse. "What am I going to do?" he said quietly to himself.

"You'll have to make other arrangements," the waitress said, warming up his coffee. "It happens to everyone at some point."

"Call up and cancel," the tow man said.

"I can't cancel."

"Sure you can," he said, lifting the cup toward Bob in a mock toast. "Everyone can cancel. Shit, I've canceled more than I care to think about. I've canceled work. I've canceled weddings. I've even canceled one marriage. I've canceled just about anything a man can cancel.''

''Amen,'' the waitress said.

Bob was laughing and looking at the phone. It was time to do something. Time to say he didn't like the way he looked. Time to admit everything ached. Sure, he could cancel. He would cancel. He said it, ''Yeah, I'll cancel.''

''That's the spirit,'' the tow man said.

''All right,'' the waitress said. ''You're in no condition to work today.'' She set the phone in front of Bob.

''Wait, it's only five-thirty,'' he said.

''All the better.'' She grinned at him and held the receiver out. ''Reach out and cancel someone.''

Bob took it. He started to dial a number, the first toll-free number that came to mind. It rang and rang, and then a recording came on.

''The corporate offices of P&V are open from eight until five weekdays. If you have a message, please leave it, and a number where you can be reached during business hours, at the beep.''

Bob lifted the receiver from his ear. The beep was audible to the tow man and the waitress.

''Go ahead,'' the waitress said. ''Tell 'em you're canceling.''

''Your car's a mess,'' the tow man said. ''Tell your boss that. And tell him you're not in such hot shape, either.''

''I can't do it today,'' Bob said into the phone. ''Not anymore, either. I have to cancel. Bob Bodewicz is canceling with P&V.'' He held the receiver away from his mouth and looked down at the empty plate, realizing that he was hungry for the first time that day. Then he said it again. Repeated the entire message. It sounded better the second time. It sounded like the truth.

About the Author

A graduate of the Creative Writing program at Syracuse University, Christopher Zenowich has worked as a college traveler and as an advertising copywriter. He lives in upstate New York with his wife and daughter. *The Cost of Living* is his first novel.